A novel by
Baltimore Russell
and
Jennifer Pallanich
Art by Alex Sanchez

Published by Pair Tree Ink

An original publication of Pair Tree Ink

ISBN: 978-0-9864104-2-0

We invite you to move your disbelief to the side and enjoy the tale that is about to unfold. After all, if you wanted reality, you wouldn't have picked out a book about superheroes. We've taken certain liberties with science, geographies, and powers in the service of creating an entertaining story. All events and characters are fictional, and superpowers have not been proven in a court of law to be real.

DEDICATION

To
The woman who taught us to read
The man who gave us roots and wings
And the authors who transported us into other worlds

CHARACTERS

Base 47
Rami Kazemi, super inoculation/immunity
Josh "Hollywood" Grant, metamorph/shapeshifter
Emma Sheehy, telepathy
Courtney "CoCo" Cooper, misdirection/illusion
Emilio Diego Santos, probability manipulation
Etienne DuBois, intangibility and invisibility
Katrina McGee, psychokinesis
James Chege, super speed
Sun Luli, force field
Waleed Gandapur, teleportation
Jiya, healing
Captain Warren G. Pierce, retired, Base 47 trainer

The Ascendancy
Henry Hastings, member of The Ascendancy, founder of
    The Hastings Foundation
Elise Springchild, member of The Ascendancy
Anabel Wong, member of The Ascendancy
Maksim Wong, member of The Ascendancy
Redheaded Man, occasional employee of The Ascendancy
Dr. Roger Martin, climatologist at The Hastings Foundation

Dr. Thierry Giraud, molecular biologist/chemist at The
    Hastings Foundation
Dr. Nicola Patel, engineer at The Hastings Foundation

Travel Now
Maggie Adams, Travel Now journalist-turned-
    TheModsBlog blogger
Wally "Focus" Jones, Travel Now videographer
Robin "The Pigeon" Middleton, Travel Now producer

Other Mods
Taneesha "The Flame" Jackson, pyrokinesis
Maru Tamatoa, weather manipulation
Ericka Zavatsky, green bio-blasts generation
Margaux Vu, metal manipulation
Dmitri Toumanoff, peak physical athlete and physical
    mimicry
Timothy Ellery, electricity manipulation

CHAPTER
1

20 June

It wasn't a particularly difficult climb, but it was a long walk. Uphill. At least it wasn't snowing. Once the sun came, Colleen would be able to see the glacier, something she had dreamt of seeing in person for years. Mount Kilimanjaro.

Until today, it hadn't been a physically demanding climb. Until today, it had been a long, slow, beautiful walk uphill.

Since day one, the guides had been saying something that sounded like "po-lay, po-lay," which she understood meant "slowly, slowly" in Swahili. The first evening, a fellow hiker had informed her "po-lay" was spelled "Pole." However it looked on paper, it translated to one foot in front of the other in real life.

Photographs documented her rise up the mountain's Marangu Route, showing vertical progress by how little or how much she was wearing.

She hadn't realized the final ascent to what was sometimes called the Roof of Africa would be such a mental game. The scree was devilishly difficult to walk in, sinking under her every step but not giving in the same satisfying way loose beach sand gives, and made her long for the wide and foot-friendly path of the days before. Colleen tried not to think about whether it would be more difficult to pick her way back down the rocky trail.

She needn't have worried.

Colleen thought the group must be a sight—silent and coat-clad, each with a headlamp beam dancing in the dark, illuminating just the next few steps.

Starting to feel a bit sweaty, she partially unzipped her jacket and consulted her watch. They had been on the climb for six hours already, since midnight, with the goal of cresting Uhuru Peak at sunrise.

Not long after, the first notes of the day's light began to brighten the sky. The beauty of the moment stopped her in her tracks, causing the climber behind her to grunt when he bumped into her.

"Sorry, Gary," she said. "You okay?"

He grunted again, and she resumed her crunchy uphill trudge through the scree, breathing in the cool, crisp air.

Finally, she was at the top, and her guide, Henry, welcomed her to Uhuru Peak at 19,341 feet, the tallest point in Africa.

The air coming off the Furtwängler Glacier felt a little frosty now that she wasn't walking, but she didn't rezip her coat as she approached the glacier.

"That glacier is huge," she said.

"It's only a fraction of its former size," said Gary. "Once, that glacier covered the whole summit."

The morning light brought out the blues trapped in the ice, and she gazed in wonder at the glacier before removing her gloves to snap a few photos. She hunkered down on a boulder to eat a small snack of granola and jerky—she was starved after hours of climbing in the dark. She wriggled her toes in her hiking boots. Despite two pairs of socks and hours of action, her toes had felt like little frozen ice cubes the first few hours of the hike up. Now that she was relaxed and feeling the elation of achievement, her feet were warm, nearly sweaty, and she contemplated removing the second pair of socks. Come to think of it, the boulder itself felt weirdly warm, as though she were in her car with its heated seat warmers.

The sun was showing its full face, and the mountain air felt much more welcoming. Colleen removed her hat and fully unzipped her coat, noticing several of the other climbers had done the same.

In the distance, small droplets of meltwater coursed down the side of the glacier. They dripped onto the mountain rock below and rolled away into nothingness.

Colleen spotted Henry, her guide, in a tight cluster of chattering, gesticulating guides. She watched them in turn touch the ground with ungloved hands before rejoining the conversation with renewed vigor. Figuring the animation for the Tanzanian version of old home week, she returned her attention to the glacier. It glistened deep blues that reminded Colleen of her grandfather's eyes. If her trail mates were quiet on the way up the mountain, now they were talking in quietly awed tones:

"It's gorgeous."

And "I can't believe we made it—it was so worth the money."

And "This is the most amazing thing I've ever seen."

And "I expected it to be colder on the Roof of Africa." This hiker shucked his coat off.

Taking his cue, Colleen removed her own coat and scarf, and returned her gaze to the glacier.

The small droplets of meltwater turned into large droplets. Puddles formed at the base of the glacier as rivulets sought and found lower ground. Colleen could hear the droplets landing in the small puddles at the foot of the glacier.

"Is it supposed to be doing this?" Gary said.

Looking to her left, Colleen saw he, too, had removed his hat and coat. It seemed unreasonably unseasonably warm.

When no one answered, he repeated his question, pointing at Furtwängler Glacier with ungloved hands, gun-style. This time, Gary's outburst drew the attention of the other climbers as well as his guide, who was still huddled with the other guides. The Tanzanians, too, had removed most of their cold-weather gear.

The quantity of water coming off the glacier each minute increased. Small puddles doubled in size. Rivulets swelled and traveled farther and farther before petering out. Finally, one of the rivulets reached a knot of climbers.

All the guides looked unnerved in the bright hot sunlight. They were speaking urgently in some incomprehensible tongue—was it Swahili, Colleen wondered, or the language of their tribe?

The huddle broke and each guide hurried to his client and pointed down the mountain.

Gary's guide, alarm creasing his face, trotted over to him.

"We must go," he said. The short guide grabbed Gary's arm and tried to lead him away from the summit.

Gary stood his ground. "What's going on?" he asked.

His guide said nothing.

"It looks like it's melting," Gary said. "Is it melting?"

That, of course, was the very question in every climber's mind now.

Furtwängler Glacier, one of the most photographed glaciers in the world, was indeed melting. Had been melting for over a century, so that wasn't exactly a news flash. The news element—what would shortly attract the world's attention—was the way and pace at which the glacier finally melted.

In 1976, the Furtwängler Glacier covered nearly 1.2 million square feet. A quarter-century later, the twenty-foot tall glacier claimed 650,000 square feet. On this fine morning in late May, the glacier spanned a mere 92,000 square feet.

And on this otherwise unnoteworthy day, the Furtwängler Glacier would cease to exist.

Almost as one, the guides rounded up their clients, grimly herding them back down the mountain. The climbers chattered nervously as they descended, speculating. Colleen rewound the hike up in her mind. She had begun to get warm when they were close to the peak, had begun removing some of her cold weather gear at a point when she should have been her coldest. Her feet were warm, and the boulder had been oddly warm when she sat to enjoy her jerky and granola. Then she realized what the guides had been excited about when they touched their bare hands to the ground. Not some sort of guide-group ritual, but feeling the temperature of the ground. Talk about global warming, she thought.

It was bad enough the glacier was now melting from the top due to the sun's heat, but now she understood it must also be melting from the bottom, with the ground no longer maintaining subfreezing temperatures. She touched her own ungloved hand to the ground and jerked it away in alarm. The earth radiated a toasty heat and brought to mind blistering summertime asphalt that could scorch bare feet.

She recalled from her pre-trip research that the mountain held a dormant volcano and wondered if the warming ground was a sign of increased magma activity.

Actually, she thought sourly, it didn't matter much why

it was heating. What mattered was the likely effect of the heating. Colleen went white as an understanding of the danger they were all in crystallized in her mind.

She and the other hikers had put less than fifteen minutes between them and the glacier, and water rivulets were already streaming past them. Colleen tried to focus on moving as fast as she dared, on not twisting her ankle in the ever-shifting scree, on moving the opposite of "pole, pole."

Fellow hikers had quit speculating out loud, probably to conserve their energy for the scramble down Kili. Colleen tried to simply listen to their footsteps to take her mind off the looming danger of a potentially unstable glacier. In this quiet she heard the glacier calve. It was a tremendous sound that made her think of both the twenty-one-gun salute at her uncle's funeral and spinning balls striking pins at the bowling alley, but amplified tenfold.

Colleen whirled in panic, expecting to see part of this newly detached glacier bearing down on them. Seeing no immediate threat, she turned to continue her hasty retreat down the mountain.

Two minutes later, a new stream chose the path of least resistance, following the hiking path the climbers were on. The hikers in the back squealed in surprise as the glacial meltwater rolled past them, soaking their shoes and the lower five or six inches of their pants, chilling them despite the summer heat beating down from above and the heat radiating from the earth below.

At the squeal, Colleen reeled around again. The next instant, her own feet were soaked, and she could feel the undeniable force of water following gravity's pull. In a panicked effort to get out of the deepening stream, she slipped on slick rocks. As she landed on her side, the frigid water soaked her through. The cold spiked through her, and she dully wished she were still wearing her coat, gloves, and hat. Why had she wrapped the coat around her waist instead of wearing the darn thing? How could she have felt so warm just half an hour ago?

A moment later, one of her trail mates stumbled over her shivering body. The impact shocked her into motion, and she tried to rise. She had to get off the mountain. But the unrelenting, growing stream gathered her into itself and began pulling her down the mountain.

She was too cold to panic; her fear of death felt tiny, like dying was something she had already accepted. Would the water ever stop coming? Where would the water take her? Her fingers were so cold she thought they might snap if they even brushed against ground.

Above her, Colleen didn't hear the glacier calve again and again. The ice was no longer anchored to the ground, given the rapidity of the melting layer at the glacier's base.

In an almost detached way, Colleen began to wonder how she would die. Which method she would prefer. Sudden impact into a rock or tree, which was immediately fatal, was her top choice, if she had to die this day. Hypothermia vied with drowning for last place. In the end, it was a rock, and it was immediate.

The meltwater stream deepened, sped up on its downward journey. It carried a lifeless Colleen along with it.

Colleen was one of the first victims the melting glaciers took. In all, a hundred and fourteen people died the day Mount Kilimanjaro was stripped of its crowning glacial glory. The disaster took mere hours to unfold, with broken-off glaciers speeding toward the bottom of the mountain, bouncing and bucking and gouging, leaving behind a nightmarish series of scars on the famous mountain.

CHAPTER 2

20 June

Rami felt the warmth of the late-afternoon sun dance across his face as he climbed toward the plateau in the Zagros Mountains in northeast Iran. He stood upright and reached his arms high above his head, smiling. It was the first time in over eight months he had been so free.

Rami Kazemi

"No delay," Ken Malloy said as he passed Rami by. "I know it's been a long trek, but we can't stop yet."

"Of course." Rami snapped out of his daze and followed the American to whom he owed his freedom. "I'm just glad the cave bottoms out at about a half mile. I don't know if I have the stamina to go much deeper than that."

"Everest of caves, Ghar Parau is most certainly not," Ken joked.

Rami knew the group's frequent stops were a concession to his poor physical condition. He was down about twenty-five pounds, and he was in no kind of shape to go off exploring the cave system.

"Besides, you've got Hassan here," Rami said as he pointed to the pudgy Iranian guide. He did not completely trust a guide who wore such terrible footwear.

"Hassan is helping the expedition, but where we're going, we'll need you," Ken said. He slung his bag off his back as they neared their campsite. "Besides, it is no longer correct that Ghar Parau only goes half a mile deep."

Rami snapped his head up. "Is there a new passage? What happened?"

All Ken would say is he would see when they got down to the bottom of the cave.

Rami stopped near him and looked at the ragtag team of men assembled near the campfire. He had been a free man for less than twelve hours, and he did not understand how he was going to be of any help on the cave expedition. That he did not understand the point of the expedition did not lessen his enjoyment of the fresh air and the magnitude of the wide-open space around him.

Hassan dropped his satchel, took out a steel pot, and set out to heat up goulash for dinner.

Rami slowly took off his heavy pack. Given his frailer health, it was lighter than everyone else's. It carried the bare minimum: his own extra flashlights, his clothes, water bottle, and jacket. He carried none of the supplies required for the expedition itself, such as ropes and food. This was already a source of contention between him and the members of the expedition.

He twisted his back and heard several cracks. He grinned at the release. He felt his ribs rubbing against his arms and frowned with the reminder of how much weight he had lost. Just then, the faintest aroma of the goulash wafted over, and his stomach roared. After months of surviving on broth and rotted meat, the hearty stew was a feast for his senses.

While he waited for the meal, he let his mind drift over memories of previous explorations. He had always felt there was more to the cave beyond the sump that blocked them out. If the cave had opened up, maybe he would be able to explore the new passage.

The men's voices dragged him back to reality. He sat unassumingly on a log next to a man with a long ponytail, who was nose deep in a book about the region's topography, and waited for the food to be served up.

"And can you believe it? Just today the entire glacier on top of that mountain melted. No one lived," Chris, a Polish caver with a thin mustache, said.

"I saw that too. World's gone crazy," a man named Sergei said in a heavy Russian accent.

"How is that even possible?" The question came from Fitz, a man with a very full beard.

"The particulars are a little vague, but remember that the mountain is an actual volcano," an American said. Rami looked at him and recognized a familiar logo on his fleece jacket.

"Dormant," Rex Adamsen, another American, added quickly.

"Formerly dormant, maybe," Peter Miller said with a nod. "The magma vents must have superheated the glacier and caused a catastrophic collapse."

Rami had seen pictures of the glacier many times, but hearing the scientists talk about the disaster mystified him. He had asked Ken about the Kili disaster but he was light on details.

"How could that happen if the volcano was dormant?" Rami asked as the others craned their necks to look at him. Rami noted the Americans were peculiarly dressed for a caving expedition and seemed like they would be more at home in a laboratory than on a mountain. They ignored his question and turned back around.

"Make sure that you check out all those rigs, belays, chisels, torches, and ropes before the morning, mate. Can't have any mishaps along the way down," the British man with the ponytail said as he pointed to the large mound of supply bags.

The Russian and the bearded guy huffed a bit, but rose to ensure the supplies were in order.

"Peter, Rex, come here for a moment," Ken said. The two Americans joined him near the makeshift rock table a few yards away. Rami could not hear what they were saying, but felt he was the topic of conversation by the way they kept flicking their eyes in his direction.

Rami knelt near Hassan as he stirred the pot of goulash. Rami's stomach rumbled, and Hassan heard it. He looked at Rami and grinned.

"I'll serve you first," he said.

The look on Rami's face was purest appreciation. "Thanks. What is this I hear about the cave opening up?"

Hassan looked strangely at Rami and stirred a moment longer. "You really don't know what this is about, do you?"

"Tell me."

Hassan's eyes darted to the two Americans, then back to Rami, then back at the other men gathered near them.

"Hassan," Rami said in a hushed tone. "Why am I here?"

"Astara must have been harder on you than you let on."

Rami was stunned. Did everyone in this party know about his political imprisonment? He glanced over at the packs and saw the logo for The Hastings Foundation and wondered exactly how far-reaching the organization was. But what was his role here?

Hassan ladled goulash into Rami's bowl and waited for the gaunt Persian to eat. Rami fought the urge to devour the food. He needed answers. He deserved answers.

"Why am I here?" Rami repeated.

Hassan peered into the pot and looked over his shoulder at Rami. He whispered, "Look, my friend, all I know is that the cave has opened up and that The Hastings Foundation is leading this expedition. Pays much more than any of the other foreign explorers—and I need that for my kids."

"But what does that have to do with me? Why get me out of Astara?"

"Just eat. Ken will explain everything." Hassan pushed the bowl closer to Rami.

The scent of the goulash combined with his prolonged hunger made it tempting to eat instead of pressing the question. Curiosity won over his appetite. "No. Everyone, you included, knows more than you are letting on."

Hassan stewed for a moment and then relented. "Because of your experience in the cave, they believe that you ought to be the first to truly explore it. Allah knows you are luckier than most in Ghar Parau."

Rami frowned at Hassan's reference to deaths inside the cave. They had even named the drops after them. He thought it was a proper honor for those who had not made it as far into the cave. If he was honest with himself, it also gave him more motivation to keep going.

Partially satisfied with the answer, he happily spooned the food to his mouth.

"Tasty."

"You'll need all your strength for tomorrow," Hassan said as he poured another helping into Rami's bowl.

Rami greedily ate but his mind dwelled on his fortunate extraction from a prison he had been sure he would die in.

Sergei walked over to them, scowling at Rami. "And what about you? Why are you so special to this expedition?"

"What do you mean?" Rami asked.

"The Foundation picked all of us for a specific reason. So what do you bring? We don't need a guide," he said as he pointed to Hassan, who was dishing out goulash to the rest of the team.

"This new passage that's opened up promises to reignite the Iranian caving phenomenon. Might make this the deepest cave," the ponytailed man said.

"We've got the Brit cave master and the American scientists and the geologists. So what about you?" Sergei again pressed.

"That's enough, Sergei," Ken interjected as he walked back toward the campfire. "Rami is here on loan from the Iranian government. He's our personal assurance that the expedition will be handled professionally."

With Ken's sharp words, the Russian huffed and stuck a spoonful into his mouth.

They ate in relative silence as Ken briefed them on the next day's expedition.

After dinner, they toasted fallen cave explorers and asked for blessings for a safe adventure.

"To those who travel deep but never return," the man with the thin mustache said as he raised his cup.

"For all those who blazed the trail further and inspire our own journey," Willy Brown, the renowned British caver, said.

"May our packs be easy, our ropes be true, and our footing be sure," Fitz said.

"And may our lights never go out!" Willy added, and his long ponytail slid off his shoulder as he lifted his glass.

"Let's scoop some booty!" Sergei laughed as they all took

their drinks and settled in for the night.

"Scoop booty!" the other experienced cavers cheered.

"Scoop booty?" Rex asked Willy.

"Entering virgin cave, new passages," the Brit answered.

"Oh."

"We'll get started bright and early tomorrow morning. We've got to scrape the bottom of the cave," Ken said as he patted Rami on the back and slipped into his own sleeping bag.

The other men shuffled away and took their spots inside their sleeping bags. It was a brisk night, and the stars shone bright and clear in the cold evening air.

Rami opened his sleeping bag and zipped himself snugly inside. He looked up at the night sky, his first in many months. He spotted Aquila, the celestial eagle, and was comforted. He smiled, recalling the joy he'd felt on spotting the wings and the head stretching off to the southwest through the telescope he built with his father so many years ago. He closed his eyes and, as always, thought of his love, Arian.

Picturing her, he whispered a sonnet they both loved, a ritual he had carried out nightly since his first day in Astara. Even though he was out of that prison, he was still far away from her. How many more nights would they spend apart?

But his normal nighttime shut-down process was not leading him to sleep. His mind kept coming back to the campfire discussion of Kilimanjaro. A glacier melting. It was as if he had heard this all before. What was it? He could almost hear a story playing out in his head. As if he had known certain events were happening or going to happen.

But that would be impossible.

How would he know?

A broken dream he had many times as a teenager rushed

back to him, overloading all his senses. If he hadn't been lying in his sleeping bag already, he felt sure he would have crumpled to the ground from the force of the recollection. It was more than just a dream. The words not thought of in so many years manifested and filled him with dread.

The mountain will flood.
The flames will smother the island.
The ground will steal the living.
The river will break the bank.
The illumination will reveal all.
The Sentinel will awaken.
And the tide will break new and old.

CHAPTER 3

20 June

"Come, come, looking is free."

Maggie turned toward the melodic voice. A beaming young woman waved at her.

"Best price. Local price, not tourist price."

Maggie returned the young woman's smile, shrugged at her

Maggie Adams

companion, and entered a shop smaller than her tiny New York City kitchen. There was scarcely room for the two of them inside, so Focus remained in the open-air market's main aisle. Maggie knew Focus was thinking about angles and lighting. She should have been thinking about content. Instead, she was thinking about the beaded red necklace that looked like something CoCo might like for her next birthday.

"See, purses. See, sandals. See, soapstone. See, carvings."

Inwardly, Maggie smiled. Most of the shopkeepers at the market seemed compelled to verbally catalog their inventory for her, even though it was readily apparent what she was seeing. In the woman's defense, the tiny shop was so full of inventory that it would be easy to overlook an entire category of goods.

"See, baskets. See, jewelry. You like?"

"Yes, this." Maggie pointed at the red necklace, and the woman deftly removed it from the display and handed it to her.

"Best price, just for you." The grinning woman held up a mirror.

Dutifully, Maggie held the necklace up around her neck and peered into the mirror. Yes, it would do for CoCo.

"Are there any matching earrings?"

"Yes, yes, I have, in my other shop. I am coming right back." She left before Maggie could object.

Maggie knew from yesterday's shopping excursion in another outdoor market in Arusha, Tanzania, that "in my other shop" was code for "one of my pals probably does" and the wait could be ten or fifteen minutes while the shopkeeper furiously searched for something suitable that the *mzungu*, or white lady, might agree to purchase at an egregiously inflated tourist price. Best price, ha. As she settled in to wait, she called to Focus, who hadn't seemed to notice the woman's departure.

"Do you think this market will be easier to shoot than the other?"

He shrugged. "Pros and cons."

"Which are you leaning toward?"

"Pretty even. Which do you like?"

"Hmm. That's tough. This one is cleaner and there are more shops. But the other one is more picturesque."

"That's kind of what I was thinking. I suppose I could video the outside of the other one and then do interior shots here, where the walkways are better and there's better light.

That is, if you don't mind including both in your field report."

"Works for me. Let's plan that for after lunch. I want to get my souvenirs taken care of first."

"Of course. Play first, right? I mean, research. Then you know what to say when it's time to work. I can't believe The Pigeon falls for that."

"Every time," Maggie said, before saying in a throaty voice, "No wiener-wanking substitute for legwork."

The spot-on imitation of their boss surprised a laugh out of Focus. "Speaking of which, did she say anything about our having to delay the Kili climb to next week?"

"Something about a shit-o-gram from the bean counters because of the delay."

"Of course."

"And she said we'd better hurry up. The Tanzania trip of a lifetime segment is supposed to air a few days after we finish the climb and get back to the US."

Focus stood at attention and gave a mock salute.

Maggie grinned, just as the shopkeeper returned, triumphantly displaying three different pairs of beaded red earrings. Maggie accepted all three pairs and peered into the mirror, holding them up to her ears, one by one, along with the necklace for comparison. Choice made, she laid the rejects in the woman's palm and held up the items she wanted. "How much for these?"

"Best price."

"What is the best price?"

The young Tanzanian woman quoted an obscenely high number. It was more than five times the first price at some of the shops they'd stopped at yesterday, and Maggie reconsidered whether to include this particular outdoor market in her travel piece after all.

"Ah, that is not best price," Maggie countered.

The shopkeeper was opening her mouth for a counteroffer when her phone buzzed. She glanced at the screen and smiled apologetically to Maggie while holding up a "just a minute" finger. Maggie nodded and sighed about the further delay while the woman answered her phone. Maggie listened idly to her side of the melodic conversation—she couldn't tell if it was in Swahili or the mother tongue of the woman's tribe. She saw dismay, disbelief, and fear flit across the woman's face before despair settled in, accompanied by a wail. The woman crumpled to the floor sobbing.

As Maggie watched in sympathy and wondered what terrible news had just been delivered, a nearby shopkeeper entered the little shop and pushed Maggie out of the way. He looked at the fallen crying woman and at her phone for a moment and decisively snatched the phone out of her hands. He spoke into it for a few moments and Maggie saw some of the same emotions flicker across his face. Maggie and Focus watched him intently as he hung up.

"What happened?" Maggie asked.

The man ignored her and instead hugged the crying woman to him.

For the first time in her journalistic career, Maggie felt like a voyeur and she wasn't even reporting this. The feeling was nowhere near sufficient to drive down her curiosity, however.

"What happened?"

He frowned at her and spoke gently to the woman. With his help, she stood on trembling legs. The last thing Maggie heard her say was "asante sana" as she fled. Maggie had little Swahili but as a good traveler had learned the basics while planning her trip to East Africa. *Asante sana* meant thank you.

The man straightened himself and looked squarely at Maggie and Focus.

"What happened?" Maggie thought maybe the third time would be the charm.

"This shop is closed. You must shop elsewhere."

"But what happened?"

"Big tragedy. On mountain. Many die."

"On Mount Kilimanjaro?"

"Yes."

"How?"

"The glacier. It fell. It kill many. It maybe kill her brother."

"What?" The question came from both Maggie and Focus.

"The glacier. It fell. It kill many. Her brother's porter on mountain. He may be killed."

That explained the grief, Maggie thought, but how had they not heard about this?

"When?"

"Today morning."

"Thank you—I mean, asante sana." Maggie shoved the jewelry she'd planned to buy CoCo into the man's hands, grabbed Focus' shirtsleeve, and took off down the aisle.

"We're leaving, right?" Focus asked, following her.

"Of course. We have to see if he's right."

He stopped. She squinted at him. He smiled gently. "Exit's that way," he said, pointing back the way they'd come.

She stood there, looking forward and backward. "Right. Lead on, oh trusty navigator."

"Let's hoof it."

When they finally emerged from the interior of the open-air market, Focus hailed a taxi and negotiated a rate back to their hotel. They slid into the back seat and settled in for a bumpy and nerve-wracking journey. The taxi driver had the radio on at top volume, playing local music.

"Think it's true?" she asked Focus.

He shrugged. "Why lie?"

"That's what I thought." She chewed her lower lip, trying to figure out what this meant for the travel piece. "First things first. We have to figure out what really happened. We're going to have to go to Kili today, I think."

"Whoa. Wait a minute. If what he said is true, then it might not be safe."

"You're probably right. But—" She halted when an excited news report in English replaced the music.

"The glacier on the top of Mount Kilimanjaro has ceased to be. Much of it has melted, causing it to skid and crash down the mountainside. Reports indicate many have been killed in this breaking tragedy. Stay tuned for further details as they become available," the newscaster's voice said. Without further commentary, a jingle for one of the local washing powders came on. The taxi driver picked up his cell phone. With one hand he dialed and with the other he expertly navigated the traffic and potholes, judiciously applying his horn as needed.

Maggie sighed. "Well, that settles that."

"Guess so."

"Only one thing to do."

"Leave?"

"No, doofus. Have to call The Pigeon. I don't know how you can have the trip of a lifetime to Tanzania that doesn't include climbing Mount Kilimanjaro. Or at least traveling around its perimeter. We'll need new marching orders."

And then Maggie's local cell phone rang. She answered.

"What kind of ball-gobbling nonsense is this?"

Maggie sighed. Focus raised his eyebrows in question and flapped his arms in imitation of a bird despite the close quarters of the taxi. She nodded at him. She wouldn't have to call The Pigeon after all.

"Hi, Robin," Maggie said. "I was going to call you as soon as we got back to the hotel and had a better idea what was going on."

"No fart-knocker excuses. This is a pure-d disaster. Is it true? This glacier. Did it really go tits-up?"

"That seems to be the case."

"Well, then get your asses back here. There's no Tanzania trip of a lifetime without Kili."

"Robin, I disagree. I think we can still pull this off. We could be the first to do a segment on a changed Kili. And we could even document some of the news elements. In fact, since we're close, we could cover it from a news angle for a few days for one of the other programs. No one else is situated for this. We're here. What do you say?"

Maggie held her phone away from her ear. Robin had blown a big raspberry in her ear.

"Stick to what you're good at. You're the face of Travel Now. I want your asses on the first plane out of Arusha."

"We can pull this off. I'm here. I can get to the base of Mount Kilimanjaro in a couple of hours. Everyone's going to want in on this action, Robin." Maggie closed her eyes and drew in a deep breath. "I don't want to go over your head on this, but I think the right thing to do is go and cover it and offer the footage to our sister programs. And we can still do a helluva segment on the Tanzania trip of a lifetime."

For a few long moments, Maggie could hear nothing on the other end, but she felt frigid air coming out of her phone.

"Don't mess this up. Misery and shit, Maggie, they both roll downhill. And don't threaten me again."

"Okay—" Maggie realized she was speaking to dead air. She grinned to Focus. "Let's go to Kili."

CHAPTER
4

21 June

"Can't believe we're going to spend the longest day of sunlight way down here in darkness," Rex grumbled as the entire expedition came up to a very steep pitch.

"This is the *eroica*," Hassan told the Americans as he began attaching and securing the ropes and belays so they could descend.

"Erotica?" Peter laughed as his light bobbed up and down.

"No. *Eroica*. From Beethoven's third symphony." Willy hummed a few bars. "Means heroic, like we will be making it down in one piece."

"Whatever, sounds like a funeral song to me," the Russian squelched as he leaned back and dropped toward the bottom.

Rami silently agreed with the Russian and shivered superstitiously at the bad luck his comment might bring. He breathed in the cool cave air and tried to soothe away the worry that he had traded his tiny prison cell for an earthly tomb. He wondered what this trip would be like.

Rex affixed a relay transponder to the wall.

"What are you doing, mate?" Willy asked.

"It's so the transmission can bounce back up in real time," Rex explained. "Keep the bosses happy."

"Right-o," Willy said as he continued on.

Rami was much less fit now than on his last visit, thanks to a prolonged diet of prison food. He knew he would struggle with the belays and rope ties that he once operated with ease.

Of the expedition members, Ken Malloy, who had helped free him from Astara, and the pudgy guide, Hassan, were the two he was closest with.

Willy, a renowned British spelunker, was charged with keeping the two scientists from The Hastings Foundation safe.

Judging by their fair skin and heavy breathing, Rami thought they spent far more time in the lab than the field. He'd been in the cave with newcomers before, and he knew Peter and Rex would face down some serious fear before the end of the trip. Peter was filming the expedition, while Rex was taking notes on his tablet. Somehow, Rami understood, they were syncing and transmitting the data back to their bosses.

Rami and Ken took up the number two and three spots at the front of the group, directly behind Hassan. Eventually, the guide stopped and directed them to crawl through a tunnel no taller than three feet.

As Hassan waited with Rami and Ken for the rest of the crew to slither through the tunnel, the guide decided to share a bit of history with them, in a tone that made Rami think of ghost stories and campfires.

"Legend has it the cave used to be larger. Before the British expedition in the seventies, the locals had done some exploration before finally being scared off. They said the cave just vanished off into nothing. One time, a group of kids made their way down the cave and managed to reach the sump, although they claim there was no sump, but a collection of rocks that led to another large chamber. They were about to continue exploring when they all vanished without a trace. No gear, no bodies. Nothing."

Willy laughed as he pulled himself out of the tunnel. "Urban myths always make me chuckle. They end with 'and they were never heard from again' or some bloody shit like that. But if that's true, who's telling the story? How did the others know what to warn against if someone did not survive?"

"That's the story I heard," Hassan said.

Fitz huffed a bit and saw his breath cloud in front of his beard, a sure sign that they were descending further down deeper into the cave.

"Yeah, noticed it too," Chris said as he looked at his altimeter.

The jokes and stories were not helping Rami one bit. He was tired, and his body was running on fumes, despite the extra helpings of last night's goulash and that morning's eggs and oatmeal. They were about two hours into what was expected to be a six-hour journey to the sump. Rami wasn't sure if he would be able to make it. The totally weird idea that the Foundation would send him back to Astara if he failed them helped him access a reserve of energy he didn't know he had.

There was little joking among the team as they trudged toward the next obstacle, which they reached about an hour later. A ledge half a shoe wide extended for about ninety paces above a twenty-yard drop. Here, authorities had installed thick rope to help people remain on the ledge and avoid falling into the chasm. If the cave were in America, the ledge would probably have been fully enclosed, but this was Iran. This was adventure.

Before allowing them to cross, Hassan talked them through the best approach.

"Remember, the most common cause of caving accidents is when multiple problems compound upon each other," Hassan said. "Just like a plane never crashes for one reason, multiple things have to go wrong. So take it slowly. Use your arms to counterbalance your weight. Shift your feet forward and make sure you are on solid footing." Hassan demonstrated, then motioned to Rami to cross first.

"Isn't this Vitoria's Falling Place?" Chris asked as he pointed his light in the general direction.

"Yep. This should be it," Fitz confirmed.

"What do you mean?" Rex asked.

"A few years ago a caver fell to her death here," Hassan said matter-of-factly.

"What? Here?" Rex's voice squeaked the question.

"Cavers have a dry sense of humor, huh?" Sergei said.

Rex looked panicked.

"Don't mind them. Focus one hand in front of the other. One foot in front of the other," Willy said kindly to Rex, as if he were a grandfather teaching his grandson how to hook a lure on a line.

One by one, they started on the path. Peter stepped on a shoelace and flailed his arms, trying to remain on the ledge and keep hold of the video equipment.

"Careful there, mate!" Willy said, coming to the rescue. He grabbed Peter's arm and pulled the scientist and his video gear into a steady stance on the ledge. Willy took in the look of terror on Peter's face.

"Just breathe. You don't have to do this fast. Breathe. Look. Step."

Finally, they all safely crossed the ledge at Vitoria's Falling Place.

As they continued the descent, the group became quieter. Not even Hassan had much to say.

"How much longer?" Peter asked as if he were a kid in the back seat on the way to a much-anticipated destination.

"About three more hours to the sump," Hassan said.

"In the second expedition," Willy said to a confused Rex, "they tried to dive through it but they came to a part where the cave just ended. That was the end of Ghar Parau. What a bloody disappointment!"

Hassan shot a look back at Willy, and the British explorer shut up.

They continued on in silence. The further they descended, the more time that passed, the larger the gnawing pit in Rami's stomach seemed. A nagging ache at the base of his skull chimed in. What made him so uneasy? It couldn't have been his last trip here with Arian. No one had been hurt, and they had laughed at their close call. What was so unnerving this time?

"Feel that?" Willy said to the burly Russian.

"Getting warmer, huh?"

"Strange," Fitz said as he passed by them.

The three hours passed uneventfully, although all the experienced cavers were a bit unsettled by not needing their jackets at depth. It should have been much colder.

"We're here," Hassan announced finally. He dropped his pack. The team gathered around him, nine lights showing the end of the cave. The cave walls seemed to bend and take different shapes. Then it became clear the end wasn't actually a wall, but a series of rocks stacked on top of one another.

"I think this is what they wanted information about," Rex said. He set up the last relay transponder and was relieved to see the tablet was still connected to the dedicated

Hastings Foundation satellite.

"Nicola is going to flip over the data. More than we ever knew before, and now she can show up that smug Frenchie," Peter said.

Rex typed estimated measurements and brief descriptions about the rock formation into his tablet while Peter filmed it.

"We're lucky that Nicola's hunch about the cave turned out to be right," Rex said.

Rami wondered who this Nicola was, how she had come to discover the cave opening, and why she wasn't part of the team.

Hassan flashed his beam on the members of the group. The level of dirt and grime covering everyone was much more pronounced than normal for this portion of the cave, likely due to the new cave opening. He motioned for Rami to step closer.

Rami was tired. After almost a full six hours of descending the cave, he needed to rest. But his adrenaline wouldn't allow him a moment. And, it appeared, neither would Hassan.

Rami carefully made his way over to Hassan. As he stood near Hassan, a chill quickened down his spine. He turned and faced the darkness, his headlamp piercing the nothingness.

"This is certainly not how I left it the other day. The sump is empty. But where did all the water go?" Hassan asked urgently.

Rami shrugged.

"Notice how warm it is?" Hassan asked.

Rami saw Willy was just in a T-shirt. His own jacket had been in his backpack for the last couple of hours.

Rami turned and slowly stepped toward the rocks. Was

he imagining it or were the rocks slightly glowing? Experimentally, he swished his headlamp from side to side, watching the rocks change color as the lamp illuminated them. He started to approach them.

"Watch it there, Rami," Ken said, coming up behind Rami. "We don't know what we're dealing with."

Rami nodded, but kept walking forward, sliding off his gloves and dropping them on the cave floor. Rex motioned Peter to film Rami.

The others set about putting a base camp together while Rami moved closer to the rocks, which seemed to be arranged like a stone fence with an opening in the middle.

"After camp's ready, we'll make proper survey measurements," Rex said. Fitz and Sergei began arranging the packs.

The rocks near the edge were indeed glowing, Rami realized. They gave off a greenish light. Was he the only one seeing it?

He looked back. No one stepped closer to follow him. He inched closer to the opening where the sump had been. There, in the middle of the hollowed ground, his shoe hit a rock. It cascaded past the edge and leapt off into nothingness without a sound. The new chamber beyond must be deep.

Rami's hands burned and itched. When he looked, he discovered they were also glowing with the same greenish haze emanating from his walls. He looked at the rocks and his hands and felt a deep impulse to touch the rocks. He knelt and pushed his glowing hands close to the glowing rocks. The closer he got, the quieter everything became. He stared out into the abyss and connected his hand to the cave.

Flesh met rock and an outrageous flash of light exploded in the cave. A hundred-year-old stench gusted from the rocks, pushed by a gurgling wind rushing from deep within the cave. It hit with the force of a wall, pushing everyone to the ground. Try as he might, Rami could not remove his hands from the glowing stones. The sound was deafening, and Rami couldn't keep his eyes open against the light and wind. But before he closed them, he thought, impossibly, he had seen a figure in the dark distance in front of him.

Ridiculous, he thought, just the light and his mind playing tricks on him. He tried to scream but no sound emerged. He felt the hairs on his neck stand up as if a predatory presence had just passed through him.

He looked down to his bony hands. Strange coin-sized shapes were flying out of, or through, his hands, he couldn't tell. Rocks? Giant dust particles? Spores? He didn't know.

Lightheadedness took away his ability to reason. He felt queasy and fell to the cave floor. He looked back at the group and saw the other expedition members also lying prone on the cave floor. Queasiness turned to dry heaving. Rami buckled in pain and blacked out, at last halting his physical connection with the rock.

Unhindered by the break in contact, the phosphorescent light that had sparked from Rami's hand traveled far from deep inside the Iranian cave. The light raced to all points above ground, giving rise to a strange new world, filled with strange new powers.

From the bowels of the earth, Rami was the catalyst for a metamorphosis that would modify and enhance the chosen. In a way, he was the father of a new people.

CHAPTER
5

21 June

Henry walked toward the worn-down building on the river. Pools of streetlights dotted the riverfront, giving just enough brightness to guide him along the trails. The Philadelphia Electric Company Delaware Station was long past its prime, and the

Henry Hastings

graffiti on the pale brick facade signified a sharp decline in the neighborhood. The summer heat wore heavily on him, but he did not remove his slate-gray tailored suit jacket. He felt more out of place than he bargained for, but he would never run into anyone here who would recognize him.

Kids gathered by the chain-link fence smoking and drinking eyed Henry as he walked by them. He hoped they would leave him be.

"You a little out of place, Gramps!" the one wearing a black bandanna shouted at him. Henry put his head down and walked faster.

"What's your rush, Morebucks?" another taunted as he

pushed himself off the fence. Henry turned toward them.

"No rush. Just taking a stroll," he said with a calm he did not feel.

"Bad for you," a tall man said as he stepped toward the out-of-place visitor. "Because this is our territory, and you in the wrong place."

They crowded Henry, forcing him against the chain-link fence. Henry's lip quivered as he frantically looked around, regretting his choice of meeting spot and wishing desperately to see someone, anyone, he knew.

Five guys surrounded him and each pulled out a weapon—blade, brass knuckles, a lead pipe—and taunted the older man.

"Please. Whatever you want, I'll give it to you," Henry stammered as he reached into his pocket.

"You know, we see your type here all the time. Think that you're entitled to this place. Changing it. Condos, coffee shops, fresh markets. It's bullshit," the bandanna wearer said, leaning in close to Henry's face. The punk's breath smelled of chili dog. Henry felt the cold steel of a blade on his neck and gulped.

"That's quite enough," a voice called out from behind them. "Leave the man alone."

They turned to see a redheaded man in a sharp navy suit taking a drag off a cigarette.

"Well, it's two of you against the five of us. I think we'll do the ordering," the leader wearing the bandanna said. He pointed the blade at the newcomer.

Henry stared at the redheaded man, daring to hope.

"This won't take long," the one with the bandanna said. He shoved Henry to the ground.

The group surrounded the newcomer, who flicked his cigarette away and grabbed the leader's arm. He twisted the punk's arm, causing him to drop the blade. When the others stepped toward him, he pulled the guy's arm harder. The punk screamed in pain.

"By all means, keep coming. I'll break his arm." He pulled his arm back further and squeezed harder, and the pack leader howled.

"S-s-s-stop!"

"Call off your little gang and get out of here," the redheaded man said in a low voice. He squeezed more. The tearing of shoulder muscle could be heard, sounding like a piece of celery broken in half. A slight smile danced across his face before he stared down the men. "And don't let me catch you back here again."

He released the arm, and the leader fell to the ground with a thud. His friends picked him up and rushed away.

"Th—thank you." Henry slumped as his pulse slowly returned to normal.

"Why all the cloak-and-dagger?" the redheaded man asked as he pulled Henry toward a streetlight on the pier. "What's with you? You really think the pier is the place to meet? Better a place where you blend in completely. Here, you're an odd one out."

"I suppose you're right. I just didn't want to be seen by anyone I know. I should have been more careful," Henry said as he wiped his brow.

"What do you need?"

"The Ascendancy has need of your … skills." Henry looked around. "Let's go somewhere more civilized."

"I told you I was through with your fanatical quests and fanciful journeys. I'm done." The redheaded man stopped and turned toward the river.

"I know the last mission didn't go as well as we hoped, but that's no reason to quit."

"Henry, remember how you felt not two minutes ago?" The man pointed toward the still-running thugs. "That you might not see another sunrise? That's the spot I was in on the last mission. I'm not risking my life for your obsession again."

"There is one last piece to this puzzle. One I know you are particularly suited for."

The redheaded man stared in disbelief at Henry. "You never take no for an answer."

"You've been well compensated for helping the Ascendancy retrieve certain artifacts," Henry said.

"Yeah, and the last time I helped you, the Hopi captured me and I thought I might die helping you pursue your damned quest."

"There is a painting in the San Telmo Museum that we need."

"Another Flores? The last one wasn't good enough?"

"It was, and it provided invaluable clues. But we now need the last known painting by Bernardo Flores."

The redheaded man stopped and fished out a silver case from his jacket pocket. He pulled out a cigarette and put it to his lips. He took out his lighter, lit the cigarette, and inhaled deeply.

"Not sure if I want to do this. Too risky for me."

"Then find someone else to do it. There's no time to waste."

"You sure this isn't just some other crazed clue in your never-ending pursuit of something that will never happen? It's been, what, five hundred years since this prophecy was given." The redheaded man smiled as he exhaled slowly.

"Think what you will. The prophecy has never steered us wrong. Only our interpretation is limited."

"And what about the others? How will they feel when

they find out you've been hiding artifacts from them?" He knew that for every two items he retrieved for the Ascendancy, Henry kept one to himself.

"They know what they need to know. And I've earned a certain amount of leeway to pursue our goals. Especially since the Jakarta Incident." The redheaded man nodded.

"Will you do it?" Henry asked.

The redheaded man took a final drag on his cigarette as the city lights twinkled in the distance. He bobbed his head from side to side, expelling the last of his smoke slowly.

"Not sure it's worth my time," he said as he looked at Henry. "Or the risk."

"I understand that the last mission was ... challenging."

"Challenging I can handle. Even capture. It's whatever this is heading toward that I'm uneasy with," he said as leaned against the railing. "I don't know much about this prophecy, but what I do know about the Sentinel, the paintings, the weird Earth changes, are they all point toward something big."

"And I would implore you to stay on the right side of the equation. Anywhere else could be ... deadly."

The redheaded man took the threat in stride with a simple nod.

"The usual amount in the same account will do?" Henry asked.

"Double the amount. By tomorrow." The redheaded man sighed. "I'll get it done. You just get out of here. No place for you."

"Thank you. This is a final test that will bring about the Reckoning that we've been waiting so long for. When that is accomplished, we can move toward the endgame." Henry leaned in toward the redheaded man and whispered, "The Sentinel will save us all."

As they walked in separate directions, a most peculiar thing happened overhead. Racing from east to west a bright light illuminated the sky and small, almost marble-sized particulates flowed through the air. Henry looked up and smiled into the light.

CHAPTER 6

21 June

It was another sleepless night for Josh. He sipped the Macallan twenty-five-year-old Sherry Oak Scotch, given by his agent after winning his most recent Golden Globe. Wearing only loose linen pants over his chiseled tan body, Josh walked across the balcony of the Spanish Colonial he'd bought in

Josh Grant
"Hollywood"

Hollywood Hills two years before. He touched his chin and felt a small scar running horizontally across—a souvenir from his fifth birthday party, when he went down a slide face first.

He pulled his phone from his pocket and resisted immediately looking at the text waiting for him. It would only sour his night and mood. A cool breeze pushed his dark brown hair out of his face as he enjoyed the view of Los Angeles. His balcony overlooked the constant stream of red taillights that connected the valley and city.

Wanting to relax, he sat in a lounge chair and gazed at

the faint stars dotting the night sky. He poured a thumb of Scotch, looked around, shrugged, and filled the crystal tumbler to the top. He didn't have anything to do the next day, and his film wouldn't start for another month. And besides, there was no girlfriend. He had just broken up with his most recent starlet, a PR relationship staged to gain buzz for his latest movie.

He stared at his phone and promised himself he wouldn't drunk dial. He took a swig before opening the dreaded text.

YOU CAN'T PRETEND THAT YOUR ACTIONS DON'T HAVE CONSEQUENCES. YOU HAVE BROKEN ME IN WAYS I NEVER KNEW SOMEONE COULD. YOU CAN FOOL YOURSELF AND BELIEVE THAT THIS WASN'T MORE, BUT I KNOW BETTER.

It was exactly the message you'd expect from a scorned lover. Against his better judgment, Josh dialed. It went straight to voice mail.

"Hey, it's Josh. I know last time we talked it was … tense. I wish I could say that I am sorry and that I have changed, but the truth is that it happened just like I wanted it to. I couldn't continue with the lies and the deception any longer." Josh took a swig of his Scotch. He paced on the balcony as he tried to figure out what else he wanted to say. "It's not something I'm particularly proud of, but that's what it is. I hope someday you can find a way to forgive me. Maybe." Josh looked out into the sky and realized he had nothing left to add.

He ended his call and looked at the screen of his phone. Was it already that late? Clarita would arrive in a few hours. The chubby maid had often found him passed out. He didn't care much as long as she adhered to the nondisclosure agreement and kept the house clean. The amount he was paying her was enough to move her family out of East LA and into a nice school district.

Josh took another sip of Scotch and scrolled through his contact list. Finding the name he sought, he pressed call, hoping to go directly to voice mail. The service kicked in, and he prepared to leave another message.

A blinding light caught his attention as it raced across the sky from east to west. The light seemed to consume the entire night sky and he tried to shield his eyes. For a moment he thought he was well past three sheets to the wind. He tried to focus on what it could be.

Searchlight? Too large for that. A meteor? Not loud enough.

The entire sky was white, and he could make out nothing but the light. Everything merged into white nothingness. There was something beautiful about the darkness turning to light, as if the world had been given a second chance, a way to right the wrongs perpetrated against itself.

Josh felt an unseen force hurtling toward him. Marble-sized particles flew at him and he put up his arms in self-defense. The particles pulsed through his body. As they passed through him, he felt nauseous. The scent of sulfur filled his nostrils.

Josh's breathing shallowed and he realized he was lightheaded. He dropped his phone and stumbled across the balcony, barely making it to his bathroom before the retching turned into violent vomiting. Although he hadn't eaten much this evening, he could not control his stomach. He barely pushed himself off the toilet before falling to the floor. His last thoughts before passing out were of the light and the physical revulsion following its passing.

As quickly as the brilliant light came, it blinked out, leaving an overwhelming stillness in its dark wake.

Many hours later, Josh could hear his maid bounding up

the stairs and belting out a Selena song. Clarita was way off-key and his head pounded. He groaned. He couldn't move or open his eyes. He tried to remember what had happened to him last night and why he was on the bathroom floor. He could piece some of it together, but his head hurt too much to focus.

An odd sensation ran over his body, and he convulsed. Josh thought he could hear his bones and muscles contract and redistribute as he contorted.

He put his hand to his forehead, trying to calm his throbbing head. His hair felt shorter than he remembered it. Did he cut his own hair last night?

Cautiously, he ran his fingers down his face. It felt like a mask: whiskerless, older, wrinkled, and chubby.

He opened his eyes just as Clarita rounded the corner. He was picking himself off the ground when he heard her scream, not unlike how she had shrieked when he pranked her with the clowns. The difference this time was that her normally dark skin turned white, her eyes rolled back, and she promptly fainted.

If his head weren't hurting so much, Josh would have found this hilarious. He finally managed to stand.

As he spoke, he realized his throat was too hoarse and dry to utter anything coherent. He swallowed hard.

"Clarita, are you okay?" Josh asked. Stunned, he shook his head, which only made his head hurt more. Somehow, her voice had come from his lips.

He shuffled toward the bathroom mirror, unprepared for the face that greeted him from the mirror. He looked. Blinked. Rubbed his eyes. Looked again.

Josh thought he was hallucinating. He could not see himself, but Clarita standing where he stood. Each time he took a step closer, so did she.

He looked across the room to confirm that Clarita was indeed passed out on the floor.

He—she—looked back in the mirror. As he screamed, he recalled this was exactly her scream from moments ago.

Was this some elaborate prank? Was she getting him back for all the times he spooked her? He twisted around, searching for a camera. There was nothing.

Panic set in and Josh tried to breathe, but his entire body felt odd, strange, and full of conflicting sensations. His feet were numb, but his hands were on fire.

He slowly lifted his hands to his eyes, as if to block the terrifying and incomprehensible image reflected in the mirror. What he saw was that his strong, manly hands had been replaced with brown stubby fingers. He inched closer to the mirror, taking in the sight. He could not see himself. All that was there was Clarita. His six-foot-three frame had shrunk to fit her five-foot-two size.

"What the—"

Before he could utter the final word, he—or was it she?—passed out, joining the real Clarita on the floor.

CHAPTER

7

21 June

Rami came to in a precarious situation. He lay on his side, one hand dangling over the edge of the abyss before him. The cave had become something new. Something dangerous. Though he wasn't in pain, Rami did a slow body check. He had everything he entered the cave with.

He strained to recall how he'd gotten into his current predicament, but it was difficult to concentrate. He was absolutely and without measure terrified. He had never before been afraid of the dark. Of course, that was on the surface, where electricity allowed him to flick a switch to scare away the shadows. Here, almost half a mile below ground, Rami had no way of shutting off the utterly quiet darkness, save his headlamp, and even that seemed frightened to penetrate the thick darkness of the cave.

Even when humans are absolutely still and quiet, the world is still full of noise. Bugs move across the ground. Wind pushes against leaves. Streams trickle. The sounds that nature provides are constant above ground. Deep inside Earth, noises become fainter, almost nonexistent. At half a mile below the surface, it is deadly quiet. The natural sounds that give rise to the known world are absent so far down. Here, the sounds are made by human intruders. The scuffing of shoes along the dirt-hardened ground. The reverberation of a voice bouncing off rock formations. The ticking of a watch to signify the passage of time. Otherwise, the silence owns the depths.

Rami counted eight other beams of light pointing in different directions. Their odd, still angles unnerved him. His own beam was the only one moving. He uttered a silent prayer that he was not the only one alive, that the rest were sleeping. He opened his mouth, but no words escaped his lips. His throat was intensely sore. His inability to call out to his fellow explorers only fed his mounting terror.

Peering into the dark of the newly revealed cave, he sensed something familiar, yet alien. Rami reached out with trepidation to determine if there was anything out there. Nothing. His beam of light pierced the darkness, but the shadows trapped the light and gave Rami no peace.

He tried to swallow again, but his mouth was bone dry. He swung his arms down to his belt to retrieve his water bottle. He took gulps, not sips, as if he had not had a drink in hours. Wait, he thought, what time is it? He turned his arm and looked at his watch. It read 17:37. He'd been out for at least four hours, and it would take at least six hours just to get out of this cave. Even if this was the longest day of the year, he didn't want to make his escape into the night.

Facing the new passage, Rami slowly slid backward. He did not want to look around and confirm his fears. He scooted a few feet back, only to bump into something. He reached back to feel the obstacle, but it was not a stone. It was a body, cold and lifeless. He had momentarily forgotten the eight men he had trekked down this cave with. Rami mustered the courage to peek at the face of the man behind him.

It was Ken, the man who had brought him from a prison to the cave. His eyes were wide open in abject fear and his mouth was hanging open. Rami could not move.

He wanted to scream. He wanted to cry out for mercy. He did neither. He reluctantly placed his fingers on Ken's neck. The lack of pulse confirmed his fears. He knew the rest of the crew were also probably dead. Slowly, he made his way from body to body, placed his fingers where a pulse should be on seven more cold necks, and knew he was the lone survivor. He had no idea what had killed the others or why he alone had been spared in this deep chamber of death.

As he made his rounds, he found Peter's camera. The green light indicated the camera was still recording. Rami moved it and stood where the camera was aimed. He glanced at his watch again and began speaking.

"This is Rami Kazemi, and I am the only survivor of the Ghar Parau expedition. It is 17:47. We made it down to the sump about four hours ago. As we got to the sump, I noticed the rocks that were staggered near the opening of the new passage were glowing with phosphorescence. I also saw my hands giving off a slight glow. I lifted my hand to touch the rocks, and without warning, the cave started to split. I was hit with a foul stench. Like rotten eggs and spoiled cabbage. I felt an unseen force barrel past us. In its wake, it left what can only be described as some sort of dust. Large, coin-sized dust particles that began filling my lungs."

Rami now realized why his mouth was so dry.

"I immediately passed out. I came to only minutes ago. The entire rest of the crew is dead. Everyone is gone but me. I don't know what killed them. I am going to make my way out of the cave. I don't know what happened and I can only hope that when I reach the top, the world hasn't gone mad and that I will still be a free man. That whatever came through the rocks, through me, hasn't killed the world. Mr. Hastings, if you see this recording, please send someone to come get me. Save me. I cannot go back to Astara."

Rami grabbed the camera. He retraced his steps to Ken and took the man's satellite phone and water bottle. He grabbed a few other supplies and said a small prayer for the dead. As he turned to leave, a strange sensation started at the base of his skull and traveled down his spine, as though he wasn't alone after all. He froze dead in his tracks, straining to hear whether something was approaching him. Then he heard it, a whisper floating in the air. Quiet, but familiar.

How long I have waited for you.
All these years reaching out to you,
Helping you achieve your dreams,
Creating a destiny for you.

CHAPTER
8

22 June

Dr. Roger Martin flipped on his office television and raised the volume slightly. He saw travel reporter Maggie Adams speaking about her impression of the Kilimanjaro disaster. She was easy on the eyes, Roger thought. He wanted to watch but didn't want

Dr. Roger Martin

to be distracted from the mounds of scientific data reviews scattered across his desk. He had a goal to accomplish and a short time frame.

Roger lifted his coffee mug to his mouth—was it his third cup of the day?—and looked around his sparsely decorated office, with the morning sun bleeding through his floor-to-ceiling windows high up in the downtown Philadelphia skyscraper that held the entirety of The Hastings Foundation for Scientific Research and Development.

He tried to imagine actually speaking with Maggie. But before he could envision the interview, Dr. Nicola Patel knocked at his door.

"Roger, these readings you must come and look at." In her excitement, Nicola's Indian accent came out heavier than normal. She held out a paper. "The calculations we provided for the synthesized particle stabilizer are correct. Heat fluctuations are interfering with the proper functions of the helix matrix."

"Nicola, I told you not to bother me until you had an answer for the disastrous trial last week." Roger stood and slid his graying hair back. Rather than take the paper from her, he crossed his office to a short bookcase that held the one personal touch in his office—a well-worn stuffed koala he'd brought when he left Australia. It sat slightly askew, and Roger shifted it around until it sat upright again.

"But I have checked and rechecked the math. We weren't wrong." She waved the paper again. "Something else is the problem."

She thrust the report toward Roger and he reluctantly took it. Roger scanned the numbers, which confirmed the trial failure was physical, not computational. Roger slowly sat back down in his chair.

"And what about—" Roger said.

"Way ahead of you. See here in the stress test"—Nicola leaned over the desk and flipped the page in front of him—"the results are the same."

She beamed. "Then again, I'm not sure why we are working on this helix matrix to begin with. It doesn't combine with any of our current or past projects." Nicola watched Roger review the pages.

"Did you tell anyone else about this?" Roger motioned her to close the door.

She did so. "No. You are the first." Nicola paused. "But I did ask Thierry to meet me here."

"And what did Thierry have to say?"

"He's on his way."

"I just want to make sure that nothing else happens to us." Roger muted the television as he leaned closer to his colleague. "We have to make absolutely certain these findings are sound. We cannot afford any mistakes, or we'll all wind up like Kaczmarzyk."

How low they had fallen. The four scientists, all working at the climate problem from different areas of focus, had come to the same result: Earth was significantly changing, and quickly. They concluded the speed was much too fast to be due to nature, and must be caused by another culprit. Man.

The documented changes included increased severe storm activity, rising sea levels, increased salinization and temperature of the oceans, and far-reaching droughts. The four took painstaking research showing the changes were tied directly to man's activities to the UN Economic and Social Council. Quantitative data and photographic evidence demonstrated that in less than fifty years, climate change would wreak catastrophic disasters on Earth unless steps were taken immediately.

The UN Economic and Social Council was unmoved. The scientific community's response was far harsher.

They'd been blacklisted.

The response was far beyond the blowback and harsh criticisms they had expected. No organization or agency would touch them. In desperation, they approached The Hastings Foundation.

They made their case to the Philadelphia-based think tank's board, which included a who's who of the city's elite in addition to Henry Hastings. Hastings, who could trace his family back to colonial America and then back across the Atlantic several generations, was a mysterious champion of free thought and pushed for his scientists to come at problems from many different angles. In fact, it was his pioneering approaches at the Foundation that divined slight geothermal changes that led to reliable predictions of earthquakes hours in advance—giving countless millions more time to prepare for the devastation. Halfway through their presentation to the board that long-ago day, Henry interrupted.

"We can all agree that the public is not quite up to the challenge of understanding why the world is changing around them. It is incumbent upon us in the scientific community to bear this burden. We must wake the world up so we can save them."

As Henry spoke, each of the scientists nodded in agreement. They had finally found someone to believe in them and their research. They had found a home that would not just help them continue their efforts to save the world from a climate-related disaster but also give them a chance to mend their scientific reputations.

Dr. Thierry Giraud crashed into the office and immediately Roger could smell his musky cologne.

"What did you call me about, Nicola?" Thierry asked, closing the door.

"The helix matrix. If we can narrow down the specific changes, we can have this machine ready for use very soon."

"Well, what are we waiting for?" Thierry asked in his soft French accent. Smiling, Thierry whipped out his red yo-yo and slung it down and up. He didn't notice Roger squint at him. "Did you see the lights last night? Some bright light just blew through town like nothing. Crazy, huh?"

Roger cleared his throat and Thierry stopped talking.

"We are waiting for precise data to come back to confirm what the problem is within the physical device," Roger said.

"Of course," Thierry said as he wound up his favorite yo-yo and returned it to his coat pocket. "But we don't even really know what this device is for. You made us stop all of our projects on seawater reclamation and artificial ice generation to work on this."

"If we could link the helix matrix with some sort of capacitor that can manage the heat fluctuations, we might be able to stabilize the machine," Nicola said. But before she could take a step away, the door opened and everyone froze.

"That sounds very logical and I suggest you get started right away. We have a lot riding on that project." Henry Hastings filled the doorway.

"Mr. Hastings. We had no idea you'd be here today," Roger stammered as he stood at attention.

"Of course," Henry said. "I would encourage you to work quickly and resourcefully on this. You don't want any unforeseen accident to befall you."

Roger saw Thierry and Nicola exchange glances and knew they were concluding The Hastings Foundation was somehow complicit in the fate of their late colleague, Dr. Kaczmarzyk.

"You've got a week to get this device operational." Henry gave a forced smile as he allowed the two scientists to pass by him. Henry shut the door.

"Mr. Hastings, we now know what the problem was that led to the explosion earlier."

"Do they know what they are actually working on?" Henry asked.

"No, of course not."

"Good, I'd hate for anything to happen to them should they find out the truth about their work here at The Hastings Foundation."

"I won't let that happen," Roger said.

"You've long been a friend to the Ascendancy and we couldn't have gotten as far as we have without you. As always, you will be rewarded handsomely for your efforts."

"Screw the money. I've enough of that," Roger said with a nerve he did not know he had.

"Then what?"

"I want in." He looked straight down into Henry's eyes.

Henry was quiet for a few moments. "You know that it is not up to me."

"I know a lot more than you think I do." Roger walked over and opened the door. "And I would be very careful with who you let know your secrets, Mr. Hastings."

"Wait!"

Roger stopped, smiled slightly, and turned around.

"If the helix matrix is successful and we can deploy it into the WaveMaker, I will bring you into the inner sanctum."

Roger swallowed a smile. After years and years of devoted service, this was the opportunity he had long sought. He wouldn't let anything get in his way.

"But we need your department's full cooperation and complete focus."

"You have it. I won't let you down," Roger said as Henry's head bobbed a bit.

"Good. I'll be in touch." As Henry walked away, Roger's body did a full shake.

CHAPTER

9

22 June

Rimbo glumly reeled in his empty line, and peered into the sloshing bucket tucked between him and Tari.

All three of the fish in there had come from Tari's hook. If Rimbo's luck didn't change soon, Tari would be full of swagger the rest of the day, having provided all the meat at dinner. And when Rimbo's son had a swelled head, well, the boy was just insufferable. Of course, Rimbo was proud of his son's luck, and grateful that the sea's bounty was jumping onto their dinner table via Tari's hooks.

Rimbo threaded fresh bait on his own hook and cast the line again. He wondered if the fish were staying away from his line because they could sense the inner turmoil he was trying desperately to squash. If he failed at that, he wanted to at least shield his son from it. Tari showed no signs of worry. Of course, he wouldn't, Rimbo thought. Tari was ten, unaware of the concerns of the adults of his house. Tari shone with the joy of youth, pleased to succeed at a difficult task that requires a certain amount of luck.

The day was as lovely as they came to his little Indonesian island, Pulau Sangeang. He watched the water glisten and dance in the sunlight. He breathed in slowly and exhaled as slowly. And yet, relaxation eluded him. The fact he'd pulled up not a single fish, that wasn't a cause for the frustration, he knew. That was just a symptom. Pragmatically, Rimbo turned his thoughts homeward. If he couldn't relax in the middle of a peaceful ocean, enjoying time with his son, then he might as well think about his problems. Perhaps the seas might offer up inspiration in addition to the fish bounty.

Rimbo was more worried than he had ever been. Or at least more than he'd been since he took up farming to supplement what he earned from taking tourists fishing.

How could he tell his wife that they were going to be poor farmers after this season ended? He'd proposed the fishing excursion with his son as a way to delay having to deliver that news. Also, he hoped a brilliant scheme would pop into his mind.

Of course, it hadn't. Although Rimbo didn't know it at the time, that wouldn't matter in the long run.

Fretting was turning his stomach sour, so he initiated a game of twenty questions with Tari.

"I'm thinking of a place," Rimbo said.

"Is it home?" Tari asked.

"No. Remember, Mentari, if you ask specifics too early in, you'll burn your questions."

"Is it in Indonesia?"

"No, but much better. Eighteen left."

"Is it in Europe?"

"Yes. Seventeen left," Rimbo said, grinning. Tari had been fascinated by all things Europe since meeting some French scuba divers a few months before. Rimbo wondered if his son would think of the iconic Eiffel Tower before he ran out of questions.

Before Tari could ask his fourth question, Rimbo heard

an explosion behind him that awakened fear in every fiber of his being. He knew instantly that Sangeang Api had let loose.

When he turned to look at the island, what he saw made all his money and crop worries moot. Gone were thoughts of fried fish and beer for dinner. Fear for his wife's life took over as the only important thing in the world. Would anyone still be alive on the island at this time tomorrow?

Rimbo realized that the volcano was exploding repeatedly. He saw lava spurting high from the cone. The stink of sulfur filled his nostrils. He felt deaf and understood that his son could be shouting in his ears and he likely wouldn't hear it. He turned to comfort Tari, who had his eyes wide open, as well as his mouth. Rimbo saw Tari didn't grasp what the jetting streams of lava meant.

But Rimbo knew what it meant. That it was too late.

Rimbo clutched his son. The gesture seemed to spur comprehension in the boy, who began to wail.

The eruption was an awesome sight, something every person living near an active volcano hopes they only ever see in pictures. Few live to walk away from the real thing.

Rimbo's survival instincts kicked in. He mentally compiled all the details he knew about Sangeang Api, facts that every resident on the island learned at an early age. That it erupted frequently in geologic terms, although that may be only a few times or never during a person's life. That it was a complex volcano with two cones. That the older cone was dormant, but the Doro Api cone was most definitely alive and kicking.

He knew the initial eruption—what he was now watching in terror—would probably be followed by a continued period of lava exploding high into the sky and fast-moving lava flows that brought ambient air temperatures to over five hundred degrees Fahrenheit, causing instant death.

His mind slid past these unhappy facts as his eyes honed in on the top of the volcano. He spotted a wide vein of lava cutting a huge pathway down the mountain. His heart went white when he realized the destructive route would eat up his wife, his home, and his failing crops, and there was nothing he could do. They were at least fifteen minutes of heavy rowing from shore. And the house was a brisk ten-minute walk inland. They'd never make it.

Tari stood in the gently rocking rowboat and forced an oar into his father's hand. Rimbo automatically clasped the oar, but sat unmoving. The oar floated uselessly atop the water.

"Row," the boy commanded. He gripped the other oar, sat on his bench, and pushed the oar through the water.

Rimbo did not row.

"Pak, we must get Bu."

Rimbo tore his focus away from the destruction and turned to his son. There, he saw a different kind of destruction. The boy's brown eyes were frantic and wide with fear. Gone were the tears of a moment ago, replaced by a grim determination to return to shore save his mother. In that moment, Rimbo saw the man his son would be, if they survived.

"We can't go back. We wouldn't make it. No one on the island will make it."

"No."

The simple negative tore Rimbo's heart.

Rimbo leaned across the bucket holding his son's three-fish catch and hugged him. Father and son watched in horrified silence as the lava smothered the life out of the land. It was moving so quickly. No one could possibly outrun it. It rolled over trees and fields. It crushed the hut of the old witch he'd feared since childhood. It surged down into the valley. It streamed right toward their farm. Steaming lava covered the very fields that had so worried him all morning.

And then the lava ate his house.

Tari screamed, and Rimbo wanted to. They were safe at sea, alive, but they would never be whole again.

The lava kept going, consuming everything that had ever mattered to Rimbo and Tari.

Rimbo held Tari closer to him. Not that a father's hug could do much to ease the loss of a mother.

"Oh, Pak," Tari said. His quiet tears turned into sobs.

Rimbo hoped he was wrong about her whereabouts. He wished she were safe off the island somewhere. That she'd had an idea to go somewhere, to take advantage of having the day to herself. But he knew she hadn't left. She'd wanted to sew a dress and cook a new recipe; she would have been at home. And so he prayed that she had died instantly, pain-free, from the intense heat that he knew, from a schoolbook lesson, that accompanies such an explosion.

Rimbo's grief was full and complete, overwhelming. He had Tari, and they were still both alive. But that was it. His precious wife was gone. Their house was gone. Their livelihood was gone. Their friends and relatives were gone. It felt like all his vital insides had been turned inside out. He felt so empty.

He watched the trajectory of the projectile lava. They were safe in the rowboat for now, but if the wind shifted, they might be in danger.

Despair waged battle with common sense and Rimbo's remaining survival instinct. He didn't want to contemplate what it would take to live through the aftermath of the eruption. But Rimbo couldn't send Tari to death simply because he himself was too heartbroken to go on. In his despair, his lungs seemed to quit on him. He couldn't get a decent breath, and the ash would soon complicate that. They couldn't go back to the island, but getting back to the next closest island, Sumbawa, would take some serious rowing.

"Mentari, son, you realize we can't go back to the island?"

"Yes, Pak," Tari said, still sobbing.

"Son, we are going to have to leave, if we want to survive. Do you understand?"

Fresh sobs greeted this.

"I want to say good-bye," Tari said.

"Of course you do. I do too. Why don't I go first?" Rimbo waited for his son's nod before proceeding. "Cinta, my dear wife, you were the sun and moon in my life. From the time we met, no day was complete without you. I was honored to love you and be loved by you. Proud to be chosen by you, to be the father of your son." His voice wavered as he lost the battle against tears, and he fell to his knees. In response, the rowboat rocked perilously. For a moment, Rimbo hoped the little rowboat, the one that had been his pride, would dump him out, sending him to the bottom of the sea as a gift, so he could reunite with Cinta.

"Pak," the boy shouted. Tari grabbed the side of the boat and held on. When Rimbo looked at his son, he was ashamed not just for furthering Tari's fright but also of his selfish grief. At last, Rimbo was able to speak again.

"I tried very hard to be the best husband I could, and I hope I made you as happy as you made me. I will do my best to guide Tari through his life, but please watch over us. We'll need some help. I will miss you until the end of my days."

Rimbo was sobbing by the time he finished his impromptu eulogy. He knew thousands of things would occur to him in the days ahead, if they survived, that he would wish he had said at this moment. But that was okay, he decided, because all he had said was heartfelt and honest. He wasn't even embarrassed for his son to see him reduced to tears in the wake of this disaster.

"I love you, Bu, and I wish we were still together. I hope it didn't hurt too much and that you will wait for me. I miss you already," Tari said.

They turned their backs on Pulau Sangeang and its destructive volcano. Vast quantities of magma continued to boil underground. Sangeang Api's surprise eruption killed virtually every inhabitant of the island. Streams of lava slid down the slope of the volcano, entombing those unfortunates killed by the heat and laying down a deep blanket of rock over the island's native flora and fauna.

CHAPTER 10

22 June

"This better not be another one of your off-the-wall theories that I can punch holes the size of—"

"Take a look at this, Rog, before you finish your eloquent thought." Thierry tossed an envelope at Roger, who slapped his hands together to catch it.

Dr. Nicola Patel

Nicola smoothed back her hair and leaned against her chair, waiting for Roger to read the contents of the envelope.

"Oh! Did you see this?" Thierry asked. He held up his phone to show Roger and Nicola a low-quality video. "See, there's a man running so fast—even keeping up with that car."

"Must be some sort of special effect," Roger said, barely glancing at the video. Nicola stared at the images.

"I thought so too, but it doesn't seem so. And I saw another where a guy jumps from a building but instead of plunging to his death, he flew!" Thierry said with a wide incredulous grin.

"Are you quite done?" Roger asked.

Thierry reluctantly put his phone away and bumped Roger slightly as he settled into the main chair. He spun his red-and-blue yo-yo while Roger skimmed the notes.

"I've been thinking about Kilimanjaro and Sangeang Api and how there has been a significant uptick in the size and scope of these disasters," Thierry said, playing with the yo-yo he kept in his lab coat. "I kept trying to think linearly with each of these events. Not to mention the Bright Light Incident that just happened." Thierry looked lost in thought as he manipulated the yo-yo into the Houdini Drop Mount.

"Bright Light Incident?" Roger said impatiently as he kicked his clunky black shoes together.

"You know, that crazy white light that passed through last night," Thierry said as Roger rolled his eyes.

The office phone rang and Roger snatched it up. He turned his back to his colleagues and began speaking in a hushed tone.

"I was thinking that there could be some sort of connection between the lights and these videos," Thierry said to Nicola.

"Why would you say that?" Nicola asked.

"The reports I've read and the footage I saw of the lights show suggest that it's some special particle-based manipulation. Plus, there are some images and videos showing the particles passing through people."

"Really?" she asked, fascinated.

Roger briefly turned toward them as if to shut them up. Thierry and Nicola stood and moved toward the door to continue their conversation.

"Have there been any credible reports of the effects of the particles passing through them? Any symptoms or strange responses?" Nicola asked.

"Nothing that has come out yet. But I have to believe that this could possibly have some effect on them. One video from a club in Montreal shows the particles passing over a large crowd and then heading straight through one person," Thierry said.

"So if somehow this ... light ... particle is responsible for changing or manipulating people, then it stands to reason that there is some way for us to determine a link between them," Nicola said, using her hands more expressively. "And if we can determine the link, we could, theoretically, discover the origin of the light particles. That would give us a starting point to calculate the expanse and range and then we can extrapolate the number of people who were affected. A signature of sorts." Nicola pulled out her tablet and entered in a series of commands that pulled up satellite images. She cross-referenced the time range and waited for the machine to compute the request.

"Thanks for the update," Roger said. He hung up the phone and turned back toward them and scanned the notes on his desk. "So what exactly are you showing me here?"

"Of course, Rog. Getting to it." Thierry returned the yo-yo to his pocket. "Nicola and I have been wracking our brains for the past two days poring over the data. And then it occurs to me that the extreme natural disasters follow a complex pattern. A series of small events that we wouldn't even think to connect followed by a large one. Then a few more small ones and then another larger one."

"Stop wasting The Hastings Foundation's time on these disasters and that blasted white light. You want to pursue it? Fine. But on your own time. When you're here, your full attention needs to be on the helix matrix. We've a schedule to keep." The veins on the side of Roger's head bulged.

Nicola and Thierry looked at Roger and then continued.

"I think that if there is a pattern to all these events and we find it, then we can make the logical leap that these disasters are building to something," Thierry said, eyeing Nicola, and pulling his yo-yo out of his pocket again.

"So there's also a notion that the particulate substance and subsequent change could also be related to the violent uptick in ecological disasters. It's not too much of a reach to come to that conclusion, right, Roger?" Nicola asked. They turned to look at their agitated boss, whose blue eyes seemed fixated on Thierry's yo-yo. Slowly, Thierry slipped the toy back into his lab coat, and the squint lines around Roger's eyes relaxed minutely.

"And?" Roger asked.

"We came up with a hypothesis. One that combines both the, uh, White Light Wave"—Nicola smiled at Thierry, who nodded in agreement at the name—"and the recent disasters. I think we can come up with an accurate forecast of what will happen next."

At this point, Roger leaned closer. He wondered if Thierry and Nicola could have actually cracked the delicate balance of natural and unnatural disasters.

"There were little, almost imperceptible changes in the thermal energy deep in the core of the earth. If you weren't looking for it, you'd never see it. I just so happened to be looking for ... you know, never mind. Listen, though, I followed a hunch and figured out there was also a substantial, localized release that coincides with the Pale Particle Explosion ... Nope, that's not the right name for it either."

"Just get to the point."

"The point is, we know where the incident originated and how to monitor it," Nicola butted in as her tablet dinged to life. The satellite map narrowed around northwestern Iran and again on the Zagros Mountains. "See this here," she said as they watched a video of a very fast-moving explosive light display emanating from a cave.

"Where is this?" Roger asked.

"That's Ghar Parau."

Roger collapsed against the back of the chair. It is happening, he thought. After a moment, he asked, "So what are we to make out of this?"

"Best as I can guess is that the thermal energy that has changed during each of the disasters is directly related to the—"

"White Light Wave event," Thierry interrupted.

"I do like that name for it," Nicola said and continued, "Where it emerged after some considerable agitation."

"Why do you think there was some sort of agitation?" Roger asked.

"I have some knowledge of caving and this particular cave has baffled spelunkers for years. They always believed that it was deeper than they could go. If that still holds true, then the energy must have had a catalyst to escape." Nicola trailed off, a faraway look in her eyes. The two scientists eyed her; they'd seen that look before and it usually presaged a leap of genius.

"We even had an expedition to Ghar Parau with Rex and Peter leading a group to discover if the sump had opened. We lost contact with them, and since I knew they were going to the cave, I had tasked the satellites to monitor the region."

Roger's eyes widened at the connection Nicola made.

"I didn't know you knew about the expedition."

"Of course, Peter told me about it since he knew I had actually been there," Nicola said, fidgeting as she mentioned his name.

"So what is it you aren't saying?" Thierry asked.

"These events are connected. But we need to discern the origins. They all lead back to one place. One location that is of particular interest to us," Nicola said. She held up an index finger over her mouth in a "be quiet" gesture and with her other hand mimicked the talking gesture.

Understanding what she was after, Thierry turned to his tablet and activated a sonic harmonics program that would scramble their conversation into benign, idle chatter so they could speak without fear of being monitored by their higher-ups at The Hastings Foundation. He then activated a hard-light hologram program that could similarly fool the video surveillance. She nodded and held up three fingers. Three minutes.

"Could the thermal energy radiation changes *and* the white light be connected? This would allow us to explain the disasters, determine who was affected by the white particles as well as give us a road map to predicting future disasters," Nicola said.

"This is more complicated than I anticipated," Roger said.

"What do you mean? More complicated than the circumstances that originally led us to The Hastings Foundation?" Nicola asked.

"We have been looking at this problem the wrong way. We weren't asking the right questions. Instead of asking how the climate has been changing or how drastic the disasters are, we should have been asking why. Or more precisely, who." Thierry let that last word hang a few moments.

"Are you saying that someone is causing these changes?" Roger asked.

"Someone or something," Nicola shot back, nodding.

Thierry motioned to them closer. They leaned over Roger's desk.

"Ghar Parau must have opened up a new passage. Peter

must have found the opening. I know that this seems all sorts of unlikely, but I'd stake my life on the cause of these problems coming directly from that cave," Thierry said.

"I know that we have looked for the origin of this so-called White Light Wave event, and all the surveillance points to its beginning here," Nicola said as they looked at her tablet, which showed the inexplicable light emerging from the earth and speeding westward.

"I hope that you covered your tracks," Roger said.

"Don't worry."

"You could get in so much trouble for this. Remember Kaczmarzyk?" Roger warned.

"I'm not going to let you scare me. This is important."

"Earlier you said who," Roger said, turning to Thierry as he changed his point of attack.

"What? Oh, right. You're not going to believe me," Thierry said.

"Who," Roger repeated.

"I think the earth itself is crying out, and that all of these are reactions to a sickness," Thierry said.

"Are you saying Earth has a consciousness?" Roger asked.

"That is your problem with this?" Thierry said. "We can easily accept extraterrestrial beings flitting about the cosmos, but is it so hard to think that this earth of ours could have a consciousness? And that after years and years of abuse from humans it is finally striking back?"

Roger took a breath, stood and folded his arms.

"I am not saying I buy into this, but if this cave has something to do with these reactions, then it behooves us to explore the possibility of an Earth consciousness." Roger could hardly believe the words that were coming out of his mouth.

"What aren't you telling us?" Nicola asked.

"It's true that Peter and Rex led an expedition to discover the full depth of Ghar Parau," Roger said as he grabbed his tablet.

"So you already knew that the cave was somehow involved in this?" Thierry asked, grinning and spinning his yo-yo.

"Not exactly. And I urge you both to return to working on the helix matrix. We have to give Hastings results. We can't end up like Kaczmarzyk." Roger looked at the clock, which confirmed that their covert moment was up.

Thierry and Nicola exchanged terse looks, picked up their respective devices, and left.

"Remember. Bring results next time. And leave this White Light Wave event and weird Earth happenings alone," Roger said as he sat back and twirled his thumbs. He thought he'd kicked this nervous habit, but stress had brought it back. Whatever, this was not the time to lose focus. He had a goal and there was no stopping him.

CHAPTER
11

22 June

A chill swallowed Rami's body as he recognized the voice from his dreams. Instinctively, he understood this voice, somehow, had been responsible for his entire life. Guiding him, helping him, pushing him toward his destiny. This thought scared him. Did he have no free will? Was his life predetermined? Was he always destined to be in this cave when the rest of his crew died?

Rami yelled to drown out these thoughts. He hadn't shouted like this since before he arrived at Astara prison. It felt good. For a moment. Then the silence returned.

He took one more look around and started making his way back along the trail. Despite being emotionally drained, Rami felt invigorated in a way that he had not felt in almost a year. Energy coursed through him, and he focused solely on placing one foot in front of the other. His blood pumped with determination. He no longer wanted to be in this cave. Rami was not about to trade one prison for another. He would reclaim his life so he was no longer an involuntary participant.

He came upon one of the most treacherous parts of the

cave. The small passage required crawling on the rough ground and then making a ninety-degree turn to climb up the steep wall. He took the existing ropes and hooked himself into the belay system. He strapped his right foot into the roped hook and tugged at the bolts. He felt good about their security but he was violating the cardinal rule of caving. Never cave alone. How easy it had seemed to pass this point with the entire crew, he thought. Now, as he stood solo in the area where other cavers had died, he was uneasy. If he fell, there was no one to help him.

He made steady progress, but lost concentration when he thought about how the belay system had once failed when he and Arian were exploring. Now, he slipped a few feet. His fingers dug into the wall, finding a few crevices, and stopped his drop. He lifted himself back up to the edge with strength he didn't think he possessed.

In his mind's eye, Rami saw Arian's long, flowing dark hair during their last visit to Ghar Parau. They had been dangling over a ledge. Twenty-six feet below were glistening tidal pools, formed by spring rains. Those same rains had damaged some of the rope and rigging, and one of Rami's ropes had started to fail. He had made a speedy but controlled descent and landed in one of the pools.

"Just a moment, love," Arian had shouted as she twisted herself upside down to connect her rope to the hook. She had lowered herself until she was face to face with Rami. "Looks like this is two you owe me."

Rami had smiled and pecked her cheek. It was the second time, this trip, she had come to the rescue. He had sloshed around in the tidal pool as she lowered the rope to him and he latched on. His head lamp had caught the dripping water, and he had grinned at the resulting rainbow arching across the cave. There's no better moment than this, he had thought.

"What are you smiling about?"

At that moment, a clip on Arian's rigging had given way. As she fell, she had screamed, "Rami." Before the cry was fully out of her mouth, Rami had caught her and was cradling her in his arms.

He had breathlessly patted both of them to make sure they were okay. Once she had smiled and nodded her head, they had broken into deep relieved laughter that echoed throughout the cave. They had reclined against the rocks to catch their breath.

"I trust no one but you to spend the rest of my life exploring with. You have me here," Rami had said, pointing to his heart.

"Why, Rami Kazemi, are you proposing to me?"

He had panicked. It was not at all how he planned to pop the question. He had wanted wine and their favorite dessert and the perfect day.

"I had a plan for proposing and it didn't involve this blasted cave." Rami had laughed and caressed her hand. "I wasn't whole until I met you. You gave me a purpose. Loving you gave me life and something to hang on to."

"Shut up and kiss me," Arian had said as she pulled him close and their lips met.

Focus, Rami, he chastised himself. Face reality. Arian wasn't here. Everyone deep in the cave was dead. His own hands were scraped, cut and bleeding from his slip. With little water remaining in his water bottle and none from the bottle he had taken from Ken and no first-aid kit, he couldn't disinfect the wounds. He didn't even have extra fabric to wrap around his wounds to protect them from the dirt in the cave.

In the second level of the cave, his light played across something he had not seen before. Writing. In a script he was unfamiliar with. After a few minutes of study, he determined it wasn't graffiti. It was actually carved into the rock. The carvings looked sophisticated and deliberate. He was intrigued. He took the camera and filmed the entire wall. He was surprised no one had noticed the markings on the descent. As he ran his fingers over the rough edges of the markings, he decided they were relatively new. Maybe from the last year or so. Perhaps Hassan would have known about them. In that moment, Rami remembered that all of his compatriots had died down in the cave, and his stomach clenched.

He eventually came to the part of the cave that, while unpleasant, was not treacherous. He began to slither through the crawl space on his belly. He was about halfway through when his light began to flicker. He cursed his failure to grab an extra headlamp before setting off. He'd never make it back to the top with no light. He lightly knocked against the light and the beam thickened. He let out a breath of pure relief. His thoughts turned to Arian and their reunion. If I get out of this alive, I'll ask her to marry me.

"Shit!" Rami shouted as he cut his side on a rock that jutted out. He pressed his shirt into the wound. "Idiot."

He pulled his hand away from the wound and examined his fingertips. They were dripping with blood. Rami hesitated, then tentatively placed his fingers inside his cut to see how deep it was. He winced as he put one knuckle deep in the cut. Rami closed his eyes and counted back from ten. With the severity of this cut he wasn't sure how he'd manage the rest of the climb. Most cave injuries and death resulted from compounding problems, with three or four things going wrong. His crew was dead, he only had a few more drops of water on him, his headlight was failing him, and now he was hurt. The end for him could come quickly.

He slowly made his way out of the crawl space and into the next chamber. He sat up and breathed.

Rami sipped a little of the water and looked at his arms. Covered, absolutely caked in dirt. Perhaps he ought to rinse the wounds out after all, no matter how little water he had left. He held up his bloody hands, but the cuts and scrapes from his fall seemed to have vanished, leaving just dried, caked-on bloodstains. Had he imagined injured hands? He opened his shirt and looked at his stomach, which had been very bloody. Rami only found a faint, light scratch. Confused, he rebuttoned his shirt.

"I can't believe how quickly I've gotten this far," Rami said out loud. "I always thought getting out of a cave was harder than going down, but not this time."

He was coming up to the highest climb of Ghar Parau and he wasn't even winded.

As Rami scurried up the ladder at the eroica, he felt Ken's sat phone bang against his side. He might be able to get a signal now. Rami dialed a preprogrammed number. It rang several times before anyone picked up, and there was only static on the other end. He decided to try again when he got closer to the entrance. Rami put the phone back into his pack and continued his ascent.

An hour later, he reached the small crawl space that separated the cave from the outside world.

He looked around the cave one last time, thinking he would be the happiest man on earth if he never set foot inside it again.

Rami braced his arm on the stone and as the light from his headlamp bounced across the cave he thought he heard something. Not the voice from his dreams, but something else. Something stranger. Something ominous.

As I spin in my celestial tomb
You must hear my cries.
You must know my pain.
I reach out to you.
I give each of my children
New gifts.
Be wise and use with
Great caution.
But you are my chosen
You must lead them all, my Sentinel.
You must save me.

CHAPTER
1 2

22 June

The last notes of Arrested Development's "Children Play with Earth" faded, and Emma Sheehy dropped neatly to the floor, criss-cross-applesauce. She had been dancing for what felt like hours. As uncoordinated as she

Emma Sheehy

was, the skinny seven-year-old, clad from head to toe in various shades of purple, didn't much enjoy dancing. But agreeing to dance camp had been a compromise, a word she had learned early from her lawyer father. Next week was science camp and, that, she would be good at.

"Girls, that was better. Get some water and then let's go through it again. We want it perfect for the recital on Friday," Cara barked. The dozen Irish girls taking Cara's hip-hop dance classes scattered, eager for the water break.

Emma groaned, sneaking a look at her watch. At least ten minutes to go. They'd probably get through the song two more times before they were freed to start the morning's costume workshop. She predicted large amounts of glitter.

Costume time would be fun. They were going to decorate the cat masks for the "Stray Cat Strut" jazz number for the recital. But in the meantime, water. She rose from her spot on the floor and headed toward the long metal bench for her water bottle.

"Okay, girls, back in your spots," the dance instructor directed.

Emma groaned. She felt cheated. Slow off the mark to get her water bottle, she hadn't gotten halfway to the bench for her water. Cara had no tolerance for disobedience or slowpokes. Or anyone who didn't have the dance bug, Emma thought sourly. Sighing, she returned to her newly assigned spot in the back row behind a bubbly chubby girl named Darcy. Emma knew why she was in the back, and it wasn't because she was tall. At seven, she was the youngest in the class. And the second shortest.

She was in the back because she couldn't Dougie, and that was the basic dance move Cara had choreographed the song around.

Cara clapped loudly while counting fours, and "Children Play with Earth" sprang loudly from the speakers in the dance studio. Emma lifted her arms and attempted to Dougie, shaking her head so her long blond braids appeared to be dancing, too. She just wanted the song to be over in a hurry. She hoped science camp would prove worth this humiliation.

"Good movies, Darcy," Cara said over the music. "Emma, you're too tense. Be loose. Shake."

Emma scowled. She was trying to shake, but even she could see it was more of a spasming shimmy than a Dougie.

The song was picking up speed, and Emma was panting, trying to keep up. Trying to be loose and shake, something difficult at the best of times. But now, she felt weak, which was weird. She was tired, yes, and didn't want to be there. Her weakness was out of proportion with her level of effort. Her legs went rubbery under her—as though she had spent the last twenty hours Dougieing nonstop and her legs had finally gone on strike—and she tried mightily to remain upright, no longer concerned with even trying to dance.

But Emma couldn't keep her feet. As she collapsed onto the wood floor, she smelled something stinky, like overcooked broccoli, and wondered distractedly which of the girls around her had tooted. She wanted to cry but instead just closed her eyes. She was weak and rubbery all over, and now her morning porridge was trying to complicate matters. Emma concentrated on keeping her breakfast down, praying for all she was worth that she would be better at that than she had been at staying on her feet. She'd already embarrassed herself enough in hip-hop without puking her guts out.

Dimly, she could hear Darcy and the other girls asking if she was okay and gathering around her. She heard Cara ordering the other girls to move away and give Emma some room.

"Emma, child, what's wrong?" Cara asked gently. Emma opened her eyes and saw concern etching Cara's face. Gone was the bossy dance teacher of five minutes past.

Emma feebly shook her head, closed her eyes again, and passed out. When she came to, Cara was still there, but the other girls were gone. It was eerily silent in the little hip-hop studio, where pumping music and barked commands were the order of the day. Cara was blotting Emma's face with a cool, damp towel.

"No, I don't need an ambulance. I'm okay."

Cara's forehead creased in confusion. "Emma, what happened?" In her worry, Cara's voice was low and gently melodic. Emma hadn't considered that the loud, brassy voice that bossed her around for an hour a day could sound any other way.

Slowly, the room came to focus around Emma, and she realized she was still lying on the floor, only now her head was in Cara's lap. Before answering the question, Emma took a quick inventory. Her head hurt a little, but that pain seemed to be fading. She didn't smell any vomit, so she assumed she had managed to keep her porridge down. On further inspection, Emma realized her stomach no longer felt queasy at all. She felt an unidentifiable energy coursing through her arms, her legs, and her head, and she was alert like never before to the world around her. Her traitorous legs, which had started all this nonsense, felt like they normally did. And so Emma sat up.

"No, I'm not hurt," Emma said.

Cara looked sharply at the girl. "Good. But what happened?"

"I don't know."

"You really scared me. Are you sure you're okay?" Cara peered at her.

Emma nodded slowly. "I'm fine. I don't like juice. I'd love some water, though."

After giving Emma a queer look, Cara gracefully rose from the floor and retrieved a water bottle. Kneeling next to Emma, she handed over the water. Emma drank deeply, thinking water had never tasted so satisfying. She felt alive and happy and grateful not to be feeling sick any more.

"Thanks, Cara. I feel better now. But I don't think I'll ever be able to do the Dougie."

Cara started, scrutinized the girl, and for an instant Emma imagined Cara was forking the sign of the evil eye at her.

"Why would you say that?" Cara demanded. Gone was the gentle, worried voice of moments ago, supplanted by the brassy, bossy voice.

The sudden change unnerved Emma, and she stood to defend herself.

"I was just kidding."

Emma watched her teacher study her. Intuitively, she realized Cara didn't want to be alone with her, didn't want to be in the same building with her. She didn't know how she knew it, but she did. The understanding filled her with certainty and immediacy and puzzlement.

"Cara, I feel better now. Can I go on to the costume workshop? I don't want to miss making my mask for the jazz dance."

"Yes, Emma, that's a good idea. You should go," Cara said. Then, seeming to remember her teacherly duties, asked again, though none too gently, "You're sure you're okay?"

"Yes, ma'am," Emma said, crossing to the bench to gather her belongings and head over to the costume workshop.

Emma slowly walked along the corridor. She noticed none of the posters of famous dancers hung at precise intervals. She only tried to make sense of the last quarter hour.

"I don't know what just happened—" Cara said, but this was in a new voice. Not the brassy in-charge Cara, not the gentle Cara worried for a student. This was an afraid Cara.

Emma whirled around to respond, only to find what she had thought all along. She was alone in the hallway.

"That girl changed right in front of my eyes," Cara said.

Emma spun again in the hallway, two full circles, but she was alone.

"She read my thoughts. How did she do that?"

The comment with no visible source confused and scared Emma. The girl backed into a wall and slid down it into a squatting position. She placed her hands over her ears, a gesture that did nothing to block Cara's brassy, unrelenting voice, and she began rocking back and forth.

"She said she didn't like juice when I was thinking I should offer it to her, but that she'd like some water. Then she joked about not ever being able to do the Dougie, which is a simple dance that any human with half an ounce of coordination should be able to handle, just after I had thought she would never manage to figure it out, and then…and then, she just seemed to know I was getting weirded out and wanted her to be as far away as possible from me."

Emma continued rocking, her hands still over her ears. A low moan escaped her mouth.

"And she asked to leave, just like that. Like she knew. How could she know? How could she know any of it?"

Emma didn't want to hear anymore, and suddenly, blissfully, Cara's voice vanished from her mind. From her mind? Yes, that's where it had to be, the girl realized. No dance teacher would be allowed to talk like that about a camper without someone cutting in, and there was no one in the hall with her. So, Emma thought decisively, it hadn't been out loud. It was in her head.

The understanding came to her at once. She had read Cara's mind, hadn't she? Emma thought back to the moment she had said she'd like water. Cara had asked if she was okay, and Emma was about to say she was when she realized Cara was thinking that Emma probably needed some juice or something to raise her blood sugar levels. And the lame Dougie joke, that wasn't really the kind of thing she would say on her own. She certainly could have picked up on the thought that Cara thought Emma was hopeless at hip-hop.

She had been reading someone's mind. She hadn't meant to. Hadn't realized she was doing it. The idea thrilled her and dismayed her in equal parts.

Telepathy. She might be only seven, but she was pretty sure that was the word for what she had done back in the dance studio, at least according to a TV show one of her babysitters liked to watch. They'd had a long conversation about mind-reading and other strange mental powers after that television show. Her babysitter said telepathy didn't exist. But it apparently did. And if her babysitter had been wrong about this, what else might she have been wrong about? Could she maybe now move things with her mind? She couldn't remember the name for that mental power, but that seemed like a more useful and pleasant one than the ability to read other people's thoughts.

But that was all silly. Of course she couldn't read someone else's mind. Of course things like telepathy really didn't exist. She was probably just going nuts out of sheer embarrassment because she couldn't Dougie and had passed out in class. She stood and aimed herself toward the costume workshop, but didn't start walking. Echoes of Cara's panicky mental rant came back to her: "And she asked to leave, just like that. Like she knew. How could she know? How could she know any of it?"

Considering this, she walked toward the costume workshop. The other girls were happily absorbed in applying glitter to their black cat masks when she entered the room. She sat next to Darcy, who had saved her a spot.

"I'm glad you're okay," the chubby girl said to her. "I was worried."

Unsure whether Darcy had said both things or had said

one and thought the other, Emma decided a simple "thanks" would be harmless enough. Emma applied herself to the decorative task at hand, gluing bright purple glitter to the edges of her black cat mask. The girls in her group were boisterously talkative today. She didn't understand how anyone could concentrate.

"My stupid little brother—"

and

"It was so funny—"

and

"Wonder if my mum's still mad—"

and

"Chocolate ice cream—"

And, absurdly, someone singing—dreadfully off-key but exuberantly—the lyrics to "Children Play with Earth."

She looked up and saw no one was talking, let alone singing. All the other girls had their heads down and were quietly applying all colors of glitter to their masks.

Emma felt a wave of nausea try to sneak itself through her, but she steadied herself, refusing to let it gain entry. She was doing it again. She was reading their minds. It was fascinating and troubling.

Emma wondered not how she had been made able to read minds—she was pretty sure that rubbery feeling that had laid her flat in the hip-hop studio had something to do with this—but why. A question of even more significance occurred to her. Would it happen again? She hoped that if it did, she wouldn't get sick like that again. Would she get better at it? Be able to tell the difference between what a person says, and what they actually think? Be able to control it? She realized, suddenly, that the teacher's rants had stopped almost on command. So she might be able to control it, if it happened again.

She felt sneaky, knowing she was listening in on what were meant to be private thoughts. She closed her eyes, but the thoughts kept coming to her. She wished them to go away, but they kept coming, like waves coming up the beach at Dublin Bay. With force, she ordered the thoughts of others to leave her mind, but without success. With panic approaching, she recalled her father donning noise-canceling headphones when he needed to concentrate and it was noisy. She pictured ears in her mind, and then she covered those ears with a mental replica of her father's headphones.

Blessed silence.

She was again alone with her own thoughts. In her mind's eye, she saw herself lifting the right headphone from her right ear, and the golden silence shattered, replaced by the mental chatter of eleven other girls and the art teacher. Smiling, Emma slid the right headphone back in place and turned her attention to other serious matters, like glitter.

She left the mental noise-canceling headphones on for the rest of the day. It was only that night, as she lay in her purple-sheeted bed in her very purple room in Dublin, that she dared remove them. She listened, using ears and mind. She didn't expect to hear anything, and was both relieved and disappointed this was the case. She closed her eyes and thought about her parents' concern when they learned she'd passed out at dance camp. She thought she had managed to convince them she was fine, that she was only tired. But she fretted that a doctor visit might be in her immediate future. She tried not to think about that.

Just in case, she put those handy noise-canceling headphones back on her mental ears. She prayed her nightly prayer, ad-libbing a bit at the end to thank God for helping her to think of the headphones and asking Him to help her learn how to control the telepathy, if it happened again.

Emma then tried to slow her breathing so she could sleep. Just as she was about to drift off into dreamland, a mental vibration shook Emma into instant wakefulness. She wasn't alone, but she knew she was. The paradox confused her. Recalling those moments in the hallway at dance camp, when she heard but couldn't see Cara, she took off her headphones to take a peek around, so to speak. She wondered if the vibration was the mental equivalent of a ringing phone or a knock on the door.

It was.

"Who's there?" Emma asked cautiously with her mind.

The voice answered, and Emma listened for a long time. The voice made her repeat several things. Finally, she said, "Okay, I will."

Later, left alone in the dark with her thoughts, she sensed a protector in the bowels of the earth who was a man but not a man, and she sensed a powerful but unborn child. These things both frightened and comforted her.

CHAPTER
13

22 June

Rami drank deeply from the glass of water that Dr. Nicola Patel handed him. The past thirty hours had been a whirlwind. Now he sat in scrubs in a lab, attached to various monitors and recording devices. Vital signs were documented and nurses, scientists, and doctors inspected him. He had never had this much attention paid to him before.

He could barely put the facts together in a coherent fashion. When he had climbed out of the cave, he half-expected the Iranian government to haul him back to Astara for good. Instead, he found the members of the base camp lifelessly strewn about. Behind them was an Apache helicopter that had not been there when Rami entered the cave. Several professional military types quickly marched to him, followed by a man in a sharp blue suit with bright red hair who would later explain to him the nature of The Hastings Foundation.

"We're taking you back to Philadelphia," the redheaded man had said. "We saw the expedition footage in real time. We saw what happened at the bottom of the cave that killed all your companions. I'm going to keep you in isolation until we get back to the States."

Wordlessly and without making any physical contact, the military types—Rami now saw they did actually wield handguns—had bundled the terrified survivor into the rearmost section of the helicopter. One asked Rami about the blood and why he was injury-free, but Rami could give no answer that would satisfy him.

They lifted off. After clearing Iranian airspace, they switched to a private jet in what he figured was an abandoned airstrip in Turkey and set off for Philadelphia, leaving Rami with nothing to do but pray and think about the events in the cave.

At The Hastings Foundation, he'd finally been able to shower. The hot water cascaded down his body as he lathered up a washcloth. He anticipated stinging from the water on his side wound, but the water just sloshed by painlessly. As the water ran down his head, he silently felt his side and did not understand how he had healed so quickly from the damage. Something had changed him in the cave. Those spores, or whatever they were, had somehow made him heal quickly. As he traced a path down his chest to count his ribs, he could barely feel where they had been prominent days ago. He was stronger, healthier, more vital. He felt like he could run a marathon if he could just get out of this room, when while imprisoned he had struggled to lift a hanged prisoner's body.

He shut off the water and grabbed a fresh white towel. A glimpse of his face reflected in the fogged mirror confirmed his thoughts. He was not as gaunt as he'd become in Astara. As he had looked in the mirror he imagined the look on his beloved Arian's face as she saw him so lively and healthy. He hung onto that thought. The promise of seeing her again choked him up.

"You must be very hungry," Nicola said.

Her comment startled him out of his reverie about the last thirty hours, bringing him back to the here and now, in the lab at The Hastings Foundation. For a moment, he only looked quizzically at the scientist.

"Hungry? If you let me know of any dietary restrictions, I can get food sent up for you."

Rami was famished and took her up on the offer. "I appreciate all that you are doing. And I know that you are doing all you can to try to figure out what is happening to me." Rami reached out his hand to her, and she stepped back. Rami wasn't prepared for her rejection.

"Sorry, I am a bit of a germaphobe." Nicola pulled a hand sanitizer bottle out of her coat pocket. The squish the liquid made as she poured a generous helping on her hands reminded Rami that he was still in a sterile environment. The lab facility at the Foundation seemed to be far more than just a research department.

"It is important right now for you to stay calm so that we can finish the tests. You have been through a traumatic experience and we are working to discern the extent to which you have … been … changed," she said and nervously glanced at her clipboard.

Rami thought he detected hints of emotion under the calm voice. "Did you know them?" he asked. "Rex and Peter. Did you know them?"

She paused before answering. "Yes. We had been colleagues for years."

Again, Rami heard the undercurrent of pain and thought perhaps one of the deaths touched her on a level more personal than work.

"They were really brave. Fearless even. And Rex had a … peculiar sense of humor," Rami said as he tried to find a way to comfort her. "You know, he told me about the prank he pulled on you. With the chickens, Vaseline, and saran wrap."

Nicola flushed and smiled faintly.

"I am sorry for any pain caused by their loss," he said. "You know, Peter spoke very highly of you." She lit up at the mention of his name, but before he could say any more, two more doctors entered the lab.

"Rami Kazemi," one said, smiling and sticking his hand out to shake. Rami obliged him. "It's a pleasure to meet you. I am Dr. Thierry Giraud. This is Dr. Roger Martin, and you've already met Dr. Nicola Patel."

Rami sat in silence.

"I know that you've had a harrowing incident, and I'd like to say that is all over, but we've still more tests to run before I can say that with any confidence."

Rami nodded. The French scientist's smile and honesty put him at ease. "Dr. Giraud, je ne saurais vous remercier assez de m'avoir sauvé. Je vous prie d'accepter mes excuses pour mon allure négligée."

Thierry raised his eyebrows but otherwise showed no surprise at being addressed in his native language. He turned to his colleagues and translated.

"He said he does not know how to thank us enough for saving him. He wants us to please accept his apologies for his sloppy appearance." Thierry pulled his trusty yo-yo from his lab jacket pocket and turned back to Rami. Smiling, he addressed Rami. "Votre français est impressionnant. C'est que je n'ai plus vraiment l'occasion de le parler." Thierry again translated for his colleagues. "I told him his French is impressive and that I don't get to speak it very much anymore."

"That's enough, Thierry!" Roger said as he signaled to Nicola to get back on track.

"From our early reports, it seems like you've made a miraculous recovery," Nicola said as she tried to ignore the Australian scientist's outburst. "Our initial readings from Ghar Parau place the—"

"I am calling it the White Light Wave," Thierry interrupted. Roger shot him a dirty look but Thierry continued. "The footage showed you placed your hand on the rocks and some sort of phosphorous reaction took place. We believe your body acted as the catalyst for that reaction."

While the French scientist was the most forthcoming, Rami sensed the older scientist with the Australian accent was the one in charge. He felt the three scientists were in an uneasy alliance, and he wasn't sure which, if any, he should trust.

"Are you saying that I am responsible for the deaths of the crew?" Rami asked Roger.

"No. Pay Dr. Giraud no mind, Mr. Kazemi." Roger pulled a chair next to Rami's bed, sat down, and adjusted his coat. "From the footage and your personal account we knew you had physical damage to your hands and your stomach, but when our crew came to your rescue, somehow most of your major wounds had been healed. We need to know the limits of your healing ability. Can you just heal yourself? Is the healing agent in your blood? What about limbs? The applications are unending."

Rami took the information in and slid back against the chair. He knew he was changed and that somehow him touching the rocks at the bottom of Ghar Parau sparked an evolution, no, a revolution, within him. The scientist's voice brought him back.

"What happened in that cave was not your fault. But we believe you were the activating agent for the chemical reaction. It looks like your body has been supercharged.

From what we've been able to discern, your immunity, healing, and recovery systems are reading at above-record capacity. In a sense, you can't get sick. We extrapolate from this data that your body will heal from almost any injury, and it seems you can recover your stamina in a fifth of the time it would take an Olympic athlete," Roger said as he swiped through Rami's charts on his tablet.

Rami silently fidgeted with his hands as they stared at him. While he was grateful for the medical assistance and their dedication to understanding his situation, he was reminded of his father's repeated maxim that anything that sounded too good to be true often was.

"Of course, we will still need more testing to discover the full extent of your, ahem, powers," Nicola said as she stepped toward him.

Rami looked at them blankly. What was so special about him that he could be responsible for what they called the "White Light Wave?" Rami felt as though he were a commodity that The Hastings Foundation would exploit. Would he never be free? Even though he wanted the answers to all these questions, he was hesitant to be a guinea pig.

"Rami, you are quite special and we are going to take care of you—and make sure your family is looked after. The Hastings Foundation can offer you their protection," Roger said as he put down his tablet.

A shadow darkened the doorway behind the Persian man.

"Why do I need protection? And how could a science organization possibly guarantee my protection?"

"Because we are more, much more, than just a science organization."

The answer surprised all of them, for different reasons.

The scientists squirmed at the unexpected appearance of the top boss. Rami, who hadn't heard the man enter the doorway, turned. He was stunned to see the ill-fated cave trip's benefactor standing before him.

CHAPTER
14

22 June

Henry Hastings stepped fully into the room, and the three scientists froze. The tall, slim man with slightly graying hair was impeccably dressed in a gray pinstriped suit.

"I believe you all have important work that needs your attention," Henry said as he dismissed the entire staff. He waited until he and Rami were alone to continue.

"Rami, as you are aware, The Hastings Foundation is a world-class scientific think tank and lab dedicated to exploring all avenues of climate change. We have funded, researched and created many cutting-edge technologies. Not to mention supplying your cave expedition to Ghar Parau," Henry said, loosening his tie.

As Henry spoke Rami thought about how much he owed the man standing before him. "Yes, Mr. Hastings. I should thank you for securing my release from Astara and for bringing me here—"

"But you feel you've traded one prison for another?" Henry said. "And please call me Henry."

"Mr.—Henry, I don't know what has happened, what it all means," Rami said. "But I am indebted to you for saving me."

"What do you know about the Hopi people?"

Rami was puzzled by the jump in topics and paused before answering. "The Native Americans? Not much. Why?"

"A fascinating people. Strong. Brilliant. Very spiritual," Henry said. He removed three manila file folders of varying thicknesses from his briefcase.

Rami could only make out the name on the first overstuffed folder: "Project: Purify."

"The Hopi are revered for their uncanny ability for prophecy. The CIA employed the Hopi for years in hopes of getting an edge during the Cold War. Spectacularly seen in the abysmal failure of the Bay of Pigs. There are even top-secret reports that the government has tried to artificially induce mental powers. But what I want to talk to you about is their thoughts about the Great Purification."

Rami waited patiently—a skill he'd gained in caving and perfected in Astara. Sooner or later, someone would answer the questions he had, even if he had to listen to a lecture on the Hopi before they got there. Besides, the courtesy of listening to him was a small trade-off for his release from prison.

"The Hopi elders have long talked about the natural resources of Earth running out, saying the machinery will begin to fail and that extraordinary events in nature will take place. Even though secrecy has guarded many Hopi traditions and beliefs, I have recently learned of rare and concerning visions. One of them is *koyaanisqatsi*, which means 'world out of balance,' and you can certainly see that happening now with all these unnatural disasters. Freak storms, the Kilimanjaro glacier melt, and the extreme volcanic explosion in Indonesia. These are just the latest disasters," Henry said as he sat on the edge of the metal table. "They claim that the key to human survival is communicating with an unseen earthly force. They say a 'singularity' will push mankind into the fifth world. The Hopi also talk about land falling into oceans and land rising from oceans, which will signify our emergence into the fifth world through the ashes of the fourth world."

Henry spread the folders out and Rami caught a glimpse of the name of the second folder: "Theories on the Great Energy Spore." This one only had a few papers inside it.

"The Hastings Foundation looks to outside sources in our quest to understand the world. In fact, without investing in the mythic creation theories of civilization, we can't truly know how to proceed in these times. As you know, science will find answers to questions we can't even ask yet. With an open mind we can solve the problems at hand." Henry casually moved the folders on the table. "We, at the Foundation, have figured out the cause. We know why these events are happening. We know how to stop them."

"That's great. What are—"

"I'm not finished yet," Henry said harshly. Then, resuming his lecturing tone, he continued. "There is more to the story. The old order we've known is essentially over. The global political dynamic is changing. Together we can help the world realize its new place."

Rami's concern about the motives of the organization grew with every word Henry spoke.

"We have been watching over you for many years. You are important to the world, Rami. Surely you know that by now." Henry smiled. "What you did in the cave was extraordinary. I don't think that you know the effect you have had on the world. That you will have on the world."

Rami felt his stomach quench. Was he merely a pawn? They'd been watching him?

"I can't help but to think that it was no accident you

being in that cave. That you are part of some prophecy handed down over the years. You released the energies from the cave during the solstice. That energy raced through the world. Finally, this long game of dominos has begun." Henry seemed to be struggling to play it cool.

Rami wondered exactly how long Henry and The Hastings Foundation had been watching him, involved in his life. Was he more bound to them than he realized? What would that mean for Arian? Or his parents?

Henry held up the last file folder and continued speaking.

"You must feel that things are different now. You are changed. You are no longer the man you once were. You are now brimming with incalculable power. You will purify the world. You are the first."

Rami drew his eyebrows together in concern. Once, in Iran, a small group of people wrested control of power from the many and ruled with ruthless abandon. He did not want to see that applied on a global scale.

"You see, the Hopi legend talks of a … guardian of the fifth world, a skeleton man of sorts that is a Spirit of Death. We have another name for him … the Sentinel."

That word made Rami freeze. He tried to dismiss the wave of anxiety rushing over him as Henry continued.

Henry placed the folder on the table. Rami looked at Henry for a moment before glancing down at the folder. Its label shook him to his core.

Project: Sentinel

As he stared at the folder title, he recalled words from the dream that had haunted him his entire life: "The Sentinel will awaken."

Then he recalled the words he heard as he climbed out of Ghar Parau: "You must lead them all, my Sentinel. You must save me."

CHAPTER

15

24 June

"Which way is it?" Maggie stopped and looked up and down the avenue in confusion.

"This way." The Pigeon pointed to the east, and they crossed with the light.

"What's the house specialty?"

"Don't know. I had the veal parm last time. Might do that again."

"Yum. I'm starved," Maggie said.

They walked companionably and passed the statue that had inspired Focus to dub their boss "The Pigeon" so long ago. Well, actually, Maggie reflected, it wasn't so much the statue as the birds that always perched on it and left behind a mess of droppings.

"That," Focus had said, pointing at the statue, "is kind of how I feel when Robin rants. I'm the statue. She's the pigeon."

And the name stuck. Maggie grinned, then frowned, hoping this little bit of memory lane wouldn't hex her. "So, I was thinking that maybe—"

"No."

"Robin, you don't even know what I was going to say."

"I do, and the answer's no."

"How could you possibly—"

"Know that you were going to ask for the umpteenth pecker-twistin' time to cover the people with powers? Hmm. I wonder."

Maggie's face fell. She'd hoped that during a walk, while getting fresh air and being away from the office, The Pigeon would be more approachable, more open to this proposed expansion of her work duties. "It's a good story, and it's not going away. There are more and more reports every day about these people, and I want to cover it."

"You're a travel reporter, not a news reporter. End of the weasel-shootin' story. Whoa, here we are."

The Pigeon stopped in front of an intricately carved wooden door, flanked by large windows. The place was simply called For Italian. The Pigeon heaved the heavy door open, and they stepped into a world of garlic and tomatoes and noise. Though late for lunch, the restaurant was packed almost wall to wall. A flustered maître d' seated them and rushed away.

Maggie resumed the conversation where they'd left off. "It is a good story, and maybe it's not mine—at least for now—but who is covering it?"

"No one."

"Why are you pigeonholing me, Robin?"

"Gee, let me think a cotton-pickin' minute. Could it be, oh, let's see, because you're the face of the most highly rated travel series on air? Maggie, you've got a good thing going. Don't mess with it."

"But I did a great job with the Kili coverage."

"Anyone could have done that. You only did it because you were there. And you blackmailed me into being allowed. I haven't forgotten that."

Maggie gulped. Of course her boss hadn't forgotten that. Would never forget that. Would never forgive that. "Where's that server?"

"He'll be along."

Maggie fidgeted with her napkin, decided a change of conversation was in order. "So, is it true this place has mob connections?"

"No. It's owned by a cheapskate couple who don't want to pay credit card fees. They were even too cheap to come up with a real name for this place. Food's delicious, though." The server approached with menus and Robin held her hand out for hers.

"Thanks," Maggie said, nodding at the server as she accepted her menu. She flipped open the folder and glanced at the entrees. She'd been starved, but she was so angry at Robin she could barely imagine eating. She lay the folder on the table and looked around, so she was one of the first to see a tall white man and his average-height companion enter the restaurant.

As soon as the beautiful wooden door closed behind them, the tall one pointed at the back wall. Maggie followed the direction of his finger and spotted a framed painting of a voluptuous woman, and below her the legend "Everything you see I owe to spaghetti." For a moment, anyway. One minute it was there on the back wall. The next, there was a crack and pieces of the painting floated through air like confetti. For a moment, Maggie was bewildered, but understanding set in, all at once. The tall man was a Mod. On the wall was a faint blueish outline where the poster had once touted the benefits of pasta. Some of the patrons close to the poster looked up in confusion, but only Maggie had seen and understood what the tall man had done. This was her chance.

"Robin, remember what I want to cover?"

"Not another snot-munchin' time."

"Well, they're here."

"Huh?"

Maggie was about to tell The Pigeon to check out the back wall when the maître d' stand exploded. Wooden shrapnel flew through the restaurant, chunks knocking into some of the patrons, splinters driving into others. Almost everyone was screaming, some in pain, and some were jumping from their chairs in fright.

"Silence." The tall man's command resulted in further screams.

Ignoring the commotion around her, Maggie studied the two, who were dressed identically in jeans and white T-shirts. Both carried sizable backpacks. The tall man was smiling, but judging by the manic look in his eyes, he had only the barest hold on his temper. The other man looked slightly more relaxed.

"Silence." This time, the boomed command brought instant quiet. "Good. That's very good." The tall man surveyed the restaurant. "Okay, here's what we're gonna do—and by we're, I mean you. You're gonna take all your wallets out and put them on the table in front of you. All your jewelry. Your cell phones. Any other electronics. In a nice little pile on the table in front of you. My buddy here is going to collect the protection fee." Here, the tall man uttered a shrill laugh that gave Maggie goose bumps. "Oh, you want to know what the protection fee is? It is what you pay us so my amigo here doesn't use his power on you. I can blow things up. It's kind of fun."

Here he grinned and demonstrated again. He pointed at the swinging door that divided the dining area from the kitchen. It shattered. When it did, alarmed screams from the kitchen staff joined those of the diners. The tall man held his finger in front of his mouth, and he had instant silence from the dining room.

"But my friend here, he's truly remarkable. He can make you want to do whatever he wants you to do. He can make you want to empty your wallet. He can make you want to jump from the Brooklyn Bridge with cement blocks tied to your feet. He can make you want to hump a hungry crocodile. So when you give us your money and jewelry and precious electronics, you're paying for protection from my friend here. Now, today, I think he would just ask for you to give us the things we've already asked for because he's in a good mood. If you were to try anything, to make him in a bad mood, well," he trailed off and shrugged. "I'm going to watch. Nobody speaks. Nobody touches him. Nobody makes a move. Anybody who does, well," he nodded at the empty chair next to Maggie and waved his hand at it.

Maggie sucked in a deep breath in nervous anticipation and the chair exploded with a crack. Pieces of wood and leather padding flew across the table, narrowly missing Maggie, but the caster on one of the chair legs hit Robin square in the eye. The force of it knocked her head back, and she bellowed in pain and immediately covered the damaged eye with her palm, as though that would make the ache go away.

"Ow, you monkey-licking devil. That hurts like a—"

The sounds of the tall man's tsks halted The Pigeon's rant in midstream. Maggie wished she had that kind of power against her boss. Falsely sweet, he asked, "Did you forget the part about nobody speaks? No, don't say a word. Just nod or shake your head."

Slowly, inaudibly, Maggie let her breath out. She waited to see if The Pigeon would be able to hold her tongue or if her inventive cursing would get them in more trouble. The Pigeon waited a long moment, apparently weighing her options, shook her head.

"Okay, then. For the crime of calling me a, what was it?" The tall man scratched his head, as if trying to remember. "Oh, yes, for the crime of calling me a monkey-licking devil, I am going to let my amigo here treat you to a dose of his power." He looked at his partner in crime. "You know what to do."

The entire restaurant went utterly silent.

The shorter man grinned and advanced on Maggie's table. He squinted and playfully pointed both of his index fingers at Robin, who could only see him with one eye. Nothing happened for a moment, and Maggie relaxed a fraction. The short man looked back at the tall man. "The usual?"

The tall man nodded.

"All right then," the shorter man said, grinning. He was still squinting and pointing at Robin.

The change in the woman was immediate. She dropped her hand from her injured eye and looked around the room. Puzzled, she asked the short man, "Where are the monkeys?"

"You're confused, my dear," he said silkily. "You are the monkey."

"I am?" She felt her arms, as though seeking a fur coat.

"Yes."

"But, I don't know how to be a monkey." She looked close to tears.

"It involves slinging shit, and you seem pretty good at that already."

At the suggestion, Robin stood, her hands moving toward her waistband.

"Not now, you idiot." The short man looked at his

partner. "Sheesh, monkeys." He turned back to her and told her to sit down. She did. "You're not a very popular monkey. No one will groom you. You have to pick off all your lice yourself. Crush them and eat them. Do this until five minutes after I leave this place."

Robin spotted something on her left arm and grimaced. She deftly picked it off with her right index finger and thumb. She pinched them together and smiled, as though feeling liquid burst out from a ruptured louse. She popped it into her mouth and moaned. She located another imaginary intruder, this time on her left knee, captured it, squished it, and tossed it back as well.

Maggie tried hard to dismiss the schadenfreude that coursed through her as the hard-nosed Pigeon complied, but couldn't quite manage.

At all the other tables, patrons watched the drama unfold in silent fascination.

"People, people, you have a job to do. Shouldn't you be pulling out all your goodies, placing them on the tables for my friend, here? For protection?" The tall man giggled. "Monkey see, monkey do."

As one, it seemed, the patrons hastily started or finished emptying out their pockets and purses and briefcases. They were pulling earrings from ears, rings off fingers, bracelets from wrists and necklaces from necks.

"It seems you understand the basics. Good, good. Now, amigo, go collect the protection fee." He smiled at his joke while the shorter man set about his duty with happy determination. He watched his amigo silently gathering the goods into his backpack. About halfway through the restaurant, the amigo returned to Maggie and Robin's table. He swooped their few items off the table and watched Robin, who ignored him as she intently rid her body of nonexistent lice. He charged back to the tall man, and they swapped backpacks. Finally, the amigo had visited the last table and returned to stand by the tall man.

"You know the drill. No one leaves for five minutes. We have your wallets. We know who you are. If we feel threatened from this—uh—this transaction, we will find you." The tall man pointed up at the trio of crystal chandeliers and they exploded. People shrieked and ducked, hoping to avoid cuts and damage from the dropping and potentially fatal falling glass. Maggie dove under the table but Robin remained blissfully in place, picking off imagined lice. No one saw the two men leave.

"Robin, seriously, let me cover this."

Robin looked at her puzzled, and held her hand out to Maggie, offering her latest catch.

Maggie wanted to laugh, knowing the image of The Pigeon picking imaginary lice off of herself would be with her to the end of her days. On the other hand, she'd just been robbed, although it could have been much worse. She could be eating her own louse lunch. Or the Mod robbers could have forced them to harm themselves. No matter what, she would find a way to cover the Mods.

CHAPTER 16

24 June

Roger quietly sipped his coffee as he walked through the lobby of 1818 Market Street, grateful for the silence before the chaos that would erupt around him. He entered the elevator, relieved it was empty, and pushed sixty-

Dr. Thierry Giraud

seven. He was in no mood for small talk today. Thierry slid his skinny arm through the closing doors. Roger groaned.

"Hold the door, please," Thierry said. He pushed himself through the doors. "Oh, Rog. How is your morning going?"

"Fine," Roger said. Until now, he thought. The French scientist annoyed him to no end, starting with his propensity for exaggerating his accent whenever pressed for answers he couldn't give.

Thierry slapped the already lit button for the sixty-seventh floor and the doors closed.

"I've been thinking about Rami," Thierry said as he pulled a yo-yo out of his pocket and let it spin to the floor. "And why his healing is somehow stimulated by an increase in dopamine levels. You have any idea about that?"

"Oy! Stop right there, Thierry. We have to tread very carefully from here on out. We must do what we can to secure our interests along with THF. We are no longer in charge of our destiny, and we must accept the circumstances."

Roger had grown more irritable with each passing day. He wasn't sure if he was really just becoming less of a people person than before.

"Fine. Then let's talk about the disasters. Every other week there is a catastrophe on a larger scale than ever before. The frequency and damage is greater and we can't turn a blind eye to this any longer."

"Why can't you understand? We have to deliver results on this helix matrix. There is no other option for us to work on these climate changes. Our deal with The Hastings Foundation charges us to create their designs, not our own. Suck it up and get on the helix matrix. We're up against a deadline."

Finally, they arrived at the sixty-seventh floor, home to their lab and where Roger had spent the last thirty-odd years dedicated to understanding global climate change.

"You know that it's all connected, right? The disasters, Ghar Parau, the White Light Wave event, Rami, these reports of powered people emerging. It's only a matter of time before—uff—" Thierry grunted as Dr. Nicola Patel, dressed in blue scrubs and white lab coat, ran into him. She fumbled and almost dropped several pieces of metal coil.

"Close call," she said, then looked up. "Oh Roger, I'm glad you're here. I think I've discovered a coating that will reduce the friction and solve the combustion issue."

"Nicola, that sounds good, but I really need results, not updates. I've got to get ready to present the forward momentum on the helix matrix to the board." The thought of Nicola tagging along to his office made Roger even more agitated. He turned to address them, and both Nicola and Thierry almost ran straight into him.

"About that, Roger, I think we are moving too fast. While I can solve the friction issue, I am not sure we are that close to actual testing," Nicola said. "It needs redundancy to ensure smooth revolutions."

"That's not the main focus. Work on the—"

"What is this project anyway? We know that the helix matrix we are working on is just the power component of another device," Thierry said, gesturing at the coils in Nicola's hands. "If we find out that this is something nefarious, I swear, Rog."

"Look, you two, we've been given this opportunity to still work within the realm of climate science here. I urge you both to do just that. Use your science to peer into the whys of the project at hand—the helix matrix."

Thierry and Nicola looked at each other as Roger grew more agitated.

"Just work on what you know. We don't want to give the Foundation any reason to treat us like Dr. Kaczmarzyk," Roger commanded in a hushed whisper, knowing video cameras recorded their every move.

"Please make sure that the problem is solved. I can't go to them with another failure," Roger said as rubbed his temples in exasperation.

Thierry took out his yo-yo and furiously played with it as Nicola awkwardly shuffled a few small sample pieces of the helix matrix in her hands.

"Fine, Rog, we'll work on the helix matrix and get it in working shape by the deadline. But we still have to consider all the other parameters. We can't just turn a blind eye to it all," Thierry said. Roger's entire body tensed up.

"Have you made any headway into trying to determine the causes of these—" Roger paused, unsure how to describe the strange happenings.

"Earth Reactions," Thierry said.

"What?"

"I've taken to calling them Earth Reactions. As if the earth is sick and these disasters are a reaction or symptom of the underlying disease or sickness," Thierry said, swinging his yo-yo up and down.

"That is the stupidest thing I have ever heard. Do not ever refer to them as that again." Roger abruptly turned and walked away. "And get to work on a project that actually has merit."

Stunned, Nicola and Thierry looked at each other.

"I think Earth Reactions has a nice ring to it," Nicola offered.

CHAPTER
17

24 June

Emilio barreled through the
crowded streets of San
Sebastian, Spain. Four police
officers were hot on his heels.
The sun shone brightly, leaving
no room for shadows that might
obscure his escape. He knew the

Emilio Diego Santos

streets well, ducking between fruit and vegetable vendors
and tiny, old ladies dressed in all black, their hair pulled back
into headscarves. He wove through a group of nuns,
stopping to wink at the last one.

"Hola, sister." He took another look back and thought
that if she hadn't dedicated herself to God they might have
had something special. But he couldn't distract himself any
further. He had to lose these cops.

They had been tracking him for almost a dozen blocks
since he jumped out of the second-floor window of the San
Telmo Museum. Emilio didn't know why the buyer wanted
the *El Ultimo Extasis de la Tierra* painting, but for 10 million
euros he wasn't going to ask questions.

He felt the rolled-up Basque painting clinging to his back and leapt over a small stone wall. He turned to see one cop trip over the wall and land face first in a basket of laundry waiting to be hung on the line. A middle-aged woman smacked the officer on the shoulder and began yelling at him for ruining her freshly laundered clothes.

Emilio laughed and ducked into a small alley to give the other cops the slip. But another cop managed to grab his jacket. Emilio slipped out of it and used it to wrap the cop inside out on a street lamp.

He walked nonchalantly toward a bar. On the way there, he caught his reflection in the window. With his square jaw, bright blues, and short blond hair, he looked good. He had charm he couldn't turn off and as a result he never had any trouble getting anyone to help him out.

As he looked at his reflected image, he noticed something on the ground. He reached to pick it up just as a cop lunged at him. The cop slid over Emilio's back and right into a couple sitting at a cafe table.

"Nice try, gordo!" Emilio laughed, turned around, and took off down an alley. Three cops down, one left.

"Para!" The last cop yelled. He raised a gun at Emilio.

"Mierda!" Emilio stopped dead in his tracks. He was trapped in an alleyway with no out. The other cops joined him. Emilio was done for, all for some silly piece of art. He prayed for a miracle as the cops closed in on him.

A clothesline swinging above them broke, and the clothes fell on the cops. Emilio capitalized on their temporary blindness and used his parkour skills to jump over their heads. Two blocks away and across the street was a bookstore with adjoining access to a bar. If he could get there he would be home free.

He smiled at a girl near the bookstore and grabbed her

toward him. She feigned resistance but once he locked eyes with her, she smiled and kissed him. As he walked toward the store, he admired her thin gold chain, which reminded him of how he had changed so fundamentally.

Two nights ago, after he had been thrown into a bullring, Emilio tried to convince his capturers to let him go. He tried explaining he hadn't meant to hit on his boss's daughter. Or sleep with his boss's wife. But how could he explain being caught leaving the wife's room that morning without also having to fess up to lifting three of her favorite necklaces? There was no way to win. Which is why he had been staring down a charging bull when a burst of blinding light spread across the clear night and a gust of unimaginable force dove into his body.

The other men collapsed to the ground. Emilio shook his head and was suddenly acutely reminded of his surroundings. He waited for the bull to come closer and then jumped, spread his legs wide, and pushed the bull's head down with his hands to vault over the beast. The bull continued running, hitting the back wall with a deep thud and collapsing. Before Emilio could even process what happened, the bull stood and snorted angrily at his prey. Emilio spotted a barrel about ten yards away. If he could make it to the barrel before the bull did, he could use it against the bull. Emilio darted toward the barrel with the bull bearing down on him. He made it there without a moment to spare. He dove behind it, as the horns broke through the wood and came with an inch of goring Emilio. He took a broken piece of the barrel to use as a shield. The bull made a quick spin and came right back at him. Emilio shuffled backward as the bull lunged at him. He fell back, his heart pounding as the lethal horns sought victory. Emilio heard the horns lodge into the wood.

"Que suerte!" Emilio checked his body for blood. None. Satisfied, he jumped out of the ring and escaped. This latest tangle with the police made it two escapes in just a couple of days. He was living right.

Emilio arrived at the designated meeting place at a quarter past four. There was no sign of the redheaded man who had hired him for the heist on the Zurriola Bridge over the Urumea River.

The redheaded man showed up five minutes later, carrying a briefcase. He approached Emilio.

"Emilio, so good to see you." The man looked out over the bridge at the river. Emilio turned to the man slightly, checking out the briefcase and estimating whether the size meant it contained the promised ten million euros.

"Not to be impolite, but I think it might be best if we take care of all this. I've got some places to be." Emilio picked up his traveling bag, which contained the Basque painting. "I'm sure you'll be happy with the item."

"I'm glad to be working with you again. Have you been through Zurich lately?"

"Not likely! The Swiss police are still twiddling their thumbs trying to figure out how I got away from them at the Kunsthaus," Emilio said with a laugh as the redheaded man quickly and surreptitiously examined the painting.

"Absolutely exquisite," he pronounced. "Are you familiar with Bernardo Flores' work?"

"Not to cut off what I am sure would be a fascinating story, but there is the lingering concern of my money," Emilio said as he leaned back against the low wall.

"Of course." The redheaded man's smoky voice tightened with annoyance. "As promised. Plus an extra twenty percent." Now, the redheaded man grinned sourly. In that grin, Emilio saw years of sacrifice and an unfilled yearning for appreciation.

"Twenty percent?"

"Think of it as a bonus. For your extra efforts and accelerated turnaround time," the redheaded man said.

"Gracias."

"My employers could use someone of your considerable … talent," he said, shaking Emilio's hand.

"That sounds all well and good, but I'm not looking for anything long-term. If you need something in a pinch, you know how to contact me," Emilio said. He grabbed the briefcase and jumped over the bridge, landing perfectly on a boat passing through. He turned back to the astonished redheaded man, smiled, and was soon out of sight.

CHAPTER
18

25 June

Elise Springchild, a charming middle-aged blonde in an impeccable dark blue Chanel suit, walked into the deserted upscale restaurant on the Upper East Side of Manhattan. As the doors opened, cool air kicked in, chilling

Elise Springchild

the room even more. Elise took no notice of the tall, bald black woman who extended her arm, showing the intended dining area.

Henry had rented out the entirety of the Michelin-rated three-star Le Petite Jardin for the evening. The French bistro aesthetic was complete with burnt mustard-colored walls, vintage equestrian photos, and large antique mirrors that lined the red banquettes on one side. Henry stood up from the round table in the center of the dining room and smiled at his guest.

The shipping magnate represented the only Ascendancy family in Europe. Elise's reputation as a world-renowned art critic specializing in Renaissance art had given her unprecedented access to valuable archives and museums, allowing the Ascendancy a better chance at gathering the remaining Sentinel clues hidden in classical art.

"Elise, it's wonderful to see you," Henry said as she held out her hand to his.

"Thank you Henry. It's been far too long since what was it? A year? Year and a half ago in Dubai?" Elise said in the indeterminate European accent she cultivated to give her an extra mystique. Henry helped her down the steps of the empty dining room.

"You know it's not safe for us to meet often," Henry said as he pulled out a chair for her to sit in.

"You bore me already with your paranoia, old man!"

Henry clenched his teeth and forced a smile as he turned toward the other two guests for whom they'd been waiting. He knew this would only be the first of many insults Maksim slung at him tonight.

Maksim and Anabel Wong glided over to Henry and Elise. The red neon sign posting the restaurant's name bathed all four in a bloody hue.

"Brother, you know that we must be clandestine in all our endeavors if we want to succeed," Anabel said as she put her arm around her twin and strode toward the table.

Henry and Elise had discussed the likelihood that the beautiful twins had killed their father to ascend to power. It was said Maks was just a playboy and that Anabel was the real power behind the name. Their father had often claimed that whenever the stocks rose in the east, it was because he had given permission to do just that. They followed their late father's example and ruled Hong Kong with an iron fist.

"Elise, pleasure to see you again," Anabel said as they greeted each other with air kisses.

"This is all well and good, but can we get down to business?"

Maks wore a Tom Ford tux with shirt unbuttoned and bow tie dangling on either side. He yawned and drank champagne from the bottle he brought. "I've got a party to get to."

"You must forgive Maks," Anabel said. She folded her arms in her black jacket and gray pencil skirt.

Henry waited until they all sat down at the exquisitely ornate cherrywood table that was set up for them.

"Of course. Our time together is limited." Henry instructed the woman to pour them all a glass of champagne from the bottle resting in the stand. "I have recently uncovered critical intelligence that sheds light onto the Sentinel. According to the manifest, the four Earth events must take place before the Sentinel can awaken. We have monitored the situations in each tragedy and all of the parameters and signs are exactly as foretold. The glacier melting on Kilimanjaro was the first sign we were waiting for. The solstice successfully altered our target, triggering the White Light Wave event that raced around the world. There are many reports of the empowered awakening to their new abilities."

"We've seen the reports of these individuals utilizing their powers. Where are we on identifying and containing them?" Elise interrupted.

"We are making headway. It's all in the reports you've seen," Henry said.

"You said that once the newly manifested emerged that we would be able to track them," Anabel said as she took a sip.

"And we will be able to. It is just taking a bit longer to calibrate our monitoring devices," Henry responded as he turned on his tablet, which showed about two dozen blips on a global map.

"And what of the scientists? Do we have anything to worry about?" Elise asked.

"They're all on board and will do all that is asked of them. The disasters all followed the signs the scrolls outlined. The WaveMaker is progressing as planned and the scientists are ready for the first test."

"You better be right, Hastings," Maks said. "We don't have the time or the resources to wait another five hundred years for this to happen."

Henry looked to Elise, who cocked her head slightly as if she was in agreement with the twins.

"There will be serious ramifications if we do not succeed. Remember what our late father said about failing to bring about the endgame." Maks pulled his bow tie from around his collar and wrapped it around his hands as if he was strangling them. "Complete and utter personal ruination."

"Of course. And since my organization is bearing the brunt of this, give me a little leeway," Henry said. He thought Elise had his back. They had known each other for a long time. But a fragile alliance had existed among the families since Shin's death.

"Henry, we all thank you for all that you have done so far. This is no easy task. You have had to play the long game in a dicey environment," Elise said as the waitress refilled their champagne glasses. "Now, of the currently identified empowered people, how many do we know we can control?"

"Thanks to your efforts and tracking," Henry said as he tapped the tablet, "we've been able to identify about ten, even though we don't have proper testing for their energy signatures. The rest were identified through news reports and social media." He did not mention he was unsure how he was going to get the newly empowered people to work for him, but that is what Project Ghost was for.

"So, I think all that is left is to agree that we are all on board for the next phase of the plan, correct?" Elise said.

"Of course," Anabel said. "The items you requested, Henry, are already on their way to your scientists. I believe you will find the materials as specified."

"Thank you. Once the wave accelerator test run has been completed, we can calibrate the device to wreak havoc upon the coasts as foretold," Henry said. "Then, and only then, can our true goal of world domination come to fruition."

"Why do we need to force the prophecy? Doesn't prophecy mean that it will eventually happen on its own?" Maks interjected.

"This is the way the Ascendancy has operated since its inception. Follow the prophecy and our goals will be reached," Henry said. "But why wait longer than we have to? We have a way to speed up destiny. By creating the disasters revealed in the prophecy ourselves, we can manipulate the earth into releasing the Sentinel to us and bring about our true mission."

"I'm real tired of hearing about this prophecy. If the Ascendancy is so great, why haven't we taken over the world already? We've accumulated plenty of wealth and power to do just that," Maks said.

"Maks."

"No, Anabel. What is the point?"

"Of what?" Elise asked.

"Of this entire thing? What is the point of killing millions of people? Just to subjugate them to our will? We can do that through far easier means." Maks threw his bow tie on the table like a gauntlet.

"What my brother means is why are we waiting for the prophecy anyway? How do we even know it's going to come true? That we aren't just chasing our tails?" Anabel said.

Henry felt his alliance slipping. He had to restore the

delicate balance and quickly. "I hear what you are saying, but we've been over this before. The prophecy is essential to our plans and, yes that means it's a waiting game. But that doesn't mean it has to stay that way. With the WaveMaker and the scientists on our side, we can make this happen now."

Elise let out a sigh. Maks and Anabel exchanged a look and seemed appeased.

"Then I think we are done here," Maks said as he downed the rest of his champagne.

"I am pleased with the way things are going, Henry. Keep it up and know that you have all of our support. Anything that you may need will be at your disposal," Anabel said.

"Any last developments?" Elise asked.

Henry's tablet lit up with a new message.

"THE FLORES PAINTING IS WAITING FOR YOU IN YOUR SANCTUM."

Henry looked back at them and lied. "No. Nothing else to report."

The twins stood and left. Elise hugged Henry and whispered, "The Sentinel will save us all."

Like a well-rehearsed call-and-response, Henry reflexively replied the same, even though his thoughts were only on the secrets he would pry from the Flores painting.

CHAPTER
19

25 June

The full-length mirror was unforgiving. Every imperfection showed under these lights and the mirror made complete detail of it. Young. Starlet. Neither word was true. She hadn't had a hit in three years and she had lied about her age by at least eight years. And as she stepped closer to the mirror, the lines exaggerated to reveal further imperfections.

She smiled. Then she laughed and her body bowled over and a strange transformation took place. Her shoulders broadened, her muscles inflated, and she grew half a foot in height. Her shoulder-length red hair retreated into a dirty blond mess and scruff appeared on the face. Suddenly, the starlet was no more. Josh stood naked in her place.

"Twenty-six, my ass. I should have known better," Josh said as his deep, gravelly voice manifested. "Last time I let my agent set up a relationship for me." He reached for a green robe and slowly put it on as he stared at the mirror. He grabbed the glass of whiskey on the counter and gulped it down. He stepped toward the mirror and his features began to morph again. This time, his skin smoothed out and became tanner, and his fine hair changed into a thick, perfectly coiffed short do. His body shrank and he became slender. His green eyes morphed into beautiful but sad almond-shaped brown ones. He reached out. His hand touched the mirrored reflection. The sadness in the eyes was his, not the Asian man he was impersonating.

"I'm sorry," Josh muttered as he tried to stop his mind from replaying the last time he saw the man in the mirror. Even though his heart sank, he marveled there was no pain when transitioning from one form to the next. Either he had figured out how to maneuver his features or he was just more malleable now. In the days that followed his first transformation into his maid, Josh stayed cooped up in his Hollywood Hills home. Refusing to even let his maid return, he turned away his agent and his manager when they banged on his front door.

Josh took one last look at the mirror and began shifting his body back to his prime form. He walked out of the bathroom toward the balcony.

As soon as Josh heard the spry voice springing from nowhere, he stood completely still. He looked over to the television and saw it was off. He scanned to see if his phone was suddenly on speaker, but it wasn't. He dared to take a step and the voice called back to him.

"Josh. I need your help."

Josh spun around and frantically tried to figure out where the voice was coming from.

"I'm in your head."

"Oh God. This can't be good," Josh muttered as he fumbled over to his bar, grabbed a bottle of Scotch, and poured an almost full glass. He quickly took a swig and wiped his mouth.

"Look, I don't know who you are or what you want, but just leave me alone," Josh said as he took another drink. He wasn't sure what scared him more, the fact that he was hearing a voice or that it was a young girl's voice calling out to him. He'd been in one too many movies where the monster was actually a little girl; he didn't trust her sweet lilt.

"I know this is a bit confusing for you, and it's strange for me too. But I need you to help," the voice replied in his head.

"I am going to need another drink," Josh thought as he reached for the bottle.

"That's really a lot to be drinking," the voice said.

"That's not any of your concern," Josh said as he slammed the bottle back down.

"Let's start over," the voice said, seeming to sense Josh needed to calm down. "I'm Emma. And I know that you are changed."

That word stopped Josh mid-drink. Forget for the moment that he's actually speaking to a voice inside his head. How in the world would she know that he was different now?

"I can tell that you are suspicious," the voice continued.

"That's one way of putting it." Josh walked over to the balcony rail and gazed out.

"Until a few days ago I was just a normal seven-year-old girl … Well, not normal, but you know." Emma sped on about how she discovered she had powers, but all Josh could hear was something about a dance teacher and some guy named Dougie before he had had enough.

"Okay! Okay! I give up," Josh said aloud. His shouting scared off a mockingbird resting on one of the branches of the coral tree in his backyard. "What is it you want?"

"I need your help finding the others. We have to join up and help save the world."

"Stop right there. I don't want any part of this. I have

way too much going on right now to just—"

"Why are you lying?" She asked as only a child could.

"Why would you say that?"

"Because I know you, Josh. You are a good person. And you've seen what's happening around us. The world is changing. We are changing. The earth is crying out to be saved and there is only so much I can do by myself."

Josh was silent for a moment. He knew that things were bad around the world—the sudden glacier melting, the volcanic explosion that rocked South Asia, not to mention the countless other climate disasters.

"Look, I'm just an actor. What can I do?" Josh said, trying to deflect her plea.

"You can actually become anyone you want to be and yet you choose to just throw your life away?"

"How do you know so much?" Josh asked as he balanced his body between the doorframe with his arms.

"I can project my thoughts and read minds."

"Nothing creepy about a little girl who reads minds."

"But I have a connection to the earth that tells me about other people with powers. He's asked me to gather them together to save the world."

"And how do you think I can help you?"

"You can help me gather the others. I can reach them but we've no place to go."

"I'm not going to have strangers in my house."

"We're not strangers. We're connected. We're the Children of the Solstice. We are charged with saving the world. You have to help."

"I don't know where you get off telling adults what to do, but it's rude and I don't appreciate you creeping around in my mind either," Josh said. He walked back to the bar and poured another drink. "I'm just not right for this."

"I should have known better than to pick you. You're too scared to even try to make a difference," Emma said as her voice deepened. "I guess this is why you shouldn't meet your heroes."

And just as suddenly as the voice manifested in Josh's mind it was quiet again. Too quiet. He picked up his remote control and pressed a button and immediately a song played by his favorite sultry songstress.

Josh finished off his drink and sort of stumbled toward the bed. He leaned back against the pillow and wondered what he could do to help. The only real skills he had were ones he learned for the films. He could fake being a weapons expert or a skilled computer tech. It was all smoke and mirrors for him. He was a product of the studios and his value waxed and waned according to the box office numbers.

He kicked off his shoes and curled up in the bed as another sad song rolled by. Why was he letting a seven-year-old get to him? Like she knew the demands he had to deal with. The rigid structure meant he had a life half lived. Never able to fully give in to his authentic self. Maybe helping others would finally allow him to be the man he always wanted to be.

On the other hand, hiding his truth was second nature to him and it had gotten him this far. He hadn't noticed before, and maybe it was due to the Scotch or maybe the fact that there was someone in his mind, but his head throbbed in pain. He put his head in his hands and rocked back.

How could someone so selfish be a Child of the Solstice, be entrusted with saving the world?

CHAPTER
2 0

25 June

Henry could not press his five-digit security code into the
alarm keypad of his spacious mansion quickly enough. His
excitement at the retrieval of the final Flores painting was
almost too much. He opened the heavy oak door and made
his way past the eighteenth-century escritoire and into the
restored Louis XIV drawing room. He tilted an old, well-
read copy of *The Prince* and a secret passage revealed itself.
He entered and the passage closed tightly after him.

About ten yards into the passage he reached a staircase.
He descended the stairs and made his way to the room he
prized more than any other. There were paintings from
classic artists, photographic copies of a mural from the Hopi
tribe, and many scrolls and half-burned documents, all
hermetically sealed and preserved. He had collected these
items over decades of intense search, but they didn't even
represent half of his holdings. These were directly related to
the Sentinel. All the records, found texts, and clues indicated
the Sentinel would awaken in the twenty-first century. Each
generation had made painstaking sacrifices to complete the
series of tasks necessary to bring about the right conditions.

Sooner or later, he was going to have to bring his son in on this. He sagged at the thought. He wanted to save Arthur from this secluded life of lies and deception, but knew that before too long he would have to explain to Arthur their past and how they would help shape the future. Henry knew the upcoming disaster would change the face of the globe forever, but he never flinched from the Herculean effort of preparing for the Sentinel.

But for now, Henry focused on the tasks at hand. He set his briefcase down and stepped over to the latest addition to his collection, *El Ultimo Extasis de la Tierra*. It was an exquisite painting by a little-known sixteenth-century Basque artist. The painting showed three soldiers at the edge of the world screaming at the black void below as a faint white light emerged under them. The style and deft stroke work was decades ahead of his contemporaries. Bernardo Flores should have been known as widely as other artists of his day, but scandal and intrigue besieged his life.

Henry walked by the walled glass-front wine refrigerator and admired his exquisite collection. He was tempted to reach for a glass from the nearby shelf and enjoy a sample but knew that delaying his gratification always made the prize taste better.

For over four hundred years the Ascendancy had used his art to ferry information and details throughout the world. The painting recently stolen from the San Telmo Museum was the last known painting remaining in public view. What would happen next to the painting would infuriate art historians.

Henry carefully donned white gloves and laid the painting on the table in front of him. He removed a special enzymatic solution from the cabinet and dabbed a swab into it. The specially formulated compound would reveal the centuries-old secret to him alone. He decided to start at the bottom left corner of the painting and carefully blotted the swab on it. Too little solution would produce no effect. Too much could destroy the canvas completely. With the painting gone, so too would the final secrets of the Sentinel be erased.

The dark, earthy colors began to dissipate. Henry stepped away from the table and brought the table lamp closer.

Nothing.

He moved toward the bottom right corner and repeated his methodic actions. Again nothing appeared from the recently cleared paint.

"Damn you, where is the code?" he muttered.

He poured more of the solution onto a new swab and gently scrubbed away the thick oil paint on the canvas. Still Henry was frustrated. This painting held the last clue about the secrets of the Sentinel's true directive, he was sure of it.

Henry stood and removed his slate-gray jacket. He slung it behind his chair, accidentally knocking the solution bottle over onto the painting.

"No!"

Henry grabbed a nearby towel and blotted and rubbed as he desperately tried to keep the solution from eating away the canvas. For a few heart-stopping seconds, he was sure the damage was permanent. But instead of ruining his chances, the landscape faded under the concentrated solution, revealing what seemed to be coordinates and a complex binary code.

Henry loosened his tie and smiled. He used his phone to take a picture of the canvas for his records. He studied the code.

Eventually, he walked to the glass-front refrigerator and

removed a bottle of vintage Dom Pérignon. He uncorked it and selected an ornate crystal-cut flute. He carefully poured it three-quarters full. He had been saving this bottle for thirty years for this occasion. He lifted the glass to his lips and took a deep, satisfying drink.

Henry sat back in the King George high-back chair and looked at the wall of monitors. As he savored his drink he saw his tablet pulse. The message was only eight words but the next stage of the Ascendancy's plans was just a few hours from culmination.

THE WAVEMAKER IS READY FOR PHASE ONE TRIAL.

CHAPTER
21

26 June

"Honey, could ya get us a coupla more beers?"

It was Jimmy Ray. Tammie and Dolly groaned in unison, as they did most things, but neither woman moved. It was too hot, really, to move, even in the shade of the cabana.

"Could ya, could ya, could ya," Tammie mimicked her husband, sitting up in her hammock.

"I know. Mine too once the first beer's down the hatch." Dolly sat up also, and her hammock swayed. She looked at her cousin. They had been best friends all their lives. The hammock's netting had imprinted its criss-cross on Tammie's back, despite the cushioning of the towel she'd been lying on. Dolly knew her own back bore the same pattern.

"If they knew how hard it is to get in and out of these thangs, they'd quit asking for beers every fifteen minutes," Tammie said.

"Whose idea was it again? To come here?" Dolly asked for what seemed like the fortieth time, fanning herself. She was looking not at Tammie but out at the brownish waters of the Gulf of Mexico. She'd thought there would be more of a breeze on the beach, even during the height of summer.

"Could'a been Cleetus. Could'a been Jimmy Ray. Either way, happy anniversary, right? At least we're at the beach and not back in Grove Hill." Tammie looked at their empty cocktail glasses, sitting in puddles of condensation on the wooden table between them. Hers had been a piña colada, Dolly's a banana daiquiri. "You want innithing?"

"Does that look like low tide? I thought the water was coming in for high tide."

"Hey, about those beers. They coming? Remember, we only tip for tit-top service." This time, it was Cleetus.

Dolly was sure if anyone complained, her husband would call it a slip of the tongue because of all that beer. It may only be midafternoon, but they were probably at eight a piece already. She always lost count when Cleetus and Jimmy Ray started drinking. As long as they didn't utter the words every redneck wife fears above all others—"Hey, y'all, watch this!"—she didn't worry too much about the beer load.

"Maybe they know just how tricky it is," Dolly said, tearing her attention away from the shoreline.

"Huh?" Tammie wrinkled her nose at Dolly in perfect confusion.

"Cleetus and Jimmy Ray. I bet they watch us every time we crawl out of these darn things."

Confusion, understanding, irritation, pride, more irritation, and grudging agreement flitted across Tammie's face, making Dolly laugh. Dolly turned to regard her husband, standing not far away on the beach with his hands up in the air, as though signaling "what gives?" It was a pose he struck often, although she'd never seen him standing like that while stark naked.

"Who's winning?" Dolly called back to the men.

Cleetus shrugged and pointed at Jimmy Ray.

"That's a change," Dolly said.

"To the victor goes the beer?" Jimmy Ray asked hopefully.

Dolly laughed again. "Come on, let's give them the show they've been waiting for."

They climbed out of their hammocks as sensuously as they could manage.

"That's what I'm talking about." Jimmy Ray catcalled and started to whistle, but Cleetus shushed him.

"You wanna get kicked out of here?" Cleetus demanded. "No lewd behavior. They said that when we checked in."

"That wasn't lewd. That was appreciation." Jimmy Ray may have been talking to Cleetus, but he wouldn't take his eyes off of their wives, swinging the gifts the good lord had blessed them with as they made their way to the little bar at the end of the beach.

"Was lewd. Lascivious too."

"Lascivious?" Jimmy Ray finally took his eyes off their nekkid wives and looked at Cleetus. He pronounced this exotic word carefully, taking it for praise. "Really?"

As Dolly and Tammie strutted their stuff on the way to the beach bar, Dolly glanced uneasily at the gulf.

"Something's not right."

"Yeah, we're way too sober to be dealing with those two," Tammie said.

"No, that's not what I mean. Doesn't it seem like the tide is awfully low? It wasn't that low yesterday."

Tammie looked around at the few other guests of the Bare Beach Resort. Most were lolling in hammocks, as she and Dolly had been doing a few minutes ago, although a few guests were engaged in a vigorous beach volleyball game. Tammie openly stared at all those jiggly body parts, moving willy-nilly as the players strove valiantly to make their shots.

"Gawd, I can't image playing beach v-ball nekkid. Sand gets everywhere as it is."

"Tammie, the tide?"

"Nobody seems worried about it but you. You gonna get another daiquiri?" she asked as they neared the bar.

Dolly shrugged. "Maybe. Probably. But not banana again."

They ordered a pair of beers, a piña colada, and a strawberry daiquiri and lounged in the shade while Mindy worked her blender magic behind the bar.

"Hey, Mindy, does the tide seem lower than normal?" Dolly asked.

"Give it a rest, already," Tammie said.

The bartender held up a finger and kept blending Tammie's piña colada. As she passed the frosty cocktail over the bar, she looked out to the shoreline and frowned. "That doesn't seem right."

"What do you mean?" Dolly asked.

Mindy didn't respond, nor did she begin making Dolly's daiquiri.

"What do you mean, that doesn't seem right?"

Again, there was no response. In irritation, Dolly turned to the bar, only to find it vacant. The girl had come out to stand next to them. Like other employees of the Bare Beach Resort, Mindy was wearing clothes, and Dolly, standing there nekkid, felt trapped in an old nightmare for a moment.

Mindy studied the water and thought about her all-too-brief orientation at the beginning of the summer. What had her manager said to do if the water receded beyond a certain point?

"It, uh, it shouldn't be that low," Mindy finally said. She was pale, paler than she had been moments ago. "I think we have a problem."

"Yeah, we sure as hell do. You didn't make Dolly her daiquiri yet," Tammie said.

Mindy shook her head slowly. "Bigger than that." And then she yelled and sprung into motion. "Run!" The bartender ran down the beach hollering at all the guests.

"What?" Dolly asked.

"Tsunami coming. Run, get inside. Now, now, now!"

"Why?" And then Dolly saw it, off in the horizon. That was one huge wave. Larger by far than anything she'd seen since they'd arrived at the beach. And it was moving in one ripping roar of a hurry.

She grabbed Tammie's hand and tried to pull her toward the resort. "Come on!"

"Stop it. You spilled my drink." Tammie dug her heels into the sand.

With growing panic, Dolly spun Tammie so she was facing the gulf. She pointed at the wave. "You see that?"

"Yeah."

"We gotta get out of here."

"Why?"

"Tammie, I think Mindy's right. That's a tsunami."

"A what?"

"A humongous wave that will wipe us out if we don't get to safety. Right. Now."

Tammie studied the wave for a moment. "It does look awfully big."

"And it's moving awfully fast. We need to go. Now."

"But what about Jimmy Ray and Cleetus?"

"Oh, shit!" Dolly looked down the beach and saw Mindy's progress. The bartender was still yelling her warning and alarming the naked beach guests into panicked action. Dolly watched one old man get twisted up and fumble around before finally managing to exit his hammock, not at all gracefully. It was a move that, given the ridiculous floppiness of his body, normally would have sent her into fits of laughter. Briefly, she noted the cross-hatch imprint on his backside, as well. She rather hoped it looked better on her and Tammie than it did on the old fella. "Mindy's going to get them. Let's go!"

Tammie crossed her arms and shook her head. "Not without Jimmy Ray and Cleetus."

Dolly looked at their husbands, who seemed undistracted by all the ruckus along the beach, and then at the resort building and back at the looming wave. She calculated speeds and angles like she was about to sink a combo on the pool table.

"Let's go get them, then." Again, Dolly grabbed Tammie's hand, but this time found no resistance. They ran toward their husbands. Despite her panic, Dolly felt a perverse pleasure in running nekkid across the beach, her breasts, small though they were, jouncing with each step.

Mindy, with her head start, got to them well before Dolly and Tammie did.

"We kinda expected beers," Jimmy Ray said.

"Tsunami coming. Got to get inside." Mindy was winded and panting.

"What? No beers?" Jimmy Ray slumped in disappointment.

Mindy looked at Cleetus. "You see that big wave?" He nodded. "Tsunami. Got to get inside. Okay? Your wives already know." Once the news had been delivered, she turned tail and ran madly toward the resort, still yelling her warning.

"Here they come!" Jimmy Ray said. "Babe, where's my beer?"

"Jimmy Ray, Dolly says it's a big-ass wave and we gotta get inside." Tammie's words were urgent, but not her manner. She paused to take a long pull from her piña colada, which, miraculously, had survived her hell-bent dash across the beach.

Dolly stared out at the rushing wave with fascination. It had been at the far end of the horizon when they'd left the beach bar to run back to their little spot on the beach. Now it seemed halfway to shore, and it seemed to stretch across the entire width of the Gulf.

"It's moving fast. We gotta go," Dolly urged.

Tammie, Jimmy Ray, and Cleetus stood transfixed watching the wall of water rushing toward them.

"Run, for the love of God. Just go!" Dolly's scream surprised them all into motion, and the four raced across the beach back toward the resort. All around them, screaming and panicked nudists ran, flopping and flailing, for the presumed safety of the resort's main building.

Jimmy Ray and Tammie and Cletus and Dolly ran like mad. Dolly had to keep fighting the urge to look back and see how close the wave had come. Doing so would only slow her down. But she could hear the tsunami, monstrously loud. Seeing Mindy and a few of the other resort clients reach the building stoked hope in Dolly's heart.

They might just make it.

But they were still thirty yards from the building's doors when Dolly felt the first spray from the wave and understood they wouldn't.

"No!" The negative, full of denial and terror, came out in a yell that Dolly's husband couldn't hear over the pounding of the deadly wave. She sucked in a last lungful of air and reached out for her husband's hand but found nothing but water as the tsunami roared over them and folded them into itself on its race inland.

CHAPTER

2 2

26 June

Rami did his best to rest, but his mind was elsewhere. He couldn't shake the feeling that something was just not right. Not with himself. Not with The Hastings Foundation. Not with the scientists. And certainly not with Henry. After days in Philadelphia he was still uneasy. There was a scratch at the back of his mind he couldn't quite understand either.

Employing a skill he honed over his time in Astara, he discreetly eavesdropped on a few of the nurses talking about the tsunami that had just ravaged the Gulf of Mexico. This made three events so far. Maybe the prophecy and the predictions Henry had talked about before were more true than he realized.

Sensing no nap in his future, Rami sat up and made his way to the electric kettle in the room's kitchenette. He checked the water level and flipped the switch to boil. He considered the tea options and settled on jasmine chamomile. He set out a cup and emptied two sugar packets into it.

As he waited for the water to boil, he ran a hand over his newly strong forearm and thought of the voice that called him the Sentinel. The idea that his life was predestined bothered him only slightly less than the fact that he might never see his beloved Arian again.

The kettle clicked off and Rami poured the water into his cup. Through the slender window in the door, he saw doctors wheeling a stretcher into the critical care unit across the hall.

He walked to the window and peered out while the tea brewed. He saw the French scientist glance at him and say something to the nurse. She closed the curtain.

Rami cursed his isolation.

Across the hall, Thierry watched a medical doctor work urgently on a young woman who was bleeding from her nose, eyes, and ears. The doctor checked her vitals and then tried to stop her bleeding.

"How did she get here?" Thierry asked.

The doctor shrugged. "Roger found her."

"I was waiting for some test results when she burst through the door. She was mumbling and flailing about. So I called for you," Roger said.

"You think she's gifted? Like Rami?" Thierry asked. "I've been seeing viral videos about people with powers, and I'm following a blog about them."

"Don't believe in coincidences," Roger said.

"She's not the first you've brought here," Thierry said as Roger grew more agitated.

"Let's stabilize her and question her later. How is she?"

"Her heart rate has dropped. Her breathing seems to have slowed, and she is not accepting the oxygen bath," the doctor said. "She's lost a lot of blood. We aren't equipped to give her what she needs."

"Don't let her die," Roger said.

The doctor measured the patient's ribs and made an

incision between her fifth and sixth ribs. He inserted a small plastic tube into her lung and began to make slight compressions, allowing the girl to breathe.

"Oh, thank God," the nurse said.

"But not a permanent fix," the doctor cautioned.

"You've got to save her," Roger told the doctor.

"And you've got to tell me where you keep finding these people," Thierry said as he braced himself on the gurney.

"Where she came from is of no concern to you."

"If you don't tell us what she is … what she can do, then I don't know if there is anything the doctor can do to save her," Thierry said as he slouched over the girl.

"Use me."

Thierry and Roger turned to see Rami standing at the curtain.

"You shouldn't be here. You need to leave," Roger said. He lunged toward Rami.

"Are you kidding me? This girl is about to die and you're going to push away the one person who might be able to save her?"

"What are you on about?" Roger asked.

"I've got some sort of immunity, right? That's what you called it. Take my blood and give it to her," Rami said as he rolled up his shirtsleeve.

"We don't even know if you're a match," Thierry said.

"I am your last, best chance," Rami said. He held out his arm.

"Nurse, please test their blood for compatibility," the doctor said.

"There's no time," Roger barked as he instructed the nurse to start the process.

"Rog, we just can't go at this on a hope and a prayer," Thierry said.

"We lost that luxury. Do it. Now." The vein in the Australian's neck bulged.

"Okay. Clear some space." The doctor pointed Rami to a wheelchair, and he sat. The nurse efficiently swabbed Rami's arm with alcohol and deftly inserted the needle.

"Go on, Roger. Make the report," Thierry said.

Roger turned to the nurse and asked her to bring him his tablet.

"Do we have any identification on her?" Thierry asked.

"None so far. She has no purse or wallet, but I have someone running her information down," Roger said.

"So, she is unknown to us, in identity as well as in powers," Thierry said, watching the line transfer Rami's blood to the girl. Rami appeared to have gone to sleep or passed out.

"Yes, but not for long," the nurse said. "She is already starting to regain her color."

Thierry grinned with satisfaction. They were still in the discovery phase with Rami, but if his blood could save this girl, then the potential lifesaving treatments were astounding.

"The rapid cellular characterization test turned up an abnormality in the girl's cells. Cellular fluctuation," Roger said, consulting his tablet.

"What does that mean?" Thierry asked.

"I'm not sure. There was a near-constant splitting and replicating of her cells. Thierry?" Roger asked.

Thierry closed his eyes to consider this and was starting to answer when the young girl started to seize again.

The doctor sprang into action. "Grab the crash cart!" Thierry said.

"Nurse, make sure you watch her. Make sure that she doesn't do anything ... strange. And get him out of here!"

Roger said, pointing at Rami. She quickly pushed Rami's wheelchair out of the room and back into his own room.

The other nurse placed the paddles on the girl's chest and waited for the charge. But before the doctor could shout for everyone to clear the body, the entire lab complex shut down. Even the emergency lights were out. Now, in the dark, they saw a blue-white light emanating from the girl.

They were all mesmerized by the light and a sense of calm poured over them. It was as if all worries, misgivings, and prejudices simply slipped out of their bodies. For a long moment Thierry could feel the azure light wash over him. Questions and theories he'd long forgotten about bubbled to the surface of his mind fully solved. It was like the emanations somehow gave him the clarity to figure out problems he never thought he would conquer. Out of nowhere, Henry charged into the room.

"What is going on? Call security to check on the emergency backup power," Henry said as the nurse ran to the phone.

And just like that, the bluish white light retreated into the girl's body.

"What are you doing here?" Thierry asked as the lights flickered.

"Dr. Martin called me as soon as the girl … arrived," Henry said as the backup generator kicked in.

Thierry looked at the girl on the stretcher, her life drained away. "She's … she's gone," he said.

"You can all leave now. I will take care of her," Henry said as he motioned to a nurse to pull the sheet over her body. "You did all you could."

"Even with Rami's healing blood the doctor couldn't save her," Thierry said as he reached into his pocket and palmed his yo-yo.

"You should not have let the doctor use Rami like that. You don't know what kind of interaction it could have. And in the end it did no good, except deplete his resources. You have to think, Dr. Giraud. We are on the precipice here," Henry said as Thierry let the yo-yo slip toward the floor and back up.

"You weren't there. I did what I thought best, and don't forget, he offered. There was little time to figure out how else to save her." Thierry put the yo-yo back in his pocket.

"We don't know the extent of his abilities. You should get some rest now. I can take it from here." Henry pointed to the exit.

Thierry thought to protest, but he was exhausted and still couldn't wrap his head around what just happened. He left the room, leaving only Henry and the nurse behind.

"Take her to the Dark Past Room. We aren't done with her yet," Henry said.

CHAPTER
2 3

26 June

Henry slid back in the King George high-back chair with a devilish smile as he surveyed photographs showing damage on the Mississippi coastline. He sipped from his crystal goblet and let the Malbec swish around in his mouth as he

Maks Wong

glanced at the top monitor showing a news report.

Before he could finish his wine, a light flashed signifying that the other members were coming online for the meeting. After taking all the standard precautions to ensure that the communication lines were secure and no one else could monitor their conversation, Henry flipped the switch to start the meeting.

First up were the twins, Maks and Anabel. He was clad in a thin robe, barely tied at the waist. She draped her arms around him and peered over his left shoulder.

"Let's get this over with. The Asian markets are about to open and we have some work to do." Maks yawned and Anabel nudged him.

"Of course, wouldn't want to disrupt our main revenue stream." Henry wished they didn't have to rely on the twins for their financial security, but at the moment the stock manipulation covered their growing shortfall.

"Apologies for the delay. I was just getting in from a gala," Elise said as she threw her mink stole across the back of her chair.

"Elise, I sure hope you weren't spending too much of our money. We know how you love the high life," Anabel teased as she flipped her jet-black hair off her shoulder.

"My dear Anabel, do not attempt to lecture me. I have little patience left," Elise said as she pointed toward the screen.

"Now, ladies, we'll have none of that. We're stronger together. This infighting only threatens our plans," Henry said. The animosity that had been growing between those two troubled him, and he knew any distraction could allow mistakes to surface. And they were too close to the end to be blindsided.

"My apologies, Henry," Anabel said as she lowered her head and looked askance at her brother, who nodded as well.

"Good. Now I am sure you have all seen the rousing success of the initial test of the WaveMaker," Henry said as he pointed to the screen behind him, which showed the recording of the device powering up and igniting the hydrodynamic pulse. It quickly cut away to a split screen of two buoy cameras in the direct path of the tsunami, then cut again to a stationary camera on the Mississippi beach that was devastated.

The sheer destructive power of the water left them in awe. The screen behind Henry went black, and it was another moment before any of them spoke.

"I trust there are no more concerns about the WaveMaker or

the accelerator. As you saw, the helix matrix maintained the directional mandate and contained the destruction to the imprinted coordinates," Henry said. He could see they were all slack-jawed as the video repeated itself.

"And we have confirmation that the distance can be increased as well as the intensity?" Elise asked. "We can leave nothing to chance. Our entire plan hinges on the obliteration of just about anything the Atlantic touches."

"Don't worry. Everything will proceed as planned. Just hold up your end of the operation," Henry said.

"Everything is in play, we just need the location for the final phase," Elise said.

"I have uncovered the last remaining ciphers to determine the place. And once it's revealed to the world, we can make our move," Henry said.

"And how exactly have you come in possession of this location?" Anabel asked as she leaned forward.

Henry froze momentarily before deciding how to respond.

"It was part of the Flores venture," Henry said as he turned slightly to Elise, who picked up on his need for her support.

"We can't rush anything at this point. Caution is the rule, not the exception. We're in the end game of our centuries-old plan to bring about the reckoning. The world will drown as we rise to power," Elise said as she swiped right on her tablet to send the data to her confederates.

They each opened their screens to see the simulation that showed the projected decimation of the east coast of America and the west coast of Europe.

"The new center of power will be ours as we claim our rightful place in history," Elise said. Her piercing blue eyes danced with glee.

"You have Rami in your possession so he can be used as the power source, correct?" Anabel asked.

"Rami is going nowhere. He has been subjected to a battery of tests and we have managed to intermix his genetic makeup with that of the helix matrix so that it won't function without him. He is now intrinsically tied to the WaveMaker and will be the central power source for the Reckoning."

"And does he suspect?" Elise asked.

"What? That he is the power source for our tsunami device?" Henry asked.

"No, that we were the ones who put him in Astara?" Elise said.

"Does it even matter?"

"I applaud your tenacity and your dedication, Henry, but we cannot be too careful. Our destiny has been thwarted before. We must not let anything interfere," Elise said as she fidgeted with her teardrop diamond earrings.

"And that's where I come in, right?" Maks said as he lifted his tablet and tapped on the folder marked Project Ghost. The app opened and five faces appeared. "I've already got my team set up. Just say the word and they can be ready to enforce our directive." His tablet lit up and a video popped up of several empowered people sparring with Yakuza soldiers.

"Very good, Maks," Henry said as one of the powered people decapitated one of his attackers.

"Brutal, right?" Maks smiled.

"And the next disaster? When should we expect it?" Anabel asked. "We have to maneuver the eco-based securities to increase our margin."

Henry recited the archaic text from memory:

The mountain will flood.

The flames will smother the island.
The ground will steal the living.
The river will break the bank.
The illumination will reveal all.
The Sentinel will awaken.
And the tide will break new and old.

"We are waiting on the sinkhole and the sandstorms," Henry added. "Then we will be able to create the world we are destined to rule."

"Then we'll leave it to you, Henry. Our time is near," Elise said.

"Until the next time," Anabel said.

"The Sentinel will save us all," they said in unison.

CHAPTER
24

27 June

Rami stared at the open pages of the book he wasn't reading. He simply couldn't concentrate. It didn't help that his eyes were leaking grief onto the pages of *One Hundred Years of Solitude*, blurring the ink.

For the last day, everything had made his eyes teary. The guilt he felt over the strange girl's death threatened to suffocate him. Praying didn't help. Meditation didn't help. Pacing didn't help. Sleeping didn't help—nightmares catapulted him into panicked wakefulness.

He knew little more now about his powers than he did when he first arrived at The Hastings Foundation's large downtown laboratory facility in Philadelphia. The scientists seemed to be working harder at keeping him in the dark than at finding out exactly how his ability to resist infection worked. No one had spoken to him yet today, and it was past the lunch hour. At noon a young woman, likely an intern, had brought salad, kebabs, bread, and an enormous sweet tea, which he had developed a real liking for, to his room.

Rami decided to try reading again. He had just reseated

himself on a green love seat and picked up the large glass of sweet tea when it felt like his mind would vibrate out of his skull.

"Rami, I'm Emma," he heard in his head. "Don't be scared."

Rami immediately dropped the sweet tea and the glass shattered on the floor, sending shards across the room. Rami looked around the room, trying to determine the source of the voice.

"No, Rami, they didn't put drugs in the sweet tea. I am like you. I have powers. From the solstice," the voice said. Rami quite liked the little girl's Irish lilt, but her presence in his head worried him even more than the terrifying solo journey out of the cave had.

"I know this is strange to you," the girl said. "I have been given a task to find others like me—like you—who can do amazing things. The earth is crying out in pain and we have to come together to save the world."

Rami was still trying to wrap his head around his own new ability. He was relieved there were more people who were changed. After all, he was able to regenerate his body. How much of a leap was it for someone to converse with him mentally? He sat back in the love seat, feeling a bit more comfortable with Emma inside his head.

"I can find others who have powers and talk to them in their heads, like I'm doing now. I can also read the minds of people around me. And you can't get sick, right? You can heal yourself?"

"Yes, I can heal myself, but I don't see what good that does. It's selfish. I couldn't even help that girl who came in here a few days ago," he said.

"What girl?"

"They found someone else with powers. They don't

know who she is, or at least didn't when they found her. They may have figured that out by now. Not that it matters. She's dead. I think her body couldn't handle the new power. She was bleeding, and I tried to help. I gave her some of my blood, hoping it would confer on her some of the same healing abilities it has given me. But I failed. I couldn't help her. It's strange but it's like a part of me is lost now." Rami sank deep into the love seat. His eyes stung, threatening more tears. Still? Shouldn't he be done weeping for the loss of a girl he hadn't known?

"Rami, do not feel guilt. You were not meant to save her." Emma could feel his mental resistance to this idea.

"It is my fault. I tried, but I couldn't save her." He drew up his knees into his arms and dropped his head onto his knees. His body trembled as he cried silently.

"You tried to save her. That's what counts."

Rami said nothing. His breath was catching and chest was heaving.

"What makes you think you were to save her? That's not your gift. Had you been meant to save her, it would have worked. Her part on Earth has finished, and she's in heaven now."

Rami felt a wonderful thing. The sadness of the loss flowed through him, but the guilt evaporated. He kept his head drawn into his knees, but found the overwhelming need to cry had lifted. His breathing evened out. Eventually, he raised his head and let his legs drop to the floor. He sat a little taller in the love seat.

"Rami, you and I still have work to do."

"Hey, wait, how can you speak Farsi?"

"It's just my power. From the solstice. I can find people who also got powers and speak with them in their head. I can speak in whatever language they can speak in."

"Oh," he said, considering this. "Do you realize this is

the first time since jail and the cave that I have been able to fully express myself?"

"Cave?"

"I don't want to relive it. Can you look at my memories?"

Emma paused, considering. "I could, but I don't like to. It feels like snooping."

"It's okay."

And so Emma looked, and she saw. She saw Rami in a tiny jail cell. She saw him cut down prisoners who had been hung to death. She saw him survive beatings from prison guards. She saw him eat moldy bread when there was no other food. She saw him pine for his beloved. She saw the first hope of months when he met a man from The Hastings Foundation. She saw him released from prison but sent immediately to participate in a cave expedition. She saw the phosphorescent light in the cave, and, hours later, Rami regaining consciousness to find all the other members of the group had died. She saw him escape this earthly tomb only to be whisked away by The Hastings Foundation. She saw him poked and prodded and fed. She saw white-coated doctors ignore his questions. She felt his distress as she sifted through suppressed memories.

"I see, Rami. I'm so sorry."

For a long moment, he said nothing. "What kind of work do you mean?"

Emma explained what she understood from the voice that had filled her head off and on since the solstice.

"But how can I help with that?"

"You will be part of the team. You are very important. You were there at the center of it all, in that cave. And you will be the one who can stop the struggles."

"There's something you should know. There's a prophecy that says—"

"Yes, I know all about the prophecy, I've spoken to the one who's given it to you," Emma said.

Rami's eyes widened. "What? You know the one who speaks in riddles about the Sentinel?"

"The voice? He didn't speak of a Sentinel to me. He spoke of you. You're far more important than you understand."

"How can this be? I never asked for this."

"The voice picked us both. We have to do the best we can."

"Are you sure we can trust the voice?"

"Of course."

"You have much faith. The prophecy speaks of great troubles."

"Yes, the coming struggles, and a reckoning."

For a long time, Rami said nothing else, taking all this in.

"Now tell me about the place where you are. The Hastings Foundation. Can you leave when it's time to join us?"

"No, I don't think I'll be able to. I'm not exactly a prisoner like I was in Iran, but I don't have the freedom to come and go as I like. They won't even give me proper shoes. I have asked to see the Liberty Bell and they've promised me that they will take me soon. But the scientists want me around for testing. Not that they worked with me much."

"Okay, I'll work on a way to get you out of there. I know a teleporter who may be able to get you out without the people there knowing you're gone until it's too late. I've been talking to others like us. Others who want to help. I'm learning more every day. Will you come and help us? Please?"

Rami considered for a moment. The Hastings Foundation

was extremely powerful and they had certainly gone out of their way to keep him safe. They wouldn't give him up easily and would not be happy if he escaped out from under their noses. But Rami also had his doubts about the integrity and motives of the operation. On the other hand, there was this little Irish girl who was impossibly in his head, who wanted him to help, who believed he could help. Who had soothed his guilt over the bleeding girl who had died. He decided to throw his lot in with Emma and her group. It was a decision he knew his family and Arian would support—he just hoped The Hastings Foundation didn't take out their displeasure on them.

"Yes, I'll help. But do you think we can ensure my family's safety? And that of my beloved Arian?"

Emma was silent for a moment, considering. "I think we can probably help keep them safe. Rami, I'll do whatever I can to help you. Do you think you can manage a few more days with the scientists?"

"Yes, probably. Two of them aren't so bad. I don't really trust Dr. Martin, but Dr. Patel and Dr. Giraud seem okay. Actually, they don't seem to get along with Dr. Martin either. I will just let them continue to think they're in control. I'll give them no reason to think I have any plans that don't involve them. If something changes here or I need to talk to you, how do I find you?"

"Just think of me. If you want, you can knock, like I did."

"Knock? That was a knock? It felt like my brain was going to vibrate out of my skull," Rami said, lightly rubbing his head at the memory. "Please don't knock so hard in the future."

"Oh, sorry. I just wanted to be sure that you heard me. I'll be gentle next time. Like this." She demonstrated a light knock that didn't rattle Rami's brains. "I'll call again when I know about the training place and when we will be able to come get you. Good luck."

And just like that, the girl dropped out of his mind. He considered their conversation for a few minutes, then reopened the book. He found his mind clear enough that now he could read.

CHAPTER
2 5

6 July

"Did Jill give you much grief about coming to meet me?" CoCo asked Maggie.

"Hours of it. Or it felt like that." The travel reporter, wearing a light blue sundress dotted with white daisies, smiled. "Then the truth came out. She

Courtney Cooper "CoCo"

already had lunch plans today anyway. So, here I am, ready to be your confessor." Maggie laughed.

"Lucky me." CoCo rolled her eyes. "Otherwise, Jill would have tagged along. It's going to be hard enough to tell you."

"And what do you want me to know, but not your own dear sister?" Maggie reached across the table and grabbed CoCo's hands. Grinning, she said, "Your secret is safe with me."

"So, um, how was your flight?"

Maggie wrinkled her nose at CoCo. "Upgrades all the way. Job perk. Now, you didn't ask me down here to make small talk. Come on, give."

"Well, uh—"

Before CoCo could decide what to say next, a waiter appeared with menus and two tall glasses of iced tea and said he'd be back in a few minutes to take their lunch order. CoCo looked frustrated and relieved by the delay.

"Maggie, you should try the grilled catfish. It's delicious. It's what I always get." CoCo, not needing the menu, left it sitting closed in front of her. She was wearing a hot pink blouse and white jean shorts with hot pink lace-up sandals. Even though she couldn't have gotten more than five hours of sleep between the late night at Pole and the early hour of their lunch, CoCo was her normal perky self.

"Right," Maggie said, studying the menu before closing it decisively. "Grilled catfish sounds like a winner. I haven't had any since my last trip to Jackson."

"Can't go wrong."

"So, how much longer you going to be at Pole?"

"Couple more months, I think. I have almost enough money saved to start my fashion line." CoCo sipped some of her tea, then pointed at her blouse. "One of mine, but for me, not for the line."

"Looks great. I'd like one of those in teal."

"I might could oblige."

"But you've got the designs ready?"

"Yup. Just a funds issue at this point."

The waiter returned and CoCo ordered a grilled catfish platter with a double side of veggies. Maggie opted for the grilled catfish Caesar salad. The waiter retreated.

"Spill it."

CoCo just grinned, still uncertain now how to begin. "I've been thinking about this since I called you and asked you to come to town. And I still don't know how to say it."

"Say what?"

Maggie sipped some iced tea and waited as CoCo organized her thoughts. After thousands of interviews and talks with sources, Maggie recognized the signs, knew when to push and when to wait. This was a time for waiting. When Maggie saw a moment of decision flash onto CoCo's face, she smiled encouragingly.

"First, Maggie, this is totally between us. You can't tell anyone. It's got to be our secret. Not your job, not my sister, nobody. You can't tell anyone."

"Of course," Maggie replied instantly. Mentally, she opened up the part of her brain that she thought of as "extremely confidential info" and nodded at her sorority sister's little sister. The utter seriousness and need for secrecy piqued her interest. Usually, CoCo was straightforward about everything she did or thought. Not one for secrets, that girl.

But CoCo seemed unsure how to proceed. Then, she looked toward a table across the way and seemed to forget Maggie was in town, after all the trouble she'd taken to get her here. CoCo's intent gaze prompted Maggie to look over at the lovebirds at that table as well.

Maggie looked at the pair. They were about CoCo's age. She could see a tiny bit of sculpted, hairless chest under his white short-sleeved shirt. She was in cherry red short-shorts and a black halter top. They were young, good looking, and in lust. As Maggie watched, the young woman took off her halter top and rose gracefully from her chair. The man pushed his chair away from the table, and she straddled his lap, kissing him, her arms wrapped tightly around him.

"Get a room," Maggie muttered, turning back to CoCo.

"No, keep watching," CoCo said in a low but playful voice.

"I didn't think this was that kind of establishment."

"You're the crack reporter. What's wrong with this picture?"

It was only a slight jab, but it stung. No one thought she was a real reporter. Maggie widened her attention from the lovebirds and considered the restaurant's dining area. Then it hit her. No one else was paying the slightest bit of attention to the nudity or make-out session. No gawking. No dirty old men staring at the young blonde's near-nakedness. And not just out of feigned politeness. It was like they didn't see anything out of the ordinary. Then, without warning, the young woman was back in her chair, taking a bite of chicken fried steak, and the young man was talking.

"What?"

"Exactly."

"No, seriously, what just happened?"

"That's what I wanted to talk to you about. I figured it was easier to show you than to tell you."

For a long second, Maggie said nothing. Then, slowly, "Did you somehow do that?"

CoCo nodded.

"That never happened?"

"Nope."

"So I'm the only one who saw her do that? Or did she do it?" Maggie struggled, but thought she had her voice under control. Internally, however, was a different story. Just the week before she'd joked with Focus about interviewing people with powers. Now, it seemed, here was one, whether she was off-limits or not.

"Like I said, she never did that. You just saw what I wanted you to see."

"We can discuss your R-rated tendencies later, CoCo. How did you ... Why did you do that?"

"I can make illusions. I can make people see what I want

them to see. She never moved, never stripped, never made out with him."

"But how?"

"I don't know, Maggie, and that's the problem." CoCo propped her chin on her palms.

Wonder spread across Maggie's face. "You're a Mod."

"A what?" CoCo looked confused.

"A Mod, you know, someone with powers." She saw that CoCo still didn't understand. "There have been some weird news reports the last few weeks, about unusual things happening. Rumors that there were people with powers. Someone, somewhere, started calling them Mods, for modified, and it kind of stuck. You, you're a Mod."

"Mods," CoCo mused, considering the term.

They slipped into silence as the waiter made another untimely appearance to deposit their lunch plates at the table and returned quickly to refill their iced teas.

CoCo grinned as she took her first bite of grilled catfish. "Heavenly."

Maggie, however, sat quietly, staring at her Caesar salad topped with grilled catfish. She was working through what had just happened and trying to put it together with rumors she'd heard over the last few weeks.

"Come on, eat," CoCo said, her eyes wide and dancing. "It's best hot."

"You didn't realize there were others?"

"Can they also make illusions?" she asked, with relief and excitement bubbling through her voice.

"You seriously don't keep up with current events. Do you?"

CoCo shook her head.

"Ever, uh, ever read my new blog? I e-mailed you about it."

Blushing, CoCo shook her head.

"But you've seen me reporting. Some of my travel shows, right?"

Finally, an affirmative.

"Well, CoCo, if you bothered to read the papers, or watch the news, or even just read my e-mails to you from time to time, you'd know about the Mods."

"Sorry. Working, trying to launch a fashion line. No time for things like news."

"So, tell me about it. Everything, from how you first discovered you could make illusions, to how it feels, what kinds of things you've made other people see, how you've practiced, everything."

And so CoCo did, talking quietly and intensely as Maggie slowly ate her meal, interrupting only twice with questions. CoCo told about casting her first illusion and, later, using them to amp up her tips at Pole. As the young woman spoke, her voice was first full of anxiety, but by the time she was done, CoCo sounded confident again.

"Now it's my turn. Who are the other Mods? What can they do?"

Maggie spent the rest of the meal filling CoCo in on how the Kili disaster and the lunch robbery at For Italian had convinced her she should be covering something that mattered, rather than just doing travel features. She'd wanted to get back to her journalism roots, but her contract with Travel Now had certain restrictions in it. None prohibited her from running a blog, so she'd started TheModsBlog in her time off, and its membership had grown rapidly. People were hungry for news about the Mods and the disasters, she told CoCo.

"You think it's all connected, don't you?" CoCo asked, her voice starting to rise with excitement.

Maggie nodded. "I'm assuming you've kept this new little power of yours a secret. You haven't shown anyone, have you?"

"No, just you. And there for a minute, I wasn't sure I was going to be able to tell you without seeing myself on some news program."

"Don't be silly. As amazing as this is, as much as it might make a mind-blowing item for my blog, I'd never violate your request for privacy. Plus, you're my little sister, almost, and I don't want to see you dealing with the aftermath of what would happen if you revealed this new gift of yours. Understood?"

CoCo nodded.

"Not that I don't want to report on these new powers, because I do. This is amazing stuff. But your secret is safe with me. I'll find another way to cover it for my blog. Okay?"

Again, CoCo nodded, and she relaxed into her chair. "I've been trying to figure out why I can make illusions, why I got this great gift." CoCo beamed. "But if I'm not the only one, that changes everything."

"It does?"

"Yes, don't you see? It's like there's some sort of master plan."

"What?"

"Don't worry." CoCo grinned and winked. "I'll only use my powers for good."

CHAPTER
2 6

7 July

What looked like an entry to hell sprawled across the Interstate 80 and Highway 395 interchange in Reno, Nevada. Thirty cars were thought to be in the sinkhole, and nearly a hundred other vehicles had wrecked, trying to avoid the gaping hole that had suddenly appeared right after the earth shook.

Three enormous cranes worked in tandem to hoist cars up from what the locals had already started calling The Devil's Slide.

Josh pulled up alongside the interstate, silently cursing himself. An hour ago he had been about to pull into his cabin in Lake Tahoe and now he was rushing into what the news had called the worst sinkhole disaster in history. He blamed the Irish girl for this burst of bravery.

"Really, what can I do?" Josh asked himself as he hopped out of his scarlet Tesla Roadster. "I can just change my face. How is that any help?"

Josh raced past an ambulance that had five stretchers lined up with victims in various states of medical care. He picked up speed as he dodged several police officers who had set a perimeter about twenty yards from the edge of the sinkhole.

On one of the officers' walkie-talkies, Josh heard an urgent call for all units to move to the southern edge of the disaster, followed by a peculiar word that sent chills coursing through him, despite the summer heat.

"All units to the southern point. Fallen officer in police cruiser. There is a Mod on site. Proceed with caution."

Josh took off in a flash toward the southern tip of the sinkhole. He wasn't sure what he was going to do, but he had to help somehow. The Irish girl's words haunted him. He was a Mod, and he should help others like him. He could be more than just an actor. He skidded to a stop near the cranes that were tasked with lifting cars from the bottom.

The rescue workers were grimly efficient. Josh watched as one of the cranes brought up a badly mangled police cruiser. There seemed to be no sign of life inside. Ponderously, the crane turned and deposited the wreck in what was clearly that crane's landing zone. Josh expected to hear the car hit the pavement, but the crane operator gently lowered the vehicle to the ground.

Immediately, two police officers rushed to the car and peered in the driver's side window. Josh saw their shoulders slump and knew The Devil's Slide had claimed another victim. The officers tried to open the door, but couldn't.

Josh looked intently at the officers, studying their positions and trying to discern the whereabouts of the Mod he had heard was on the scene.

At last, Josh saw other officers converge on a nearby spot with guns drawn. No one was paying any attention to him, so Josh willed his face to change into someone who would have reason to be on the scene. As Reno Mayor Luis Cruz, Josh approached them slowly.

"Just stay still, kid," an out-of-shape captain said as he inched closer to the suspected Mod. The kid huddled against a crushed car. He was covered in scratches and blood, and his short brown hair stood up in spikes.

"Leave me alone! Don't come any closer!" the boy yelled at them. Tears streamed down his face. The ground trembled. The officers hesitantly stayed their footing as rubble from the fallen highway broke around them. The crane began to sway back and forth and, even from a distance, the operator looked close to panic. After a moment everything was eerily still again.

Josh let out a loud whistle and the officers looked back. "That's enough, officers. I'll take it from here." They looked stunned to be addressed by Mayor Cruz.

"What are you doing here?" one of the officers asked.

"Taking control of a situation you were about to escalate."

"But this kid's a freak. Probably started this disaster," the out-of-shape captain said.

"Yeah, every time we step closer to him, the ground starts shaking. Just like before," his partner added, his voice wavering in what Josh interpreted as fear.

"That's enough. He's scared and confused. Call off your men and get the hell out of here," Josh said in his disguised voice. Josh could see their hesitation to leave him alone with the Mod fighting with desire to get far, far away from the Mod.

"We can't leave you here alone. Where's your security detail?"

"I'll be fine. There are others in danger on the other side of the sinkhole. I'll take care of this." Josh pointed the police in the other direction.

The captain reluctantly waved his officers away as the

mayor stepped closer to the kid.

"It's okay, you're okay now," Josh said as he crept down. He carefully made sure that he was on secure footing before moving farther down.

"I'm alone and I won't hurt you," Josh said nervously as he felt a low rumble beneath him.

"No! You don't understand! This is all my fault! I did this. I killed my family," he said with a sob.

Josh wanted to interrupt, but he knew instinctively that his best bet was to keep the kid talking. He looked through the crushed blue sedan's window and saw a woman slouched over the steering wheel and a little girl in a car seat with eyes wide open. Josh swallowed hard and looked at the kid, whose dingy T-shirt was bloodstained.

"What's your name?"

"Pete."

"It's going to be okay, Pete. I promise," Josh said. He put his arm around the boy he thought might be about ten years old and sat down.

Through the sobs, the boy began his story. "I told my sister to stop bothering me. She kept singing that stupid Princess What's-Her-Name song. My mother was driving and told us to be quiet and the next thing I know my head is pounding and the car starts shaking. I get real scared and I slam my hands on the seat, and then out of nowhere a hole opens up in front of us. Don't you see? I killed my family."

Josh looked out toward the sinkhole, taking in the sheer catastrophic damage.

"Aren't you scared of me?"

"No, Pete. I'm like you," Josh said as Pete looked blankly at him. "How long have you been able to shake things?"

"For a few weeks. I got a really bad headache one night and the next thing I know is I could shake the ground," he said through tears. "I didn't mean to do this. You have to believe me."

"I do. It's going to be okay. I promise," Josh said as the boy sobbed into his bloody hands. He looked around to ensure they were still alone. "This isn't your fault. I don't think you are capable of this."

"How can you say that? I can make earthquakes," he said.

"Lots of strange things happening these days," Josh said, trying to keep Pete's mind off of the disaster.

Pete seemed to wrestle with the hope Josh's view offered. The tears welled again. Pete put his head down again, and Josh knew he was losing him.

"I can change my face," Josh said as he morphed his face back to normal, looking at the kid as the Hollywood star that all the boys idolized and the women lusted after.

"You're ... You're—"

"That's right. Let that be our secret," Josh said as Pete muscled a smile. They sat in silence for a few minutes before speaking again.

"Are they dead?"

"I'm going to make sure you are taken care of."

"I'm all alone now," Pete cried.

"What about your dad?"

He shrugged. "New wife, new life."

"Growing up's rough, isn't it?"

"I thought that this would make me special. That these powers would make me a hero, with a cape and all," Pete said. New tears trailed down his cheek.

"Who says you can't be," Josh said. "This doesn't have to be your whole story."

"What's going to happen to me? Are they going to arrest me?"

Out of the corner of his eye, Josh saw the police officers

close in on them again. "I won't let that happen to you," Josh said as Pete leaned his head against him.

Josh let his own head fall back against the car and tried to figure out how to get out of this. He could hear helicopters buzzing above him and saw a news crew set up about twenty yards away. Maybe there was a way to salvage this. Even if it meant giving up his life.

"Guess Emma was right all along," Josh said. He stood and put his finger to his mouth, shushing Pete as he changed his face once again. "Just follow my lead." Josh led Pete toward the news crew, passing right by the police officers, who seemed more petrified than normal. Josh wished someone had written some lines for him. Improvisation terrified him.

The newsman stood in front of what was effectively a mass grave. He looked like a classic Norman Rockwell painting come to life.

"Good afternoon. I'm Glenn Whitfield reporting from Reno, Nevada, for National News Now. Behind me is the giant sinkhole that swallowed up the interchange at Interstate 80 and Highway 395, killing dozens of people and injuring scores more. Dubbed The Devil's Slide by locals, this sinkhole measures two hundred feet wide and is estimated at six hundred and fifty feet deep. To put this in perspective, the hole is more than twice as deep as a football field is long."

"Excuse me," the mayor said as he and the boy entered Glenn's frame. "Sorry to interrupt your broadcast, but we have something very important to say."

Glenn looked at his cameraman and then back at the mayor before nodding and tilting the microphone toward Mayor Cruz.

"I know you have heard a lot of things lately. The world

is going through some serious changes and I think all these disasters are evidence of that," Josh-as-the-mayor said as the kid grabbed his hand so tightly the tips of his fingers began to feel cold.

"A tremendous White Light Wave engulfed the world a few weeks back, on the summer solstice. And that wave has modified some people, giving them some very special gifts. By now you may have heard about these Mods, as they are called. I am here to tell you that you don't have to be afraid. You don't have to be scared of—"

"Excuse me, Mr. Mayor, but how can you be so sure of that?" Glenn interrupted, as if prompted by a voice in ear.

Josh looked at the reporter and then straight into the camera. "Because I am one of them." With those words, the face and body contorted and morphed into the *Extreme Warrior* actor. The cops just on the edge of the frame drew their guns on the newly revealed Mod.

"I'm Josh Grant," he said as he barely blinked. "And I'm a Mod. No special effects needed."

The police officers to the side dropped their jaws, but never took their guns off of him.

"This boy was as much a victim of the sinkhole as anyone else. I'm standing here right now to give all the Mods a voice. If you're different, if you can do incredible things, then you should come with me. I'm not afraid of my abilities. The White Light Wave event on the solstice granted us gifts specifically so we could help save the earth. Any Mod who wants to use their powers for good should come to me. No need to be afraid. You have my guarantee of protection and safety for all Mods."

"But how would they get in touch with you?" Glenn asked before Josh could walk away.

"I've a special friend that can reach out to all Mods. Call

out for Emma and she can get you where you need to be."
Josh turned around and walked past the dumbfounded cops
as the camera followed him.

CHAPTER
27

7 July

Sun Luli felt nothing like the dewy jasmine she was named for. The summer had brought hotter-than-average temperatures to San Francisco, and she was clad in a pale blue business suit that was sticking unpleasantly to her skin. Between the

Sun Luli

heat spike and the Chinese emigrant's pregnancy, sweaty jasmine more appropriately described how she felt. Despite this, Luli stood patiently waiting at the crosswalk for the signal to change to "Walk." Her left hand rested comfortably, protectively, on the baby bulge.

Her body might be on its way to a meeting with a client, but her mind was directed inward and downward. It was something she'd been doing ever since she found out she was pregnant. Something she'd done when she was pregnant with her daughter, Sying, as well. She sent reassurances and love to the baby boy growing inside her. Tried to ascertain if she was giving him everything he needed. She wasn't sure about that, since for the last two weeks or so she'd had fitful sleep full of unusually vibrant dreams. This morning, she had woken up feeling achy all over, but her body seemed to have worked its way through whatever had bothered her. Again, she sent her mind inward and downward, trying to get a sense of who he was, so she and Yi could name him properly. To make sure he was developing healthfully, happily, peacefully. To let him know that he was loved, and wanted.

The light flashed to "Walk," and the petite public relations professional, still absorbed with the tiny life inside her, stepped into the crosswalk. As she crossed the street, she watched her feet appear and disappear under her bulging stomach and grinned.

Six more steps and her life would change forever.

Coming from the opposite direction sped a man in a dark green Dodge Dakota pickup.

Luli, thinking of cooing babies with dark black hair, heard a woman yell and looked up. Her entire world immediately expanded from the tiny child growing inside her belly to the green pickup truck less than five feet away from her. Instinct took over.

She screamed.

Her left hand remained protectively on her stomach.

Her right hand flew up in a frantic "Stop" gesture.

And for a wonder, the old Dodge Dakota, a rolling heap that had just barely passed its most recent safety inspection, did just that.

Still screaming, Luli watched the truck make what would probably be its last stop. It seemed to slam into an invisible wall. The front end crumpled in a shriek of mangling metal and the engine died. Luli saw the driver remove his seat belt, exit the truck, and race toward the Dakota's front end. He, too, seemed to smash nose-first into an invisible wall. Luli saw, rather than heard, as he cursed and backed up a step, rubbing his nose.

Finally, she heard him ask if she was okay, but she kept screaming.

Ever so slowly, he tried to step toward her. Again, he encountered that invisible barrier.

All around, frustrated drivers honked their horns and flipped birds as they tried to pass the wreckage in the intersection.

Luli finally stopped screaming. She opened her eyes and saw the badly twisted front end of the green truck, and then she saw the bystanders. She patted her belly, as though checking on its resident, and dropped her other arm. When she did, the front license plate dropped off the clunker.

What had just happened?

She spotted the driver, and he stepped toward her. Instinctively, she backed away a step.

"What did you do to my truck?"

"Me?" Disbelief dripped thick in her voice. A public relations professional to the core, she knew when to spin, when to make nice, and most importantly, when to go on the offensive. "What did I do to your truck? Are you kidding? You almost hit me. Me and my baby."

Flustered, Luli turned to go. She couldn't understand what had just happened, but she felt a deep need to get away from the scene of the near-accident as soon as possible.

"Hey, come back here," the driver yelled.

Ignoring him, she picked up her pace, and as she walked as quickly as her legs would take her, she tried to figure out what had saved her from being run over by that old clunker.

Two blocks later, she spotted an ice cream shop and thought chocolate might ease the worst of her nerves. Within minutes, a more collected Luli was holding a chocolate ice cream cone, licking it as she made her way to the client meeting. Thoughts about her unborn son vied with wonder at the miracle that had saved her life.

Later that day, Luli would tell Yi that it never occurred to her to run forward or backward while the truck was bearing down on her.

Yi had come home, panicked, after hearing about the near-accident. Seeing Luli and their soon-to-be-born boy were truly okay, he kissed her deeply, love mingled with relief. Then, without missing a beat, Yi picked up their four-year-old daughter, Sying, swung her around, and hugged her tight before kissing her forehead and depositing her on the couch. By unspoken agreement, which seems to happen so often when a couple is attuned to each other, they didn't discuss what had happened until after the dinner dishes had been cleared and Sying was tucked away in bed. But Luli could think of little else.

They sat at the square wooden kitchen table, in their normal seats, where they held all serious discussions.

"I'm relieved you're okay, my love," Yi said, brushing tendrils of Luli's long, straight hair out of her face. "But now I want you to tell me again what happened."

He was a computer programmer, and he liked things orderly. To Yi, everything could be understood if arranged appropriately and approached logically.

She gently and patiently explained the whole incident again, leaving out no details.

"I know you had the light, but you must be more alert. You are so often careless." At this last, he frowned and his eyes turned hard with fear he had yet to release. "What do I always tell you?"

Luli sighed. "We must always look out for ourselves. No one else will."

"And were you looking out for yourself? For our son?"

"I was thinking about our son, about our growing family. I was thinking of the future, not of protecting him," she said. Her voice was quiet, reluctant.

Her admission softened his features. "Luli, I worry. I couldn't bear to lose any of you."

"Look, today we got lucky."

"Yes, we did."

"Does it make any sense to you?" she asked. When Yi still looked blank, she elaborated, "The crashed truck?"

Frowning, Yi shook his head. The unexplained didn't fit in well with his worldview, and he refused to discuss this incomprehensible turn of events further.

That night, they gently and quietly loved each other, as much a celebration of safety as of their continued happiness. After, Yi wrapped his arms around Luli, and he slept.

Luli, troubled by the afternoon's events, lay still in his arms, mulling over possibilities and rejecting them. Considering and beginning to embrace the only obvious possibility before discarding it, repeatedly. She was doing what the Americans called waffling.

But no matter how she looked at it, there only seemed to be one answer.

She had put her hand up, in panic, wanting desperately for the truck not to hit her and kill her. And the truck had stopped. Instantly. But it had run into something. The front of that green Dodge looked like an accordion after slamming into something. In fact, now that she fully replayed the memory, hadn't she heard an impact that for one dreadful moment she had thought were her own bones being crushed by the truck?

So the truck had definitely hit something, Luli thought. But she had been looking at the truck, and she could see nothing between her and what had looked like sure death. So whatever the Dodge had hit was invisible. But maybe not permanent, she thought, as she remembered how the license plate had dropped off the truck well after the accident.

The timing of her action and the truck's response left little room for doubt: she had caused something invisible to protect her. The conclusion both reassured and unnerved her.

The question was what, precisely, had she done. And whether she could do it again. Maybe an experiment or two, she thought.

With these thoughts filling her head, Luli slid out of bed, closed the bedroom door, and padded into the living room. But when she got there, she just looked around. How was she to arrange an experiment of this nature? And would the fact that she herself had arranged it affect the outcome? She didn't know. Feeling uninspired, she decided to light a candle and meditate. Graceful despite her bulging midsection, Luli dropped to the ground, cross-legged, and looked at the taper candle. She breathed in for a slow count of five and out for a slow count of five. Staring at the flickering flame, she repeated this breathing pattern until she felt centered and relaxed.

Thinking clearly, she knew she couldn't single-handedly force a situation that truly threatened her life, and that of her son's, not without having her husband there to save her if the experiment went wrong. But she was pretty sure he'd never agree to let her initiate such an experiment in the first place.

She reconsidered the elements of the incident: panic, stop hand gesture, overwhelming want to protect her unborn child and thirst for own survival.

The easiest of those to replicate would be the hand

gesture. Now she just needed something that might respond. Feeling foolish, Luli rose from her cross-legged position and extended her hand in the stop gesture. She walked toward the taper candle. The flame flickered as she approached. When her outstretched hand was three inches away from the flame, she watched, slack-jawed, as it continued flickering, but at the same time bent away from her, as though it were diverting around an obstacle.

She pulled her hand back, and the flame sprang back to its normal upright stance. Luli moved her hand back toward the flame, and it bent away from her.

"Wow," she said in quiet awe.

Fascinated, she repeated this back and forth motion with her hands and her arms until the taper candle had lost a little of its height.

"It doesn't have anything to do with want. Or panic," she murmured. Whatever she was doing, it was involuntary, and it was protective. The understanding energized her and she decided to make a cup of chamomile tea, so she headed into the kitchen.

Actually, she wanted another chocolate shake. But she didn't want the extra calories, and it would be difficult to explain to Yi why she had chosen to leave their comfortable bed to run the loud blender and make midnight dessert. So she compromised: lots of honey in her tea. While the water heated, she wondered what she would tell Yi in the morning about her newfound protective barrier. How would she show him? Once the water hit a boil, she poured it over the chamomile to let it steep. Then, she tilted the kettle over the sink with her right hand and poured a trickle of the boiling water out. Timidly, she brought her left hand under the stream. Instead of pain, delight filled her as she watched the steaming water arc around her hand, as though protected by a globe, and spatter into the sink.

Tomorrow, she would show Yi what she could do. Maybe he'd quit worrying about her so much.

CHAPTER
2 8

20 July

"Say cheese."

Maggie was already smiling, so she turned to look at her companion for the evening. As usual, The Pigeon looked stern. She elbowed her boss and grinned when the woman drew in her eyebrows in consternation.

"I am, you llama-loving—"

"Be nice. You promised," Maggie whispered.

The Pigeon groaned. "How am I supposed to smile when I look like the lowest of sphincter barnacles wearing this—"

Again, Maggie cut her off. "We're holding up the line. Just smile, and you can take the funny mustache off and we can go eat."

The Pigeon frowned and touched the offending prop. "Fine."

Maggie watched as The Pigeon worked to transform her stern expression into a patently fake smile under the handlebar mustache. Maggie shrugged, offered her eighty-watt smile and tilted her head, hoping it made her own Fu Manchu look jaunty. The short and balding photographer, seeming to sense The Pigeon's smile wouldn't last long, snapped the picture.

"Very good, ladies. Quite lovely. My assistant will give you copies of the photo. Ah, next," the photographer said to the next couple in line for pictures in front of the green screen. Maggie glanced back and nodded at Hank, a fellow travel journalist, and his date for the evening, who were further back in the souvenir photo line. She grimaced when Hank flashed a thumbs-down sign at her.

Carefully but quickly, The Pigeon removed her mustache and Maggie followed suit.

"So, Robin, what background should we choose for our photo?" Maggie asked.

The Pigeon scrolled through the options, which ranged from the pyramids in Egypt to Machu Picchu in Peru to the Eiffel Tower in Paris and everything in between. If it could be a travel photo setting, it was an option for the souvenir photos being taken at the awards banquet. As The Pigeon sifted through the possibilities, the photographer shot pictures of four other pairs, and they were all waiting for their own turn at the background-choosing station.

"This," The Pigeon finally said, pointing to what Maggie first took to be a crystal palace. On closer inspection, she realized it was a bar inside an ice hotel in Scandinavia she'd visited the year before and wondered how she possibly could have mistaken it.

"I like it."

"It seemed right."

The photographer's assistant noted the request, added the background to the mustached image of The Pigeon and Maggie and hit print. Moments later, two copies of the souvenir picture slid out of the printer. The assistant handed one to The Pigeon.

"Good luck," the assistant said, smiling shyly as she handed Maggie her copy. "I saw your piece on the ice hotel. I'd like to go there some time."

"Fingers crossed," Maggie said as she and The Pigeon strolled off. She was surprised that the photographer knew who she was.

As she walked away, Maggie inspected the photograph. Clearly she hadn't worn a fake mustache when she covered the ice hotel the year before. Nor had she worn a pale pink Dior evening gown. Despite the elegance of the venue, formal wear would not have been appropriate.

"I like your odds," The Pigeon said.

"Huh? Oh, right. Thanks. I'd love to beat that snake Hank and win. You think I have a good chance?" But, before her boss could answer, Maggie asked another question. "Is Focus at our table? I lost him when we decided to take the souvenir picture."

"Probably. Listen, before we go in there, I need to say something to you."

Her boss's tone snapped tension into Maggie's lower back. She stood stock-still and tried to keep her voice calm. "Oh? What's that?"

"Whether you win this award or not, you have to stop blogging about the Mods. I can't have you dividing your attention. This whole whale-wanking blog of yours is causing me problems I can't even begin to describe."

In a play for time, Maggie turned and walked into the dining room, where her name would or wouldn't blare from speakers later that evening as the winner of the travel documentarian of the year. At the moment, though, the possibility of winning paled in comparison to the possibility of having to quit the most meaningful work she had done in years. The Pigeon caught up to her and grabbed her elbow.

Fuming, Maggie squinted at her boss. "You're kidding. I can't just stop. That's an important story, and I'm doing it on my own time."

"Doesn't matter. TheModsBlog goes, or you do," The Pigeon said and steered Maggie toward their table. "Now, let's go win."

Maggie shook free from The Pigeon's clutches and looked at her boss. Could she give up meaningful work to toe the company line?

CHAPTER
29

21 July

When Xi Chang sat down at his monitoring desk and futzed with the knob controlling the video recording of hydraulic pumps, he saw water dripping from the ceiling. Despite the torrential amounts of rain the region had received, the rainy season wouldn't start officially for another three weeks. The Three Gorges Dam staff had recorded and patched the leak during last year's monsoon season.

Xi had just returned from inspecting the rotators and gear shifts deep inside the Three Gorges Dam. While concerned about the rising floodwaters in the Yangtze River region, he was confident the dam would hold. The region's administrators weren't as confident. They had declared a state of emergency.

While watching the minor leak, the middle-aged Xi opened a small silver box in front of him and removed a container of rice and a matching container of diced chicken in sauce. He reached across his desk and brought a plate toward him, dumping the rice and chicken onto it. He rummaged through his drawer for matching chopsticks and mixed his food together.

The large beige phone rang as he brought his first bite to his mouth. He dropped the sticks and answered it.

"Yes, I checked the pumps and the gear compressors," Xi said dryly into the receiver. "Of course I saw the report from last night about the generators and the spillway concerns. But honestly, it is not a problem. We are prepared for extra water above what is already in our reservoir and there are redundancies upon redundancies in place for just this sort of weather situation."

Xi confidently lifted a piece of chicken with rice and popped it into his mouth. As he listened to his superior drone on about safety protocols and procedures, he felt a tremor beneath his chair.

He wasn't sure if he imagined the vibration or not, so he put the phone on the desk and stood, looking at the monitors that showed measurements for critical elements of the dam. He checked each of the readings carefully.

Then he felt it again and understood what was happening. The unlikely timing of the fault line moving along with triple the amount of water in the reservoir meant disaster. An instant after the realization struck, he reached to trigger the klaxon alarm. He might have a few seconds to escape.

But he knew it was already too late.

He thought of his wife and daughter at home completely unaware of the fate hurtling toward them.

In the coming weeks scientists and environmentalists would debate the cause of the catastrophe. There was plenty of blame to go around. The earthquake exposed a fatal flaw in the design of the dam. The flood raged down the river, destroying everything in its path.

All told, 1.3 million died in the Three Gorge Dam Disaster, including Xi and his fellow co-workers and most of the residents along the river's edge. There had been no warning about the earthquake or the deluge of the reservoir. A perfect storm of serendipity and ineptitude caused the fatal tragedy along the Yangzte River.

CHAPTER
3 0

22 July

Under the unforgiving West
Texas sun, two men walked
alongside a lonely stretch of
barbed wire near a large
converted hangar. The
parched desert compound
held many secrets, but this

Capt. Warren G. Pierce

one, just a few miles from civilization, told a tale that twisted
and turned so much that its actual history was less interesting
than the legend around it.

"How are the reorganization and conversions going?"
the man in the gray T-shirt asked as the wind blew sand at
their faces.

"Everything is going better than I anticipated. The
training complex, as you'll see, has been working for a week
now. Communications are up and running and the housing
facilities are ready. I even worked on the special War Room
you requested," the older man in green army fatigues said.
He chomped on the cigar as they walked.

"Sounds like Base 47 is coming along very nicely. I'm

looking forward to the training. I'm sure you'll have your hands full. Most don't have any training at all." The younger man waved smoke from his face.

"I'm ready for whatever you throw at me," he said as he took off his green hat to wipe the sweat from his brow. Josh glanced over and saw a large circular scar on the left side of the other man's head.

"You came highly recommended for training. Tom speaks well of you," Josh said.

"He's dedicated, that's for sure. Hate the Hollywood thing, but it made up for a few harsh years," he said before quickly adding, "No offense."

"Don't worry, Captain Pierce, I get it. The business is a strange beast."

Warren Grant Pierce, named for his parents' favorite presidents, came from a long line of servicemen. Captain Pierce had been in the Army since he turned eighteen, making his mark throughout his career and rising to prominence in the Green Berets. The scars covering his body showed a history of service in the world's hot spots, some while he was in the Green Berets, some after he retired. A thin, badly healed knife scar from Myanmar stretched across his left forearm and a bullet wound from Iraq puckered his neck. Another scar, earned jumping a fence topped with razor wire in Russia, spanned his back.

"How many more are you expecting?" Pierce asked as he put his cigar out and threw it in the nearby trash bin.

"There's three of us here now, and four others are on their way, that I know of." Josh pressed the passcode to open the hangar door.

"You're not bringing in that kid from Reno, are you?"

"What, Pete?" Josh said as he struggled to remember. "Nah, he's off to live with an uncle, I think."

"Good. This is no business for a kid."

The two men entered Base 47, a seven-story underground facility that housed a large training complex, communications room, dormitory rooms, an infirmary, and a commissary, among other designated spaces.

"I've got my unit working with CoCo and Emilio right now," Pierce said as the elevator doors opened on sub-level 7 and they walked toward the observation room.

Under the training and instruction of Captain Pierce, the first recruits were being pushed to their limits already.

"Now that the systems are all in place and Base 47 is up and running, you have to start your training too. Can't just rely on your powers. You need actual skills to back them up," Pierce said as they entered the observation room and he looked at the scenario unfolding. In the training room, they played a deadly game of tag. Pierce was never one to make things fair, so the two recruits were up against four of his ex-soldiers with real weapons.

"I need your assurance that I will have full control of the group with regard to training and field work. You may have deep pockets, but besides acting in a lousy war film, you don't know what it takes create a team," Pierce said.

The words stung, even though Josh had heard far worse reviews. He understood the value of chain of command. "You got it." Besides, he'd rather that people have someone else to yell at. He quickly forgot about this as he watched the first two Mods in action against Pierce's men.

"We've got you pinned down, Santos," Sawyer said as he and three in his unit closed in on Emilio's location. They had been tracking him through an elaborate obstacle course Captain Pierce had designed for training.

"You've no hope for escape. Better to give up now," Marquez taunted, inching closer. They each checked their weapons to make sure they were set to stun. The guns were a recent addition to their arsenal, provided through a black-market deal that Captain Pierce engineered. The guns were cutting-edge, not only using fingerprint operation fail-safes, but also a stun feature that emitted vertigo-inducing symptoms. That feature was not fully tested.

Emilio ducked behind a low wall with just a bo staff to defend himself. He heard the click of their weapons just a few yards from him. He was wearing the official Base 47 training gear, all black, with protection pads to guard against impact and combat boots.

"You just got caught in my trap, amigos," Emilio said as the first ex-soldier's foot passed by him. He stuck the end of the staff between the man's legs and jerked it forward, causing him to fall flat on his face.

Emilio laughed and jumped back, dodging the stun-gun shots from his opponents.

"I don't go down easy, boys," Emilio said. He spun his staff, warding off the encroaching ex-soldiers. He slammed the staff down and used it to leap over Sawyer's head as they sent shots at him. Each blast missed the intended target.

"Damn it!" Sawyer said. He steadied his hands on his weapon. "I can't let this freak show me up."

"Freak, huh?" a voice called out. Sawyer looked around but found no body to claim the sound.

"Be careful who you call a freak."

A small fog rolled in.

"Watch out, guys. Looks like we have a live one on our hands," Sawyer warned. He and his fellow mercenaries placed their backs against each other so each covered a point of the compass.

"It must be that girl," Marquez said as he recovered.

"We can't trust anything we see. Use your goggles," Sawyer said.

"It's no help. Everything is the same," Marquez said.

"Use the thermo setting. She can't fool us that way," Sawyer said.

Emilio dropped down from above, knocking all of them to the ground.

"See, if the entirety of the Euro Intel Division can't stop me, what chance do you have?" Emilio taunted. He placed the end of his staff on Sawyer's throat. "You may be good, but I'm so much better. Game over."

"Not yet!" CoCo called out. She leapt from a nearby ledge and collared Emilio, taking him down hard. As they rolled around on the ground she landed on top. "Tag. You're it."

"You think I will just lay down for you?" Emilio asked. He struggled to gain the upper hand.

Emilio and CoCo concentrated hard, each trying to dominate the other. Energy crackled around them. The lights started to flicker above them.

Sawyer motioned his fellow ex-soldiers to move away, but it was too late. In a blinding flash of light, they were all thrown about the course. The emergency lights slammed on, and the blaring klaxon alarm sent Pierce and Josh from the observatory to the floor.

"What the hell happened?" Pierce demanded. He waved his men for a break and pointed at the trainees. "Up on your feet. Now."

Sawyer and his group shuffled off. Emilio extended his hand to help CoCo stand.

"I don't need your help, Eurotrash!" CoCo said. She rose on her own strength.

Emilio grinned.

"What happened?" Pierce asked CoCo.

She shrugged and rubbed her temples with her palms.

"There's something peculiar about their powers," Josh said, approaching Pierce. "I was watching them with you—"

Pierce looked at his men, who were dusting themselves off. Washington, Pierce's number two man, gave him a look that let Pierce know that the men were all right.

"What the hell kind of maneuver was that? You both could have seriously injured my men," Pierce said.

"Injured? You're the one who sent your goons out with real weapons," CoCo said.

"They're in nonlethal setting. You were completely safe," Pierce said as he folded his arms across his chest.

"I think I know why their powers did what they did," the actor-turned-would-be-hero said.

CoCo and Emilio both looked at Josh.

"He can make things always go his way and she can craft fully immersive illusions. They probably operate on the same frequency. As if they are drawing from the same source." He looked at the others but saw no sense of understanding on their faces. He sighed and tried again. "He manipulates probability. While it gives him good luck, it must also draw energy from somewhere. She manipulates your senses, causing you to see what she wants you to. That means her energy to do that comes from somewhere else."

"What does that mean? Plainly," Pierce asked.

"I think it's not a stretch to think that drawing from the same energy source could be, well, explosive. Using their powers against each other probably agitated the frequency and caused the backfire. But if they used their powers in concert, I expect the results, well—they could be astonishing," Josh said.

"How would you even know all this?" CoCo asked.

"I played a rocket scientist in my last movie. Had to be convincing, so I researched a bit," Josh said as CoCo rolled her eyes. Emilio caught her look and muffled his laugh.

"All this stuff is new to everyone. But it's all energy and energy has to come from somewhere," Josh said.

Pierce considered Josh's hypothesis before stepping toward the cocky Spaniard.

"Careful, hombre, last time a guy got that close to me, he ended up in the hospital." Emilio smirked.

Pierce took a breath. Never in his twenty years of training had a cadet gotten to him the way Emilio had.

"Why are you such a jerk?" CoCo asked Emilio as she jutted her hip out.

"You know, you're cute when you're angry." Emilio playfully tapped her nose.

"Are you kidding me?" She turned to Captain Pierce with outstretched arms.

"Okay, you two! I bet that when your powers interact the consequences can be either amazing or disastrous. It seems to me that it might be in everyone's best interests to keep you separated," Pierce said.

"I couldn't agree more," CoCo said. She sauntered off.

Emilio came up between Pierce and Josh and put his arms around their shoulders.

"That woman," he said as he looked at each of them for a response. Pierce saw Emilio looking at the large scar that spiraled around the left side of Pierce's skull. He knew the rumors: Some said it was from a brain tumor operation while others thought it was from a shrapnel scar from a bomb explosion. Few knew it was actually a reminder of a far more sinister and vicious battle Pierce would rather forget.

"I've got to tend to my boys. Make sure you are both prepared for the next training session," Pierce said he walked toward the section of Base 47 that was off-limits to the empowered trainees.

"I don't think he likes us much," Emilio said, his arm still slung over Josh's shoulders. "Must be something I did."

Josh looked at Emilio and could hardly speak for a moment. His cheeks became rosy and he quickly looked away.

"Don't worry, it happens to everyone," Emilio assured his new friend. It wasn't the first time his charm had affected guys before, but he was man enough to know it wasn't really about him. "How did you come across this place?"

"I was shooting a movie out here a few years back and thought about setting up a studio here so I bought it. I didn't know at the time that it housed an abandoned military base. I lost interest in all the intricacies of putting a studio together outside of Hollywood, and just let it lie here. But when this whole thing started I figured this would be the right place for a group of us to come together," Josh said as he realized just how much he needed somewhere to belong.

"I'm glad you made that announcement about Mods after the sinkhole in Reno."

"Why's that?"

"Let's just say that I was no longer welcome in Barcelona."

"What does that mean?"

"I may have accidentally offended quite a few people back home."

"Are you on the run?"

"Not anymore," Emilio snickered as he pushed the elevator button.

CHAPTER
31

26 July

Captain Pierce and three of his ex-soldiers waited patiently at the gate of Base 47 to greet the recruits, who would arrive shortly in a van that struggled under the extreme Texas heat. While they waited, Pierce studied a series of folders.

Etienne DuBois

"Summer in Texas, am I right?" Washington said. He wiped his sweaty brow.

The van trembled and stopped about fifty yards away. Pierce motioned the ex-soldiers to follow him. They had no sooner started trotting toward the jeep when they heard three quick pops and metal scraping against metal. A huge blaze erupted from the van's engine.

"Get them out of there!" Pierce shouted.

A lot of things happened at once.

A dark-skinned African sprinted out the van door carrying an elderly Indian woman.

"There are still three more in there!" the man yelled. He

eased the woman to the ground.

"What happened?" Pierce asked.

"He wanted to change the music station, and then the engine just exploded," the man said.

Two ex-soldiers approached the van, spraying it with fire extinguishers from the nearby hangar.

Pierce looked at the van. Two more people exited the van, although they didn't go through any door. A man carried a goth-looking girl in his arms.

"What did you do?" Pierce asked.

"Nothing. I don't know," the young man said in a heavy French-Canadian accent. "The driver is still in there. We have to get him out!"

The African man sprinted back to the burning vehicle.

The van exploded, sending auto parts flying across the desert. The force of the blast laid everyone flat on the ground.

"No!" the goth girl screamed. She threw her hands up. Pieces of the van flew into the air, but none of the debris hit the new trainees or Pierce's men.

"Is everyone okay?" Pierce asked. His ears were still ringing, but he picked himself off the ground and surveyed the damage.

Slowly, people began to respond. The area looked like a war zone. The van was charred to a crisp.

"What about the driver?" Pierce asked.

"No sign. The blaze is too hot to control right now. I'll call into the town for assistance, but they're probably forty minutes out," Washington said.

Pierce felt a breeze as the Kenyan screeched to a halt in front of him, carrying the portly driver over his left shoulder, fireman-style. He set the driver on the ground. The man was bleeding from a chest wound.

"Almost didn't make it," the Kenyan panted as he stretched out his back from side to side. "You Americans eat too much hamburgers."

"Good moves. The driver is hurt. Is anyone else hurt?" Pierce asked.

The old Indian woman hobbled over to the driver. Pierce knew from her file that the short woman had suffered from polio as a child and as a result walked with great difficulty on the withered leg.

"Rest easy, child," she said and knelt by the injured driver. She put her tiny hands on the top of his large chest and closed her eyes, whispering a chant she learned long ago.

An orange hue emanated from the old woman's hands, and Pierce thought he smelled jasmine as the color started returning to the driver's face.

After a long while, the Indian woman whispered, "There, there." It seemed the driver breathed easily. She leaned back, tired.

Pierce pulled the man's shirt off and saw the gash was gone completely.

"How … what happened?" The driver slowly rolled over onto his side. He slid his hands over his body, checking it for wounds. Finding none, he stared quizzically at the old woman, who smiled at him.

"That is quite impressive—" Pierce said, halting when he couldn't recall her name.

"Jiya. No last name. I am orphan."

"Jiya, thank you," Pierce said. "This healing gift you have, why have you not healed your leg? If I could make myself better, that would be the first thing I would do."

She smiled. "I did heal my eyes. Good to see clearly, but leg is burden to bear. I could not change my course too much. Karma."

Pierce nodded and motioned to Sawyer. "Get a chair for her."

Sawyer quickly brought her a chair from the hangar and sat it in the shade of a mesquite tree. Jiya limped over to it and smiled her thanks as she sank into rest.

Pierce studied the group. On first glance, the goth chick and the elderly Indian left a lot to be desired. The Kenyan and the French-Canadian had some potential, though. They were powerful and had displayed quick thinking under pressure. His training would make them all the more capable.

"So what exactly happened back there?" Pierce asked, wiping his brow.

"My fault," Etienne said in his heavy French accent.

Katrina grinned at him, seeming to like what she saw.

"Sir," Pierce said.

"Sir." Etienne sighed and rolled his eyes. "I can phase my body through solid objects. I was trying to find something to listen to on the radio—the music here sucks—when we hit a bump in the road and my arm accidentally phased through the van. I guess the engine got mucked up and then the fire started."

"Huh," Pierce muttered as he considered the story. "DuBois 1, Van 0."

"I guess so. Sorry about that. I didn't know—"

"You can phase the molecules of your body through solid substances. It seems a side effect is that you will disrupt electronics and mechanical devices," Pierce said. The French-Canadian's gift was highly weaponizable, he thought.

"Oh, and I can also do this," Etienne smiled as his body slowly faded from sight.

Pierce watched him, holding back a grin. He almost

expected Etienne's smile to linger like the Cheshire cat's smile from Alice in Wonderland.

"Invisibility, too? That will come in very handy." Pierce looked at the group and paced in front of them. "I am Captain Pierce. I'll be your guide, your mentor, and your trainer. I will whip you into fighting shape. I will refer to you by your last names. McGee."

The goth chick shrugged. "That's me."

"Sir."

"Huh?"

"When you address me, you will call me sir."

"Uh. Okay. Sir."

Pierce consulted one of the folders he held. "McGee, it says in here you can move things with your mind."

"Yes."

Pierce stared at her.

"Sir."

"Good. Show me."

"It's, uh, a little complicated," she stuttered, running a hand with black-painted fingernails through her dyed jet-black hair. "I haven't been really able to do it again."

"That kind of weakness will get you killed on the field," Pierce screamed. He stepped toward her.

Instinctively, Katrina put up her hands up. Pierce flew backward toward the bunker wall and landed on his butt. One of the ex-soldiers aimed a gun toward the girl. Pierce got back on his feet and motioned him to lower the weapon. Pierce walked back to the recruits.

"McGee, it seems you need to be scared or angry to harness your powers."

"But I'm scared of them," Katrina said as she pushed back a stripe of blue hair behind her ear.

"Get over it. There is no room for self-doubt here. You

need to remember this so you can be effective as a group. I am here to train you to control your powers. But you can't rely solely on them. You will have a complete boot camp training so you can operate smoothly in any area you are challenged on," Pierce said.

"And what exactly are we being trained for? I mean we all saw what happened in Reno and the call for us to gather here," the speedster said. "But how are we going to save the world?"

"We've entered a new age. One where anyone has the potential to wield fantastical powers. That makes each of you unique, but also paints a big target on your backs. My job is to prepare you for any eventuality that comes your way. Whether it's search and rescue, reconnaissance, or direct action engagement," Pierce said. He smirked. "Or saving the world."

Katrina seemed to consider this as the rest of the group nodded.

Pierce turned his attention to the Kenyan. Pierce wondered how this skinny African could maintain the energy needed to sustain his high speeds.

"Your quick thinking saved not only your teammate's life but also the driver. Good work. What is your top speed?"

"I haven't had any way to really figure it out. It's just really fast," James said as his grin reached ear to ear.

"You see that fence over there?" Pierce asked, pointing at it. The fence was about four hundred yards away.

"Of course."

"When I say go, go and come back." Pierce set his watch to time James.

"Sure thing." James smiled, readied himself.

"Go."

James took off in a blur of pumping arms and legs. The

others shielded themselves from the dust he kicked up as he sped past them. In less than ten seconds, he skidded to a stop at his starting spot. He was panting and placed his hands on his knees, breathing deeply. "How was that?"

"Not bad. Not bad at all." Pierce smiled. He wondered how much training would improve his speed. Could they get it to supersonic levels? "Sawyer! Go and get him some protein bars."

Sawyer disappeared into the hangar, passing Josh, flanked by Emilio and CoCo, who were approaching the newcomers.

"You're ... You're ..." Katrina stammered as though she couldn't believe that the star of the *Extreme Warrior* series and *Don't Look Behind You* was actually standing in front of her.

"I know," Josh said as he winked at Katrina.

"I'm glad you all heeded Josh's call," Pierce said.

"I couldn't believe when you announced you were a Mod. I mean, *the* Josh Grant is a Mod." Katrina looked at the star and blushed furiously. "And you asked us to join you."

"Welcome to Base 47, ladies and gentlemen," Pierce said.

"Wait! What are we supposed to do?" Katrina asked as they watched Pierce walk back toward the hangar.

"Don't die," Pierce said.

CHAPTER
3 2

28 July

The clang of metal on metal echoed through Independence Square as the bell rang noon. Dozens of pigeons flew up in fright and settled on a nearby hundred-year-old oak. The summer sun baked the tourists as

Redheaded Man

Rami and the redheaded man made their way through the park.

Rami was uncomfortable in the preppy pleated khakis and short-sleeve polo given to him. He looked around and saw he was surrounded by men dressed in the same casual style.

Even though he was miles away from the lab, he still felt some strange connection pulling him back. As if there were some part of him left in the lab. He tried not to think too hard about it and instead turned his thoughts to Arian. His last image of her was of her screaming and crying as the Iranian police ripped him from her arms. He hoped Emma's teleporter friend would help him visit her.

He had been in America, Philadelphia specifically, for over a month and this was the first day he had actually set foot outside of The Hastings Foundation. He had long begged the scientists for a chance to explore the city, and they finally relented.

Rami took a deep breath and looked at the city, enjoying the chance to see it without a glass window in between. He smelled the blooming flowers. The city was busy around Independence Hall.

He thought about what Arian would think of America. Maybe when she came they could visit Philadelphia, but the tainted memories of The Hastings Foundation might be too much. He hoped his extraction would be sooner rather than later. He'd be that much closer to seeing Arian again. Rami sighed and smiled slightly, feeling so much closer to having Arian again in his arms.

He walked toward the Liberty Bell and hoped his redheaded chaperone would allow him to study this icon of freedom in silence. That would not be the case.

"The Liberty Bell first came into use in the 1750s to call the lawmakers into their meetings. And the crack appeared almost ninety years later on George Washington's birthday. They decided to retire the bell from use and replace it with another that is currently atop Independence Hall," the man said. He shuffled close to Rami, and Rami saw the man was sweating in his blazer.

Rami, who suspected the man wore his blazer only to conceal a gun, had not wanted a history lesson. His main goal for the outing was really for some time to try to contact Emma. He worried she had forgotten him. He'd been afraid to call out to her from the lab in case they had devices that could monitor more than just video and audio. He nodded at the man while he called out to Emma.

He swallowed a smile when she answered him.

"Oh, thank Allah you are there. I worried you had abandoned me," Rami thought to her. He tried to keep his face neutral as he drifted alongside the manicured landscape.

"Could never happen, friend," the Irish girl's voice assured him. "I will get you out. It's taking a bit longer to plan than I expected. I am trying to get my parents to understand how important our mission is. It's not like the voice speaks to them, only me. It's not that easy to convince them when they are scared I'll mind-talk them into agreement. As if I could actually make people do what I want." She snorted.

Rami wondered for a moment if Emma did have the capability to manipulate people. He shook his head and the idea disappeared.

"Whatever you have planned, please do it as soon as you are can. I fear for my safety here. I long to be with the people you mentioned the other time we shared thoughts. I even looked up Texas in the map," Rami told her. For the redheaded man's benefit, he stared at the information tablet on the lawn.

"I will. Have patience, Rami. I will come for you. We will rescue you so you can lead us to save the world," she said in a reassuring voice. "Now, I have to go. My dad is coming up to tuck me into bed."

"Thanks, Emma. I will wait for you. Be quick." Rami signed off and turned his attention to his chaperone.

"Is it possible to have this Philly-del-fia cheesy steak sandwich?" Rami asked, overemphasizing the words.

"Of course. I know the perfect place for that." The man smiled and led Rami down the street.

If I can make it through months in Astara, I can certainly make it through the next couple of days in Philadelphia, Rami thought as they stopped at the street vendor.

CHAPTER
3 3

30 July

Beneath the arid Texas desert, the
Mods trained to save the world
from itself.

Nearby, Josh said, "Come on,
Etienne, you've got this." He was
spotting the young Quebecois,
who struggled with the bench

Jiya

press but finally managed to lift it back up to the bar release.
Josh, clad in a fitted tank top and shorts, secured the bar on
the hooks.

"Don't feel bad. I remember on my first set I had to train
with an Israeli drill sergeant. I am much nicer than she was,"
Josh joked.

Etienne sat up and wiped his sweaty face with a gym
towel. He wished he weren't working out with Josh, whose
proximity unsettled him.

"Or maybe you need proper motivation," Josh quipped
as he transformed into a svelte Israeli trainer, complete with
long brown hair pulled back in a ponytail and heavy
eyebrows.

"What in the——?" Etienne jumped back as he tried to make sense of the transformation. One moment a man had stood in front of him and now there was a woman.

"Too much?" Josh laughed as he morphed back into his natural form. "I was just trying to help you out."

"It's okay. I know what you were trying to do," Etienne said. He spotted Jiya and crossed to join her.

"What's that?"

"A blanket for Luli's child." Jiya assessed him as she continued knitting. "What's wrong, *beta*?"

He kicked out a chair at the table across from her, sat, and looked at her quizzically. "Beta?"

She smiled. "It's Hindi, affectionate, means young one."

He nodded. Then, finally said, "I don't fit in here."

"Do you wish to be here? A part of"—Jiya paused and gestured around them at the training area—"this?"

Etienne shrugged.

"That is a decision only you can make."

"But I don't fit in here," he repeated.

"Maybe you are too hard on yourself," Jiya said. "Why are you always so uncomfortable? You have a special heart but you won't let anyone see it."

"But——"

"You don't have to close yourself off. You can let us in." Jiya grinned as she cupped her weathered hands together and brought them close to her heart. Her hands began glowing warm and she placed them on top of his head. "You don't have to push anymore."

"Jiya, what are you doing? I don't need to be healed," Etienne said as he instinctively tried to phase into intangibility to avoid her touch.

"I am not healing you. Just peace."

Etienne felt a calmness rush down his spine, accompanied by

a strength he hadn't before. He looked into the old woman's gray eyes and smiled.

"No longer alone." Jiya looked at him with great tenderness, then picked up her needles and returned her attention to knitting.

Energized, Etienne stood. He smiled at her, though she didn't see it, and strolled back toward the obstacle area. Katrina looked longingly at Etienne as he passed her. The elevator opened and a pregnant Chinese woman walked out with Pierce.

"I don't know why you're here. I won't let you out in the field," Pierce said. Instead of his usual cigar, he was holding a Golden Delicious apple.

"I'm answering Josh's and Emma's call, like everyone else. We all have powers. I can help."

"Luli, I'm so glad you're here," Josh called out as he rushed over.

"You're still not going out in the field," Pierce said.

"Emma brought us all together for a reason. Luli's force field won't let anything happen to her," Josh said.

"Thank you." Luli smiled at Josh.

While her attention was diverted, Pierce lobbed the apple at her head. Midair, it bounced off an invisible wall and dropped to the ground. Surprised, Luli turned back to Pierce.

"What just happened?"

"Your force field just ruined my snack."

She looked down, spotted the bruised apple, and grinned. "See. Nothing can hurt me. Just because I'm pregnant doesn't mean I can't help out," Luli said. "Let me stay."

"And what does your husband say?"

"He understands that I have to do this," she said

Pierce looked at Josh, then back to her. "Fine. But I won't put a pregnant woman out in the field." He sighed and walked away.

"I know that my being pregnant is troubling, but I can do this."

"I know. It's going to be okay," Josh said.

***

Pierce made his way to the elevator so he could go topside to check on the Kenyan speedster. As the elevator doors closed, Washington slid a hand between them.

"Sir, I have to talk with you," he said as he slipped inside.

"Where are we on the neural disrupters? We need something to take these people out should things go south."

"We've made serious advances, but the science division is struggling."

"Anything else?" Pierce asked.

Washington said nothing.

"Make the neural disrupters priority one," Pierce said. "I want them by the end of the week."

The elevator dinged and the doors opened. They walked outside into the bright, desert heat.

"And if Josh asks about the scientists on the payroll?" Washington asked.

"Say nothing. Send him to me," Pierce said. From his side pouch, Pierce took out a half-smoked cigar and chomped on it. He lit a match off the bunker wall and puffed his cigar to life as his encrypted phone rang.

"You go on. I need to take this." Pierce waited for Washington to leave before answering. "Hello?"

He listened a moment before speaking again into the phone. "Yes, everything is going according to plan," Pierce said.

Another pause, and then he said, "I am putting all the pieces together as you requested. There will be no surprises."

Pierce listened intently to the modulated voice on the other end. "I await your orders."

Another pause.

"May the Sentinel save us all." He switched off the phone and took an extra-long drag off the Cuban cigar.

CHAPTER
34

30 July

As soon as Timothy Ellery walked out of the gym into the Miami summer, the hairs on his arms prickled. He could feel the barest hints of electricity pulsing through the air. The twenty-five-year-old gazed skyward, assessing the storm

Timothy Ellery

clouds on the horizon. Yes, there would be another lightning storm, and soon. He'd be able to practice.

Timothy whistled as he opened the driver door of his black Camaro, got in, and turned the car on. Where should he go to throw around lightning? Should he stay home and work from his apartment balcony? Or should he go somewhere wide open, where he'd have better visibility but would likely get wet once the rain started? Since his balcony faced the clouds, he opted for the comforts of home. He pointed the Camaro toward his apartment and thought about the last few weeks. He still didn't understand what had happened in June, but he was certainly enjoying the effects. And so had Gina last night, apparently. She had called sex with him electrifying. If she only knew.

It had started small. At first, all he could do was cause lightbulbs to flicker. Soon after, in a fit of frustration, he had tripped his breakers, shutting down the lights in his apartment. Over the following weeks, he had learned how to switch on and off electrical appliances with his mind. When he walked into a new place, he was instantly aware of all the electrical outlets in the room and had begun purposely sitting or standing near them. The hair on his arms, legs, the back of his neck all stood on end and pointed in the direction of a potential energy boost. He felt better just being by the outlets, and he had been able to draw electrical energy from those outlets to boost his own sagging energy levels, like after a severe workout at the gym. He'd even conducted energy without being electrocuted.

Timothy had the idea he might be able to do direct or redirect lightning during a storm, and sometime that night he'd have the chance to try to move lightning bolts around the sky.

While he waited for the storm to approach, he showered off the gym sweat and stink and changed into a pair of tight Levis and a T-shirt that showed off his biceps. Finally, he dried his hair, mussed it until it looked like he'd just gotten out of bed, and judged the overall results in the mirror. Yes, he was definitely date-ready. He might just call Gina later, see if she was up for more fun after he wrangled some electricity. He peeked out the sliding glass door and saw the clouds closing in. From the fridge he grabbed a Red Stripe beer and the box of pizza leftover from last night's dinner. Timothy headed out to his third-floor balcony to watch the storm come in.

He settled into one of the cheap plastic lawn chairs on his balcony, popped the bottle cap off, and drank deeply. He chose a slice of the sausage pizza and inhaled it in four bites, washing down his first bit of dinner with a guzzle of beer. He was always starved after the gym. The second and third slices of pizza took six bites each. He ate the final slice more slowly and tried not to think about what he was going to try soon. And it would be soon. Every hair on his body was standing on end. The promise of electricity was thick in the air. He drank down the remainder of the beer in a few long gulps and set the bottle down. He watched the sky with a concentration he normally reserved for surfing, sports, and sex.

In a few moments, he felt what he was waiting for. He felt the energy gather itself. The southern sky lit up, and he thought of a spot on the northern side of the sky, willing the lightning to stretch across the sky.

It didn't.

The thunder boomed, and he jumped.

He waited patiently for another bolt of lightning. It wasn't long in coming. Again, it lit up the southern portion of the sky. The moment it appeared, Timothy pointed his right hand to the northern sky, where he wished to send the energy.

Nothing.

Almost simultaneously, the thunder from the last lightning strike arrived just as the third bolt of lightning hit to the south. Surprised, Timothy jumped, flinging his right arm wide and toward the horizon. In stupid amazement, he watched as the lightning grew out of its originally planned route and slammed into the ground well north of his apartment complex.

So, he thought, he needed to send it to ground. Or he needed to act more quickly. For the next thirty minutes, he experimented until he got the timing down. He felt energized by the practice and wanted to try something bigger. But what was bigger than lightning? He knew he couldn't create it, he could only work with what existed. He'd think about that later. For now, he should just focus on what was happening in the skies above.

Another bolt started to form, and Timothy negligently pointed toward a spot about four miles northwest of his apartment building. Immediately, the bolt landed there, with the loudest explosion of thunder yet thick on its heels.

All of Miami went dark. At least everything Timothy could see from his balcony. Surprised, he watched for a few minutes, waiting to see if the lights would come back on. He walked back inside his tidy but dark apartment and felt no electricity vibrating at the outlets. He felt like he'd been abandoned by a buddy. He found a flashlight in his junk drawer, grabbed another Red Stripe out of the fridge and his cell phone off the counter, and made his way back to the balcony. He nursed the beer while he waited for the lights to come back on. While the electrical storm had continued for some time, he had lost his enthusiasm for moving bolts around the sky. But it sure had been fun while it lasted. He pulled out his phone, thinking he'd call Gina and see if she wanted to get together, but the phone was dead. Battery probably shot.

He drank a third beer while he pondered what had gone wrong. Just where had he sent that last bolt? For the first time it occurred to him that any one of those bolts he'd flung across the sky may have hurt someone. He hoped he hadn't. Mostly, though, he wanted the lights back on. He felt diminished, lonely without that friendly hum of electricity keeping him company.

When he awoke the next morning—late because his alarm was on his phone, which needed some serious juice—

his apartment was still without electricity. He felt even more powerless than he would have before he'd become a Mod. He mulled the label and the changes his new power had brought to his life as he lay in bed, procrastinating against the day ahead. Finally, he rose and took a hasty cold shower, dressed, and headed out for a long day of selling Chevys.

Traffic was excruciating. Every stoplight was off, and it was still raining. It would have been faster to walk, Timothy thought. When he finally arrived at the dealership, he found it was running on generators. He found David in the break room, reading the morning paper, legs propped up on the table.

"You believe this mess?" David asked.

"Crazy. Took forever to get in this morning," Timothy said.

"I know. You're late."

"Stuff it. Does the paper say what caused all the lights to go out?"

"Yeah. You're not going to believe this," David said. "They think an EMP hit us, here in downtown Miami."

"What?"

"Yeah. Apparently there was what they call a 'non-nuclear electromagnetic pulse weapon' at a warehouse on the outskirts of downtown. And I'm not sure just how it happened—it seems to defy logic—but lightning struck the warehouse and triggered the weapon."

"What?"

"Dude, you're stuck on repeat. Grow a vocabulary."

Timothy collapsed into the chair opposite David at the break room table. "What does this mean?"

"They don't know. The paper had a helluva time getting today's issue out. The EMP wiped out their computers. There's a note at the top of page two saying what they went through to get the paper out today. They borrowed space at—"

"Computers are out? What about electricity? When do they think that's going to be up and going again?" Panic strained the edges of Timothy's voice.

"Here," David said, thrusting the paper at Timothy. "I'm done with it. Nothing else to do here. We've got no coffee. We have a few things hooked up to the generators, but our computers are out. We can't even do the paperwork if we managed to get a buyer in the rain today. I'm not sure why we're here."

"Yeah, thanks."

He read the coverage with growing horror. Power was out over most of the city. He had caused that. People had died in car wrecks when the stoplights failed, and he was responsible for that, too.

He felt a regret deeper than he had ever experienced. What had he done?

Slowly, he reread the story, looking for clues that the authorities might have any idea that a person could be behind this unbelievable turn of events.

Timothy was still reading and rereading sections of the paper an hour later when David returned to the break room.

"Dude, they're telling us to go home. They think there will be rioting as soon as the rain stops, and yesterday's forecast had the rain stopping around lunchtime. So, go home. Or at least get out of here. I'm going home."

Timothy looked up. His tanned face looked pale in the dim break room. "What?" He hadn't heard a single word David said. Obligingly, David repeated himself.

"Oh, okay," Timothy said with a remarkable lack of enthusiasm.

"Dude, you okay?" David asked.

"No, I don't think so."

"What, one of your girlfriends pregnant?"

"What? Uh, no. I think maybe I'm coming down with a bug. I better go," Timothy said, standing. He rolled up the paper and carried it with him out of the dealership and out to his car.

Oh, God, what had he done?

CHAPTER 3 5

30 July

Waleed Gandapur

"How is practice going on Waleed's Teleporting Taxi Service?"

"Emma," Waleed nearly shouted, sounding pleased to be hearing the little girl in his head. "It is good. I'm able to go far now, even if I can't see the place, as long as I have been there before. Yesterday, I teleported from London back to my old apartment in Pakistan. Had to leave in a hurry—the new occupant thought I was an intruder. I mean, I was, I guess. Anyway, I got out of there no problem. I think I can probably manage people now. Maybe. I've carried things— like books—and animals. Made my friend's cat sick a bit, but the dog got through it just fine. Wagging his tail on the whole journey."

"And you haven't asked a human to go somewhere with you because?"

"Because I don't really know how to make that kind of offer. What do I say? Who would I say it to?"

"Me. Or someone else with powers."

"And what if something goes wrong? The cat—"

"Was a cat. Finicky creatures, cats, my pa says. Sicking up all the time for no good reason. It's why he won't let me have a kitten. The dog did just fine."

"I don't think I'm quite ready to port a human yet."

"You can do it. I'll be your first real passenger. Come get me," she said. Then remembered where she was and what she was wearing. "In five minutes, I mean."

"I don't know."

"It'll be great. You know where I am and how to find me, right?" Emma was already out of bed and stripping off her purple pajamas.

"Well, yes. We have a connection, so I can teleport to you, even though I can't see you."

Emma heard his reluctance and knew she needed to come up with a reason to make him commit before he chickened out. "You want to meet me, right? See the Irish girl who can talk in your head?"

"Yes." This answer, at least, was immediate and enthusiastic.

Emma found the clothes she'd been wearing earlier in the day and put them back on. "Then come get me. I'm ready. We'll just have a little practice."

"Sure, just let me drop my fare off. Five, ten minutes, and I'll be there."

The girl felt Waleed disconnect. Soon, glittering black spots appeared in her room. She watched in awe as the black spots grew from a small circle to a large oval almost the size of her bedroom door. Slowly, a man wearing baggy jeans and a white cotton shirt stepped through the teleportal into her lilac bedroom and grinned. He stuck out his right hand.

"Hello, Emma, I'm Waleed. Pleased to meet you."

She ignored the hand and hugged him instead. Then she stepped back and looked at the man who had emigrated to London from Pakistan years ago. He was younger than her parents, but she wasn't sure by how much. She hugged him again.

"How do you want to try this?" she asked him.

"I'm not sure that I do."

"What?"

"Want to, that is."

"Don't be silly. You're here. Want to just try moving the both of us from one end of my room to another or is that too easy? After all, you did come from London to a place you'd only ever seen in your head. Or are you ready for a bigger challenge, like Australia? I've always wanted to go there."

Waleed surveyed her room, then crossed to the bedroom window and looked out on the cottage's backyard. He beckoned her to the window.

"Let's go right there," he said, pointing to a spot near the stone fence.

"Okay. So how does this work?" She looked up at him. "Do we need to hold hands or something?"

He nodded. She lightly clasped his hand, but when she felt his grip tighten on hers, she responded in kind.

"You sure you want to be the first test?" he asked her.

"You can do this, Waleed."

"All right. All you have to do is walk with me through that little portal. It's just like walking through any other door," he instructed.

Holding his hand, she skipped through the glistening oval portal that divided her lilac bedroom from the garden. She shivered as cool air raised goose bumps on her skin. They were standing by the stone fence in the chilly night air.

"How was that? You okay?"

"That was so cool." She threw her arms around him and hugged him again. "See, no reason to be worried."

Waleed grinned faintly at her.

"You're sure?"

"Yes. Now, let's go a bit further. Can you show me one of the pyramids in Egypt?"

"What? No."

"Why not?"

He sputtered, unable to defend his hasty refusal.

"Come on, Waleed, it'll be fun."

"No."

"You need to practice more. And maybe even with more people than just me."

"I'm sure, little one, but not tonight. I dare not take you somewhere where I might be accused of kidnapping a child."

"But that was so fun. We should go somewhere else."

This last entreaty was so beseeching that Waleed relented. "Not to the pyramids."

"The Eiffel Tower?"

"Way too many people there." He frowned, thinking, and then brightened. "How do you feel about dinosaurs?"

"You can't time travel."

"Next best thing. There's a museum. Locked up tight for the night. But we can go and check out some old bones. What do you say?"

She nodded and grinned. They clasped hands again, less tightly this time, and she closed her eyes. Moments later, Emma heard Waleed grunt, followed immediately by what sounded like chunks of wood dropping onto a marble floor. She opened her eyes to see the huge bones of a tyrannosaurus rex at the Natural History Museum of London. The size of the dino surprised a squeal from her. And then she noticed it was nowhere near intact. Now, part of the oversized dinosaur hung suspended in air, while many of the bones from the lower part of the body lay in a heap underneath.

"Oh, I hope they don't have cameras or an alarm in here," Waleed said, looking around at the empty museum hall.

"What happened?"

"Misjudged the landing a bit. I always worry about that when it's a new place or out of sight." Waleed knelt to pick up one of the fallen bones. "Hey, this isn't even really bone. It's a replica. Good. I'd hate to have damaged a perfectly good dinosaur skeleton."

"But we didn't trip or fall on the landing. High marks, Waleed."

"Still gotta work on the landing, though." He sagged onto a bench and watched with a big smile as Emma ran around admiring the different dinosaurs. When she came back to his bench, he said, "You know, it's harder to move you with me than it is to just move myself."

Emma cocked her head at him and jumped forward to hug him again. "You're okay though, right? You can take me back home?"

"Of course. Just need to rest a bit first. Or maybe a snack. Go see some dinosaurs."

She studied him for a moment, nodded, and skipped off to examine a triceratops.

Not long after, Waleed called for her. "What did you learn about the triceratops?"

"Um, it lived sixty-five million years ago."

"And what did it eat?"

"Plants, I think."

"That's right. And why did it need the horns?"

She shrugged.

"To defend itself from other dinosaurs. It lived at the same time as the T. rex."

"Oh. You talk like a teacher sometimes."

"I am a teacher. Was a teacher. In Pakistan. Science and math."

"But not here?"

"No. I don't have the right permits to teach in the UK."

"Do you like driving the taxi or teaching better?"

He shrugged. "They're very different jobs, but taxi driving pays better. Enough fun here, and I feel ready again. I think we better go before we get caught."

Emma nodded reluctantly, and he returned them back to her room. This time, the landing was uneventful. Immediately, Waleed wedged himself into her desk chair and panted.

"It makes you too tired, doesn't it? Teleporting more than just yourself?"

"Yes, it takes more energy. I think if I eat something after I port, I might be able to recover faster."

"Chocolate? Ooh, I have some," Emma said. She rummaged in her backpack and triumphantly held up a slightly battered candy bar. "Here."

Waleed ate the candy bar in four bites. "Thanks. Actually, I think this is already helping."

"Good. I'm going to tell Rami that you will soon be able to rescue him from that dreadful place in Philadelphia and take him to Base 47." Emma saw the beginnings of alarm stretch across his face. "No, you can do this, Waleed. It's why you were chosen. And I'll help you all along the way. I'll be mentally connected to you and to Rami."

"That poor dinosaur," he said, shaking his head.

"Replica. And you can do it. Just practice. Now go, so I

can call Rami and tell him the good news."

"I'm so eager to join everyone at Base 47," Waleed said.

"Soon, we have to wait until the time is right."

"Okay, I'll wait." Waleed leaned down, gently hugged the girl, and vanished.

Emma stared at the spot he had just vacated for a moment. Then she swapped her regular clothes for her purple pajamas and called out to Rami to tell him the good news.

CHAPTER 36

1 August

"Are you sure this is where we are supposed to be?" Katrina asked as she joined her four teammates against a concrete pillar separating them from the large industrial park they were surveying. They were there to snag the Refractory Lobe, which

Taneesha Jackson
"The Flame"

could decrease friction and heat in nuclear warheads, making them more portable. Certainly don't want that to wind up in the wrong hands, she thought. This was the first mission Pierce had organized for the Mods, and she was nervous she might lose control of her power if something went wrong in the field.

"These are the coordinates Pierce gave us," James said.

"Shouldn't Emilio be here for this? I mean he's the thief, right?" Katrina asked.

"Don't worry about Emilio, he's doing what Pierce wants elsewhere. We can do this," CoCo said.

Nothing CoCo said made Katrina feel more at ease. Josh

looked over his shoulder and spotted two guards. Their timing had to work out perfectly. His body began to warp and his face changed into that of a guard's. As many times as Katrina had witnessed Josh change forms, the momentary blend of features creeped her out.

"CoCo, you're up," Josh said. He walked toward the guard station. CoCo smiled and closed her eyes. She cast an illusion on the guard, making him see a stranded car in the lot.

Josh approached the guard station and waved.

"Hey there, Owens, here for the guard switch," the fake guard said as he swiped his card.

"What's happening out there?" the other guard asked as he looked out.

"Looks like someone got a flat tire. You should check it out," Josh said. The guard sighed and walked out. As he neared the illusionary car, the rest of the team walked right through the guard station unnoticed.

"Good job, CoCo," Katrina said in a rare moment of camaraderie.

"Thanks, Kat," CoCo said as they quietly ran through the corridor.

"Don't call me that!" Katrina scrunched her eyebrows together.

Josh stopped them at the large glass door at the front door and motioned them to stay low. He swiped his card and the door opened. They followed him through the labyrinth of hallways until they reached the last door. It was steel plated and this was where the key card would be of no use. Josh looked at Katrina, who approached the door.

Katrina closed her eyes and concentrated on the steel door. For several long seconds, nothing happened, and Josh began to fear they'd need to find another way into the room. Then Josh heard a series of metallic rumbles and clicks from inside the door, and it gently swung open. She wiped her brow. Figuring out how to psychokinetically unlock the door took a lot more precision than she had expected.

"Good job, Kat," Josh said.

"Don't call me Kat!" she said. But this time she smiled at him and didn't sound quite as irritated.

The team walked into the lab complex. Josh took the tablet from James and pushed a few buttons to get him to the screen they needed. He looked up and pointed to a section in the far end.

"It's over there."

"All right, y'all, be careful not to trigger any ..." CoCo halted, sensing something coming from behind them.

"Danger!" James shouted as a short-haired blond man launched himself at the team. James tried to tackle the man but the blond used his momentum to throw him against the wall.

"And that's how we say hello in Ukraine," the blond said as he dusted off his dark camo pants.

Josh edged closer to the locked chamber in the center of the lab as four compatriots joined the blond man. A beautiful black girl, an Asian girl, a Pacific islander, and a young woman who appeared to be swathed in green light stood menacingly next to the blond.

"Josh, who are these guys?" Katrina asked as she cowered behind him. "What do you think they want?" She knew that there were more Mods than the ones at Base 47 and figured sooner or later they would meet up. But she had hoped that whatever had sent the Mods their powers through the White Light Wave had the sense not to give powers to bad people.

"Don't know, and frankly don't care. Get James," Josh said.

Katrina used her power to lift James and float him back to them.

"Watch your sixes, everyone," Josh said.

As they pressed their backs against each other, Katrina studied their opponents. She thought they seemed to revel in their powers, and that frightened and intrigued her. The women seemed strong and self-assured—it made Katrina feel like she was right back in high school in Canada with the popular girls bullying her because of her pale skin and the blue streak through her dyed black hair. Her skin heated as she remembered the taunts. She took two deep breaths, just like Jiya taught her. It helped. Some.

"It looks like you are out for something tonight," the beautiful black girl said. She clenched her fists and flames ignited around them.

"I think they need to be taught a lesson, oui?" The Asian girl crossed her arms over her chest.

"They crossed the wrong people," said the islander. He seemed to be levitating in the air.

"Let's not be too hasty here," said a girl with strange, green energy emanating from her fingers.

"What's your problem?" the blond Ukrainian asked as he joined his team.

"Just because we were hired to stop them doesn't mean we have to use excessive force," the green energy girl said.

Katrina looked toward CoCo then to Josh, hoping they would have an idea about how to retrieve the Refractory Lobe and defeat the Mods who had descended upon them.

"I don't know who you are or who hired you, but we are leaving with this," Josh said. He used his shape-shifting powers to increase the density of his muscles and make himself taller. He looked at Katrina and CoCo and they readied themselves.

"James, are you all right?" Katrina asked.

He nodded and took a defensive stance.

"Enough of this talk. You may be leaving, but not all of you will be leaving in one piece!" the floating islander said. Outside, thunder clapped and rattled the building's walls. "Yeah, that's my doing!" He smirked as he punched his hand at them. A hurricane gust of wind blew at them.

"Watch out!" Katrina said. She raised a psychokinetic shield around them as the wind howled, and chairs flew around them as a spectrograph whipped past their heads.

"I thought we were the only ones with powers," James said, grateful to be inside Katrina's protective dome.

"That's ridiculous," Josh said. "There must be some other agency that is gathering other Mods like us for their own end."

"Not to be a wet blanket, but we've got to get the Refractory Lobe and get out of here," CoCo said as they all inched closer together.

"You're right. First things first, CoCo make an illusion and get the Refractory Lobe. We'll hold them off. Once you get it we'll contact Pierce for an extraction," Josh said. Maybe, he thought, taking on the team leader position is exactly what he needed. "Oh, and, CoCo, be careful out there. This weather guy seems pretty intense."

"Thanks. I'm on it," CoCo said as she closed her eyes and planted an illusion in her opponents' minds that she was still in the protective bubble when she was really heading straight to the secured zone to pick up the Refractory Lobe. She dodged the flying debris and slid toward the door with the key card entrance.

"Take them on one by one, just like Pierce taught us. Don't let them overwhelm you," Josh said as stepped forward.

"Let's do it!" Josh said as Katrina let down the field. He and James charged the group, sending them scattering.

"You take the fast one and I'll take the stud," the black pyrokinetic said, igniting the oxygen around her hands. As Josh approached she threw fire balls at him. He easily dodged them and continued toward her.

"You may have some quick moves, Josh Grant, but I've got your number!" She raised her hand and a wall of fire separated them from the rest of the group.

"I don't know how you know us, but—"

"Are you kidding? You went on national television outing yourself as a Mod. We know exactly who you are. All of you." Fire crackled off her body.

***

"Mon Dieu!" The Asian girl reached her arm out and pulled back. Across the room the metal beam ripped from the wall and was magnetically launched at James.

"Umph!" James said as he scrunched down and let the beam hit him. As it bounced off of him, he eyed the girl and shook his head.

"Look, we don't want to hurt you. Just leave this place," the short auburn-haired girl said as she projected green energy beams from her hands.

"Doesn't seem that way," Katrina countered as she jumped away from the blasts.

"Enough with the warning shots, Ericka. Blast her. We've got our orders, same as you," the Ukrainian said.

"Dmitri, we don't have to harm them, we can just disable them long enough to get the Refractory Lobe," Ericka said.

As Katrina heard them bicker, she realized she might be able to exploit their divergent views. But before she could act, a tornado formed in the room and raced toward them. The

223

air chilled around the two as several broken pieces of steel rebar swung wildly in the air. Katrina ducked and screamed.

"Let's see how you do against me!" The islander laughed.

Katrina focused her energies and the air around her began to crackle.

"Who are you? What do you want?" Josh asked. Sweat streamed down his face.

"I'm Taneesha. But you can call me The Flame. For obvious reasons. As for what we want, that's pretty easy. To stop you." The ring of fire surrounding them closed in. "You can give up any time now." She laughed as Josh dropped to his knees in the unbelievable heat.

***

"Too fast for you to blast me!" James laughed as he ran circles dodging Ericka's green energy shots.

"Lucky for me I don't have to hit you to stop you."

"What?" James looked back at her and tripped over rubble from her blast. He tumbled, hard.

"See, nonlethal. Just stay down," Ericka said as she emitted a knock-out blast to his head.

***

"Maru!" the magnetically empowered girl called out to the Pacific islander floating in the air. "Use these in your tornado!" She lobbed pieces of metal girders toward him.

"Thanks, Margaux. A nice deadly combination!" Maru laughed as he summoned a localized tornado inside the building. The winds howled as the tornado sucked the girder pieces into the vortex and spit them out in every direction, causing mass destruction to the complex.

Katrina hid from the tornado. CoCo appeared next to her.

"Kat, you got to help us. We won't be able to make it without you."

"I'm scared."

"We all are. But we've got these powers for a reason. You can do this. I believe in you," CoCo said as Katrina reached out to hold her hand. Just as she made contact, CoCo vaporized from view, and Katrina realized it was just an illusion. But she knew the words and sentiment were real. Katrina swallowed her fear and psychokinetically grabbed the bits of girders flying around, crushing them into harmless powder.

***

"You should stop now. It won't end well for you!" Josh panted as he picked himself up.

"I'd say the same to you, but I really don't care." The flames grew around her. Flames engulfed her hands and she swung wildly at Josh.

She landed a punch on Josh and burned straight through his protective gear.

"See what I mean?" She leered at him.

"Not going to let you have a second shot," he said as he bent down and followed through with a devastating uppercut, sending her a few feet in the air before crashing on the floor. "I used to have issues with hitting a woman, but in your case I made an exception." Josh quickly touched his chest, where his adversary had burned through his armor, relieved it was just scorch marks.

"Let's end this quick!" Dmitri charged the stationary CoCo. He passed right through her. He shook his head when he realized how they'd been duped.

"She's got some mental powers. Makes us see what she wants to. Tricky bitch, where are you?" He surveyed the room. Near the back of the room he saw a barely perceptible glow. He suddenly realized what he was looking at.

"She's got the Lobe! Stop her!" he shouted as he charged toward where CoCo actually was.

"Maru, keep up the attacks!" the black pyrokinetic said as she pulled herself off the ground. The fire in her hands may have been out, but not the fire in her heart. She would not let these amateurs defeat her.

"On it, Taneesha!" Maru sent out three more tornadoes toward his attackers.

"CoCo, watch out!" James shouted.

"What are you talking about?"

The Ukrainian man slide-tackled CoCo. She crumpled to the floor hard.

Across the room Katrina pushed back at the Margaux and The Flame.

"I've got your number," Katrina said as she psychokinetically trapped her two opponents in a force field.

James tried a special maneuver against Maru while Josh and Ericka traded blows.

"I can tell you're different. You aren't like your friends," Josh said to her. The energy blasts she wielded tingled and there was a strange sensation behind them, as if she was deliberately pulling her punches or, in this case, her blasts.

"What the hell are you talking about? Just because I don't want to hurt you doesn't mean ..." She sent three short blasts, hitting him square in the chest. Josh fell backward as she continued toward him.

"It doesn't have to be like this. You can come with us."

James sped in from the right and then from the left, confusing the weather manipulator and managing to grab him. With his concentration shattered, the tornadoes quickly dissipated.

Just when it seemed like the Base 47 team had the upper hand, a voice called out for them to stop.

"If you value your friend's life you'll stop right now!" Dmitri held CoCo by her brown hair. She was unconscious.

Immediately, Katrina dropped the field trapping the two girls. James let go of Maru. Both Josh and Ericka stopped as well.

"Glad I have your attention." He laughed as he let go of CoCo's hair and she fell to the floor. He walked toward the others. "We got what we came for. Let's get out of here."

"The hell you will," Josh said.

"Did I forget to mention? We set the building with explosives. You've got three minutes to get out of here. Margaux, if you please?"

She magnetically ripped the wall open and then loosened all the rivets, causing the steel beams to bend and quake.

"If I were you, I'd get out while you can. Doesn't look too safe," he said.

Maru used his power to call a wind to lift them up and fly away.

The building started to crash around them.

"James, bring CoCo over. Katrina, move that slab over there," Josh said, pointing.

James raced over to retrieve the unconscious CoCo while Katrina floated the slab toward them.

Rubble came down around them in loud smashes.

"All right, get close to this piece," James directed as they scooted in tight together. "Katrina, push yourself and create a shield strong enough to survive the explosion."

"I can't do that. I'm scared."

"I know. It's okay. We all are. But you can do this. And you don't have to do it alone." He grabbed her hands and let his faith in her flow into her.

She closed her eyes and reached out her hands, encasing them all in an impenetrable bubble.

Around them the building fell apart. They heard the series of bombs explode. Fire swept through the ruined structure and pushed them out toward the parking lot. Only through sheer force of will did Katrina contain the psychokinetic sphere that held her friends. As the fire raged on she held on, protecting them from the heat, the debris, and fire. The irony that the Refractory Lobe would have given them more protection from the heat was not lost on Josh.

CHAPTER
3 7

1 August

Nicola and Thierry trudged silently along the empty hallway of The Hastings Foundation lab toward Roger's office. The automated lights flickered to life as they neared the door.

"I think that the strange electromagnetic pulse that took out Miami the other day may be the result of another Mod," Nicola said, breaking the minutes-long silence between them.

Thierry gave no response. He removed his trusty yo-yo from his coat pocket. He fiddled with the toy for a moment before letting it slowly drop from his hand toward the ground and quickly flicking his wrist to return it.

"And it seems like there are more going to that Base 47 that the actor set up for those with powers," Nicola said as she tried to loosen her cohort up. She had never seen him so tense, but the last few weeks had been an extraordinary strain, given the Mods showing up after the White Light Wave, the environmental disasters, and their mounting concerns about the work they were really doing.

"Oui, but you both know that's not what's concerning me," Thierry said.

"I don't think this is something that we can really talk about here." Nicola put a calming hand on his shoulder.

"That's just it, Nicola. We've worked for The Hastings Foundation for how long? And how many times have we just let them explain away our projects?" Thierry shook his head and continued walking.

Roger opened the door to his office. "It's about bloody time," he said to them. He glanced up and down the hall and saw they were truly alone. After they entered his office he closed the door tightly.

Roger fired up the sonic harmonic device, along with the hard-light hologram, to give them privacy. He sat and ran his fingers through his white hair and sighed.

"I know that you have been restless and upset lately, and of course I feel the same way." Roger offered them a seat, which they both refused. "And I know that you have concerns about the helix matrix. But I have to have your promise that you will not do anything rash after I tell you the truth."

Nicola thought the last time Roger had been this serious he had been explaining the truth behind Dr. Kaczmarzyk's death.

Not long after they joined The Hastings Foundation, Dr. Kaczmarzyk discovered her desalinization project had been weaponized and was being sold to an Asian dictator. She demanded, in front of her colleagues, that the board not sell her patented projects or she would expose the Foundation. The next morning joggers discovered her body in a park near her home. Police reports called her a victim of a robbery gone wrong, but the three remaining scientists knew different. She had crossed the Foundation and the Foundation had crossed her off. Nicola had long suspected that the Foundation was not as noble or magnanimous as she once thought, and from discussions with Thierry, knew he had similar concerns. Their lives were intertwined with the Foundation, and they had to watch each other's backs.

"Just spit it out, Roger, for Christ's sake," Thierry said as he put his hands on the back of the chair.

"All right. You deserve to know the truth behind The Hastings Foundation and what we are really here for. What our designs and experiments are truly doing," Roger said.

Nicola took a breath and glanced at Thierry.

"When we joined the Foundation all those years ago it was to restore our names and prove that man was having an adverse effect on the climate. While we were right, I knew that just pointing to the ice shelf disappearance and the uptick of violent storms would not be enough to convince people … governments … to do anything. So, Henry and I formulated a plan to unleash disasters on the world to push the politicians to take a stance."

"You what?" In her shock, Nicola's voice was harsh and brassy. She leaned against the metal filing cabinet as though trying to put more distance between herself and the Australian scientist.

"We created and manipulated natural events that would help prove our theories of manmade climate change. And it worked. You know that. But what you may not know is that all of the research you have done throughout the years has been in direct relation to this goal. Many of your projects and designs have been perverted into weaponized instruments of destruction. You have been working toward this since day one. I've held this secret from you for so many years."

As Roger spoke, Nicola felt fainter and sicker. Now she knew the answer to this question: was it better to only suspect or to truly know you were involved in something nefarious?

"And the helix matrix?" Thierry asked.

"Charges a powerful device that can create tsunamis," Roger said.

"Like the one that just destroyed Mississippi?" Nicola demanded. Anger welled up inside her.

Roger nodded.

"You manipulated us! Forced us to work on these experiments when you knew exactly what the result would be," Nicola shouted. She was shaking with fury and despair. She looked away from Roger.

"You've made us complicit in murder!" Thierry hissed, the veins on his forehead pulsing. "How many deaths are we responsible for?"

"What have you done? What have we done?" Nicola asked. She sagged with newfound guilt.

"Everything that I have done, I have done in the name of science," Roger said.

"Why are you telling us now?" Thierry stared Roger down.

"You needed to know the truth."

"The truth?" Nicola asked. Her eyes welled with tears as the guilt of years wasted washed over her. So much time away from her family and husband, so little good accomplished, and so much damage.

"Yes. The truth."

"Why?" Thierry asked.

Nicola saw his chest heave.

"Why what?" Roger asked.

"Why now? Why tell us this now? You've clearly hid all this from us for decades. Why are you telling us now?" Thierry sounded icily calm.

"I had no choice. You would have found out about the tsunami device soon enough," Roger said. "I protected you for as long as I could. I did all of this for you. So you wouldn't have to."

"But you've done it in all of our names!" Thierry shouted. He dropped his yo-yo and lunged at Roger.

"Thierry! No! Stop!" Nicola struggled to hold Thierry before he could take a swing. As she held him, she had a better idea. She let go of Thierry, who stood watching, gape-mouthed, as she snatched up the sonic harmonic device and the hard-light hologram and threw them against the wall, destroying the anti-surveillance equipment.

"Are you kidding me? That equipment is the only thing that kept our conversations private," Roger hissed.

"We are done," she said. "This is over."

"You know it isn't safe for you outside this building. They will find you and—" Roger grimaced. "At least stay here where I can at least protect you."

Nicola and Thierry burst out of the office, leaving Roger all alone.

"That went better than I expected," Roger said as he closed the door behind them. "One day, they'll understand what I've sacrificed for them. And one day, what I've done to them will get me into the Ascendancy." He spotted the yo-yo Thierry had dropped on the floor. He picked it up and set it on the edge of his desk, studied it a moment, and slowly but deliberately pushed it off the desk into the trash can below.

He lifted a file from a desk drawer marked Phase Two and set it on the edge of the desk.

CHAPTER 3 8

3 August

The Atlantic waves crashed onto South Beach as Timothy jogged along the edge. He was rocking out to the Foo Fighters when he spied two women jogging toward him. One was a beautiful Asian girl in matching gray sports bra

Margaux Vu

and shorts and the other girl, rather plain, wore a sleeveless T-shirt and black jogging shorts.

"Morning, ladies." Timothy smiled and bowed his head a little. They laughed and returned the greeting as they passed each other. Timothy turned around and jogged backward, watching them from behind.

"Watch it!" a jogger with a heavy accent said as Timothy narrowly missed colliding with him.

"Sorry, bro."

"Yeah, yeah, stupid American."

Timothy looked suspiciously at the man, trying to place his accent, before peeling off of the beach and heading for a group of benches under the shade. Only eight in the morning and it was already hot as balls, Timothy thought. He took off his baseball cap and pushed his short hair back.

"Hey there, got a light?"

Timothy turned his head to see a stunning black woman—except for the cigarette in her mouth. He mouthed no as he stretched his legs.

"That's okay, brought my own." She snapped her fingers and a small flame danced above them.

"What? How did you do that?" Timothy asked as he took his earphones out and backed up. He stared, riveted, at the wavering flame. It was about the size of a flame atop a birthday candle, but seemed to come out of her fingers.

"Oh, you'd be surprised the things I can do." She took a drag off her cigarette and blew the smoke toward him. "You can call me The Flame, for obvious reasons."

Timothy backed up a bit more and bumped into the man he had almost slammed into while jogging.

"Scared, bro?" he mocked as Timothy moved in another direction, only to be met by the two joggers he had ogled earlier on the beach.

"What's going on here?" Timothy's heart pounded as he realized how neatly the group had cornered him. Suddenly, a strong wind whipped around him and a tanned guy dropped down from above him. He was stocky and Timothy thought the guy had never seen the inside of a gym.

"Look, I don't know what you want, or who you are but—"

"Oh, Timothy, you may not know who we are, but we know you," the black girl said. Her flame jumped from hand to hand. "Maru, some privacy please? We don't want the whole world to see this."

The tanned guy tilted his head back and squeezed his hands into fists. Without warning, wind swept down in a funnel, surrounding them and obscuring them from prying eyes. Timothy crouched, throwing his hands over his face as debris whipped around him. With equal parts apprehension and excitement, he realized he was not the only Mod in Miami. He wondered how they had found each other, how they had found him. As fear set in, he wished he had contacted that actor Josh Grant when he came out as a Mod.

"Thanks." Flame smirked. "Timothy, we aren't here to hurt you."

"Not so sure about that. It doesn't feel that way, the way you are hiding us." Timothy tried to keep all five of them in eyesight. Last thing he wanted was to be blindsided.

"My friend, we're here to help you," the plain girl said calmly.

"I don't need your help. I'm good on my own," Timothy said. He noticed that while they had surrounded him, their postures and stances were neutral. Years spent hitting on girls at the bars had refined his awareness of body language. He felt his phone strapped to his arm and could sense it was fully charged. Better to be safe than sorry.

"We're not here about that little blackout you caused," the black girl said.

"I don't know what you're talking about."

"That's how you're gonna play it? All right," she said as she threw a fireball into the metal trash can. Flames immediately jumped up, and Timothy instinctively shielded his eyes from the blaze.

"I mean, that was quite impressive, but we are here because we have need of your ... particular abilities," the black girl said in a tone that suggested to him that she was in charge.

"Yeah, us Mods have to stick together," the man with the heavy accent said. Timothy cocked his head and figured the guy must be Russian or maybe Ukrainian. He looked like the type of guy the clubs in Miami hire as bouncers. He wore a stern expression, as though he were about to discipline an unwanted stepchild, and Timothy shrank back from him.

As they waited for Timothy to talk, the black girl clapped her hands together and the trash can fire extinguished itself.

Timothy took a deep breath. He was outnumbered and outmatched. He had used his powers a few days ago and his reserves were low. While it had taken him almost a week to recharge after his first power display, he was now refueling more quickly. He looked around within the confines of Maru's tornado to see if there was any electricity he could siphon off and use. Nothing but his phone.

"The world is changing, Timothy. You can either jump on board, or be burned into a crisp like the rest," the black girl said and nodded toward the smoking trash can.

Timothy weighed his options and decided to play it safe. He said nothing.

"That White Light Wave that gave us all these amazing gifts also gave us a choice. We can either stand with our kind or be left behind," the Asian girl said with a slight French accent.

"Show us what you can do," the black girl said as she crossed her arms in front of him.

For a long moment, Timothy regarded the group, running potential responses and counter-responses through his head. "I can't control it very well," he finally said, injecting doubt into his voice.

"It's okay, we can help you," the plain girl said in an indeterminate Eastern European accent. She looked at the black beauty, who nodded. The plain girl knelt near Timothy and spoke softly. "I'm Ericka. These guys found me and saved me. If not for them, I'd still be stuck in a small town outside of Prague with no one to help me."

"What are you talking about?"

Ericka stood back up and rubbed her hands together. Green energy vibrated off her skin and soon wrapped around both hands. She clenched her fists and aimed at the bench next to him. He watched as the energy burst out toward the metal bench. It exploded. Shards flew everywhere. Timothy instinctively put his hands up to his face to protect himself. Nothing hit him, and curiously he looked around. He saw the Asian girl commanding the shards in midair.

"What? How?" Timothy asked as he looked toward the girl.

"You may control electricity, but anything with metal is under my control," she said. She brought her hands together and the metal shards responded to her thought. She playfully let the shards encircle Timothy before molding the metals shards into a trident.

"Whoa," Timothy said.

"That is but a glimpse of our powers," the black girl said as she threw her cigarette to the ground.

Timothy considered a moment, then opened his palm and stole the charge from his phone, transforming it into a blueish-white electric current that pulsed between his hands. The hairs on the back of his neck stood up as he felt the familiar surge of electricity throbbing through him.

"How cute," Maru said as he willed a single lightning stream down to the ground next to Timothy. "But mine's bigger."

"Thanks for that." Timothy smiled as he reached his hands toward the lightning. He directed it into his body, giving him a super charge. He manipulated the charge into a nonlethal surge of electricity and then into an arch that he sent arrowing through each of the other Mods. As one, they all fell back, unable to withstand the force of the voltage. The wind curtaining them from fellow beachgoers dropped as well. Timothy shot up and ran toward the open beach. He felt bad about mildly electrocuting them, but without using his power, he could not escape.

As long as I'm in the open, they won't do anything to me, he thought as he trudged through the sinking sand. I should have siphoned off some of the charge for me, he thought as he wiped his brow.

He made it about fifty yards before the accented blond man tackled him, hard. For a bulky, muscle-bound guy, he moved with spooky speed.

"Not polite to lash out at us. Only trying to help you," he said as he flipped Timothy over and sat above him, pinning him down. "No use struggling, we know you can't generate electricity and there's none around here. You're just a helpless Yankee."

Timothy struggled but realized that the guy was right.

"Let's try this again," the black girl said as she reached down with her left arm to pick Timothy up. As he rose up, she sucker punched him back down. He'd never been hit by a girl before, and the unexpectedness of the attack shocked him. More than that, she was strong and the punch busted his lip. He rubbed his lip, staring thoughtfully at her.

"This is how this is going to go. You either go with us right now and join us," she said as she stood over him.

"Or what?" Timothy asked as he wiped blood from his lip.

"Or we leave you here for the cops to deal with," she said as Timothy saw the police flanking them. "I'm sure they'd be very interested in knowing who the culprit for the Miami blackout is."

"Why? Why are you doing this?"

"Because. It's a new world out there. If you want to be with those losers at Base 47 go on ahead, but first you'll have to deal with them." She gestured negligently toward the nearest policeman. "But if you want to be with the people who call the shots, I think the answer's clear," she said, motioning Maru to create a wind to carry them away.

"Your choice," Maru said.

"Okay! Okay! Stop!" Timothy said as the winds picked him up. "You didn't have to hit me."

"But it was more fun to," she said as she nodded to Maru to carry them all away. The cops tried to move in, but the wind picked up the sand and prevented them from getting close.

Timothy caught the wind ride, and as they rose higher and higher his old life seemed to disappear altogether. Lifted high by the winds, he realized just how powerless he was to resist a force greater than his own.

CHAPTER
3 9

4 August

It had been two weeks since
Etienne had arrived in Texas at
Base 47. Two weeks since he had
been in the outside world. He
hadn't seen anyone except the ex-
soldiers and his teammates. He was
going stir crazy. CoCo seemed too

James Chege

hung up on Emilio. Katrina was too young. And Luli, of
course, was married and pregnant. He needed to get out of
the compound and get laid.

He remembered from the ride to Base 47 that the nearest
town was about a thirty-minute drive away. Pierce's men had
mentioned the town's only bar closed at midnight.

He knew the most recent mission had gone poorly,
although no one was really talking about it. The most he had
gotten out of James was that there were other Mods out
there and they were definitely not on the same side.

In the base's exercise area, Etienne saw Josh and Emilio
sparring. Etienne grinned as Emilio countered every strike
Josh threw. Got to be his luck, Etienne thought as he sat

down on the bench. Not a moment after he sat down, a gust of wind whipped by him and the skinny Kenyan was sitting next to him.

"You've got to stop rushing up on me. One of these days I am going to learn how to phase the ground so it's like quicksand, trap you up, and then where will you run?" Etienne said. Frowning, he fixed the bit of hair the gush of wind had mussed.

"Ha! The day you learn how to do that is the day I will run up a wall," James said, his brown eyes sparkling with mischief.

"I have got to get out of here. I am going insane without seeing a girl."

"Girl problems?"

"Yeah. There aren't any for me here. I just want to—"

"Then let's do something about it."

"Are you serious? How can we get away from here?"

"I know you're Quebecois, but surely you aren't that thick?" James laughed.

"Watch it," Etienne said.

"We've got powers. What good are they if we can't have a little fun now and then?" James smiled. "Tell you what. There's a bar not too far from here. Let's go there tonight."

"How would we even get out here?" Etienne asked.

"I've been there every night," James said.

"What?" Etienne shouted. He stood and faced his teammate. "You've been out every night since we got here? And you never took me?"

"I didn't think you would want to come with us."

"Us? Who else has gone with you?"

"At first, it was just me, then I got bored so I took Emilio and Josh and now CoCo comes, too."

"How is this possible?"

"Well, I run very fast and CoCo provides an illusion to help us sneak out," James said.

"No. Not that. I mean, how could you do this and not invite me?" Etienne was fuming.

Finished with their sparring match, Josh and Emilio joined James and Etienne.

"We on for tonight? I need an escape," Josh said. He wiped his brow with a dingy towel.

"Yep. We'll sneak out around nine, just like last time," James said.

"Great. See you later," Emilio said. He slapped James' back and walked toward the locker rooms.

"I cannot believe you!" Etienne said. He grabbed James by the arms and looked into his eyes. "I am going with you tonight, and you're buying me a shot for not including me for so long."

"Okay." James smiled and shrugged.

"That was easy."

"Just because we're going to save the world doesn't mean we can't have some fun." James dashed away. Etienne turned around and ran into Katrina.

"Sorry. Didn't see you there," he said. He gently pushed past her and continued toward the common area.

"Of course. You never see me." Katrina scowled. Behind him, the dumbbells on the rack started to twitch. The chairs started to squirm and anything that was not nailed down began to wobble.

"Katrina, you've got to calm down," Luli said.

The room begin to shake.

Katrina snapped her head at the pregnant woman and took a deep breath. "Sorry."

"It's okay. You just have to be careful," Luli said cautiously.

"Just leave me alone," Katrina said. She scowled again and walked away.

Luli shook her head and walked the opposite direction toward CoCo, who was busy with a crossword puzzle.

"Six-letter word for unembarrassed?"

"Excuse me?"

"Six-letter word for unembarrassed. That's the last one I have left," CoCo said, holding up the crossword book for her.

"Uh—"

"You barely talk to me. Do I make you uncomfortable?"

"Brazen," Luli said.

"What's that?"

"It's the word you're looking for," she said again. "Six-letter word for unembarrassed."

"Ha. Of course it is," she said as she leaned back in the chair. "Thanks."

Luli sheepishly nodded and walked away as CoCo checked her crossword.

James whooshed by and dropped a note in her hands. CoCo read it quickly and slipped it into her pocket. She smiled and looked at Emilio, who was wiping off the sweat from his brow. She looked away. She stretched her arms out and bumped into Jiya, who was walking by.

"I am so sorry. I should have looked before I—"

"It's okay, darling. I am unharmed." Jiya smiled with a faint twinkle in her eye. The elderly Indian woman struggled to sit in the chair next to CoCo. She put her weight on the cane and eased into the seat. "Do you have any more of those puzzles?"

CoCo nodded, ripped a page out of the book, and handed it to Jiya. "I've been having a bit of trouble with these. Maybe you will have better luck."

Jiya nodded and placed her hand on top of CoCo's. Immediately, a warmth came over CoCo.

"That feels amazing."

"You're welcome. I could tell you were a bit tired and could use a little recharge." Jiya's bright orange-and-red sari looked almost regal against her dark and wrinkled skin.

"Would you like any tea? I could get some for you."

"No, thank you." Jiya smiled before stopping CoCo with her hand. "Be careful tonight. I think that perhaps Captain Pierce is on to you."

"Thanks, Jiya. We'll be extra careful." CoCo grinned, turned, and skipped away to her quarters.

As CoCo neared her room, she saw Katrina lurking next to her door.

"How's it going?" CoCo asked, using her key card to open her door.

"Everything's just peachy," Katrina said.

Judging by Katrina's sour expression, things were not "just peachy." CoCo smiled.

"I'm more mad at myself for liking him. He's a jerk!" Katrina said.

CoCo chuckled. "You'll never get his attention with that look on your face. You need to show him just how special you are. Let me make you over you tonight. Kick your makeup up a notch."

"If he won't like me like I am, why should I want him?" Katrina countered.

"Sweetie, sometimes boys need a little help to see what's right in front of them. Doesn't mean you have to sacrifice who you are."

Katrina thought that over for a moment and a slight smile crept across her face.

"All right, but no blue eye shadow. I've got standards."

CHAPTER
40

4 August

"I don't want to argue about this again," Luli said. "I'm right where I should be."

Yi lifted his hand to her chin and gently turned her face toward him. "No, Luli, you should be with me. We belong together. You, me, Sying, and our baby to be."

The morning had been a sweet reunion, the first time they'd seen each other since Luli heeded the call to join Base 47. The most important people in her world were here at the base, if only for a few days.

Now, they sat stiffly on a wooden park bench on Base 47 grounds, watching Sying swing. The inches on the bench between them expanded into an emotional chasm, divided by two opposing views about duty. Yi, wearing trim khaki shorts and a polo shirt, leaned into Luli. She was in a pair of maternity shorts and a blousy T-shirt. She still felt sweaty even though it was dusk.

"Yi, what I'm doing is important. I can use my power to help them and still make a family. You just have to be patient." Her eyes were wide and earnest.

He dropped his hand, releasing her chin. She did not turn

away. Instead, she lifted a neatly manicured hand of her own and brushed his bangs out of his eyes.

"My sweet," she said, "don't you see why I am doing this?"

Yi slowly shook his head.

"What I am helping with will ultimately help protect us, our family. Whatever gave me this power, they wanted me to protect something—not just myself."

"But you're not protecting yourself." Yi's words came out flat, almost angry.

"I'm doing what's right for us. And I'm showing Sying that it's important to do what's right, not what's easy. Why have a big family if we aren't going to be good role models for them?" she asked.

"You take terrible risks, my dear," he said.

"Maybe. But I must learn what I can do so I am prepared when the time comes."

Yi shifted on the bench. "What do you think is coming?"

Luli lifted her shoulders half an inch and grimaced lightly. "Don't know, but I don't think it will be a walk in the park. What I do know is that it will be worse if I don't help. And that would be worse for us, my sweet. I wish you would understand. Could understand."

Sadly, Yi shook his head again.

"Yi, it is so hard to do this, to be away from you and Sying, even though I know it is the right thing to do. I need your support. *Qǐng chángshì.*"

In Luli's distress, the appeal slid out of her mouth in Chinese.

"English, Luli. This is our home now," he said.

"Please support me," she repeated.

"You don't even know these people. Why do you want to risk your life for them?"

"It's not for them. Or not just for them. It's for us, for our future."

Yi broke eye contact with Luli and stood. Watching him stalk toward the swings, Luli began to understand the depth of their conflict. If only her force field could protect her from emotional turmoil as easily as it did from physical danger.

"Push me, Daddy!" Sying begged. Yi did.

Luli heard Sying's delighted shrieks as the swing ascended to new heights. She knew he had come to the base to talk her into returning home, but she had thought she'd be able to sway him once he saw the team and how far they'd progressed.

She let Yi burn off some of his—what? Anger? Frustration? Fear?—by pushing Sying in the swing a few more minutes. As she watched, she breathed deeply, gathering her resources, her courage, her will—no, her need—to do this because it was right, even though it meant time away from her family.

CHAPTER
41

4 August

"We ready to go?" Etienne asked as he dusted off his shoes. He looked at the rest of the group, all gathered by the wall.

Katrina McGee

"We should be good. I planted an illusion that will fool Pierce's guys until we get back," CoCo said.

"Are you sure your illusion will maintain with you being so far away?" Etienne asked.

"It's worked for the past few nights, so, yeah, I think we'll be all right," CoCo said, surveying the sparse Texas landscape from behind the wall guarding Base 47.

"How exactly are we going to get to this bar? The town is not close. Are we going to run there?" Etienne asked.

Just then, bright lights shone on the group. Everyone was still as they watched an ex-soldier emerge from the driver's side of a van.

"What are y'all doing out here in the dark? Up to no good?" the ex-soldier said and turned his flashlight toward the twitchy group.

Etienne looked to Emilio, who merely shook his head from side to side to quiet him.

"You aren't trying to sneak off are you? 'Cause that's a no-no." The ex-soldier stopped in front of Etienne, who began to turn himself invisible.

The ex-soldier laughed and his body began changing shape. Josh, impersonating one of Pierce's men. Etienne rematerialized, his face turning redder than the Texas dirt. Playfully he slugged Josh for the trick.

"You should have seen your face!" James laughed.

"Man, you really thought you were caught!" Josh said as put his arm around Etienne. "No harm, no foul, right?"

Etienne looked uncomfortable, but seemed to realize the hazing prank for what it was.

"All right, fools. You got me. Happy?"

They all nodded.

"So, what now? We've got a van out here, but there's no gate for us."

"Where we're going we don't need no gates," Josh said.

Everyone groaned at the *Back to the Future* reference.

"That's right, Frenchie, you're going to phase us and the van through the wall and we'll keep on until the bar," Emilio said, and they all loaded into the van.

"Oh no. I don't think so. I've never phased that many people before and we all know what happened last time I phased a machine. Ka-Blouey!" Etienne threw his hands up in a mock explosion. "And don't call me Frenchie."

"We trust you. You won't kill us. Besides, I ran out of ideas for illusions to get us past the guards at the gate," CoCo said. She hung her head out the window, begging him to join.

"I'll try. I can't promise anything," Etienne said.

James sped around, picked him up, and placed him in the

front seat. Etienne looked at Emilio in the driver's seat. He revved the engine.

Etienne took another breath, reached out one hand back. "Hold on to me and take a deep breath." One by one, they grabbed one another until they were a joined mass. With his free hand, Etienne touched the dashboard of the van. He concentrated hard to establish a connectedness to all the molecules with which he was in contact. He nodded at Emilio, who dropped the gear into drive and sped toward the concrete reinforced fence separating Base 47 from the desert.

They felt like they were swimming through quicksand as they passed through the two-foot-thick concrete wall. Safely on the other side, the team cheered.

"You did it!" Josh said as he high-fived James.

"I did it," Etienne said. His voice was full of wonder.

"I knew you could do it," Katrina said, almost under her breath.

"Next stop, The Hog Pit," James said as they drove toward town.

The Hog Pit was a bar from another time. It was smelly and a little dodgy, with a touch of charm that only those who love hole-in-the-wall joints can appreciate. Empty peanut shells and sawdust covered the floor. The bar on the left side of the room had seen better, brighter days. Knife marks and bullet holes in the bar top spoke of dark and dangerous nights. The wooden stools that lined it were worn and cracked. The Hog Pit opened up a bit in the back, where the scuffed pool table served as entertainment. The lights flickered off and on and management either didn't care to replace all the bulbs or didn't seem to notice. The bar was hopping when they arrived. A lively jukebox did that in a small town. The bar was filled with the regular types—older guys still living in the past's high school glory days, middle-aged guys from the factory in town, and women on the prowl for a man or a good time.

Etienne smiled broadly when he saw the girls at the bar. Dressed in a tight black T-shirt and dark wash skinny jeans, he walked to the bar.

"What will it be?" the bartender asked as he wiped the bar down with a dirty rag.

Etienne thought for a moment, considered the state of the taps, and decided to get a bottled beer instead. "I'll take whatever import you have."

The bartender rolled his eyes, turned toward the ice chest, and pulled out a Dos Equis. Etienne smiled and took a sip.

"They're all on my tab, Stevie!" James shouted as he sat next to Etienne.

"Oh, so this one is yours?" the bartender mocked as he fist-bumped James.

"Yep, we all just needed a night out." James looked at Stevie and added, "Nice duds."

Emilio dropped money into the jukebox and selected three songs.

"What I wouldn't give for some Euro pop right now."

"Really? Euro pop? I never would have thought that would be your type of music," CoCo said.

She slid back against the wall next to Emilio. She looked around the bar and saw most of the men staring at her. She wore a backless red halter and black jeans. Emilio leaned next to her and dropped his head near hers.

"I just play whatever I like and it never seems to be a problem." He smiled as she took a deep breath. He smelled like sandalwood and, strangely, cotton candy. She smiled back at him.

James caught the bartender's attention.

"Same as before!"

Stevie set down seven shot glasses and filled them with tequila. As soon as the last shot was poured, James slammed all shots in quick succession.

"So, who's the girl?" Stevie asked, as he dried one of the glasses on the bar.

"That's CoCo. But she's out of everyone's league. Well, except Emilio. Funny thing is everyone sees it but them. Must be that kind of hate/love thing," James said. He propped himself against the bar.

Katrina, underaged and forced to drink pop, had been watching Etienne flirt with girl after girl.

"He's going to notice you," CoCo said.

"Yeah, right. Doubt it," she said. "I did everything you said. I got dressed up like you wanted. I put your makeup on and still … Nothing."

"Sometimes it just takes a bit of time. Remember, guys aren't the brightest. You just have to put yourself out there and let them think that they are just discovering you."

"You make it sound like a game," Katrina said as she twisted around.

"That's exactly what it is," CoCo said. She put her arms on Katrina's shoulders and winked at her. "Watch this."

Katrina saw Etienne putting his arm around a tall, blonde girl decked out in full cowgirl ensemble. Out of nowhere, he backed off the girl and let out an audible gasp.

"What the hell!" He spun his head around toward the two girls. CoCo laughed and elbowed Katrina in the ribs.

"What did you make him see?" she asked.

"Let's just say, he won't be thinking about her anytime soon," CoCo said as she took a sip of her drink. "You should go, talk to him." She pushed Katrina toward the well-built Quebecois.

Josh, wearing an ironically hip T-shirt and ripped jeans, joined James at the bar.

"You ever play?" Josh asked James, pointing toward the pool table. James nodded, and they headed to the back of the bar. Josh untucked his shirt, snagged a pool cue, and tossed it to his friend.

"I don't think that they're done yet," James objected as he caught the stick.

"Doesn't matter. We'll get next game," Josh said. He slapped some quarters on the well-worn pool table.

"What do you think you're doing, bud?" The challenge came from a balding redneck wearing a wifebeater and pointing his pool stick at Josh.

"Calling next game. That's how it happens all around the country," Josh said genially.

"We don't take too kindly to your type in here," the redneck said. For emphasis, he flexed his farmer-tanned arms.

"Oh, you mean people whose vocabulary is more than three syllables?" Josh said.

"Just watch it. I mean it." The redneck stepped closer.

Josh couldn't help himself. He morphed his face into that of his balding challenger. "Or what?" Josh challenged, using the other man's voice and face.

"Jezus Christ!" the redneck yelled as he stumbled back. "What kind of freak are you?"

"Just your regular type. You wouldn't get it," Josh said. He massaged his face back into his own. He turned around to smile at James.

"Josh—" James shouted and pointed past Josh. Despite his speed, the warning came too late. The redneck cracked his pool cue against the back of the actor's head. Slowly, Josh sank to the ground.

CHAPTER
4 2

4 August

When Yi turned to Luli, she saw worry and weariness etched into his face. She reached out a hand, and he clasped it gently. They turned and walked to the edge of the bed in her tiny room at the base. Sying was already sound asleep on a cot in the corner.

At last, Yi spoke.

"It's not fair for you to ask me to support you going into life-threatening situations. You're eight months pregnant. It's not just you, it's our son, our future."

"I know, my sweet. But it's also not fair of you to deny that I must do what I've been asked."

"Yeah, it pretty much sucks all the way around."

The frank assessment of the situation was so unlike Yi, it surprised a laugh out of her. When he grinned weakly back at her, she relaxed a bit. They would mend this fracture, maybe even become stronger for it, the way a broken bone knits itself together to become tougher than ever.

"Come here, Luli."

She leaned in, and he hugged her as close as her bulging belly would allow.

"Can't you understand how much this scares me? I can't be without you. I just can't. You, our family, it's my world."

Luli kissed him, slowly and tenderly, her slender hands lightly cradling his face.

"And you are my world. We will find a way to make this work. And I will be more careful. Not as light on my feet as I was two weeks ago," she joked. "I'll see if I can't invoke special Pregnant Woman Privileges with Pierce, let you stay here during the rest of the training so we don't have to be apart so long."

"That would be great, but you're forgetting one thing."

"Oh, what's that?" she asked as she nuzzled into his neck.

"My job."

"Right." She had completely forgotten about that little detail. "But weekends?"

"Luli, I won't ever be okay with you putting yourself in danger. If I thought you would stay put, I'd drag you back home."

Her breath hitched and she held him tighter, but she said nothing.

He sighed. "It's not the training part that worries me so much. It's whatever you might be training for. The thing you think is yet to come."

"My sweet, I'll have to face it one way or the other, trained or not." Her words came out almost in a whisper.

"And don't I know that?" Yi said. There was real heat in his words. "Deep in my heart, I've known this day was coming, ever since the day you almost got hit by that truck."

He put his hands on her shoulders and gently pushed her away from him and searched her eyes again. He opened his mouth to speak, but changed his mind.

"What day?"

When he finally answered, he seemed two inches shorter. "The day I would have to accept this, that you would be the protector of this family, not me."

CHAPTER
4 3

4 August

"Josh!" James said. There was a large cut in the back of the Hollywood star's head. Blood flowed freely onto the floor, mixing in with the sawdust and peanut shells. Josh's eyes rolled back in his head.

"What is wrong with you?" James, baffled by the seeming overreaction, asked the beer-bellied guy.

"I ain't gonna be made a fool of," the redneck said. He pointed the broken pool stick in James' face.

"I don't understand," James said.

"Just take your girlfriend out of here, scum," the other pool player shouted, pointing at Josh. He rolled up his sleeves to reveal two homemade tattoos, one of which read "MOM."

"That's quite enough, gentlemen," James said.

"Stay out of this, boy. You don't want to get on my bad side," the balding guy said as he flicked his finger at him.

"Does that mean you have a good side?" James countered.

"You're going to wish you hadn't said that." He threw a punch that would have broken a slower man's nose. "What the? How are you so fast?"

"You're drunk. Your reflexes are pole-pole," James said. The last had come out sounding like "po-lay."

"What did you call me?"

"Pole-pole? It's Swahili for slow. Which you are," James said as he dodged another drunken punch.

"Hey! What's going on here?" Emilio said. He jumped over the pool table to break up the near fight.

"Our fight isn't with you, man. Just leave," one of the rednecks said, eyeing Emilio.

"Afraid I can do no such thing. You see, these are my friends. And it looks like you've done enough already." Emilio clenched his fist, glancing around the bar for the nearest exit.

The commotion drew the attention of the other locals, always curious about a possible fight.

"Stevie! What's going on?" the bubbly waitress asked as she ducked near the bar.

"I have no idea. Stay close," Stevie said. She huddled near him and they watched as a bar stool flew toward them. "I'll protect you," he said and she buried her head into his shoulder.

CoCo and Katrina stepped away from the bathroom doors in time to see Etienne slowly fade from view.

"Uh oh. Things are about to get bad. Kat, stay here," CoCo said. She handed the underage Canadian her drink and rushed toward where she imagined Etienne to be.

"Hey! Don't call me that!" Katrina said as she lifted the drink in the air. She looked around, took a giant sip of the drink and spat it out. "Ugh. Gross."

"I don't know what you think you are going to do, but this isn't the time or place," CoCo said to thin air.

"We have to get Josh out of here. This is out of control." Etienne reappeared and the group of girls he was flirting with all screamed. "Can't you do something? Put everyone in a mass illusion?"

"No. Too many people," CoCo said, wishing it were that easy to defuse the situation.

"We've got to do something. Can't just let our friends get pummeled," Etienne said as looked over toward the bar.

"You're right. We can't stay here, but we've exposed ourselves too much. We have to get back to Base 47," CoCo said. "I'll figure out a way to get us out of here."

Barroom brawls can escalate exponentially. Given the group's special abilities, which they had just revealed, and their status as outsiders, this brawl could escalate into a disaster.

Out of thin air, CoCo created three hot guys, who quickly walked over to the frightened girls.

"Ladies, you should come with us. We can protect you," the first guy said as he waved the girls toward him.

"He's right, this is no place for you to be," another guy said as the girls reached for them. The phantom men quickly and safely led the girls out of the bar and told them to go home for the night.

"I'm going to cause a distraction. Have James get Josh back to base. Get Jiya to heal him. We have to defuse the situation before they become more unhinged and angry," CoCo said, speaking calmly, although her face belied any sense of peace.

"On it," Etienne said. He weaved around the patrons to the pool table. He whispered to James, who picked Josh up and sped out of the bar without anyone noticing.

"I saw what your 'friend' did. He's a freak! He made his face look like mine. That's not normal!" the balding man with the MOM tattoo said, directing all his pent-up anger at Emilio.

"Sounds like you need a drink. Let me buy you a round. And we can just call all this off," Emilio said.

"Get off of me!" the balding guy said loudly as he threw off Emilio's arm and took a swing. Emilio stepped back. The guy missed and tumbled to the floor. Emilio couldn't help but laugh.

With all the chaos going on it was getting more difficult to concentrate. CoCo thought hard as she put her left hand to her head and pointed her right hand at the men in the back area. She focused to create a fitting illusion to trap them in.

"Stop looking at our men, skank," a high-pitched bottle blonde said. She pushed CoCo into the wall, shattering her concentration.

"Big mistake," CoCo said as she flipped back her hair and planted her feet firmly on the ground. Suddenly, she saw the girl's hair stand on end.

"Uhm … What's going on?" CoCo asked, looking around the bar. People seemed to become increasingly agitated with each other. The bottle blonde lunged for her and CoCo sidestepped her. The girl tripped.

Things were getting worse by the moment. If they didn't contain this, they could all be hurt or killed. But if they could act together and use their powers in concert, they could win this fight without casualties. Any worries CoCo might have had about exposing their powers to the world flew out the window as she scrambled to contain the situation.

***

James rushed Josh past the gates at Base 47 and straight toward the infirmary.

"Jiya! I need your help," he said. He placed the wounded Josh on the examining table.

"My word, what has happened?" she asked.

"There was an accident. He was hit in the head," James said. "We have to save Hollywood. It's not his fault."

"What wasn't his fault?" Captain Pierce asked as he threw open the infirmary door. "Tell me everything."

James dodged the captain's glare as Jiya rubbed her hands together, an orange glow appearing around her.

***

"We have to get out of here," CoCo said, trying to reason with the local girls.

"No way, bitch! You messed with the wrong girls." This was from a girl, sporting a fake tan, who tried to grab CoCo's hair. CoCo stepped back and blocked her reach.

Etienne and Emilio stood back-to-back, ensuring both were protected. As the men surrounded them, Emilio jumped, collaring two guys to the floor.

"Mon Dieu!" Etienne smiled. He nodded approval for his teammate's tenacity. But before he could move, a punch came flying toward him. Instinctively he phased his body, and the stocky guy fell through him onto the floor.

"How the hell did you do that, you French freak?" the would-be puncher's friend demanded.

"I'm not French, I'm Quebecois," Etienne said. He landed a punch square in the man's chest, knocking him straight to the dirty floor. "Merde! That hurt." Etienne shook out his hand. "Have to work on punching." He looked over to his teammates and saw the jukebox rise from the ground. It began to shake and break apart.

"Oh no." CoCo saw Katrina in the corner. The goth girl was hunched against the wall with her hands covering her head, absorbing and amplifying all the negative energy in the room. What had been a small fight had grown like an aggressive cancer into a full-scale barroom brawl. Nearly everyone was involved. CoCo whistled, and Emilio looked over. She pointed at the distressed Katrina.

Emilio ran through the crowd of people who were throwing bottles and chairs at each other. He grabbed Katrina and spoke softly into her ear. She opened her eyes for a moment and he shook his head at his teammates. If they weren't able to get Katrina's emotions under control, the consequences would be devastating. The entire bar started to shake. People fell over each other and Stevie, who was holding a frantic waitress named Francine, ran out of the building alone, covering his head.

"Stevie! What the hell? Don't leave me alone!" Francine yelled. Glass broke around her. She screamed as she dropped to the floor and struggled to protect herself from the flying glass.

"Emilio!" CoCo shouted. He could barely hear her. He dodged a falling light fixture and pushed the balding redneck out of the way of a flying barstool.

Emilio, who was holding Katrina's shoulders and whispering urgently into her ear, felt the girl slide out of his grasp and fall to the ground.

All of the sudden, things stopped. Confusion settled over Emilio's face until he spotted a large syringe filled with a blue liquid sticking out of Katrina's arm. Based on the direction it was pointing, he traced the origin back to Captain Pierce, standing at the entrance with a large gun. James stood next to him, shoulders drooping.

"Party is over, everyone." Pierce's voice boomed in the now-quiet bar. The locals struggled to get to their feet.

"James? Why did you bring Pierce here?" CoCo asked. James hung his head low.

"It's a good thing he got me here as fast as he did. You

are all out of line here. If I hadn't arrived when I did, she might have destroyed the entire place," Pierce said. He walked across the bar to the now unconscious goth girl.

"Pierce! What did you do to her?" Emilio demanded.

"Just a sedative. Had to contain the situation," Pierce said as he stared everyone down. "I am so disappointed in all of you. Get out of here now."

Each of them turned and slowly walked toward the exit. Emilio tried to comfort CoCo, but she waved off his hand.

The balding redneck got to his feet and marched toward Pierce as three of his men walked into The Hog Pit.

"I don't know who you think you are, but you can't just come in here and command us," he said, jabbing his index finger in the captain's face with each word.

"Washington, you have the room. Do what you have to." Pierce looked down at the man with contempt. He motioned to his ex-soldiers.

Emilio picked up Katrina and carried her out of The Hog Pit.

Pierce did not look at them at all as they each got into the black van they used for their excursion. No one spoke during the tense drive back to Base 47.

They were in trouble. Things had gotten out of control. They had just gotten a taste of how the real world would view them.

Back at the base, Pierce's men carried Katrina to the infirmary, where the somber group saw Josh and Jiya.

"Sorry, guys, I had to tell him. Josh was in a bad way," James said again as he hung his head.

As soon as everyone was inside the main room of the Base, Captain Pierce laid into them.

"You were all so stupid and careless tonight. This is unacceptable. There are no excuses. The world is not ready for your powers. They can't handle it," Pierce screamed.

"What's going to happen to everyone who was at The Hog Pit tonight?" CoCo said.

Pierce shook his head and stood in front of her. "That's none of your concern. You exposed your powers to the world. These people can't understand it. They have no idea what is about to happen. I did what you made me do. I wiped their memories, and I would do it again."

"You did what? How did you do that? Why would you do that?" In his distress, James sputtered out all three questions one on top of the other.

"You can't expose your abilities to the world. Not like that," Pierce said as he slammed his fist on the table.

"And what would Josh say about you arbitrarily wiping people's minds?" Etienne asked.

"It doesn't matter. You are no longer just people. You are Mods. You have a duty. A responsibility. A charge to protect others."

"What kind of sedative is that? She's still out cold," Emilio asked.

"I neutralized her."

Etienne and CoCo looked at each other, both trying to figure out what that meant.

"If you've harmed her in any way—" Etienne said.

"Oh, don't get all girly on me, son. She'll be fine in a day or two," Pierce said. "I had to do what I had to do. She was going to level that place. You could have all died."

CoCo grabbed Etienne and gave him a look. He stepped back toward the group as Josh stumbled in.

"Are you okay?" Etienne asked.

"I'll be fine," Josh said slowly.

"I'm particularly upset with you, Josh. You were supposed to keep your eye on them. You were supposed to watch them and make sure they behaved themselves," Pierce said.

"What is he talking about?" CoCo asked.

"Don't worry about it," Josh said. "All we do is train and run scenarios. They—we—needed some time to just be. We aren't machines. We're humans."

"That's exactly it. You aren't human. Not anymore. That White Light Wave saw to that. You have abilities now. Powers that normal people would kill to have. And this is how you act? Like children?" Pierce yelled.

Almost as one they shrank into themselves, knowing instinctively that he was right.

"I thought you were in charge, Josh. Aren't we all here on your dime?" Etienne asked as he leaned against the wall. The others eyed the actor, waiting for him to respond.

"I hired you, Pierce," Josh said, taking a stand. "But we are equals. I asked you to prepare us and train us. Get us ready for the battle that's coming. And in return we should give you the respect you deserve for doing so."

"Thank you for that. But there will be consequences for your actions. And this little fiasco has—" Before Pierce could mete out punishment, a crackle of black floating globules appeared, circling a shimmering area of intense darkness. Everyone readied themselves, expecting a fight.

A tiny sprite of a child and her exhausted teleporting guardian stepped out.

"Hey, guys! Wow! You're all here. I'm Emma."

They each recognized the little girl. She had arrived, and just in time.

CHAPTER
44

5 August

"Yo, Mags, congrats on the big award. By the way, I've got a great idea for the blog. Call me."

Maggie deleted the voice mail from the night before and debated whether to call CoCo back. She hadn't updated TheModsBlog since the awards banquet, but that didn't mean she'd stopped gathering information or abandoned it. On the one hand, CoCo could probably tell her plenty about life at Base 47. On the other hand, she probably wouldn't be writing whatever story CoCo dangled her way. Not if she wanted to keep her job.

She burrowed deeper into the covers of her queen-sized bed. She wished for a time machine, something that would take her back to before The Pigeon's nasty ultimatum. What would she do for money without her job? Sure, she was now an award-winning travel journalist, but who would hire her if The Pigeon fired her? Did she even want to keep her job? She sighed and flopped onto her other side. Could she continue to give up writing about the one thing that seemed to give her life meaning? She flopped back over. But what about money?

The ringing phone yanked her out of her introspection, and she glanced at the caller's name. CoCo again. She slid her phone under her pillow to muffle the continued ringing. Finally, it stopped, and she assumed CoCo was leaving a message. But no, it started ringing again. Sensing there would be no peace until she spoke with CoCo, she sat up in bed. Forcing herself to sound friendly, she answered.

"Hi."

"Hi, yourself. Whatcha doin' this afternoon?" CoCo asked.

"Sorry I haven't gotten back to you." Maggie looked around her darkened room for a moment before continuing. "It's been a little busy around here."

"Yeah, I figured. You're always going. I just got too impatient to keep waiting for you to get back to me. In fact, why haven't you gotten back to me?"

"What's your idea?"

"You know how you said on your blog that people fear what they don't know, what they can't explain? Well, I saw it in action. Things, uh, they got a bit out of hand."

Curious, Maggie asked what CoCo meant.

"One of the locals got a little rowdy and we tried to use our powers to calm the situation down. But it went south. Way south."

"What? When? Are you okay? Of course you're okay. Why haven't I heard about this?"

"Pierce used some sort of memory mumbo-jumbo on everyone who was at the bar that night. Anyway, the problem is, we all saw firsthand what can happen if someone is afraid of the Mods and of our using our powers on them. We're not invincible, you know."

Maggie frowned. "What do you mean, memory mumbo-jumbo?"

"Just that. I wasn't there, I don't know what he did. All I know is that he told us later that he had wiped all of the witnesses' memories. Maggie, I'm scared."

"Is that your blog idea? The Mods are scared of the regular people now?"

"No, don't be daft. I'm worried what will happen the next time humans see Mods use their powers. That's why I called."

"Tell me."

"First, why has TheModsBlog been dark for a while? Why aren't you writing about the Mods anymore?"

"That's ... complicated. What's your idea?"

"I want you to cover Base 47. Come out, see us in training, talk to the Mods who are teaming up to help the world when things go wrong. Remember Josh? He outed himself at The Devil's Slide in Reno? He's running Base 47."

"Yeah, I know. I covered that on TheModsBlog when it happened." Maggie paused, considering the rest of what CoCo had said. "You want me to cover you as part of a public relations maneuver?"

"Well, yeah. I figure if the public can see that not all Mods are dangerous, not all of us want to hurt them, they'll be a bit more supportive. Tell the world that the Base 47 Mods are there to help. What can it hurt?"

Only my job, Maggie thought glumly. Aloud, she said, "I'll think about it."

"Cool. Can you come to Texas next week to shoot some of our training? I'll arrange it with Josh. He'll love the pub."

"Listen, let me think about this and I'll get back to you."

"What's to think about?" CoCo pressed. "This is a no-brainer. Great for the blog, great for me. Let me know when you're heading down, and I'll get it all arranged. Gotta go. Bye!"

CoCo's abrupt sign-off left Maggie sputtering. Moving slowly, as though her body ached in every joint from arthritis, she got out of bed and walked to her vanity. She looked terrible. Hadn't showered in days. Hadn't figured out how to deal with The Pigeon and that cursed ultimatum. Her job or the blog? Certainly what CoCo said was intriguing, and she'd love the chance to cover the training at Base 47. But she'd love to keep the paycheck that guaranteed she'd continue living in this lovely apartment, as well.

She spotted a quarter on the vanity and held it a moment, considering. Then she lobbed it in the air.

"Heads, the job. Tails, the blog."

She watched the coin flipping in air and wished for tails.

It landed in her palm, and she slapped it onto her other hand and looked.

Her heart sank.

CHAPTER
4 5

5 August

"Kat? Kat? It's me, CoCo. You're okay."

The goth girl's eyes swirled. A bright fluorescent bulb above her lit crisp white walls and standard medical equipment around her. She was in the infirmary at Base 47. "What happened? My head is ringing." A tear fell from her eye.

"There, there, beta. It will be all right," Jiya said as her finger caught the tear and whisked it away.

Katrina looked around. Jiya was sitting on her left side and CoCo on her right with Emilio behind her. Someone else stood at the foot of her bed. She had never met this girl, but her presence felt familiar.

"W—who are you?"

"I'm Emma."

Katrina recognized her voice. They had spoken after Josh's announcement in Reno. She smiled wanly at the child.

"You convinced me to come here. Told me that I could get help. That I would be all right." Katrina began to weep.

Emma leaned on the bed frame.

"Emma, it's okay," CoCo said. "She's just going through something really rough."

Emma slowly nodded.

"What happened?" Katrina asked as she tried to regain her composure.

"Things got a little out of hand," CoCo said, and her tone was a gentle as Jiya's. Katrina struggled to sit up in her little bed to see who else had crowded into the little area.

"That's an understatement," Emilio cracked from a spot atop the counter.

CoCo shot him a look and he shrugged. She reached over and grasped her young friend's hand. "You're okay now, Kat."

"Stop calling me Kat."

CoCo bit her lip and sighed but continued to hold her hand. "We were all out at the bar when a fight erupted. We were handling it just fine but then the heightened emotions got the better of you."

"What did I do?"

"Got a little *loca* at the bar." Emilio's Spanish accent hit hard on the "loca" part of his explanation.

"Seriously? Shut it down." CoCo spun around and pointed her finger at Emilio. He hopped off the counter and skulked out the door.

Katrina noticed there was one more person in the room, but it wasn't the guy she expected or wanted.

"Here, let me," James said as he pushed himself away from the wall. CoCo nodded at him and moved away from her friend. "You took all the negative energy in, and it was too much for you." James perched on the stool next to her bed. "You started losing control and pushing everyone away. I tried to calm you down, but you couldn't hear me over your own screams."

More tears fell from her eyes.

"I never wanted this," she cried. "These powers are too much."

"Look, I know what it's like to fall into despair." His words were gentle and full of aching for a life gone past. "What I am trying to say is that you can either roll up in a ball and be defeated, or you can stand up and say you won't let that get the better of you. If you work on handling your powers better, you will be stronger inside. These powers, these gifts we were given, they give us purpose, but we must control them, not the other way around. You can do this."

"Katrina, I am sorry this happened to you. I know that I told you to come here and that you would learn to control your powers here. Haven't you? Aren't you stronger now than when we first talked in your head? Back when you were tormented by those mean girls?" Emma said.

"Emma, I'm not sure that you're helping right now," CoCo said.

"No. She is," Katrina said as she forced a smile at the girl. "You're right, Emma. I have grown. I am stronger."

The ringing in her ears returned, and Katrina rubbed her head. She looked at CoCo. "How did I stop?"

No one answered for a moment.

"Captain Pierce did that," James said. "He's doing the best he can so that we can come together."

"Yeah, but he's still a world-class jerk," CoCo interjected.

Katrina looked away for a moment, as though searching her memory for something.

"So how did he do it?"

"He had a sedative. Quick acting and highly effective. It took you out immediately," James said.

"So that's why my head hurts so much."

"It's okay. We've already given him a mouthful," CoCo said.

"Don't," Katrina said as she struggled to lift herself up onto her elbows. "We may need to keep that in case I lose control again."

"But …"

"No, CoCo. We have to be realistic," Katrina said as she took a breath. "When my powers manifested, I did something I'm not proud of. I wish I could take it back, but what's done is done." Her eyes began to well up. "I didn't ask for these powers and I really wish I didn't have them. But James is right, and so is Emma." She psychokinetically pulled her IV out of her arm, causing the alarm to blare. "I can either let them control me or I can finally take a stand and use them."

Katrina twisted her body around and let her legs drop off the bed.

"I'm not about to lose again."

CHAPTER

4 6

6 August

Henry took a quick sip from his whiskey as he studied the large world map on his table. He plotted the coordinates from the Flores painting. He double-checked his math, shook his head, and walked away from the map.

Anabel Wong

"This doesn't make any sense. How could the Old Ones give me coordinates to a place that doesn't exist? That I can't even reach?"

He had agonized over the details from the Flores painting for weeks and felt no closer to understanding it. His ancestors had carefully hidden clues throughout many historical artifacts lost in time, and this was the last piece to be solved before the rise of the Sentinel.

Henry had shepherded the Ascendancy since his father's death, and while he didn't always understand what the information was telling him or how that would play into the game plan set up over five hundred years ago, he was determined to see this through. He had unwaveringly followed all the rules, all the rituals, and doctrine of the Ascendancy. The least he could do was figure out how to get the WaveMaker to the coordinates given by the Old Ones to herald the true power for the new world. He wondered how difficult it would be to get access to an aircraft carrier.

Everything he had read and believed in had not steered him wrong yet, so he trusted that in time the prophecy would reveal itself. For now, though, he'd have to put it on hold. He checked himself out in the mirror.

"A little worse for wear, but not bad." He straightened his deep purple tie, framing it squarely against his crisp white shirt. He eyed the wrinkles in his face and decided they made him distinguished, not old. He glanced at his watch and saw that it was time.

He carried his whiskey to the viewing station to join the video conference with the rest of the Ascendancy. He sat and pressed the video button on the pad. He was immediately joined by his fellow Ascendancy members. He initiated the conversation.

"We know our tsunami device is successful. We have made our presence known and now we can make the final preparations for the end game that is our birthright," Henry said. He tried not to let his pride show.

"What is required of us next?" Elise asked. She pulled her blond hair back into a makeshift ponytail. The look was incongruous with her cream-colored dress and slate-gray stole.

"What's the matter, Elise, running late for an opera?" Anabel asked as she flipped back her hair.

Elise's eyes tightened for a moment, then she relaxed. Henry took that cue and continued.

"We have to proclaim our intentions to the world. Claim responsibility for the tsunami and make real the threat," Henry said.

"So you are ready to announce our presence? To follow through on the prophecy's demands?" Maks asked.

"Whatever the demands are, I have always, always followed through and this will be no exception. We have secured the final piece of technology that will allow the fusion of the Sentinel blood to bond with the WaveMaker. Once the world hears our ultimatum they will know we are not to be trifled with," Henry said as he sipped deeply.

"Was it difficult to obtain the Refractory Lobe?" Elise asked as she leaned forward.

Henry calmly placed his glass on the table. "No more so than usual. Our group of Mods performed exceptionally."

"Exceptionally?" Elise snorted. "I understand that the facility went up in flames."

"Sometimes it's in our interest to play both sides against each other. You know what they say about omelets and eggs."

"And what of your Foundation? Are the scientists all on board?" Anabel asked. She swiped her blunt, black bangs from her face. "This is very late in the game for any surprises. Remember all of the sacrifices we've made to get where we are right now."

Sacrifices, Henry thought. If they only knew how much he himself had given up to get where he was today. The compromises, the blood on his hands. He smiled instead of saying what was on his mind.

"Of course. I am confident they will all remain true to our goal. And should we have any inkling of dissent, I know exactly how to remedy the situation," Henry said, thinking of Dr. Kaczmarzyk.

"And what of our precious Sentinel?" Maks asked. He sat next to his sister. Even though Maks was looking into the camera, Henry could tell he had grown tired of the conversation and was distracted by what the American imagined to be a harem of women flashing him from beyond the camera.

"Rami is still in our control. I have full confidence that he will cooperate with us. We've shown him the only kindness he's seen since he was arrested," Henry said.

"And what if he learned of the true reason he was imprisoned in Iran?" Anabel asked. "Could that cause problems for us?"

"It was a necessary move. We needed to secure him and make sure we could control his actions," Henry said.

"It was a rash move, and one that still leaves our operation vulnerable to exposure," Anabel countered. Her brother vanished from the screen.

"Our whole lives are about bold, rash moves, Anabel," Elise said. "We can't just pile on Henry. He is the one taking the most visible risks here. The rest of us are insulated against exposure, so think heavily before making accusations."

Anabel nodded and bowed her head. "Of course, Elise. My brother and I apologize for any doubt coming from us."

"It is all right. I understand your concerns, and I actually share them, as I fear the same exposure could put my family at risk," Henry said.

"Then I think that we can conclude our session now. Henry, you know what you must do next. Do not let Rami fail us," Elise said. "You have all the necessary material for the blackmail video and the means to set off the events that will lead to our full global control."

Henry shut off the secured lines. He stood and made his way back to the map. He refilled his whiskey glass and sipped. He stared at the coordinates intently, only moving his gaze to take a drink. Suddenly, an element of the map caught his eye in a new way. He dropped his glass as realization dawned. The glass broke on the floor, and his previous understanding of the prophecy shattered, replaced by new hope.

CHAPTER
47

7 August

"You've had the last two days to really think about your situation. Your powers. Your abilities. Your responsibility. You have been given the opportunity to be something greater," Pierce said. He stared down his training group, all standing in a line and wearing matching uniforms. "Yet you threatened our entire operation just so you could go to a bar. To drink? To dance?"

"That all ends now. You are soldiers. My soldiers, and you will do what I say." He towered in front of them. "I have prepared a challenge and battle location for you. This will test your teamwork. This is a simulated battle, but I want no quarter asked, none given. Treat this as if it's the real world."

"What's the prize?" James asked as he raised his hand.

Pierce turned his attention to the speedster. "Bragging rights."

"That doesn't sound like much. How about money?" Etienne countered.

"How about ice cream?" the little Irish girl added.

"Enough!" Pierce stomped, startling everyone to attention.

"Win the game and we can talk about a substantial reward. I want the best, most efficient response team, and this challenge will determine that."

Emilio looked at CoCo and smiled. She rolled her eyes at him, but stole a glance when he turned away.

"I have worked with you individually and as a group to hone your combat skills. I have shown you survival techniques, and I have helped you gain control of your abilities. This is a modified capture-the-flag challenge. In this case, you must capture these orchids. I have split you into two teams as evenly as I can with offensive and defensive powers. You will be scored on ingenuity of power use as well as on your ability to work together. The first team to get this back to me will win."

"What's the point?" Katrina asked.

"Yeah, I hope I don't break a nail," CoCo laughed.

"That's it!" Pierce shouted as he stared the two girls down. "I want your full attention."

"After the fiasco at the bar and the overwhelming failure of your first mission, you need to convince me you belong here. I need results," Pierce said.

The trainees reluctantly nodded.

"You will have to think about offense to get the opponent's orchid while defending your own." Pierce looked at Luli. "You are excused from the scenario."

"I beg your pardon?"

"I will not place a pregnant woman in harm's way, even simulated."

"Do you not get my power? I can protect myself. I survived a truck coming at me," Luli said.

He ignored her. "Emma, you're out of this one, too. And Jiya."

"No way. I am here and I will be a part of this," Emma said.

"I don't think so," he replied. "Emilio, Katrina, and James will make up the gold team defending the eastern fort. Josh, Etienne, and CoCo will make up the blue team defending the western fort."

As he said their names they each stepped toward their respective team members.

"What about me?" Waleed asked.

"You are my go-between," Pierce said. "I will need you to help me keep track of each team. Besides, your power set would give either team an unfair advantage. This sparring session is a way to test skills and inter-team development. Use each other wisely and remember that teamwork is key to taking down opponents who would otherwise overpower you."

Waleed looked disappointed.

"Let me be clear. Nonlethal and nonharmful use of your powers only. I will not abide any deliberate misuse of your powers that will injure another teammate. Remember that after this exercise is complete you will still have to live with each other. Do nothing but your best," Pierce said.

"All right," Josh said before the teams split up. "I know that we each want to win, but let's make it a clean fight. No one gets hurt."

"Whatever you say, Hollywood." James laughed, turned his back, and sprinted away.

***

Over at the western fort, Josh took lead for the blue team.

"All right, listen up. I want CoCo on defense. Make sure that no one gets near the orchid," Josh said. "CoCo, use your misdirection wisely. Etienne, let's get ready to invade. I want to win!"

"That's not a great battle cry, Hollywood," CoCo said and shook her head.

"Stop calling me that!" Josh said.

"Ready?" Etienne asked. He reluctantly grabbed Josh's shoulder and made their bodies invisible. They began phasing through the obstacles.

***

"They're going to put their quickest and sneakiest on offense, so let's prepare for that. We have to defend with everything we've got. Only trust what you can see." Emilio parsed out the orders. "James and I will take a direct approach. Katrina, you are on defense. Guard the orchid with your life. Remember, this is for the glory!"

***

Josh and Etienne made their way through an obscured area. Josh pointed toward the orchid sitting in the open about ten yards away and Etienne nodded. Etienne phased himself through the ground, emerging only a foot from the orchid. He reached out to grab it but Katrina stepped between him and the glory of claiming victory for the blue team.

For a moment, she hesitated, as though she might let him just take the orchid. Then her cheeks flashed pink and she shook her head. "You should bring flowers to girls, not try to steal them from us," she said.

The words were so unexpected he stopped moving.

***

Emilio and James snuck closer to the ledge. Emilio looked over, and saw they were now only about a yard away from the orchid. He flipped over the ledge and reached for the orchid. But his fingers just pushed through the orchid. Confused, he looked around. He saw CoCo doubling over in silent laughter.

Emilio tried to focus. As long as he was distracted, CoCo could hide the orchid. He approached her.

"Not going down without a fight!" CoCo said. She did a handstand and trapped Emilio between her legs, eventually bringing them both down to the ground.

Yes, Emilio was distracted now.

***

"Enough! I've seen enough!" Pierce said as he walked out of the side entrance toward the gold team's orchid. "You've all performed admirably, but clearly the blue team has you at a disadvantage." Pierce neared the orchid.

Katrina looked at Pierce in puzzlement.

James rushed back to the gold team's side. "That's not Pierce! It's gotta be Hollywood!"

Pierce stopped short of reaching the orchid, and his body began to contort, revealing Josh.

"Nicely figured out. But not in time!" Josh laughed. He snagged the orchid before Katrina could react. "Now you see us," Etienne became visible and grabbed Josh, making him intangible as well. "Now you don't," he said as they both disappeared.

"Kat, do something," James said.

"I can't move what I can't see," she said.

"Have you tried?"

"Oh, no, I guess not. It never occurred to me."

She concentrated, but James could see nothing happening.

"Where are they?" he asked.

"Shush. I'm working here." Then she grinned and held out her hands. It seemed that nothing was happening.

James heard both CoCo and Etienne shout and looked around in confusion.

Two orchids floated gently through the air, then landed

in Katrina's outstretched arms.

"Both? That's just kind of greedy, isn't it?" James teased.

"You wanted to win, right? Can't win if we don't have our orchid. Can't win without theirs."

***

"Good work, team. I am impressed with your tactics. I will call the exercise over and the gold team winners. You have made significant advances since your disastrous mission a few weeks ago and have learned to complement each other's abilities. There may be a day when you may have to use your powers more forcefully," the real Pierce said. The whole group came toward him as he spoke. "I am proud of you. You can count on only each other in the battlefield."

"Captain?" Emma said, standing up on the table. "There's something we all need to know."

The Green Beret looked puzzled and glanced at Josh.

"What is it?"

"I have been in contact with Earth. He told me to get all of you and that Earth was sick. That the sinkhole and the flood and the disasters are kind of like symptoms."

"Yeah, right. Some voice told you that Earth is sick and we have to do something about it?" Etienne said. "I didn't believe it the first time I heard it and I don't believe it now. That is the most ridiculous thing I've heard."

"She's right, though," Josh said. "Emma reached out to each of us and we came here for a reason. We have to trust her. Emma, show them all what you showed me." He knelt near her.

Emma linked the minds of all her friends in the facility.

Pierce watched as his trainees' eyes glowed with a purple hue that signified the girl's mind meld.

Emma shared with them the knowledge she had gained

so far. That the voice from deep inside the earth had chosen them to save the world. That the disasters that were happening all around were a symptom of the earth's illness. That what happened during the solstice and the so-called White Light Wave event changed them so they could come together and fight on the earth's behalf.

"We really aren't alone, are we?" Luli thought as she looked toward Etienne.

"Who is the Sentinel?" Emilio thought.

Pierce watched his powerful trainees. Pride warred with jealousy. What he wouldn't give for a power like theirs.

"The fate of everything rests on us," Luli thought. She hugged her belly as her unborn child moved about.

"One more thing," Emma said as the purple hue faded. She looked at Waleed. "Now!"

No sooner did Waleed hear her than he opened a portal and jumped through.

"You have to trust us. Trust me. We won't let you down," the girl said to the Green Beret.

The portal reopened in front of Pierce, and he shielded his eyes. Waleed and a mysterious figure emerged.

Everyone started speaking at once, curious about the newcomer.

"Waleed! You did it!" Emma squealed with delight at seeing them return. She composed herself as she addressed Captain Pierce.

"Now the whole team is here, Captain Pierce," Emma said. She walked to them and put her hands up to the newcomer.

Rami, dressed in blue scrubs, stretched his dark arms under Emma's armpits and lifted her to him. He smiled wide and they hugged.

Pierce struggled to figure out who the mysterious new

player was. When the newcomer set Emma back down, Pierce locked eyes with him, and he realized that everything Emma and Josh had said must be true. He was the key to stopping the disasters engulfing the world.

CHAPTER
48

10 August

Halfway between Delaware and Portugal, a patch of the Atlantic Ocean ceased its peaceful rolling. Water roiled as a volcano in the Mid-Atlantic Ridge erupted, sending lava shooting up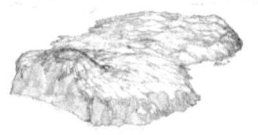

New Atlantis

through the water and into the air in a furious plume. As it made the return trip to the earth's surface, the lava cooled quickly. Pieces of volcanic rock floated momentarily and sank to the ocean's mysterious depths.

Not all lava went skyward. Some spilled down the volcano's sides, helping it grow out and up.

The volcanic mountain was only one of many that had been slowly rising up from the bottom of the ocean floor for thousands upon thousands of years as the European and North American and African and South American tectonic plates shifted and moved and ground up against each other. But for the last five hundred years, one mountain of the whole Mid-Atlantic Ridge range had grown at a steady and much accelerated rate to a point about fifty feet below the surface of the ocean.

This day, it began shooting upward from the seabed at an increasingly rapid rate.

For hours, lava spewed from the volcano's crater and out of the ocean until, at long last, the peak peeked out of the water. In the next instant, the nascent small round island doubled in size. The eruption continued for hours more, sending lava straight up in the air and flowing gently down the sides of the ascending mountain. The volcanic island, which humans would soon dub New Atlantis, grew with each spurt of lava.

The eruption column stretched ten miles into the sky. The resulting ash cloud would disrupt trans-Atlantic flights for months. Ash dumped on the decks of vessels making the ocean crossing near the 40th parallel. The resulting waves were high and fast, but not on the magnitude of a tsunami. Atlantic surfers enjoyed some of the gnarliest, record-setting waves of their lives.

During two weeks of continuous volcanic activity, New Atlantis grew as though on steroids, confounding volcanologists and other scientists around the globe. The rocky little island spread, claiming more and more area above the sea. By the time the volcano belched its last, the island was some hundred miles in diameter. The peak, crowned by a collapsed cone, stood at 1,000 feet above sea level on the southern edge of the island.

It was a devastatingly stark landscape. Nothing but black volcanic rock from shore to shore. There was no fresh water. It seemed the earth had gone to great effort to create a large, lifeless, inhospitable hunk of rock in the middle of the Atlantic.

Far away, in a land much larger but not so barren, Emma

heard a voice in her head that she hadn't heard in nearly a month. She smiled, realizing she hadn't been abandoned, after all.

I am here.

The Children of the Solstice must protect me.

I await the Sentinel.

Protect me.

Bring him to me.

Protect me to protect humanity.

CHAPTER
4 9

10 August

The doors opened and Henry strode across the newly waxed floor and past the secretary's desk. He wore a dark pinstriped suit over a crisp white shirt and a pineapple-yellow tie. As he adjusted the silk pocket square he glanced at the time on his custom Excalibur Quatuor watch.

After twenty-five years of dedication, time spent away from his wife and son, the prophecies were finally coming true. The Ascendancy had waited for over five hundred years for this new world, and it was happening. The new island was emerging in the Atlantic Ocean. Everything was going his way. Nothing would stop them from their goals.

Giddy with the coming success, Henry continued through the lab area to Rami's room. He found the room empty. His excitement slipped away, and panic filled the void. Henry grabbed the arm of a passing lab technician.

"Where is the man who is supposed to be in here?" He fought to keep his voice level, but his question came out in a near roar.

"I ... I don't know, sir," the tech said as Henry's grip tightened.

Three technicians scattered once the shouting began.

Roger, still wearing yesterday's clothes, heard the commotion from his office. He grimaced and stepped through his doorway. "Mr. Hastings. Good morning. Could you come to my office?"

Henry let go of the tech and beelined to Roger's office.

"What's going on here, Roger?"

"There's, uh, there's been an incident." Roger closed his office door.

"What do you mean, an incident?" Henry raised his voice. "I am in no mood for games."

"Of course. But first know that we are handling the situation."

"Now it's a situation? Where is Rami?" Henry slammed his hand on Roger's desk. His insides went liquid at the thought of losing the linchpin of a plan five centuries in the making.

"Last night we had just finished testing Rami's blood against the samples left in the cave, when all of the sudden we were knocked over by what I can only theorize was some sort of teleportation portal." Roger looked down and then gestured with his hands to imitate an opening portal. "A man jumped through, grabbed Rami's arm, opened another portal on the opposite wall and took Rami with him."

"Why is this the first time I am hearing of this?" Henry roared.

"I had hoped to get him back before you found out he was missing." Roger cowered behind the desk.

"What?" Henry roared.

"Maybe it's best if you look at the video," Roger said. He turned the monitor toward Henry and played the scene from the night before.

On the screen, the event unfolded just as Roger had said. Henry could scarcely believe his eyes. Henry knew there were other powered people out there with otherworldly gifts, but he had not seen many in action yet.

"Have you been able to identify the teleporter?" Henry asked, considering the potential this ability offered.

"Not yet. We didn't get a good angle of his face. We can just give a description. About five-foot-ten, a hundred and sixty pounds, maybe Indian, maybe Pakistani, something like that. Can't give you any other information. It happened so quickly."

"Have you tried to measure the radioactive spectrum for him? Can you detect or locate any quantum energies? Tachyon elementals? Anything to figure out a way to trace them?" Henry asked. He straightened his tie, trying to hold down his anger and panic.

"None of our monitoring equipment detected him coming or going. As you saw, we tried to breach the portal field before it closed up behind them."

"And what happened?" Henry asked.

"The device was cut in two. We don't know where the other part went. We have tried to ping its location, but there's nothing. Like it's not on Earth anymore."

Roger shifted in his desk chair, then stood to pace.

"So someone knew where Rami was and was able to teleport inside the building and escape with him. Is that correct?"

Roger shifted his gaze away in shame.

"Okay, forget this for a moment," Henry said and refocused on his original intention. "What I came here to talk to you about is the island. You've seen it, right?"

"Yes, I saw the initial reports. We reached out to the UN Science Division for information, but they haven't said much. We are looking for a contact within to help us out," Roger said.

"Don't worry. I'll take care of that. Find him. Find Rami," Henry said. He stood and pushed furiously past Roger and opened the door.

"Henry." Roger could barely look his superior in his eyes. "There's something else you should know."

Henry slowly turned around and closed the door.

"What is it?"

"Thierry and Nicola know."

"How much?"

"About the WaveMaker."

"And?"

"And they're missing," Roger looked down.

"Where are they?"

"They've gone underground. I've no information on them at the moment."

"So Nicola and Thierry now know about the WaveMaker and I am guessing they have some idea of our endgame. And Rami has disappeared. Have I missed anything?"

"Henry, I am doing all that I can to get all of them back."

"I am not about to let you destroy a plan that has been in motion for five hundred years." Henry stood directly in front of Roger. "Your invitation into the Ascendancy hinges on your success with the WaveMaker."

"I understand. I am taking care of it."

"Hear me, Roger. If you don't find him, if you don't find them, you'll beg for the swift kindness we gave Kaczmarzyk." Henry fixed Roger's tie and dusted his shoulders off, then stalked out of the office.

CHAPTER
50

10 August

"Rami, I think I know where the voice wants us to bring you," Emma said.

He looked at her blankly.

"From the prophecy," she clarified.

"Oh? Where's that?"

She didn't answer immediately.

Rami and Emma were in the cafeteria, holding another of their increasingly common mental conversations.

Emma focused her attention on concocting an ice cream float with just the right ratios of ice cream and soda while Rami poured himself a glass of sweet iced tea. They settled into plastic blue seats at a table with a view of a television screen that showed the training field.

For a few moments, they enjoyed their treats and watched Waleed open five pitch-black portals in various directions. Waleed then threw rocks through one portal and watched them come out of another. He then closed those portals and opened two more. One directly in front of him and one immediately behind him. He squared off and pushed his hand through. Emma and Rami watched in surprise as his hand emerged from the portal behind him. His fingers began to tickle and twist his own curly, black hair and he laughed.

Emma demolished her float before speaking mentally to Rami. Even though she didn't need her mouth for the conversation, her mother's dinner table prohibition of speaking with anything in her mouth was too strong to overcome.

"There's a new island. It just grew up in the Atlantic Ocean. That is where we're going to have to go," she finally said.

"How do you know? Did the voice tell you?"

"Yes and no," she said, smiling a bit under her troubled brow. Then she looked down at the puddled remains of her float. "I snooped. Washington. Please don't tell." She looked back up at him and the plea was huge in her eyes. "I don't snoop in your head, or any of the people who have powers." Her mouth smiled a smile that didn't reach her eyes. "Once, I did try to see into Captain Pierce's mind, but it was dark. And twisted with scars. I couldn't read his thoughts. That's never happened to me before." She paused, considering, and then continued. "It was scary in there. It reminded me of this maze I once got lost in."

Rami frowned. "You should stay out of his head."

"I will," she said solemnly.

"And out of his men's heads, too."

"I wonder why I can't read Captain Pierce's mind."

"That's a mystery for another time."

She set the glass down and nodded. "I know it was wrong. But I think this was a time to break rules."

"Why?"

"I don't trust Captain Pierce, or his men. My pa's a lawyer, and he always says it's best to hold some cards back.

I don't know if he actually would ever lie, but I thought this might be one of those times Pa wouldn't mind if I did."

"Pretty savvy for a seven-year-old. Good work," he said, sipping his sweet tea.

Sensing no scolding or disappointment from Rami, her forehead smoothed a fraction. "Thanks."

"Speaking of your pa, how did you convince them to let you come here?"

She looked down and said nothing.

"They don't know you're here, do they?"

Emma slowly shook her head. "They think I'm at summer camp."

"I'm sure they're worried about you."

"I'm sure they are," she agreed. "But this is bigger than that."

"Not to them. To them, you're everything."

She shrugged and bit her lip. "What if I let them know I'm okay, and that it's kind of like summer camp here?"

"They're your parents."

"I promise to tell them the truth, once this is over. It won't be much longer."

He frowned again. "The moment this is over, you tell them. Promise."

"Promise." She grinned and held out her pinky.

"What's that for?"

"Pinky swear. Here. Stick yours out."

He did, and they pinky swore.

"So, the island?" Rami prodded.

"I was in the study writing my nightly letter to my parents, and Washington was going on about the island. They think about you a lot. It's one of the reasons I'm so worried about you. Anyway, Washington and Pierce think the new island is connected to the disasters and to us." She paused for a moment, thinking. Reluctantly, she added, "They're probably right."

Rami frowned. "If he is, what does that mean?"

"I don't know. And last night, I heard about the Sentinel. From the voice." She paused, recalling the message, and then delivered it haltingly in her impression of an old man's voice. "It said, 'I am here. The Children of the Solstice must protect me. I await the Sentinel. Protect me. Bring him to me. Protect me to protect humanity.'" She searched his eyes. "What do you think it means?"

"Also, who is it? Where is it? What is it?"

She ignored those questions and posed one of her own. "Do you see why I think that island is where we're supposed to take the Sentinel? I mean, why I think that's where we're supposed to take you?" She considered, then added, "If you are the Sentinel. Which I think you are." Suddenly, the confident little blonde shrunk back in her seat, miserable at the prospect.

Rami said nothing.

"There's something else." Now Emma looked pale and small. Deflated.

At last, he forced the interrogative. "What?"

She pulled her knees up under her green sundress and hugged them to her chest, trembling lightly. She put her head on her knees and refused to look at him. When she spoke again, the tremble in her mental voice echoed her physical trembles.

"Pierce and Henry, that man from Philadelphia, know each other. Henry knows you're here."

15 August

"Again!" Captain Pierce shouted. "I want this perfect so we don't have another repeat of the Refractory Lobe incident. While you are doing well in training, you can't get cocky. That leads to mistakes. And mistakes cost lives."

"But we've been out here for hours!" Etienne said as he put his hands on his knees and heaved.

"And you'll stay out here until you get it right."

Josh patted the Quebecois on his shoulder, and Etienne shrugged it off.

"CoCo, you've greatly improved the number of people you can put into your illusion, so keep at it. I want you to create a rescue setup in this structure here," Pierce said as he pointed to an empty fireman's training building. He addressed the rest of the team. "There are four civilians to be rescued inside on various levels. It's your job to secure the area, reduce the flames, and get the civilians out of there. Act as a team, coordinate with each other."

"Sounds easy enough." James laughed as he pulled his calf behind his thigh for a deep stretch.

"Glad you said that," Pierce said as Katrina rolled her

eyes. "You now only have sixty seconds to complete this drill before the building explodes."

"Come on!"

"Enough. Those are the rules. Now get ready," Pierce shouted as the Base 47 heroes lined up to start their drill. CoCo closed her eyes and projected an immersive illusion into the minds of everyone topside. Suddenly, the empty building was engulfed in flames and dozens of hysterical bystanders on the ground appeared amid the chaos. But before they could start the training, two guards drove up in a black jeep, honking their horn.

"Captain, we found these two lurking around the gate. Said that they have information about the Gulf of Mexico tsunami that you and the Mods should know." The guard opened the door and urged the newcomers out.

"Well, what do we have here?" Captain Pierce said as the group closed in behind them.

"Dr. Patel? Dr. Giraud?"

"Rami?" one of the intruders replied.

"What are you doing here?"

"You know them?" Pierce asked.

"They're from The Hastings Foundation. Where I was held after my imprisonment in Astara and the caving expedition to Ghar Parau," Rami said in a rare burst of exposition. He looked at the scientists and asked, "Where's Dr. Martin?"

The scientists exchanged a look and Dr. Patel answered. "Rami, we're not with him. We didn't know anything about what the Foundation was doing. Not what they were doing in your life, or to the world."

"We were as blind to their intentions as you were," Dr. Giraud added as he wiggled out of the ex-soldier's grasp.

"It's okay, Captain. They're good people." Rami waved

the two scientists over to him.

Nicola and Thierry ran over to Rami. She hugged him as Thierry eyed her.

"What happened to you two?" Rami asked.

"Rami, you are far more of a pawn of The Hastings Foundation than you can imagine," Nicola said. As though just realizing she was still hugging him, she stepped away, dug a bottle of hand sanitizer out of her purse, and rubbed some over her hands.

"Far more than even we were." Thierry furrowed his brow and looked at Captain Pierce. "We have some news."

"That's enough for right now. We need to get you down into Base 47. Too exposed out here." Captain Pierce shooed everyone into the hangar.

"What do you think this is about?" Etienne asked.

"Whatever it is, it's not good for us," James said as he rocketed forward to be the first in.

They descended in the elevator to the heart of Base 47. Nicola and Thierry smiled at Rami. They walked out of the elevator toward the War Room to deliver their news.

Thierry walked next to CoCo and studied her outfit.

"I like the combat body armor you've got. I think some adjustments could make it easier to maneuver in," Thierry said.

"Yeah, and I have some adjustments that could make them look good," CoCo said.

The team found spots to sit or stand around the table in the War Room.

"You've got our attention, show us what you've got," Josh said.

Thierry nodded and walked toward the monitors.

"Oui, I understand your hesitation and reluctance. But we believe there is something serious going on and you are the only ones who can help," Thierry said. Nicola smiled her support at him.

"Why should we trust them? They're working for the bad guys!" Etienne shouted. He pushed back his chair. CoCo glared at him and he shrugged.

"We came to you. We have spent our lives trying to save the world!" Thierry said, the veins in his forehead bulging.

"Thierry, no. He's got a valid point. We have to prove ourselves to them," Nicola said, grabbing his shoulder.

"They don't have to prove anything," Emma said as she walked into the War Room. Everyone looked back at the seven-year-old telepath standing in the doorway.

"Please! Don't say you've seen inside their minds and that you can count on them," Etienne said.

"Why is it so hard for you to believe?" Jiya asked her teammate.

"This isn't a game anymore. This is real. We are up against a group that is highly organized and well financed, trying to accomplish God-knows-what. We don't stand a chance," Etienne said.

"It's true."

Everyone stopped in shock as Josh stood.

"It's true that they are more organized and have deeper pockets. But look at us, how far we've come. Not long ago we were strangers and today we are strong. A team. They are the ones who should be scared." Josh said.

"I trust them. Rami trusts them. We should hear what they have to say," Emma said as she climbed up on the back of a chair.

"Thank you," Nicola smiled. "We know The Hastings Foundation well enough that whatever their endgame is, it will be far more disastrous than the Gulf of Mexico tsunami."

"You have any idea what it will be?" Emilio asked as he inched over to CoCo's chair.

"Oui," Thierry said. "Over the years, the Foundation has had us create and invent several seemingly unrelated devices. Individually, they seem random. But if you put them together—"

"It's a whole other apparatus altogether," Nicola said. "They had us working on a helix matrix, which we believe powered the device that caused the tsunami. Our boss said it was just the test run." She blinked rapidly, fighting back tears. "We didn't know what we were working on."

"It's okay, Dr. Patel, we know you aren't to blame for this," CoCo said as she reached her hand across the round table.

"Thank you, dear, but I must disagree. Without my innovation in coating the matrix it would never have been able to properly function. So, yes, I am to blame," Nicola said.

"Do you have any idea what the next target will be?" Captain Pierce asked.

"Theories, yes. You've heard about the new island that appeared in the middle of the Atlantic Ocean?" Thierry asked.

"What?" James asked.

"How is that possible?" Emilio asked.

"Impossible, no? Improbable? Yes. Of course new islands are forming all the time and others are disappearing," Thierry countered. "But this one is different and the timing of its rise is suspicious. Do you mind?" He pointed at the drawing board and looked at the Green Beret for approval.

"Go on," Pierce said.

"See here," he said as he sketched the shapes of the Americas, Europe, and Africa with the ocean between them on the drawing board. "Roughly in the middle, here, an island has emerged from a prolonged volcanic eruption that caused all sorts of turmoil for airlines."

"We theorize that the Foundation will take a larger version of the tsunami device to the island and use it to cause massive destruction on the coasts," Nicola added.

"Which coasts?" Emilio asked.

"All of them."

The entire room went silent.

"Anything the Atlantic touches is in danger," Nicola clarified.

"We came to you with this because we think that you could stop them," Thierry said.

"The Hastings Foundation has already destroyed our lives. We won't let them destroy the world," Nicola added.

Josh looked at the two scientists. "You are welcome to stay here for as long as you like. We'd appreciate any guidance or advice you can give us. Pierce will set you up with labs and we will come up with a plan to stop them."

The scientists sighed in relief.

"Come with me," Pierce said, standing and waving them over. "I'll make sure to get you all set up."

CHAPTER

5 2

16 August

"Here are the items you requested," Washington said as he dropped a copy paper box on a desk in the lab. The large-screen television blared, showing one of Thierry's favorite BBC news programs.

"Oh, thank you so much!" The French scientist rushed over to go through the materials. He immediately took out a yo-yo and began twirling it.

"That's what you're most excited about?" Nicola grinned as she walked over and pulled out a spectrometer.

"It calms me," Thierry said as he walked back to his high table.

"Thank you, Washington." Nicola turned around. Unbeknownst to her, he affixed a listening device under the table.

"Best of luck." Washington smiled and left the lab.

"Thierry, talk me through the theory about the device and its range." Nicola put the spectrometer on her table.

"Like we theorized earlier, with our fix to the helix matrix allowing for a smooth revolution, the range should be in the neighborhood of three hundred to five hundred miles. So that puts the point of origin somewhere in here," Thierry said as he traced out on a large map from the Mississippi coastline to a spot in the middle of the Gulf of Mexico where the device must have been activated.

"Okay, so that gives us a pretty good idea about the current range. But the fact that it was so localized gives us an advantage. If they were able to solve the viscosity issues with a specialized liquid isotope, then we have to imagine that they could possibly gain range and—"

"Uh, Nicola, you're gonna want to see this," Thierry said as he clicked on the television's sound. A news station was playing a video that showed a bird's-eye view of the tsunami that ravaged the Gulf of Mexico. As the water rushed ashore, a man spoke, and a scroll at the bottom of the screen transcribed his words:

THE MISSISSIPPI TSUNAMI DISASTER WAS BUT THE OPENING SALVO IN OUR WAR ON THE WORLD.
OUR NEXT TARGETED ATTACK WILL BRING THE WORLD TO ITS KNEES.
NO ONE IS SAFE.
NO ONE CAN STAY THE HAND OF THE SENTINEL.
THERE IS A POWER GREATER THAN YOURS AT PLAY.
THERE WILL BE NO BARGAINING.
THERE WILL BE NO NEGOTIATING.
ONLY CONSEQUENCE.
YOU HAVE DESTROYED THE WORLD AND NOW THE WORLD WILL DESTROY YOU.
FROM THE ASHES A NEW AND GRAND WORLD WILL RISE.

The screen went back to a pale anchor, who tried to sum up the video message. Thierry and Nicola stared at each other for a moment before he threw the remote control onto the lab table.

"Merde!" Thierry slumped to the ground.

"We can fix this."

"No we can't, Nicola. We are responsible for this. All of this," Thierry said in a detached manner.

"No. They twisted what we did." She knelt beside him.

"Wrong. We were blinded by our obsession to regain our reputations and we must live with the consequences."

"Look. We can't change what happened, but we may be able to prevent it from getting worse. I can't do it alone. I need your help. It's the only way to make it work," Nicola said. She took his hands into hers.

Thierry nodded and stood. Captain Pierce walked into the lab.

"Did you see the video message?" Pierce closed the door. "Can you come up with any ideas about what they are threatening?"

"We've been searching how they got the means to increase their range and we've settled on the idea that they must have solved the friction issues that were plaguing our original trials. A specially bonded liquid isotope."

"Something viscous that could circulate throughout the device, coating it and charging the weapon," Thierry said.

"Something that could provide a semi-permanent bond that would allow for the friction to pass harmlessly through it."

"Like water? Or oil?" Pierce said as he looked through the box and snagged his finger on an errant blade. "Damn it!" he swore as his finger began to bleed.

Thierry and Nicola froze, watching the blood pool on the table.

"I always wondered why we were working with helix matrix, since it's a peculiar shape to use," Nicola said, excitement starting to ring in her voice.

"But if the machine was specifically bonded to a central person's DNA, then their blood would allow for the machine to function at the highest level," Thierry said as he finished her thought.

Pierce studied them and considered their scientific leap. "So, it's Rami. His blood."

"Of course. Why didn't we see this sooner?" Nicola said.

"Don't beat yourself up. They had us going in different directions and only gave us pieces of information to work with," Thierry said as he took the yo-yo out of his pocket and spun it a few times. "Everything was out of context."

"Mighty impressive," Pierce said. "I'll let you get back to your work. I will send someone in to help you with your research. Please take all the time here in the lab that you need." He turned toward the door.

"Captain Pierce," Thierry said and the Green Beret looked back. "I know that Josh is funding this, but we know that you are as much responsible for this base as he is. Thank you so much for allowing us to stay here. We are in your debt."

Pierce nodded slightly and walked out of the lab.

CHAPTER
53

16 August

Arian was running late, but the dream had been worth it. A morning person and light sleeper, she had not overslept in four years. She had about fifteen minutes to dress and get out the door to be on time to work. She twirled around the bathroom throwing clothes on, trying to make herself as presentable as possible. She kept going back to her dream. Her sleeping mind had tried to keep Rami with her for as long as possible, if only in dreamland. In life, she hadn't seen him in almost ten months, as she had not been permitted to visit him in prison.

Arian tied a peach-and-ivory scarf around her head and let a few strands of hair fall toward her face. A glance in the mirror said her full-sleeved cream-colored blouse and dark wash skinny jeans were impeccably maintained. She shrugged into an ivory manteau, leaving the knee-length overcoat open near the bottom. Satisfied, she grabbed her keys and the leather briefcase her parents gave her when she graduated top of her class. She was about to open the door when someone on the other side knocked.

She opened the door. Her jaw slacked and she dropped

her work briefcase to the floor.

"R—Rami?" she stuttered. "Is that really you?"

He smiled and stepped toward her.

Heart pounding, Arian looked at him up and down. He looked strong. Healthy. Fit. His hair was still curly, and his face was freshly shaved. Not at all the gaunt, weak, and listless man she imagined an inmate at Astara prison would look like after almost a year. A tear trickled from her eye, and she reached out to touch his chest.

"It's me. I'm real," he whispered. He wiped away the tear.

Arian had imagined her reunion with her love many times. Would it be her identifying the body? Would it be after years had robbed them of their youth and only a glimmer of their former selves remained? Would it be that their love wasn't strong enough and they were more strangers than lovers? This reunion banished those worries.

"How? How is this possible?" she asked, pulling him into a tight hug.

"I had to see you," Rami said.

"Rami, my love," she repeated over and over. Her tears were now falling freely. Tenderly, he kissed her face. She rested her head on his shoulder, a pose they had fallen into thousands of times before, but not in almost a year.

"Come inside." She led him into the parlor. As they touched, they felt a shock. They smiled, neither knowing nor caring if it was the static shock from the carpet or the electricity from their love.

"My Arian, I am so sorry it's been so long since we've seen each other. I've missed you so. I am on … leave for the day and I came to spend it with you," he said. He glanced around the parlor and smiled when he spotted a framed picture taken of the two of them in front of a rocky waterfall at Jamshidieh Park about a year before.

Arian hugged him tightly, not wanting to let go. He felt so warm and strong, and she whispered a silent prayer of gratitude for this good fortune.

"You are even more beautiful than I remember," Rami said. He led her to the couch and they sat together. He put his hand over hers, an affectionate gesture he often made.

"Rami, I don't understand. How are you here? Have you seen your parents?"

"No. And you must never tell anyone, especially my parents, that you saw me today. It isn't safe."

She studied him, and it seemed he had something he wanted to blurt out. "I don't understand."

He hesitated but she just held his hand. "I just want to spend one perfect day with you. Can we do that?"

She could hardly refuse her love anything, especially after their time apart. She nodded.

"I can't believe how good you look. I would have thought being in prison for almost a year would waste you away, but you look as handsome as ever. And so strong, healthier than I've ever seen you."

Rami smiled. "I brought our favorite breakfast and your favorite book of poetry for us to read together. And this," he said, lifting a bag into view.

"I didn't even realize you had a bag." Arian smiled wide and gently brushed her hand against his as if she were a schoolgirl again, scheming of ways to touch her crush.

"Would you get plates and glasses?" he asked her.

"Of course," she said, and made a swift trip to her kitchen. She deposited plates and napkins and knives on the coffee table. Rami topped the plates with flat breads and then he brought out butter, her favorite creamy spread of sarshir, and a few fruit jams.

"Rami this looks amazing!"

They ate, and took each other in.

She could see in his eyes such sadness and loneliness, and wondered if she could make it all disappear. Rami kissed her. Gently, at first, and then with each breath more passionately than the last. Arian had almost forgotten how sweet Rami smelled, a mixture of spice and leather and another scent she could never identify. She inhaled his aroma deeply, as if she might never get to hold him this close again.

"I have been in love with you since the day we met at the library. Remember, we were both in the research section, and you kept walking by me trying to get my attention," Rami said.

"That isn't at all what happened and you know it," she said, smiling. "I was sitting at the table and you ran into my chair, repeatedly! And just when I was about to yell at you, our eyes met and everything just slowed down. At that moment I couldn't even form a word."

"You took my breath away that day. And every day since." Rami gently picked Arian up and held her tight as they kissed passionately. "I have missed you so much."

She wrapped her legs around her fiancé, and he carried her back toward the bedroom. They fell into the bed. Arian pulled the soft, purple T-shirt off his body and kissed him as Rami slowly unbuttoned her cream-colored blouse. They made love, slowly, passionately, as if they both somehow knew, but would not admit, that this was the last time they would ever touch each other again. Every motion was orchestrated to give each of them the care and attention they had long since forgotten.

Rami dozed on the bed and Arian watched him, memorizing each detail of her lover. She traced his muscles and caressed the hair on his arms. Her gentle touch woke him, and he lifted his head to kiss her.

"Rami, tell me—" Arian said.

"Shh … Not now," Rami whispered.

"I have to know."

Rami sighed, and Arian's heart quickened.

"I love you so much," Rami said. His face was serious and sad. "I have to tell you something, and you must never repeat this to anyone. Not my parents, not your friends. And anything you hear on the news, you can't trust their version."

"Rami, you're scaring me," Arian said. She drew back from him and pulled the violet sheets over her body.

"I have been changed, and there are people after me," he said.

"What do you mean changed? Who's after you?" She studied him. It seemed he was holding something back. "You're scaring me."

"Please. Everything will be fine. I promise. I have been gifted with a grave responsibility. I wish that I had not been called, that I could just stay here in this room with you." He gently caressed her cheek.

"What are you saying? I don't understand."

"I just have to do this one last thing and then we can be together again," Rami said. He groped under the sheets for her hand and held it. "If everything goes as I hope, we will wake up in each other's arms for the rest of our lives. We could go anywhere you want. America or England. Live free from any regrets."

"Why can't you just stay with me?" She pulled his hand to her chest and held it over her racing heart. "Nothing can harm you when you're with me."

"If I did that, I wouldn't be the man you deserve. As much as I want to stay with you, I have a responsibility. A calling—" Rami's voice began to shake.

Arian studied him, and her eyes welled with tears.

"I can tell that whatever this is, it is weighing heavy on you. I trust you completely. Just promise me that we will meet when this is all over at our favorite spot in Jamshidieh Park," she said, hoping that Rami's honor wouldn't be his downfall.

"Of course," Rami said. He kissed her and then kissed the trail her tears had left down her cheeks. "Your love kept me alive during those horrible, long months in Astara."

He held her close to him again, then stood and, as Arian watched, he dressed again.

"I hate to leave you like this, but seeing you—being with you—has been the best thing I've ever done. I love you, Arian. I will see you soon." Rami leaned over and kissed her good-bye.

He took one last look at Arian and closed her bedroom door. He walked into Waleed's teleportation portal and back to Base 47.

CHAPTER
5 4

17 August

"Not everyone's going to be happy you're here," CoCo said.

"Yeah, I'm starting to understand just how different blogging and regular reporting are from being a travel journalist," Maggie said. Behind her, Focus snorted.

**Wally Jones
"Focus"**

"The cool part is through here." CoCo pulled a heavy metal door toward her. "Voila, the training room."

The trio stepped into a gymnasium that looked nothing like the facilities where Maggie had suffered through phys-ed classes in her school days. Then again, Maggie thought, if she'd had classmates who could shapeshift and teleport, maybe those horrible acoustically challenged fitness centers would look and sound more like this one.

"What are they doing?" Focus asked.

CoCo studied the group a second before responding. "Looks like they're practicing an earthquake rescue mission. Blue shirts are victims, black uniforms are heroes."

Maggie studied the uniforms and looked back at CoCo. "I can see your design genius at work there."

"Thanks. You should have seen the first uniforms." CoCo rolled her eyes. "But this is version two, and I got some input. So, there, the one levitating the rocks and concrete blocks? That's Katrina, she moves things with her mind. Etienne is probably around here somewhere, but you most likely wouldn't see him. He can be invisible, but he's great for stuff like this, since he can also phase himself—and other people, if they're touching—to move through solid objects."

"And me without my camera," Focus said.

"Does that make you out of Focus when you don't have a camera?" CoCo teased.

He cocked his head and grinned at her. "Actually, the nickname has nothing to do shooting. I'm a bit ADD, and when I was growing up, my mom would always tell me to focus on my homework, focus on this or that task. To focus. Eventually she'd just bark, 'Focus!' It just stuck."

She turned toward him and held up both hands in a whoa gesture. "You remember the terms, right?"

"Of course," Maggie said. "But Focus is right. What kind of segment can we put together for the blog if we don't get any of the heroes in action?"

"Oh, you'll see some of them in action during this afternoon's practice session. It'll be back in here after lunch." CoCo turned them both around and pushed them out the door. "In the meantime, I want you to meet one of our resident mad scientists."

"What?"

CoCo grinned. "You'll see. He's on the other side of the complex. While we're walking over, though, I have a question, Maggie."

"Sure, what?"

"What happened with your job?"

"Oh, that. Well, let's just say that the network and I had a difference of opinion. I wound up on the short side of the ultimatum."

"You got in trouble for TheModsBlog?"

"I'll say she did," Focus said.

"Sheesh. That seems pretty shortsighted of them."

"I thought so too. Believe me, I did a lot of soul-searching. That ultimatum is why the blog went dark for a while. But in the end, it was a story that demanded to be told. You know. It's a Mod world and we're just living in it," Maggie joked. "So I'm here." She looked at Focus and amended. "We're here."

"Ah, here we are," CoCo announced. The nameplate by the door simply read "R&D lab." Instead of barging into the room the way she had the gym, CoCo knocked. "He's a bit sensitive about interruptions."

A muffled "enter" sounded through the door, and CoCo twisted the knob.

One step into the lab, Maggie stopped short and Focus ran into her. Maggie tilted her head, taking in the scene, which was about as opposite what one would expect in a lab as one could get. Two men stood in the center of the room talking in hushed tones while two others, wearing sleek black outfits, were sword fighting a few feet away from them.

CoCo pushed them into the lab, took in the commotion, and sighed. "I never can decide whether I want Emilio to win or lose these fights."

"I thought we were going to the lab. It, uh, it said lab on the door. And the one gentleman is wearing a lab coat. But, the swords?"

"Relax, Maggie. They're just testing out the new uniforms. Hey, guys, stop for a second, will ya?"

"Sure, sweetie, anything you say." But the man's words didn't match his actions. Instead of halting his attack on the other man—who Maggie now realized was Josh—he drew his sword back and tried to swing it through Josh's midsection.

Maggie sucked in a worried breath and let it out when she saw the sword deflect off the black outfit. "Wow, what is that stuff made of?"

The man wearing the lab coat seemed to hear the whispered question. He smiled and looked at Maggie. "That, my dear, is similar to what cops wear, but better. Much stronger and lighter protection."

At the same time, Josh countered with his own thrust. The opponent's suit defended against this attack as well.

"That's enough for now," Pierce shouted to Josh and Emilio.

Josh looked up at Pierce in evident surprise and Emilio, true to form, took advantage of his opponent's break in concentration by thrusting one last shot at Josh's torso.

"Enough!" Pierce boomed.

Josh and Emilio sheathed their swords and Josh strode over to Maggie and Focus to introduce himself. "Thanks for coming, Maggie, we can use all the good pub we can get. Don't want people confusing Base 47 with a ... certain criminal element you yourself have blogged about."

"Oh, you read my little blog?"

"Started reading you even before I came out of the Mods closet," he said. "It was a lot easier to read what you wrote about me than it is to see what critics think of my films."

She grinned at him. "I look forward to working together." Later, she would tell Focus she thought Josh had finally found a role that really suited him. He looked like he had found his purpose.

"Captain Pierce, we need the public at large to see us as the good guys. Trust me, this is the way to go," Josh said.

"Maggie, I'm Captain Pierce and this is Dr. Thierry Giraud." He pointed at the man in the lab coat.

Thierry reached out to shake hands with Maggie and Focus. "I like your blog. Very informative."

"Thanks," Maggie said, grinning.

"Now, let's head up to my office, and we can go over the ground rules. Because I'm still not sold on doing this little video," Pierce said.

Focus turned to Maggie as if to ask which one was in charge. She shrugged.

"But swords? Why swords?" Maggie asked.

But Emilio answered for him. "That? Just for fun."

"Ugh, boys," CoCo said. She looked around the group. "How about let's go to Captain Pierce's office and discuss things further."

CHAPTER 55

18 August

Nicola shrugged as she straightened her cornflower-blue scrubs. She squinted into her microscope.

"I can't decide what's worse. How much Roger lied to us or us believing his lies," Thierry said as he did calculations on the dry erase board near his desk. Neither noticed an unfamiliar man with red hair slip into their lab and lock the door behind him.

"He fooled us for far too long, but now that we know about their plans and how Rami fits into it, we can defeat him," Nicola said.

"I don't think that will happen," the redheaded man said. The scientists froze in place.

That voice was familiar, but Thierry couldn't quite place it. Slowly, they both turned around.

"Pretty smart, I'd say. But maybe too smart for your own good," he said as he brandished a pistol. "Now, we can do this one of two ways."

"It's you," Thierry said.

"What?"

"You're the voice from the video," Thierry said.

"Good catch. My claim to fame will be as the voice that doomed the world." He laughed as the two scientists inched toward each other. "Let's not make this more difficult. I think it's time to come back to The Hastings Foundation, don't you?"

"What are you talking about?" Nicola said.

"We never escaped, did we?" Thierry said as started putting the pieces together.

"The Ascendancy is everywhere," the redheaded man said. He saw Thierry look to the door. "I wouldn't, if I were you. Be a shame if she had to pay for your carelessness."

"Thierry, please," Nicola said, frozen. Thierry lowered his shoulders and stayed put.

"That's the first smart decision you've made," he said. "Let's go."

"Why are you doing this?" Nicola asked as she scooted back.

"I'm not a good guy."

Nicola looked into his eyes and couldn't sense any remorse. She realized they were as good as dead.

"Nicola, remember when we worked on the post-thermo-imaging unit a few years back?" Thierry asked as they walked around the table as their opponent waved them closer.

"What?" she asked, turning to him with confusion on her face.

"And we couldn't figure out how to make the device work or reboot until we applied the wave-matter energizer?"

"Yes." The word came out hesitant and uncertain.

"That was a crazy design, right? We didn't realize the serious flaw until we were ready to hit the ignition." He looked her straight in the eye.

"I remember. It would have destroyed a two-block radius without the isotope replacement," Nicola said.

"Thought you'd remember that," Thierry said. He took

a deep breath, and looked at Nicola. He turned, pulled his hands out of his pocket, and swung his yo-yo at the redheaded man. "Run!"

As the redheaded man dodged the yo-yo, Thierry sent a right hook into his face. The distraction gave Nicola enough time to run a few feet away, but she paused and watched their struggle with growing horror.

There was a sharp bang and blood sprayed from Thierry's back. The scientist slowly put his hands on his front and looked down. His shirt was quickly becoming saturated with blood. He slowly slipped down to the ground.

"No!" Nicola screamed as she looked around the room. She was truly on her own.

"Don't get any more smart ideas. I've got to get you back to the Foundation. I don't particularly want to leave a trail of bodies, but I will," the redheaded man said as he stood.

Nicola fell to the floor and took Thierry into her arms. He tried to hug her but lacked the strength to do so. He lifted his hands up toward her and patted her, leaving a bloody handprint near her right pocket.

"It didn't have to be this way. You could have all ended up alive," the redheaded man said.

"Shh, Thierry. Don't say anything." She cried as she bent her head closer to his.

"If you don't want to end up like your friend, I suggest you get up and come with me." The redheaded man motioned the gun at her, encouraging her to stand up. Nicola gave Thierry a tearful kiss on the cheek as he took a last strained breath.

And just like that, Thierry closed his eyes.

The redheaded man dialed a number on his phone.

"I've got the target. Only one casualty. I'll have her on her way to you immediately to prepare for the Reckoning."

CHAPTER
5 6

20 August

Henry took a sip of wine, savored it, then swallowed. He hadn't felt this good in years. After the upheaval of Rami's disappearance and the scientist's defection, he was finally on the verge of success and there was nothing to stop him. Soon the Sentinel would welcome him and create the prophesied utopia.

But first, Henry needed to report back on the latest goings-on, from the emergence of the Atlantic island to the gathering at Base 47 and the Reckoning.

Because this would be the last time they would meet before the world changed, they met in Lisbon at his favorite restaurant, which would not survive the tsunami.

The restaurant was housed in a former convent, but the history of the establishment held more meaning to Henry. The former convent was a spot that many Ascendancy members throughout the years had used for safe passage as well as a go-between for passing cryptic messages.

He tightened his fantastically colored tie and checked himself in the nearby mirror. He sighed at the deeper lines appearing on his face. He stood behind a dark cherry wood high-back chair waiting for his guests to arrive. The doors in the back opened and Elise walked through. Right on her heels were the twins, Anabel and Maks.

"Welcome!" Henry raised his bottle of Chateau Margaux in the air. "I took the liberty."

Two waiters offered them glasses and they selected one each. Elise nodded at the glasses and then smiled her approval at Henry.

"Are these from the personal crystal collection of King Louis XIV?" she asked.

"Yes," Henry said. "He was quite the supporter of our little cause."

"Salut." Elise lifted the glass to her lips and drank. She was dressed impeccably in a blue Dior Provenance dress.

"Not to sound ungrateful, but don't you think you're celebrating a little too early?" Maks asked, gulping the wine. Dressed in a black, deep V-neck shirt and tight leather jeans, he seemed more ready for a night out than the sober meeting he was attending.

"After all the effort and sacrifices Henry's had to make, he's allowed a bit of happiness now," Elise said.

"What of the Sentinel?" Anabel asked. Wearing a custom Gucci gray pinstriped business suit, she was serious, stern, and attentive. "Is he prepared for his role in all of this?"

The group had spent most of the last decade working behind the scenes to push Rami Kazemi in the necessary directions to prepare him for the Reckoning.

"Yes, how is Rami doing?" Elise asked.

Before Henry would answer, he motioned for them to sit down around the solid Tuscan walnut dining table. Large enough to seat twenty, there were only four place settings. They sat down and Henry resumed speaking.

"Rami is now in Base 47 training with the other Children

of the Solstice," Henry said, knowing that this was absolutely not part of the plan. He was lucky that his contingencies had come through.

"What? You've got to be joking!" Anabel slammed her glass down. The red wine splashed out and splattered the pristine white tablecloth.

"Henry, that is not part of the plan. Rami is not supposed to interact with any of them. You know what that means!" Elise said as she pointed at Henry.

"What it *could* mean, Elise. This is not necessarily the disaster you think it will be. Believe me, I've relentlessly pored over the prophecies. He will still do everything we need him to do," Henry said.

"How can you be sure they will not taint him?" Elise asked. Her dissension troubled Henry. They had come into the Ascendancy at roughly the same time and had vowed to support each other.

"Listen. The prophecy says:

The Sentinel rises from a long slumber.
No force on Earth must intercede.
The Children of the Solstice
Turn the world from in to out.
They will face off against the Sentinel
In The Reckoning, leaving only carnage
In their wake.
At all costs they must not be allowed to
Temper a god.

"All will still go according to plan," Henry added. "Rami has been under the direct surveillance and guidance of one we can trust. Someone from the Old Guard. Remember the Swarm of 1912 and again of 1979?"

Maks and Anabel shook their heads, but Elise gently fingered a brooch her father had given her on her sixteenth birthday. She narrowed her eyes and Henry fought not to squirm for violating his pledge to never bring up the Swarm. An offshoot of the Ascendancy, the Swarm's effort to jumpstart the prophecy had ended in complete disaster. Ascendancy members of the time had quickly moved to decimate the ranks of the Swarm. And those members were referred to as the Old Guard. The Ascendancy to this day still employed various Old Guards to carry out their visions.

"The sovereigns tried to merge occult practices into the Ascendancy to disastrous effects, capping off with the murder of Franz Ferdinand. They foolishly believed the assassination would lead to a global meltdown in which they could seize control," Henry said. "Another offshoot grew in secret and emerged again during the Iran hostage crisis. They tried to manipulate the world leaders into a catastrophic disaster. Those were dark times for us. And the only thing protecting our interests were the Old Guards. If we've learned anything, it's that we must be absolutely committed to our goal."

"Enough of the damn history lessons, Hastings!" Maks said. "I'm tired of all of it."

"So there is someone with Rami now? Ready to get him where we need him to go when the time comes?" Anabel asked.

"Of course. Someone I trust implicitly. A member of the Old Guard come back to the fold," Henry said with a grin. "In fact, he's running Base 47, and he's superb at maintaining his cover."

"Nicely done," Elise said.

"Never mind that, you just better make sure that Rami is ready to perform as the prophecy requires. There is no other option," Anabel said.

"He'll be there on the island, shepherded by our member of the Old Guard. But it's probable he'll bring Mods from Base 47 with him. As such, I've set in motion plans to have an opposition team of Mods there to keep the Base 47 players from interfering with the WaveMaker," Henry said.

"And what of the scientists?" Anabel asked.

"They are ready," Henry said, deciding against telling them of their defection, followed by the killing of one and abrupt return of the other. "We will begin the operation tomorrow. In two days' time the entire face of the planet will be forever changed."

"And the potential millions of deaths this causes gives you no pause?" Elise asked.

"Millions die every day and no one bats an eye. Suddenly we care about this loss of life? The prophecy says this sacrifice must be made so we can achieve the promise. I can live with that," Henry said.

"I won't be losing any sleep over it myself." Maks slammed down his empty glass and walked out the door. Anabel followed him out, but not before leaving one last thought for the others.

"I appreciate all you have done, but we must always be vigilant. The Swarm may yet still pose a threat to us. We must never let our guard down," she said. She bowed confidently and closed the door behind her.

Henry knew the words she said were true. They had never ferreted out the remaining hardliners, but the last offensive those many years was enough to discourage anyone from picking up the embers of the dying group.

"And you?" Henry asked, turning to Elise.

"I have always maintained that what is good for us is bad for the Swarm," Elise said as she stood.

"You believe that what we've all done to push Rami on

this path is for the best?"

"We all took a vow to see this prophecy through. That meant doing all we can to shape him into the perfect vessel for our ultimate rise." She leaned over and kissed him on the cheek. "Don't lose focus now, Henry. Far too much is at stake." She turned and left him alone.

Henry sat back in his chair and looked out the window. The prophecy handed down over five hundred years ago would finally be fulfilled and the Ascendancy would be responsible for the single greatest leap in the history of mankind.

CHAPTER
57

22 August

"Watch where you're going, kid!" an annoyed Marquez said as he barely avoided decapitating the child with the container of weapons he was carrying to the staging area. Emma just smiled and waved.

Base 47 was buzzing and it would stay that way until they left for the new island in the Atlantic.

Even though the team was split up into several training groups for the next hour or so, Emma needed to connect everyone so they could formulate their plan. She mentally brought all of her teammates into her mind—the safest spot she could imagine.

"Mon Dieu!" Etienne said as his astral self entered her mind.

"Emma! What is this?" CoCo asked.

"Sorry about no warning," Emma said.

"How is this possible? I'm in the middle of a training session," James said.

"I have only taken a part of your consciousness—you won't be missed in the real world," Emma said, trying to calm her new friends. "I wasn't sure I could pull it off, but here you all are. We can talk and no one can listen in our plans."

"She is right. There is little time and much to discuss," Rami said. His astral self sat in the center of the group.

As the others struggled to acclimate to the new environment, they sat in the chairs that Emma had provided.

CoCo looked at the sprung floors and the hip-height wooden bar surrounding the astral room. "I know this place. We're in a dance studio."

"Uh, Emma, why are we in a dance studio?" James asked.

"This is where I first discovered my gift is special to me, even if I hate dancing. But don't look in the mirrors too long. I can't control what you'd see," Emma said. "It could be … unsettling."

The team watched James fight to look away from the sprinting vision of him in the reflection. They all tried not to peer into the mirrors, but few could resist.

Astral CoCo reached for the mirror, but her hand passed right through. A cold, skeletal hand grabbed hers. She yanked her hand back. When she peered again into the mirror she only saw open water followed by a fierce lightning storm and a small room. In another image she cradled a baby and smiled into the eyes of a man she could not identify. She shook her head violently and returned her thoughts to the group. The image would haunt her over the years.

"We all know about the new island in the Atlantic," Emilio said.

"Yes. It's called New Atlantis and we are going there today," Emma said with matter-of-fact calmness.

"So, you're just naming things now?" Etienne said.

"All right. You have a direct line to whoever is calling the shots. Who needs to go?" Josh asked.

"It's going to take all of us, of course. Why else would we be here? But Pierce won't want to bring everyone. We have to convince him to," Emma said. "Or arrange it so everyone shows up there, anyway."

"Maybe we can get more information from the scientists about what The Hastings Foundation made them work on," Emilio said.

"Speaking of, I haven't seen them around, have you?" CoCo asked.

Emma paused and closed her eyes. "They're not here," she slowly said. "I can't find them. Then again, I can't always find people who aren't Mods, even if we've got some sort of connection."

"What happened? Did they just disappear?" Katrina asked.

"I ... I don't know."

Josh seemed to sense her distress. "I think we should focus on getting everything we need and getting to the island," he said as Emma rubbed her head.

"Waleed, have you been practicing?" the seven-year-old asked.

"Of course. And now that I have a visual of the place, I can get us there without a problem," the teleporter said.

"Hold on. We're just going to take her word on this?" Etienne asked, looking at everyone in the astral circle.

"What is your problem with this?" Emilio asked. Out of the corner of his eye he glimpsed himself in a large palace filled with treasures but no one to share them with.

"She gets her information from voices she hears. Voices we don't even know if we can trust. And we're supposed to take her word for it?" Etienne said, snapping Emilio out of his vision of princely but solitary wealth. "Because I've seen this movie before. Creepy little girl hears voices. It never ends well. Count me out."

"Emma wouldn't lie. And I have heard this voice too," Rami said. He gently touched Etienne's shoulder.

"Sure. Of course, you're on her side. You just got here. Why should we risk our necks for these people?"

"Because we are all a part of it. The earth gave us these abilities in order to save it." Jiya spoke calmly and with certainty. "That is why I'm here. Why did you come?"

Etienne said nothing.

"Me too," CoCo said. "I realized my powers were part of something bigger, and this was my chance to make a difference."

"No man's an island. Had to do something for those who couldn't," Josh said.

"Hell, I just needed a good place to hide out until some things blew over," Emilio said. A few of the team members exchanged looks. "But I've found a reason to stay."

"Back in Pakistan I was a teacher, but when I got to London I couldn't work. I've always wanted to make a difference. The solstice has given me that chance again," Waleed said.

"I just thought it would be fun." James grinned and shrugged. "It has been. One adventure after another."

"So, Etienne, why are you here?" Josh asked.

Etienne frowned. "I guess I just hoped I could get a fresh start, make some new friends." His frown deepened. "But I haven't exactly done so well on that front."

"Hey, we can work on that," James said. "Try to have fun. Smile, once in a while."

"I'm just saying that I'm not sure I'm ready to risk my life for a bunch of people I've never met," Etienne said.

"Don't be so selfish, Etienne. There are some here who'd risk their life for yours," Katrina said.

"We have a purpose here. We come from all over the

world. We have been gathered for a reason. We have to protect and defend those who can't," CoCo said.

"I'm not so sure," Etienne said. "I mean, this whole kumbaya thing is sweet and all, but our lives are at stake here—"

"Enough, Etienne." CoCo shouted so loud that her astral presence momentarily flickered. "Emma, show us what would happen if we don't act."

"Not really how my power works," she said, discouraged.

"Maybe I can help you with that," Jiya said as she knelt beside her and held out her hands. Emma dropped her hands into the weathered Indian woman's hands and light danced between them before Emma threw back her head. Her eyes glowed purple and she stood up. Suddenly, everyone was connected to her vision. Cities under the sea, land broken, fires raging across deserts, clouds of ash circling the skies. Death as far as they could see in any direction. In the center of the shared vision stood a soaring metal contraption with spinning blades. Inside that machine was Rami, drenched in black fire and writhing in pain.

As Rami saw the vision unfold in front of him, he patted his body to make sure he was not actually on fire.

Emma fell backward as Waleed rushed over to catch her. Jiya slumped over in exhaustion and James ran over to check on her.

"Oh my God," was all CoCo could say. She looked at Rami in horror.

"Thanks, Waleed," Emma said.

"Emma what does this mean? How is Rami going to stop this?" CoCo asked.

At the mention of his name, Rami shifted uncomfortably in his astral seat. The images haunted him far more than he'd like to admit.

"I think this means Rami is the Sentinel," Emma said, and Rami slumped. "Rami has to destroy the device they created. He is the key to stopping them."

"That's not really informative," Etienne snapped. "What does your voice say?"

"Hey! Emma's doing all she can here," Waleed said.

"Yeah, and that's more than you seem to be doing," Emilio said.

"Why are you ganging up on me? I didn't show us an apocalyptic future," Etienne said.

"Seriously, Etienne. That's enough," CoCo said in a calmer though firm voice. "There is no way we can turn our backs now. If you want out, go ahead. But know that this is permanent. You turn tail now, you won't be able to come back."

Etienne seemed shocked at the force in her words. He finally nodded. He remained seated.

"What do you need us to do?" Katrina asked.

"Pierce will be coming around soon. We need to convince him to take all of us. What is coming will be difficult, but this is what we've been training for. United, nothing can stop us." Emma dissolved their astral meeting, allowing each to fully return to their physical bodies.

Etienne returned with a start, causing him to drop weights on his chest.

"Careful there, friend," Rami said. He quickly lifted the weight. "Good thing I was spotting you."

Etienne forced a gruff "thanks" and wiped his brow with the dank gym towel.

As he walked away, all Rami could think about was burning in the vision. Every atom in his body pleaded with him to escape back to the loving arms of Arian, but his mind told him he had to do everything he could to save the world, even if it meant giving the ultimate sacrifice. Would he have the courage to do it?

Katrina was working with several of the ex-soldiers as they threw boxes at her. She was psychokinetically grabbing them and pushing them back while maintaining her own personal force field.

Across the room, James and Emilio practiced jiu-jitsu techniques against the ex-soldiers.

As Etienne walked by, Josh called out to him. "So I have to ask, do you have a problem with me?" Josh tossed a bo staff at Etienne. As soon as Etienne grabbed it, Josh swung hard at him.

"What do you mean?" Etienne blocked the blow easily but winced at the strength of the blow.

"You seem distant. Well, more than normal. Did I do something?" Josh said as they began trading barbs. "I've let it go until now, but I need to know you've got my back out there, just like I've got your back."

Etienne circled his bo staff behind his back and swung hard, hitting Josh square in the shoulder.

"Oof—" Josh reeled and spun away from the blow.

"It's just ... I am not sure about you."

"Well, don't hold back," Josh said. He took his own bo staff in two hands and pushed Etienne against the wall.

"I think you are hiding something. And I'm not used to someone like you," Etienne said as he phased right through Josh and dropped his bo staff on the ground.

"Is that right?" Josh said as he let go.

"I'm not some stupid kid from the provinces. It just will take some getting used to ... you."

"Let me make it easy for you, Etienne," Josh said as he threw down his bo staff. "I spent years hiding who I was and once that White Light Wave hit, it made me realize how empty my life was." As Josh spoke he got more and more animated. He didn't realize it, but he was shifting his face from form to form. "It took some changing to do, but I am finally comfortable in my own skin—no matter what face I wear." His own features rematerialized on his face, and he walked away.

"That's not what I meant," Etienne said. But it was too little, too late.

CoCo sat on the bench, leaned her head back, and squeezed her water bottle. Emma sat down quietly next to CoCo and looked at her inquisitively. CoCo forced a smile.

"I need to talk to you," CoCo said.

"About the mirror?" Emma asked.

"What? No. I thought that we should have an ace in the hole, just in case things go bad," CoCo said as she stretched her left arm over her head.

"How do you mean?" Emma asked, mimicking CoCo's movement. CoCo gave her a look and Emma linked their minds.

"We need someone who can tell our story. Someone we can trust. To tell how we came to this place and what we are trying to do for the world," CoCo thought to Emma as she switched her arms.

"What do you have in mind?"

"I want to bring in Maggie, who interviewed us the other day. I trust her completely. With the reach of TheModsBlog it's our best shot at convincing the world we are here to help." CoCo stood and placed her left leg on the bench and leaned over, giving a good, deep stretch to her hamstrings.

"You want Waleed to get her and bring her here?" Emma asked.

"Yes. I don't trust Pierce one bit. We need an outside, objective source for our security," CoCo thought to Emma.

Emma nodded and accepted the information that CoCo provided for finding Maggie. She smiled, hugged CoCo, and turned around. As she walked past Luli, she heard not only the Chinese woman whispering to her unborn child, but for a moment she thought she heard—no, felt—the baby reach out. It unnerved her so much that she quickly put on her mental headphones for the first time in weeks.

CHAPTER

58

22 August

Captain Pierce threw open the door to the training floor. "All right, folks, it's time for action. We have gotten a call to help out," he said as the team gathered around him. "Rami, Emilio, CoCo, Etienne, and James, you're with me."

"Where are we going?" James asked.

"I'll brief you on the way to the War Room," he said, and chomped on his cigar. "I need another group ready to go as well. Josh and Katrina, you will all act as support in case of emergency."

They divided themselves into the groups, and Etienne stood as far away from Josh as possible.

"The rest of you come along too. You've got a place in the plan as well." Pierce motioned to Washington to join them as they followed Pierce out the door and toward the elevator.

As they walked, Emma mind-linked the whole team to let them in on what was surely going to happen.

"Waleed will take the first group to the island and then will come for us and bring us there too."

"And what exactly are we supposed to do there?" James thought.

"Yeah, the specifics of how we're supposed to 'save the world' aren't quite clear," Etienne quipped.

"Etienne, if you're not onboard with how, at least get onboard with why," Luli said. "I'm doing this to make sure my family is safe."

"I don't really have anybody," he said tonelessly.

"If you don't help now, you won't have the chance to have anybody to save," Luli reasoned.

"Your parents," Emma suggested. "I'm here for mine. And the voice." She paused, as if to give Etienne a chance to respond. When he didn't, she continued. "The island is where Rami will fight for all of us. And we have to help him." She dropped the mind-link.

Captain Pierce had brought all of them into what he and Josh had dubbed the War Room. "Thanks to our scientist friends, we know that we need to go the new island that emerged in the Atlantic." Pierce pointed to a three-dimensional map of New Atlantis, sitting by itself in the Atlantic Ocean.

"And do what exactly? You haven't been too forthcoming with your plan," Rami said.

"We are going to recon the area in case the scientists are right, so they can be ready if and when The Hastings Foundation shows up. We don't have any significant information due to the ash cloud, so we must get a decent visual of the island and perform an initial exploration," Pierce said.

"And where are the scientists? Haven't seen them around," Josh said.

"I have them working on a few special projects for me," Pierce said. "Now, by all accounts the island is deserted, but we aren't going to take any chances. That is why Washington and a select group of my men will accompany us."

"Captain Pierce, I think that you are making a strategic mistake not taking all of us," Emilio said, standing.

"What are you talking about?" Washington said.

"You are leaving behind significant assets. You just want Waleed to ferry people back and forth, but he can do so much more," Emilio said. "And by leaving Jiya behind, you risk one of us getting hurt, perhaps fatally. She can heal us on the battlefield and Emma has—"

"Are you kidding me? I'm not taking Emma, Luli, or Jiya into an unknown," Pierce said.

"But you said yourself that this is just an exploratory mission. Why can't we all go?" Etienne countered.

"And we all know that this isn't just an exploratory mission. We all heard the ultimatum. Every country may be working to stop this, but we are the best chance at stopping that machine. You're going to need us. All of us," Josh added, backing up Etienne, who rolled his eyes.

"Either we all go, or none of us go," Rami said, rising to stand next to Emilio.

"Fine. You can all come. Except you two," Pierce amended, pointing at Emma and Luli. He pointed Washington to the door and lit a cigar.

Luli's face turned sour. Her hidden force field began to reach out toward the Green Beret, but Jiya's calming hand on Luli's arm drew the protective field back.

"Not the time, my dear," Jiya said quietly. Luli nodded.

"Don't worry, Rami. We've got your back," Emilio said, putting his hand on Rami's shoulder.

"Yeah, bro. This'll be fun," James added, throwing his support in with a fist bump.

"We have a mandate from the United Nations to explore and discover if The Hastings Foundation is indeed operating on the island. And to be honest, given our enhanced reputation, we are the only ones who can handle this."

"And what about the bad guys with powers we faced before?" Katrina asked.

"What about them?"

"What if they show up? What if they are a part of The Hastings Foundation, too?" Katrina asked.

"We're prepared to face them." Pierce saw their apprehension grow. "So you had your asses handed to you the first time out. Okay. Now you know what to expect and you are much stronger," he said. "As far as I can discern, we will be the first to set foot on the island. Waleed, you will take us to the far eastern edge, right here." Pierce pointed at a spot on the representation of the island. "From there we will set out toward the volcano's cone, here. Mapping as we go along. If we encounter enemy combatants, let my men take the lead."

Emma looked at CoCo and nodded. She would have to reach out to the reporter to cover their story. Waleed's eye glowed light purple as Emma shared with him the plan to bring Maggie Adams and her photographer to the island to record whatever happened on New Atlantis.

"All right. I need you fresh and ready for this. Meet back in an hour," Pierce said and walked out of the War Room.

"Rami, can you stay for a moment?" Josh asked. He, Emilio and CoCo stood next to the table.

"Sure. What's this about?" Rami asked. Emma stopped and looked at them.

"There's something you should all see," Josh said as the War Room door closed. "I installed secondary security surveillance that Pierce doesn't know about."

"That's a little creepy, bro," Emilio said and Josh shot him a look.

"After CoCo mentioned this morning that we hadn't

seen our scientist friends in a few days, I went back and reviewed the footage." Josh pulled up the footage on the computer and played it on the large monitor. "We've got a problem."

The five of them watched a man confront Nicola and Thierry in their lab.

"Who is that?" CoCo asked.

"Oh, I know him. That's the redheaded man from The Hastings Foundation. They've found us!" Rami said.

"Shit," CoCo hissed.

Emilio jumped over to the computer and paused the footage on the image of the man's face. "Mierda!"

"What?" Josh asked.

"Ay Dios! You've got to be kidding me!" Emilio slammed his hands against the table next to the computer. He unpaused the image, and the onscreen confrontation continued.

"Emilio! Calm down," CoCo said.

Onscreen, the man pulled a gun on the scientists. In the muted footage they saw Thierry charge the man and then fall to the ground as blood pooled around him.

"Oh no, not Thierry," Rami said.

"Shit," CoCo repeated, this time with horror and sadness. She covered her eyes with her hands. Next to her, Emma started crying.

"We have to assume that man took Nicola. So the question is, how did he get in the base and then out without tripping any alarms?" Josh asked.

"He's one crafty bastard," Emilio said.

Josh turned to him. "You know him too?"

"In the past, I've done some things I'm not necessarily proud of."

"You were a thief. We know," Josh said.

"Right. Well, I have been employed by this man before. I procured several items for him, or his benefactors, and not too long ago."

"What are you saying?" CoCo asked.

"I'm saying what you're all thinking. I have helped The Hastings Foundation get closer to their goals. Even though I didn't know who I was helping, I knew it was wrong." Emilio's shoulders slumped and misery clouded his face.

Everyone was silent for a moment.

"Look, we can either harp on past mistakes and let that take over our lives," Josh said. "Or we can do something about it and prevent them from reaching their goals."

They nodded.

"We have two possibilities. Either Pierce has no idea what is going on, or he does and he's playing both sides. Either way, we can't let our guard down," Josh said. "This is for Thierry."

"The Hastings Foundation will never stop. They will never stop until they get what they want," Rami said, panic ringing in his voice as he slid down the wall.

"Rami, it's going to be okay. You aren't alone. We are with you," CoCo said.

"Yeah, what's the worst that could happen?" Emilio added.

"Not helping," CoCo snapped.

"You guys!" Emma shouted in their minds.

"Not so loud!"

"Sorry. But we have to be as one here. Josh is right. We have to be careful with Pierce. For some reason, I can't read his mind. And now with Thierry killed and Nicola missing, we have to act fast and make sure that we do everything we can to stop them from winning," Emma said.

"I swear, if I see that redheaded man again," Emilio said.

"And if you do, you'll make sure he pays for what he did. But we'll do this, together," Rami said.

CHAPTER

59

22 August

Nicola gripped the rails of the inflatable boat and dropped her head. With each bump she dry-heaved a little more. She wiped her mouth and slid down the inside of the inflatable boat as they raced to the new island. Nicola thought about the strange forces that had brought this island into being. For a few moments it took her mind off her guilt over Thierry's death.

She was still wearing the same cornflower-blue scrubs from four days before, but they now splattered with dried blood. The redheaded man had refused to provide her with fresh clothes.

She had not seen her family since she and Thierry left The Hastings Foundation to seek out Base 47. Her heart ached for them and the knowledge they would never be able to understand what she had done. If Roger's device did what he claimed it could do, their lives would be destroyed. Her stomach retched again as seafoam sprayed her face.

A little after sunrise, the group from The Hastings Foundation came upon New Atlantis. They had taken a series of helicopters from Philadelphia and landed on a frigate about twenty miles from the island. With media scrutiny and governmental surveillance, they didn't dare land on the island in the frigate, so they set off for New Atlantis in inflatable boats. When forced to get in the boat she was grateful to be on a different one than her former colleague, Roger.

It felt like just yesterday Nicola had watched Thierry die. She could hardly wrap her head around the details. Her worry about what was next eclipsed worries about whys and hows. Somehow the heroes of Base 47 were being used by The Hastings Foundation. How did they infiltrate the heroes and who was the traitor there? And would her new friends at Base 47 even know that she was kidnapped and Thierry killed?

Absentmindedly, she reached into her pocket and discovered something unfamiliar. It was a folded-up piece of paper. How had that gotten there, she wondered. She looked down toward her pocket and saw Thierry's bloody handprint. He hadn't been comforting her at all. He had adroitly passed her a note. Instead of taking it out while surrounded by Roger's goons, she ran her fingers over it. She stared off at the island. All she could see was her very own Death Star.

Nicola estimated the eight boats held about twenty mercenaries who must have by hired by Hastings, plus her, Roger, and the technicians responsible for building the device. She inched closer to the edge of the boat and peered into the almost-black water. The crew was distracted with the virgin island. It would be so easy to just fall overboard. Without her help, they couldn't operate the machine. She could end this. She willed herself to slide out of the boat.

"Oh, no, you don't!" one of the mercs said. He grabbed Nicola by the neck of her scrubs and dragged her to the center of the boat. "Can't have you going overboard. We've a schedule to keep here. It's the dawn of a new day, lady. And, thanks to you, the Sentinel will rise." He looked her in the eye.

She cringed as he crept closer. He touched her face with his rough, sweaty hands. Nicola felt her anger rising and swallowed hard. The boat lurched and slowed, joining the other boats as they coasted toward the edge of the island. The merc radioed to the other boats.

"The lava has cooled significantly, so we should be able to walk on the surface with no problem," another merc said as he gazed at the island through binoculars. "Look here, there are even of flocks of birds on the island."

On another boat, Roger gazed off toward the rising island.

They were going to be the first humans to set foot upon a brand-new island.

"What a sight," one of the mercenaries said.

"Indeed," Roger replied.

"How often do you get to witness an undiscovered land?" the merc asked. Roger remained silent, simply staring at the pristine island on the horizon.

They reached the westernmost point of the island and secured the boats along the shoreline. Roger wiped his hands on his pants and walked over to the technicians to supervise the building of the device. Within a few hours they could set up the machine and then start the process that would transform the world.

Nicola steadied herself on the alien terrain and watched with a heavy heart as the mercenaries emptied the boats of the equipment. She looked at the barren and rocky island outcrop in the middle of the Atlantic Ocean not with amazement and wonder, but with soulful trepidation. She fully expected this inhospitable patch of barren earth in the middle of the ocean would be her final resting place. If I'm dead either way, maybe this is better, she thought.

Roger grabbed Nicola by the arm and dragged her away. "Come on, Dr. Patel. We've a world to wreck."

***

On the far eastern side of the island, a flash of light erupted and tiny, black globules grew into a circle connecting New Atlantis to Base 47. Out of the portal stepped Captain Pierce, cigar in mouth, along with the rest of his team.

Pierce breathed in the fresh island air, threw his cigar on the ground, and walked on the barren, rocky landscape.

"I didn't think it would be so large," Rami said.

It was beautiful in its stark nakedness.

"See, I told you that if you stuck with me I'd show you the world," Emilio said with a chuckle to CoCo, who quickly looked away.

Waleed was about to close the portal when he felt someone passing through. He looked back and smiled at the two unexpected tagalongs.

CHAPTER
60

22 August

"Goddamn it, Luli!" Captain Pierce shouted when he noticed her accompanying the group. "And Emma? What the hell? How did you both get here?" he asked as the girl poked her head out from behind Luli.

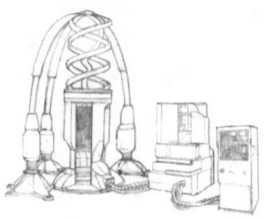

WaveMaker

"Waleed, get them back to Base 47 immediately." Pierce pointed to the two.

"No! I am not going anywhere," Luli said. She smoothed out the all-black uniform that hugged her very pregnant belly.

"The hell you aren't!" Pierce said. He rushed back toward her.

Instinctively, Luli put up her arms and Pierce bounced off the invisible force field.

James erupted in laughter.

"See. Nothing can hurt me. I am just fine." Luli smiled.

Pierce internally screamed as he got up and looked at Washington, who flanked his side.

"Whatever you may think, they'll still be an asset," Washington said into Pierce's ear. "Better to have them on our side than not."

"Fine. You can both stay. But the minute things get rough, you're out of here." Pierce was supposed to get Rami to the island and he'd done just that, but having the rest of the team there, especially the mind-reading child, complicated matters. Then again, maybe he could use this to his advantage.

"Besides, not only can I help here, I am also another pair of eyes to help watch out," Luli said.

"Watch out for what?" CoCo asked.

"Surely you don't believe that we're the only ones here, do you?" Rami asked.

"All right. Let's calm down. James, do a scout around the island. Be sure to keep yourself hidden in any case," Emilio said.

"Wait!" Pierce shouted before James could take off. They all looked at him.

"I'm in charge here. I give the orders." Pierce stared at Emilio. "James, recon the surroundings. If you see any outside forces on the island, do not engage. Be careful with the ground, it's uneven and craggy. Report back immediately."

"That's exactly what you just said, right?" CoCo giggled and Emilio winked back at her.

"Sure thing, Mr. Boss Man. BRB, as the kids say." Just like that, James was off. All they could see was a blur. When last timed, he was reaching a peak speed of three hundred miles per hour with a short start.

Emma took Rami's hand and smiled at him.

"I didn't think it was going to be so hot here. I mean the Texas desert is hot, but this ... this is ..." Lost for words,

Katrina wrapped her hair in a makeshift bun and used her hand to fan herself.

"It's hot as hell here," Etienne said, filling in the blank for her. He handed her a band for her hair. She looked at him for a moment, then accepted the band and put her hair up in a more secure bun. "I use bands on my wrists to prevent me from smoking."

"That work?"

"Haven't smoked in three years, so yeah." He smiled at her.

"'Come explore an island,' he says. 'It'll be fun,' he says. Where are the beaches?" CoCo complained.

"Well, technically beaches are formed from deposits of sediments and other materials brought from elsewhere. I would guess it would take about ten years," Waleed said, motioning with his hands the effects of the tides.

"Shut it down, nerd," CoCo said. Then, seeming to realize she had hurt his feelings, she added, "Sorry, I just get a little tense sometimes."

"It's okay. Sometimes I forget I'm no longer in a classroom," Waleed said. He checked the straps on his protective helmet. He was the only one wearing one, but he had told his teammates it made him feel better and safer.

A quick wind hit their faces and James was back and dripping wet head to toe. He did a quick spin and flung the water off his body completely.

"What happened?" CoCo asked.

"Who's here?" Rami asked, stepping closer to James.

"Looked like professional soldiers. Or maybe mercenaries. And scientists. About eight white coats and more than twenty soldier-types. They were putting together some sort of device on the far western side," James said. "About ten or so feet high, situated on some sort of tripod with a rotating center section. There are all sorts of wires connected to it. Definitely a bad thing."

"And the being all wet thing?" CoCo asked.

"Oh. Thought I could run on water. Didn't work. Wasn't fast enough. Big splash." James placed his hands on his knees and breathed deeply, trying to recover.

"Did anyone see you?" Pierce demanded.

"No. No one," James said.

Jiya stood next to him and put her hands on his chest. His breathing normalized. He gave her a quick smile and mouthed his thanks.

"This is bad. This is real bad," Rami said.

"Relax, Rami. Everything will be just fine," Luli said.

"Listen up. Here's what's going to happen now," Pierce said. "Waleed, you are going to get us closer, maybe a quarter mile southeast of their location."

"But there's really nowhere to hide. We have nothing to provide cover. Won't their mercenaries see us coming?" Waleed said.

"Not if we're invisible," Pierce said as he chomped on his cigar. "Etienne can you provide cover for us all?"

Etienne nodded and closed his eyes. One by one, the entire group became invisible. He had practiced so that those who he turned invisible could see the bends in the light where the others were.

"Then we'll separate and have the other group about three hundred yards northeast of the firefight. In case we need any support."

As Pierce gave the orders, Waleed opened up the portal to Pierce's desired location.

While the portal was open, Waleed created another one just behind it and crossed over once Pierce left in the first one. He winked at Emma and she smiled. He was getting their insurance policy.

"Make sure to put them a safe distance away," Emma said and he nodded.

Moments later, Waleed walked out of his portal and into the New York offices of Travel Now. As he looked around he saw an unattended craft services table full of snacks, veggies, and fruit. He grabbed a grilled chicken sandwich as Maggie Adams and her handy cameraman, Focus Jones, came toward him, both dressed in khakis.

"Waleed. We thought you might have forgotten us!" She grabbed her black bag and Focus pulled his gear together.

"Hurry up," he said. He looked around, saw no one, and opened a black portal next to him, all while quickly devouring his sandwich. He snagged three more sandwiches. "Let's go."

"And what happens on the other side?" Focus said as he suspiciously poked at the glowing black globules.

"You'll be safe. Out of the way, but near enough to record the action," Waleed said as he chewed with his mouth open.

They arrived seconds later.

"Whoa," Focus said, looking around at the alien-like island he had just arrived on.

"And put these on too, it will at least give you some protection," Waleed said as he handed them flak jackets and two helmets like his.

"Thanks," Maggie said, trying to decide if the potential danger warranted a helmet.

"Sorry, I have to get back. Be careful. If you need anything, just mentally shout at Emma." Waleed took another bite and walked through a newly generated portal.

He joined the rest of the team as they made their way through to the other side of the portal, where Pierce was surveying the situation. He munched one of the sandwiches and tossed two to James.

"It looks just like you reported, James. Now, does everyone remember the plan and their part in it?" Pierce asked. He turned around and frowned. "Where did you get those sandwiches?"

"Take a breath, sir. It's clear that Waleed needs to rest. He's been ferrying people back and forth. And he has to fuel himself for all the teleporting," Rami said.

"You try 'porting people and see if you aren't exhausted," Waleed added.

Pierce was about to press the issue when Josh stood in front of Waleed. Instead, he nodded.

"Five minutes. But when I finish with the briefing, we're gone," Pierce compromised. "Rami, you have to stop the device. It's likely the best way to destroy it is from the inside. CoCo will provide the distraction so James can get you close enough to the device so you can do whatever it is you are supposed to do to stop it. You told me you'll know what you have to do to prevent this machine from wreaking havoc across the hemisphere, and I'm banking on that being true. Josh will attack the mercenaries from the south, while Waleed takes Emilio and me to the north. Work together. You can do this."

"And what about me?" Luli asked, pushing her way into the planning circle.

"You stay behind," Pierce said.

"But you said that I could—" Luli protested.

"I know what I said, but I changed my mind," Pierce said as he towered over the small Chinese woman.

"Be careful, Captain. You know what happened last time I felt threatened," she said.

Pierce took three quick steps backward.

"All right you two. Enough. You are worse than my parents before they divorced," CoCo said as she came between the two of them.

"Let's keep going. There is some cover over beyond this ridge." Pierce put his cigar back in his mouth and led the way.

As they walked toward the protective ridge, Rami mentally spoke to Emma. In turn, she joined the team in her mind. Their bodies continued to march along with Pierce, but their minds were spirited back into the astral plane.

"Back to the dance floor again, huh?" CoCo said. She avoided looking in the mirrors completely.

"I'm scared and I don't know if I can do this," Rami said.

"Me too," Katrina said.

"That makes three," Luli said, touching her belly. "But we're doing this for more than just us."

The entire group looked at Rami. He said nothing.

"Rami?" Emma mentally brought him back to the group.

He nodded and seemed to summon and then share his own inner strength to give them all the courage they needed to finish their task.

"Look, life isn't worth living if there's no danger. But we've got each other. We can handle this," Emilio said.

"We don't really know what we're up against. But you've been training hard and we didn't get these powers for no reason. We must use everything Pierce taught us to win. At all costs," Rami said.

"I know some of you are skeptical of what Emma says about the voice and the prophecy, but she is the reason we've come together," Josh said. Etienne looked away. "I was too. But everything she has said has come true. We have a big job to do, and we each have our reasons for being here. We are the best shot Earth has. We cannot let The Hastings

Foundation succeed with their plan. It's not just our lives on the line, but millions of innocent people."

"Hold up," Pierce said. His voice shot through each of their minds, breaking their collective mental link. Their astral selves snapped back into their own bodies and they waited for the Green Beret to give them orders.

"We're here. This is the point of no return. We're playing for keeps. These guys are locked and loaded, and won't hesitate to use deadly force. Me and my guys will be the first line of defense as we break through their ranks. It is up to you to finish this. Destroy the device. Don't let them win," Pierce said.

He had given many such speeches and until now had felt confident of the outcome. With these newly powered people, his mind kept lowering the odds of success. He had to make sure that Rami got to where he needed to be. Above all, he had to fulfill that one demand.

"And what if we're hurt? How is Jiya supposed to take care of all of us?" Josh asked.

"You've got immediate first-aid kits inside your pouches. Use those first. We don't know how much it will take out of her to do any sort of mass healing, and I don't want her death on my hands," Pierce said.

"Emma, you have to be very careful. This all hinges on the voice you heard. We are putting everything in your hands," Waleed said.

"I'm not going to let you lot have all the fun," she said with a grin.

"I'm serious. This is not a safe place for you to be. There are mercenaries here on the island. Set to kill anyone who messes with the device," Waleed said.

Jiya took Emma's hand and brought her near. "Whatever you may do, child, you will do it here where we are protected."

Emma grudgingly agreed and walked toward a small wavy rock formation with the old Indian woman.

"I will protect you," Waleed said, and a sunny smile lit up her face as he walked to the rocky wall with them.

"So we just stay here and make sure that no one gets hurt? And if they do, we whisk them off?" James asked.

"That's what the captain said. I know that it may not be the most exciting thing—" Emilio said.

"No. It's perfect. I was a little nervous about getting into a fight once you said they had big guns," James said, looking down and stretching his quads.

"I'm sure you can outrun a bullet," Etienne teased.

"Easy for you to say since you can just let the bullets pass through you," James snapped.

"Guys. Some of us don't have a gift that will protect us from bullets, so that's why we have these uniforms to help us," Josh said. He felt the newly designed interwoven high-tech polymer that was advertised as able to resist bullets. Waleed did the same as he put his helmet back on.

"You aren't the only one worried, Josh," CoCo said. "We've just got to stick together and we'll be fine."

"All right. Let's get the Alpha team to this spot," Pierce said. He and Rami walked back to the group. Pierce pulled out the map and pointed to Waleed where they needed to go.

Once Waleed gathered up his strength, he opened a portal to bring the Alpha team to their desired location.

"Is everyone in place on the other side?" Josh asked.

"Yes. I got them all," Waleed said. He sat. "Just give me a moment."

"We don't have a lot of time here. For all we know that device could go off at any moment. We have to get a look at the area and form an attack plan," Pierce said. He and his troops readied themselves for the split mission.

Pierce wanted to say something, but before he could he heard a loud slap followed by what could only be described as metal grating on metal, a sound that no one should have to bear.

"What was that?" Josh asked. Like several of the group, he covered his ears.

"Only one way to find out," Waleed said. He opened a portal to the destination Pierce had requested. They made their way through the portal and came out near the western side of the island.

As they emerged, they saw the mercenaries hired by The Hastings Foundation. Every one of them was still clasping his hands to ears, although the grating metal sound was winding down.

Waleed gazed in wonder at the device, which appeared to be about twice as tall as the nearest men to it. A trio of spiral blades intertwined and connected at the top to three large arches anchoring the contraption to the ground. The blades were spinning, but slowing. As they crept to a halt, the grating metal sound finally died away.

"I think they tried to turn it on," Waleed said.

"Probably," Pierce agreed, looking around. There was little to block them from view. "We need cover. Now!"

The team scattered and found some refuge behind a craggy formation.

"All right, time is of the essence. Remember the plan. Don't get shot and remember to work together. That will be the difference. These opponents are well-trained. And armed. They will not hesitate to use lethal force on us. So we have to surprise them. Use their weapons and tactics against them. We have the element of surprise and the fact that each of you can do wondrous things," Pierce said. He thought it was the most inspiring he had ever been.

Before they could start the battle, each of the empowered people heard an unfamiliar voice in their heads.

As the children gather together
They must act as one in order
For The Sentinel to emerge
And restore the planet.
If they hesitate, the world will
Perish in the flood
Racing from here to the ends of the earth.

CHAPTER
61

22 August

Luli gritted her teeth in equal parts pain and dismay and excitement, her left arm automatically reaching down to her bulging belly. As she did so, she looked at the time on her watch. She had been in early labor for several hours, feeling intermittent light contractions, and had expected that to continue for weeks. After all, her son wasn't due for another month.

But this latest contraction told her something she didn't want to believe just now. Her daughter, Sying, had been born four years ago, but Luli still remembered much of the delivery very clearly. The contraction she'd just felt told the first lines of the story of active labor.

Was she really going to have this precious boy on this inhospitable patch of rock, without Yi by her side? No hospital? No epidural? No bed? She badly wanted to ask Waleed to teleport her back to the hospital. But she didn't dare. He needed to rest up in case he had to teleport to help the team complete the mission.

She was stuck here.

This couldn't be happening. Could the teleportation have

stimulated the early labor to progress? Or had she just been too optimistic about the state of her labor and her ability to help? She so badly wanted to help. But she wouldn't be in full control of her body for quite some time. How could she deliver her baby without Yi? Her heart ached that he would miss this most precious moment of his life.

She was stuck here. Even worse, this delivery might put everyone in danger. Sooner or later, she'd scream with the baby's coming, and any bad guys around would be able to home in on the campsite.

Luli closed her eyes and sent a message to her unborn son, asking him to wait just a while longer, to stay in early labor until she could find a place more suitable for the hard work of childbirth. This place was nothing but rocks.

She grimaced, thinking Pierce had been right to want to leave her back at Base 47. At least Jiya was here. She decided to wait for the next contraction to pass before alerting the healer to the coming baby. She watched her watch and waited. It wasn't long, but it brought with it the news of her water breaking. Again, she wished she'd dared ask Waleed to take her to a hospital, the one about a mile from her house, where Yi would be able to join her.

Luli struggled to stand, then slowly started to approach Jiya and Emma, who had remained at this camp as part of the support team. Waleed, who had stayed behind to protect the communications and healing functions of the team, was nearby. The rest of the team was on the other side of the island, preparing for battle. It was silent at this camp. They were far enough inland they could smell the ocean but not hear it crashing on the shore.

The campsite itself sheltered under one large, dark tent erected on arrival by Waleed, to better blend in with the dark rock. In one corner, the team had heaped standard first-aid supplies, so as to not trouble Jiya with minor injuries. Also, they had brought a pair of five-gallon water bottles for drinking and cleansing wounds, a number of blankets for any wounded to lie down on, and a milk crate full of high-calorie snacks plus some ready-to-eat meals that Pierce had insisted on bringing.

Emma sat on one of the blankets in the middle of the camp. She wore a look of intense concentration as Waleed stood sentry at one of the camp's corners, peering through binoculars as he munched his way through three granola bars.

Luli reached the old healer, who was sitting near Waleed's corner.

"Jiya, my time has come," Luli said.

Jiya's face broke out in a delighted grin before she remembered where they were.

"Relax, child. I will help. You must walk and move around as much as you can as long as you can. I will have the others prepare a spot for you for when it is time to push." Jiya gently rubbed the young woman's shoulders. She looked around the camp before speaking again. "Waleed? Please make a comfortable place for Luli. We will witness a miracle today."

This last statement finally penetrated Emma's deep concentration. She looked up at Jiya and Luli. "It's coming? Soon?"

"How far apart are the contractions?" Jiya asked.

Luli reflexively looked at her delicate gold Seiko again, though she didn't really need to. "Just under two minutes."

Jiya smiled gently. "Soon. Most likely," she told Emma. "Tell Washington to tell Captain Pierce."

The child did as bid. For a moment all over the island, Emma's mental connection snapped out of the minds of all the team but Washington. Emma told him Luli had begun labor but they didn't know how quickly it would happen. There was a pause, and Emma could hear him relaying the development to Pierce.

"Damn it," Pierce growled through Washington's walkie-talkie. He sounded furious. "Of course she did, stubborn damn woman. And we can't push Waleed to take her back to the base or a hospital. He's got to be ready for us. So she stays put. Tell Emma to keep us posted. Tell no one else that she's in labor."

"But why—" Emma started to ask, but Washington didn't bother repeating the question to Pierce. Instead, he answered her.

"It's a soft spot. A weakness. If our opponents find out about Luli, they might attack the camp."

Frowning, Emma mentally reconnected with all the team. Having Washington as a go-between to Pierce certainly slowed things down.

Luli relaxed under Jiya's direction. The old Indian woman was unobtrusive and unassuming, which made the quiet authority she took on as a healer that much more forceful.

"Jiya, it is going very fast. The contractions are quickening. My baby wants out now."

"We really should have you in a hospital. But your son will have a worthy birth story," the old woman said, gently guiding to Luli to the blankets Waleed had laid out for her.

Emma felt a wave of uneasiness and looked around. She could see four mercenaries approaching from the south, guns raised. A moment later, Emma relayed the imminent attack on the small camp to the whole group.

"Four men are closing in on the camp. They have guns," she broadcast to the team. There was a pause as Washington relayed this to Pierce, whose words Emma again heard via the walkie-talkie and broadcast to the team at large. Washington felt a weird echo as he heard Pierce's words both in the walkie and repeated moments later in Emma's Irish lilt in his head.

"Dammit, that's why I didn't want everyone here on this island. We can't spare any of Team Alpha to help you there. Waleed's going to have to protect everyone there. All at the camp, complete silence. Waleed, take the enemy down, but watch out for their guns," Pierce directed back, via Washington and Emma.

Luli strove for silence as her body continued preparing for the delivery. Jiya hugged her, rocking and soothing. "Shhhh, child."

Emma watched the four mercenaries silently approach the camp.

Waleed tried an experimental portal to get the mercenaries off the island. Instead of the black globules that heralded the appearance of his portals, there was only a slight black pop. He hadn't fully recovered from the last teleport. Gathering his courage, he fastened the chin strap to his helmet. He looked back at Luli, who was tightly gripping the ground as another contraction washed over her.

"All right, next idea," Waleed said. "Emma," he thought, "keep close to Luli and Jiya. I don't know how much I can do against them, still so weak. But I won't let them get near."

"Waleed!" Emma cried out in her head. "You can't face them on your own."

"I have to. It's my duty." His voice was full of resolve. He focused on opening a portal directly underneath one of the would-be attackers. The portal opened and the first mercenary fell through and came out on the far north side of the island. Waleed smiled, one down.

The other three mercenaries let out a barrage of bullets overhead, probably in hopes it would spook their targets into a hasty mistake. Waleed buried his body as close to the ground as he could get. Once the guns stopped shooting he could hear a deafening silence.

Waleed tightened his hands into fists and looked out again. He manifested a small portal near his right hand and the other end opened up next to the face of one of the mercenaries. He quickly jabbed through his portal, making contact with the merc's face. Laughing, he quickly closed the portal. He opened another and grabbed one of the guns and pulled it back.

Now Waleed was armed.

He panicked.

He had never fired a gun before, having sat out of the group's gun-training sessions as a conscientious protestor.

Waleed heard Luli groan as another contraction began. They were getting closer. He swallowed hard and opened a portal. He ran through it, emerging a few feet away from the remaining attackers.

They seemed surprised to see Waleed in front of them, especially the one in the middle, who was now weaponless.

"What did you do to him?" the mercenary on the left asked, lifting the gun and aiming at Waleed a bit to underscore the question.

"Who?" Waleed played dumb.

The mercenary said nothing, only glared.

Waleed shrugged.

The shorter one on the right continued glaring at Waleed, changed his aim, and fired his gun toward the camp. The sound was shockingly loud. The crack of the gunfire reverberated off the rock and echoed across the island. Pierce would not need to get this news secondhand from

Emma; he would have heard it.

The shot missed the camp entirely, but the boom scared a shriek out of Luli and broke Emma's composed concentration.

"Kill him," the shorter man shouted, pointing at Waleed.

The taller man took deliberate aim at Waleed's chest and prepared to fire. Waleed opened a tall portal in front of him as they fired. To the side of the mercenaries, the exit portal opened. They all went down, victims of their own gunfire.

As Waleed moved away from them, he heard Emma shout at him to turn around.

Horrified, Waleed heard one last crack of gunfire as a bullet ripped through the side of his neck. Blood gushed out immediately and he fell to the ground.

CHAPTER
62

22 August

"Hi, boys," CoCo said, adding extra wriggle to her walk.

The boys in question weren't boys. They were mercenaries. And they were mesmerized. If she were still stripping, they'd be shelling out cash left, right, and

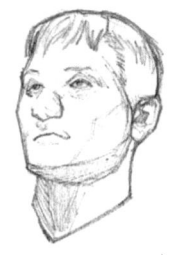

Dmitri Toumanoff

center, she thought. As she captured the mercenaries in her illusion, she spotted Dr. Patel. The scientist looked miserable and scared. A few feet away stood the redheaded man with his weapon drawn on the scientist.

"Emma, can you link Emilio and Josh to me?" CoCo asked. Emma did so, and CoCo continued. "Dr. Patel is here, along with that redheaded man."

"That son of a bitch!" Emilio said.

"Emilio. Calm down. We have to play this smart," CoCo said. "We will avenge Thierry."

"Yeah, but this is personal," Emilio said.

CoCo widened her smile. Aloud, she said to the mercenaries, "And here I thought I was all alone on this big island. I was getting lonely. But maybe one of you could keep me company?"

As if they had no control over their bodies anymore, in unison about twenty men with guns stepped forward. They stood in a ring around the civilian scientists, and despite their obvious interest in her, they maintained the circle.

Emma reached out mentally to Dr. Patel and urged her to remain calm. "Dr. Patel, we are all here. We are going to stop the Ascendancy from unleashing the WaveMaker."

"You better do something fast. I don't know how much longer before it's operational," Nicola thought back to the little girl.

***

"Oh my," CoCo said. "How will I ever choose?"

Everyone was watching, which was crucial for the plan's success, although not all of them were mercenaries. Dr. Patel looked miserable. CoCo made a big show of smiling at the mercenaries. As they focused on the illusionary CoCo flaunting her goods in the center of the circle, the real CoCo was cautiously emptying their gun cartridges.

"Emma," she thought, "I'm disabling their weapons while they're trapped in my illusion. There are a lot of lab techs too and about twenty mercenaries. I'm looking at them now. Do you see?" Emma said she did, and CoCo continued. "Keep our mental channel open."

About three hundred feet away, under the cover of rocky outcrop, an intrepid reporter and her fearless cameraman captured the intense opening gambit between the powered champions of Base 47 and their opponents.

"Focus, are you getting all of this?" Maggie asked as she tried to peer through the viewfinder.

"Maggie, I'm getting it. You need to back up. Stay hidden,"

Focus said as he watched a woman relieving mercenary after mercenary of his ammunition with no notice. On their trip to Base 47 he had seen them use their powers in practice, but this was an altogether different experience.

"Maggie, isn't that CoCo?" Focus said as he pointed to the brunette girl in full combat gear. "What is she doing?"

"I'm not worried about her. She'll be fine. It's the bad guys who should be worried," Maggie said as she leaned on Focus' shoulder.

***

Rami made his way toward the device. Every step closer made him more anxious. He crept along the rocky island, unaware that he was being followed.

"That's about far enough," the man said.

Rami froze in his tracks. He slowly turned and saw a lone opponent holding a gun at his chest.

"Look. You don't have to do this."

"But I do. I know who you are," he said as he inched closer.

"Then you must know that I can't let you stop me," Rami said as he took two steps toward the mercenary, putting him off balance. Rami jumped the mercenary and took him to the ground. He lost his grip on the gun and it clattered away. They rolled on the rocks and Rami pinned the mercenary down.

"Don't need a gun to stop you," the merc said as he pulled a six-inch serrated knife out. "And it's going to hurt."

The merc swung wildly, slashing Rami across the face.

"That was a mistake," Rami said.

"What?" The mercenary stared with disbelief as his opponent's wounds healed in moments.

"Yeah, it's time for this to be over." Rami head-butted

the merc unconscious. "I've got a device to disable. I just wish I knew how."

He tried to clear his mind as he considered the towering machine in front of him, but deep dread lingered inside.

***

To the first mercenary, CoCo said, "Do you believe in love at first sight?"

"I didn't until now," he said.

To the second, she said, "Who's your dream girl?"

"You are," the second mercenary said softly.

To the third, she said, "How do you like this?"

His blush said it all. In his mind, she was slipping off her négligée.

CoCo saw that Josh was finally in position, but couldn't tell if Emilio, Captain Pierce, and Washington were in place yet.

A few moments later, she heard Emma in her head. "Everyone's in place. Captain Pierce says Josh and Katrina should begin the attack now. CoCo, keep them distracted as long as you can."

CoCo smiled coyly at the three men. "I'm having a hard time choosing just one of you handsome boys. What's a girl to do?"

"Pick me," one of them called out.

"I bet you could make any date interesting, even here on this pile of rocks," CoCo said to one. He beamed and started to step forward to claim his prize. But CoCo wasn't done. To another, she said, "What about you? Can you make my dreams come true?"

Stealthily, Josh and Katrina crept up on the mercenaries from behind. Josh, fighting specialist that he was from his action movies, had knocked six others unconscious while

Katrina watched. None of the mercenaries were able to break away from CoCo's mesmerizing illusion.

"That's just about enough!" a voice boomed as lightning struck near the mercenaries, shocking them out of the illusion.

The group of super-powered fiends appeared on the horizon, floating in the air as the winds whipped around them.

"Should have known they'd turn up again," Josh said to Katrina when he spotted their foes. He addressed the fiends. "There's no chance you will defeat us this time. You're outnumbered and outclassed."

"That's so cute. You think you're going to win. We'll mop the floor with your little friends. Again," the pyrokinetic said as she launched several fireballs their direction. Josh and Katrina scattered away from the flames.

The lab techs started screaming once they realized their group was under attack. They were in the middle, like the bull's-eye on a dart board. Around the scientists were the mercenaries, and around them a crazy fighting force that seemed to have come out of nowhere.

Captain Pierce, Washington, and Emilio emerged from their hiding spot to join in the fray.

Apparently deciding it was best if downed mercenaries stayed down, Katrina set to work psychokinetically handcuffing their wrists and ankles with plastic zip ties, which she had begun carrying in bulk following one of weirder training sessions they'd had back at Base 47. Satisfied with her work, she mentally flung their fallen weapons beyond the battle zone into the depths of the Atlantic.

Out of the corner of her eye, she saw Maru, the weather manipulator, creating water spouts over the ocean. "Don't want to fight that crazy tornado guy again," she said as the guns splashed into the ocean.

"Maru, if you please!" a cocky brown-haired guy shouted as Maru reached to the sky and brought down several lightning strikes.

"My turn," he said as he grabbed the lightning and fashioned an electrical shield around him. He looked toward the scattered Base 47 heroes and decided to use his powers to pick them off, one by one, starting with the cowering girl to his left. He held a bolt in his hands and threw it at her. It hit her psychokinetic shield and splintered into a thousand harmless sparks.

The shield had protected Katrina, but for how long?

CoCo studied the fight, trying to decide how to best help. She turned her attention to the girl with magnetic powers. "You can't fight what you can't touch!" CoCo shouted as she landed a punch in the girl's stomach, knocking her to the ground. Wildly, the fallen girl sent magnetic waves out in hopes of hitting her unseen attacker, but in her mind she was trapped in an illusion that she was strapped to a tree and being whipped by her parents.

"Oh please, the nuns were far rougher on me than you could ever be!" She laughed as she saw through the illusion. She grabbed several metal containers near the device and threw them toward CoCo.

"Gotta watch out for her powers, could get real nasty, real quick," CoCo said as she crept behind the girl and put her in a chokehold. "Have to get her out of the fight. With her power to control metal, I don't want her to wreck the island, the device, or worse," CoCo muttered as she squeezed hard enough to make the ferrokinetic girl pass out.

Emilio used his luck to sneak in and throw some punches on the hyperkinetic Ukrainian without getting hit back in turn.

"Lucky shots, *ese*. Want to try your luck on me?" the Ukrainian said as he jumped in front of Emilio.

"And who, exactly are you supposed to be?" Emilio asked as he eyed the newcomer.

"Not just your match, but your better," the man said with a laugh as he threw a right hook. Emilio easily dodged it.

"If that's the best you can do," Emilio taunted.

"Oh no, you've yet to see my best," he replied as he flung his elbow back and landed it in Emilio's solar plexus, leaving him breathless and stunned.

The captain set about efficiently neutralizing his targets. He was near seventy and the mercenaries all looked to be in their twenties, but there was something to be said for a lifetime of experience. Pierce settled into a rhythm of knocking heads about.

"What are you doing here?" Josh asked as he ran toward the green energy-wielding girl.

"What I have to do. To stop you," she replied.

"Do you even know what's going on?" Josh asked as he dodged her blasts. "What they hope to do with this machine?"

She fired in quick succession three beams of green energy that pushed him back toward the water.

"What do they have over you? I can tell your heart isn't in this," Josh said as she stood over him.

"I owe them my life. Everything. I would be dead without them," she said, struggling to maintain her composure.

"Are you so sure? I've seen some bad things before, and I don't see that in you," Josh said as green energy crackled around her hands. "You don't have to do this."

"Yes. Yes, I do," she said as she unleashed a full blast at Josh. After the energy dissipated she saw there was no body.

She dropped to the ground in teary shock.

Etienne appeared out of nowhere into the fight and followed Emilio's lead. He threw punches at the mercenaries. Not a one was able to land a hit on Etienne. A few came close, but he phased out to avoid getting hit.

One of the mercenaries, facing imminent defeat, leveled the gun and fired three times at Etienne.

He missed, but those gunshots changed everything. Every mercenary still standing—there were still about a dozen upright—moved from nonlethal to lethal force. Their guns were no longer simple intimidation.

Pierce signaled to Washington to use extreme force. They had to thin the ranks to gain the advantage.

"Not going to let us get our asses handed to us without a fighting chance," Washington said as he cocked his gun and took aim.

With fresh enthusiasm, Pierce did what he was trained to do. Before the mercenaries realized he even had a gun, Pierce had mowed down five. Washington, too, was shooting. He managed to injure three, and there were four left. One was aiming straight at CoCo.

CHAPTER
63

22 August

Waleed cupped his hand over his neck in a futile attempt to minimize the blood loss. He was too weak to stand and too weak to teleport. He called out to Emma, who was already racing out toward him.

"Waleed!" she screamed as she knelt beside him. She held him in her arms and cried.

Jiya could help Waleed, but he was too heavy for Emma to carry and Jiya couldn't leave Luli alone to help her carry him.

"We have to get you out of here," she whispered through tears. Waleed blinked his eyes in agreement. Emma could feel him struggle to produce a portal below them. Finally, they fell through and emerged only a few feet from Jiya and Luli.

"That was real good, Waleed," Emma whispered.

With that last teleport, Waleed passed out.

"Jiya, please, you have to come help Waleed."

"What happened?" Luli asked through deep breaths.

"It's my fault. Waleed was shot. It's bad. Jiya, you have to help him," Emma said. Her hands were covered in blood and her face streaked with tears.

Jiya, carrying blankets, approached them and took control.

"Emma, spread these blankets for Waleed. Then help Luli with her delivery. I will take care of him," Jiya said. "And wash your hands."

Emma did as bid, and helped move her friend onto the blankets. At the jostling, more blood spilled from Waleed's neck. "Waleed, you did great. You saved us." Emma patted the injured man's shoulder. "I'm so sorry I couldn't keep you from getting shot. I'm so sorry." Emma reached into Jiya's bag and pulled out a water bottle and sanitizer. She rinsed her hands and applied the sanitizer. She turned to find Luli.

Jiya knelt next to Waleed and looked him over, assessing the damage and composing her thoughts. She closed her eyes a moment and held her hands over the gunshot wound while murmuring encouragement to Waleed. There was tremendous damage. As the old woman held her hands over his wound, the damage receded, repairing itself.

Luli moaned as Emma approached.

"Tell her to start pushing," Jiya called out to Emma.

She knelt next to the pregnant woman's shoulder and spoke softly to her. "Jiya says it's time to push. Can you do that?"

Luli nodded. Sweat drenched her face. Emma wiped Luli's face with the sleeve of her uniform. "Just let me know what you need from me."

She nodded again, grimacing with effort. She made little noise, although the need for silence had long passed.

Jiya looked at her hands and saw that the pale orange glow that indicated healing energy hard at work had turned a deeper and brighter shade.

She could see into Waleed's neck, and she watched in

fascination as the carotid artery knit itself back together under her healing touch. Next, the muscle put itself back together, and then the protective skin. Jiya groaned when she felt a twinge in her withered leg, but kept her healing focus on the man under her hands.

Jiya barely reacted when Luli began screaming in earnest.

"Finish helping Luli, now is her time," Jiya said over the young woman's screams. "I will be able to save Waleed. The most delicate and difficult work is done."

Emma heard the relief and satisfaction in the old Indian woman's voice, but also exhaustion and perhaps pain. She saw the baby was emerging from Luli's body. Trembling and a bit grossed out, she reached down to help pull the baby the rest of the way.

Luli shrieked as her body shuddered and relaxed. She moaned with relief and smiled wanly. She opened her mouth to speak, but nothing came out. She cleared her mouth and tried again.

"How's my baby?"

"Ew. He's covered in stuff. I need to find a towel or something to clean him up with," Emma said. She grabbed a blanket and was about to wipe down the boy's body when she found herself knocked on her butt but still holding the child. "Ow!"

"What?"

Emma studied the baby for a moment until understanding set in. "I just got force fielded!" Curiously and cautiously, she tried to bring the blanket closer to the baby. When her hand was a few inches away from him, her hand stopped, as if bumping up against a glass wall. She shrugged. "Um, Luli, you're going to have to do the honors." Emma stood and handed both the blanket and the newborn to the mother.

Emma watched a moment as Luli cradled her infant, then poured water over her hands again.

"Emma, have Washington tell Captain Pierce that Luli has given birth to a little boy." Jiya paused before adding, "Also, tell him that I was able to save Waleed."

Jiya lifted herself from the healing pose and struggled to stand. Emma thought she looked tired and weak.

Waleed sat up, rubbing the spot on the left side of his neck where a bullet had pierced him. Nothing hurt there.

"Jiya, I can't believe you did it," Waleed said, grinning widely. "Thank you."

Jiya wobbled on her weak polio-damaged leg and collapsed.

CHAPTER
6 4

22 August

Nicola looked, shock etched into her dark face, as the firefight between the Mods and the mercenaries waged beside her. She hoped the Base 47 heroes could stop the armed men and also help her stop the doomsday weapon that would ravage the coastlines of the Americas and Europe by creating a tsunami.

The lab techs were hard at work constructing the twelve-by-six-foot WaveMaker. The checked the platform to ensure it would raise and lower properly. Nicola saw another lab tech installing the helix matrix at the bottom of the WaveMaker. The only missing piece was the specially formulated DNA-infused liquid that would make it run. Nicola had tried every way she knew to slow the process despite Roger's dogged monitoring and the gun-wielding redhead man's glare.

Nicola tinkered with a few levers and sensors on the control board. Roger scrutinized her every move.

"Keep at it. We must not be deterred from our goal," Roger barked at Nicola from under a makeshift barrier of boxed crates.

"Not my goal, you murderous bastard," Nicola growled as she shifted in her shoes. "You are as responsible for Thierry's death as he is." She pointed to the redheaded man, who leaned against a large crate smoking. She saw Roger take a moment. "You didn't know. It's not too late to stop this. You don't have to go through this."

"There are forces at play here, Nicola, that you have no idea about. And, as for Thierry, he made his choice. Look where it got him. Use this time to complete the task at hand. And don't get any clever ideas. I'll be watching you closely." Roger towered over her. "Get back to work."

While she knew that there was little possibility to stop the device, she still thought furiously about ways that it might be done. The heat from the tropical island sent sweat beading down her face. She wiped her brow with a dirty beige scarf. Then the inconceivable happened. The inside of her skull seemed to vibrate, and she heard a voice inside her head.

"It's Emma, again. Sorry I had to break off earlier. We're going to help you," Emma said in Nicola's mind.

"Oh thank God," she said, half out loud, half to herself. Nicola had feared she would have to stop Roger by herself, even after she saw the heroes arrive. "I was worried when I couldn't hear you anymore."

"It's okay. I will help you stop the device," Emma said.

"I am trying to do that. It's difficult since the others are watching my every move," Nicola said. "You have to know that we were taken and Thierry—" Her mind locked on the image of Thierry bleeding in the lab and she closed her eyes hard and shook her head.

"I know. We know what happened. Everything will be okay. We have to stop the WaveMaker from coming online," Emma thought to Nicola.

The novelty of mentally talking to someone momentarily stopped Nicola from thinking about the death of Thierry and her guilt over her unwitting part in the deaths of so many.

Under Nicola's hands, the second light on the control board turned green, accompanied by a click and a whir as the pistons and rotators in the WaveMaker roared to life.

"We have six or seven minutes to stop it before the third light turns green and the WaveMaker comes online," Nicola thought to Emma. "Once that happens, it will be fully powered except for the outside energy source, which is Rami."

In hours, the coasts of America and Europe would be irrevocably altered if they couldn't stop the machine from being activated.

Nicola felt in her pockets. Her fingers located the folded-up piece of paper. She stealthily took it out and read it. Thank you, Thierry, she thought as she looked over at the island. Even though he was not here, Thierry was still looking out for her. She put the paper back into her pocket and dashed toward the machine. She knew what she had to do. A tech stretched out his hand to grab her.

"Get back here," the tech shouted.

"If you want the machine to explode, by all means stop me," Nicola said. She gave the tech a knowing look. "We have to make sure that the isotope is properly replaced. Otherwise, the pneumatic blast won't be directed outward but inward. Meaning that they will be picking the pieces of your brain off the ground for months."

The tech stood his ground.

"Before we can hit the ignition, we have to recalibrate the intake. Otherwise, big bang, you're dead," Nicola said to the tech.

The tech released her and she stumbled toward the

device. She took one of the circuit boards out of the device and quickly rearranged the wires.

Roger spotted this and yelled at the redheaded man to stop her.

The redheaded man ran toward Nicola. "Just what do you think you're doing?" He raised his gun at the scientist.

CHAPTER

65

22 August

Emilio only had moments to react when he saw the mercenary shoot at CoCo. He jumped up and ran past the hail of gunfire in an attempt to push her out of the way of the bullets. She turned to him and smiled. But before she

Ericka Zavatsky

could move, she saw out of the corner of her eye one of the mercenaries aim for them. She paused for a moment and then three bullets ripped through her chest.

Emilio screamed as CoCo fell to the ground in a bloody heap. He crouched over her. Then, out of nowhere, CoCo appeared at his side.

"What's wrong, sugah? Looks like you've seen a ghost!" She laughed and planted a kiss on his lips.

"But ... how? I just saw you—" Emilio stammered.

"Misdirection, my dear Emilio." She laughed and ran toward the mercenary who had shot her illusion. She slammed him to the ground.

"That woman." Emilio grabbed his chest and blew a kiss to her.

"Get up, Romeo. We've got work to do!" Pierce shouted. He threw Emilio a gun.

"Thanks, Pierce, but guns really aren't my style," Emilio said, tossing the gun back to the captain and charging at one of the mercenaries. The foe tried to fire the gun and Emilio's probability field swept over him. The gun misfired, blowing up in the unfortunate man's hands. Emilio looked back at Pierce and winked.

"Then take care of your powered opponents." Pierce shook his head and rolled his eyes at Emilio. He took aim at the mercenaries guarding the techs near the device and let loose a spray of bullets.

Washington stood back-to-back with Pierce and covered him as they tried to reduce the threat the mercenaries presented.

***

Timothy strode toward the crouched girl near the beach, throwing bolts of electricity at her.

"Can't stay tucked inside that force field all that long, girlie," he said as he edged near her.

"You're right, I can't stay tucked in here," she said as she looked in his eyes. "I just needed to get you closer."

"For what?"

"For this!" She dropped her field and psychokinetically grabbed his neck and squeezed. He lay there convulsing, grasping at the unseen hands throttling his throat.

"I don't know who you are, but your little sparks can't compare to me. You may be a firecracker, but I'm an atom bomb," Katrina said as she lorded over the fallen Timothy, eyes full of rage. She gritted her teeth and clenched her hands. At last, she released her psychokinetic hold on his neck and walked away, leaving him coughing but alive.

***

"What happened?" Josh said as he rested against the lapping water.

"You were about to be toast and I sped through and saved you," James said, smiling.

"That girl must be hysterical now."

"Well, Hollywood, she's something all right. Really tore up that she vaporized you."

"Except she clearly didn't," Josh said as he stood up next to the Kenyan. "I want you to take her out of the battle and get her with Jiya and Emma. She's not like them. She needs to be saved," Josh said.

"She thinks she killed you. I'm not sure sending her to Jiya and Emma is the best idea," James said.

"Fine. Then form a vortex around her to get her to pass out. Don't want her in harm's way."

James reluctantly agreed. "Whatever you say, Hollywood. I'll take care of ..." The rest of his words were lost to Josh as the speedster sprinted away. Josh mentally called out to Emma, letting her know that the next phase of the plan was ready to begin. He cracked his knuckles and twisted his neck from side to side.

"Here goes everything."

***

"Round two. You ready?" CoCo asked as she walked calmly toward the pyrokinetic.

"It's going to end with your ass on the ground, so why not?" Taneesha sneered as flames danced in her hands. "And I'm prepared for your mind games. You won't get to me."

"We'll see about that," CoCo said as she charged her.

"You'll have to do better than that!" Taneesha shouted

as her flames shot clear through CoCo. "What?"

"Thought you said you were prepared for me. Guess not!" CoCo said as ten of her surrounded her opponent. "You call yourself The Flame? How appropriate, since you're about to be smothered!"

Taneesha struggled to sort out which was the real CoCo. She shot flames out in all directions. Each CoCo came out unscathed.

"Where are you?" The Flame shouted as she frantically backed up. She tripped and fell. From nowhere, dozens of rocks seemed to collapse on her, burying her. She screamed and writhed but no one could hear her.

"That illusion ought to hold her for a while," CoCo said. She smiled as she ran toward the group.

***

Maru glided next to Timothy to check on him.

"Just underestimated the girl. Now I'm out of juice," Timothy said as he struggled to stand, still coughing. Maru looked over his shoulder and saw the girl in question.

"I'm coming for you now!" the weather manipulator said. The skies darkened and lightning began crashing on the island. Katrina screamed and tried to dodge the lightning. Etienne heard her, turned invisible, and ran toward her. As he neared her, the hairs on his neck stood on end. Lightning was about to strike them. Etienne solidified his arm and pushed Katrina out of the way as the lightning bolt hit him directly.

"Shhhh!" Etienne yelled as his body surged with electricity. As he fell to the ground, the fiend who had summoned the lightning floated over him.

"Now that is a direct hit! You're sunk," he crowed as Etienne's body shook. As the electricity coursed through him, Etienne alternated between being visible and not, being tangible and not.

Katrina saw her crush, the guy who saved her, suffering and convulsing. She screamed, and used her psychokinetic powers to squeeze the culprit.

"What the hell?" Maru said as he struggled to free himself from the unseen force holding him.

"Not hell. It's me," she shouted as anger swept across her face. She pushed her hands together, squeezing him further.

Maru whipped the winds into a frenzy, but they just bounced off her psychokinetic shield.

"Hope you can swim, you son of a bitch!" she said as she launched him in the sky toward the open water. As he screamed, she knelt down next to an unconscious Etienne. She didn't notice the Ukrainian sneaking up on her.

"How sweet, found your soft spot!" he said as he launched himself on her.

"Get away!" Katrina said as she tried to force the bad guy off of her.

"Don't think so, girlie! Dmitri wants a fight," he said as he swung wildly, hitting her across the face. She dropped to the ground. Her eyes raged and the loose rocks on the ground began to shake.

"I'll take care of him," James said as he rushed to her side. "Don't think you'll like this," he said as he grabbed him and raced around in circles, then used his momentum to launch the Ukrainian about forty feet in the air. James quickly caught him as the Ukrainian struggled to focus.

"You are one very lucky guy. Now, can I trust you to be good?" James asked. Since the villain could barely put two syllables together James was almost satisfied. "But just to make sure…" He speed-punched the Ukrainian until he passed out. James looked around and darted off.

***

"For a group that just came together a few weeks ago, they fight well together," Focus said. Both he and Maggie were flat to the ground, using the craggy rocks as cover. "So the other powered people they are fighting, they must be a part of the evil prophecy group?"

"That's the prevailing thought."

"Is there any specific angle you want?" Focus asked as he glanced at her.

"Just get it all," Maggie said. She rose up a bit to check on the fight.

"That's far enough," a voice called out behind her. "Stand up, both of you, and put the camera down."

The end of a machine gun tapped against Maggie's back. She looked toward the heroes, all engaged in their own combat, then at her cameraman. Slowly, she said, "Focus, do as he says." Just as they were about to put down their equipment, the mercenary fell to the ground, spraying them with his blood. Maggie screamed in revulsion and looked around. She saw Captain Pierce firing off shots and the former soldier standing next to him nod and smile.

***

"I may have gotten smacked around, but I can certainly handle a goth chick like you any day," Taneesha said as she shot flames out of her hands toward Katrina.

"Think again!" Katrina said as she lifted a psychokinetic shield around her and the fallen Etienne. "Come on, Etienne, come on. You've got to come out of this."

"I can do this all day. Can you?" she yelled as the flames smothered Katrina's shield. "Eventually you'll have to come out for air."

The odious Mod was right. There was only so much

oxygen left in there and Etienne seemed severely injured. Katrina screamed, letting out a concussive psychokinetic blast that knocked The Flame to the ground.

"Looks like you got smacked down again." Katrina laughed. "Not bad for a goth chick."

***

One of the fallen mercenaries had come to. He located a utility knife in the uniform of one of his fellow mercs. Within minutes, he had severed the zip ties holding not just himself but all of his fallen comrades. As they regained consciousness, they returned to the fight, even if they did so without their high-powered weapons. It was now a battle on two fronts, one with the powered villains and one with the mercenaries.

Pierce asked Washington to have Emma connect everyone. Once she'd established the link, Washington repeated Pierce's words for Emma to share with the rest of the group. The number of mercenaries was down from the initial count. She passed that information through to her teammates.

"All right. Now is the time we put an end to this. They don't seem to mind using lethal force and we must react in kind," Pierce shouted. "This is a kill-or-be-killed situation. I know that most of you aren't killers and I respect that, but this is war. And there will be casualties. Don't let it be you."

Katrina, seemingly feeling guilty about the escaped mercenaries, spotted the two bad guys guarding the device. Pointing at them, she lifted them both from the ground and flew them through the air over a mile from the shore. They'd live. If they could swim. For now, at least, those two were out of the fight. She knelt and tried to lift Etienne up, but her hands just phased right through him. He wasn't solidifying after the lightning attack. Something was dreadfully wrong with him.

***

"James!" Rami shouted as the speedster skidded to a stop near him.

"You ready?"

"Just get me a little closer to the device. It's now or never." Rami took a deep breath and grabbed on to James.

***

"That's far enough, monsieur," Margaux said as she magnetically grabbed all the metal weapons and aimed them at the heroes and Pierce's men. "You don't want to test me. You may have bested some of my team, but not me."

Emilio and his team froze. Emilio motioned all of them to stand down.

"Ericka! Get your head in the game!" Margaux said as she gestured to her. Ericka struggled to focus and looked blankly at her opponents as green energy began to form at her fingertips. She raised her hands, prepared to blast the heroes.

Washington looked at Pierce, who shook his head. Washington tensed his muscles and sprung out to tackle Ericka. In response, Margaux unleashed the guns on him and riddled Washington with bullets. He thudded to the ground, clasping at his chest.

"No!" Pierce shouted.

"I told you to stay where you were," she said as Pierce struggled to remain still. "Flame, you got this handled?"

"Oh yeah, I got this!" The Flame said as the fire raged and she twisted her arms and contorted the flames into a giant ball.

"Shouldn't we be doing something about that?" Etienne breathily asked as Katrina helped him up.

CHAPTER 66

22 August

"I'll take care of this," said a voice few recognized.

Maru Tamatoa

They all turned to see Henry Hastings standing about fifteen feet away from them, holding an unconscious Waleed.

"Ah-ah. I wouldn't do that if I were you," he said when he saw the gifted clench their fists. "Let's all calm down." He dropped Waleed to the ground and walked toward the scientists.

"You too, girls," Henry said. They looked to each other and powered down.

Emilio and CoCo looked to each other and called out to Emma for help. Suddenly, a wave of peace rushed over them. Far from their view, the young Irish girl had triggered within almost every person on the island a tranquility unknown to them in their adult lives.

One mercenary struggled violently against the halcyon waves, fighting to fire his weapon. His brow creased, and he slowly lowered his gun. He looked at the other men, who were similarly placing their weapons on the ground.

With his foot, Henry Hastings rolled the unconscious Pakistani teleporter over on the ground and walked through the submitting mercenaries and hired gifted goons.

Pierce, who seemed unaffected by the calm wave, artfully reloaded his weapon and aimed.

"Ah-ah-ah. I'd be very careful with your next move, Captain," Henry said as he walked toward him.

Timothy stood next to his cohorts behind Henry and smiled. He looked up to the skies and nodded at Maru, who called down lightning. Timothy reached out for it and twisted the bolt in his hands before casting it toward each of the Base 47 heroes. Massive currents coursed through them. One by one, they flopped convulsing to the ground.

Henry watched the Base 47 team members writhe in pain.

"I'm shocked you didn't see this coming," Timothy said as he crept toward a still shaking Emilio. "It's okay. I know how you feel. But it seems a few of you are missing." Timothy looked around and spotted the speedster, who had apparently managed to outrun a highly charged situation and was still on the move. He grinned. "Not so fast. I've got you now."

"Do what you will to speedy there, but spare Rami. He's important," Henry said.

CHAPTER
67

22 August

James dashed, with Rami on his back, from side to side, avoiding the lightning bolts zigzagging across the island. Timothy's electrical charge had incapacitated all the other heroes. As James avoided the shocks, he grabbed the mercenaries' guns and threw them into the ocean, then doubled back. He smiled at the baffled looks on their faces as they held up their inexplicably empty hands.

"I need to get to the WaveMaker. Can you clear a way for me?"

"Thought you'd never ask, my friend!" James said. "We're off."

In a flash, James sped off with Rami, blazing a corkscrew trail to avoid Timothy's continued shots of electricity. Rami, lightheaded from the motion, thought he might have inhaled a bug or two before they stopped about ten yards in front of the device.

Rami looked in awe at the WaveMaker. From afar it looked tiny, but from just a few yards away he saw it was twice his size. His fear grew twice as large. He stepped back and took several breaths, coming to terms with the knowledge that he must climb inside the monster machine. This is exactly where he'd known he'd end up. The prophecy would finally be fulfilled when he took his place in the device.

As he looked at the WaveMaker, time seemed to stop around him. He became aware of a presence he hadn't felt since he left the cave. His heart sank.

"This is it, isn't it?" Rami said, speaking to himself.

"It is," the voice agreed.

Rami felt deep foreboding in that voice, one he'd only heard in dreamy prophecy. "Why me?"

"The world has gone mad. The device has been imbued with your blood. If you don't do anything, the coasts will be destroyed."

"And if I stop the device?"

"Then the energies expelled will bring peace to nature."

"There's no real choice is there?" Rami fought to accept the prophecy.

"There's always a choice, my child."

Rami looked down and clenched his fists. Suddenly, time sped back up.

"I think this is as far as I can get you. Can you manage?" James asked. He looked around to see if any of the others could help out. But all of his teammates were still passed out on the ground. At least they were no longer convulsing. With the exception of James and Pierce, who were oddly silent, he was alone. Rami motioned to the other side of the WaveMaker, so James sped him off to that side.

As they circled the device, Rami's head pounded. The closer he got to it, the worse his head felt. James halted with Rami about a yard from the WaveMaker. Just as James was about to leave Rami, he spotted the redheaded man holding a gun on Nicola.

"I don't know who that ginger baddie is, but I'm not going to let him hurt her. Stay here," James said. He ran toward the redheaded man. He began to speed punch the redheaded man, who blocked the punches by closing his arms over his torso and face.

"You aren't going to get the jump on me, Mod! I know all about you freaks and how to deal with you." He landed a lucky punch to James' solar plexus, and the speedster dropped like a rock. From his pocket, the redheaded man removed a syringe filled with the same blue liquid that Pierce shot Katrina with in the bar. James eyed the syringe and scooted away from the man.

The redheaded man knelt over James and raised the syringe over his head. Out of nowhere Emilio tackled the redheaded man, and they rolled away from James.

"You and I—we have unfinished business," Emilio said. He gained the upper hand, pinning the redheaded man to the ground. "You used me to help find a way to destroy the world. You're going to pay for that."

"I thought you were electrocuted?"

"Lucky me, I guess," Emilio said as they rolled on the rocky ground.

"If I recall, you took the cash quite happily. So you've no moral authority over me." The redheaded man struggled as Emilio wrenched the syringe out of his hands.

"I know what this does to us Mods when we get it, but I'd love to see what happens to a plain guy." Emilio plunged the needle into the redheaded man's chest and pushed the blue liquid all the way in. The man's eyes widened in pain. Emilio grinned.

"What have you done?" he gasped.

Emilio stood over the man, watching as he lost consciousness, and one of Timothy's electrical bolts blasted him. He fell and landed next to his adversary.

Nicola used the opportunity to try and further sabotage the machine through the control panel, but it was too late. The third light turned green.

***

Timothy spotted James at a standstill and realized this was his chance. He aimed a blast at the speedster, but nothing came out. He was out of charge. He felt around for a top-up and sensed energy pulsing from the WaveMaker. It was a vast energy source, and he tapped into it.

The surge of electricity overflowed, and the machine sparked and roared. In a spectacular flash, the WaveMaker whisked to life, sucking into itself the very air around them.

Timothy felt dazed and lightheaded, and breathing became a struggle. He watched as Maru created pockets of air around himself, his comrade Mods, and many of the people from The Hastings Foundation, including Roger, Nicola, and the redheaded man, along with as many of the mercenaries as he could see. Lucidity began to return to Timothy as his breathing eased. One of the mercenaries Maru had been unable to protect seemed to have suffocated.

***

Waves of dizziness washed over Rami. He fought to remain conscious as the quantity of air diminished all around him. He felt a moment of oblivion, then wakefulness as his body fought asphyxiation. Nearby, he could see Nicola and Emilio standing stock-still in fright as James ran a counterclockwise vortex around her to contain some breathable air the pair of them could share. Further afield, he saw enemies encapsulated in air pockets similar to the one James was creating, and he recognized Maru's power in action.

Unfortunately, the rest of his teammates all seemed to be down for the count. His heart cried out for Emilio, CoCo, Etienne, Katrina, Waleed, Josh, and Pierce and his men. But what of Emma and his teammates at the other camp? He established a feeble connection with Emma. Her thoughts were spotty and he could barely make out what she was thinking. Through her eyes he could see Luli and her wailing newborn, tight within their force field. Emma was clinging to Jiya as they struggled to remain conscious while crawling toward the protective bubble. The device had a far reach, he thought, but it seemed distance lessened its effects. At least the people at the camp were still conscious, but how long would that last? He wondered how Maggie and Focus were faring.

A gruesome grinding sound yanked him back to the crisis unfolding around him. Horror settled into his stomach when he spotted an empty sneaker and spatters of blood not three feet from him. He looked up and saw the spiral blades of the WaveMaker swallow up the last fraction of one of the technician's legs. Blood shot out of the device as it pulverized the man.

Just how had the technician gotten entangled in the blades? And where had the rest of him gone? Rami didn't want to know. He tried to beat down his rising gorge when one of his team members caught his eye. Katrina was no longer curled up with Etienne. She was hovering about two feet above the ground, though Rami couldn't figure out how or why. As she started flying toward him, and the machine, he suddenly understood. He could feel the device's insatiable intake of air and instantly worked out how the technician must have been drawn into the WaveMaker. He couldn't let the same fate befall Katrina.

Not only would everyone on this rock die, and soon,

should he do nothing, but also the tsunami would claim millions of lives if he didn't stop the device.

In the dullness of the moment he heard the voice calling out to him in the whipping wind.

This is the moment to stand for the children.

This is the time to show the world who you are.

All is not lost.

Your life can save millions.

This is not the end.

The next step is yours.

Rami saw no option but to try to disable the machine. But first, he had to save Katrina, who was flying toward the WaveMaker. He leapt, reaching for Katrina. For one heart-stopping moment, he thought he'd missed her. Then his hand closed around her ankle. He landed, pulling her down with him and fighting the force trying to suck them both into the spiral blade intake. Calling on every ounce of power in his body, he jumped to the side and felt the force lessen. It no longer pulled at them, and he propped Katrina up next to him as he considered what to do next. He looked around and spotted James. A smile of relief crawled across his face.

"James," Rami called. "Come get Katrina."

In a rush of air, James did just that. He lifted the unconscious girl over his shoulder in a fireman's carry and dashed back to Nicola. He handed the girl over to her and resumed his lifesaving vortex.

Rami saw his team was as safe as they could be in an environment with diminishing amounts of air. His own body had constantly been cycling through near-asphyxiation and resuscitation, but his team members couldn't do that. He had to stop the device, or everyone would die.

His life for millions. He thought that would go down as one of history's best deals.

Rami cocked his head as he looked at the WaveMaker. Nicola had told him his blood was essential to the machine's operation. Perhaps, he thought, his blood could also disable it.

"This ends now," Rami said as he reached his hand out to the device. He stepped into the WaveMaker and rode a hydraulic lift up to the platform. Rami stepped onto the platform of the device, and what was left of the air crackled around them as the energy expelled by the WaveMaker and its power source made tentative contact. A hush settled over the island. As Rami stepped inside the enclosure made by the spiral blades, a black beam of energy shot straight up into the sky.

CHAPTER
68

22 August

Rami and the device began to merge. The energy being swept up into the device crackled and sparked with preternatural sounds. It was impossible to tell where the machine ended and Rami began.

As Rami stabilized the device, the air returned to the area with an explosive gust that knocked down everyone still conscious. James found himself on hands and knees, his vortex gone. Yet he was breathing. Maru was struggling to stand. His air pockets had vanished, and blood dripped from his nose. He'd bashed it on a rock when the blast of air pushed him down. Those he'd been protecting seemed to be breathing just fine. Many of them were themselves tumbled on the ground. Others, on regaining consciousness, found themselves rolled several yards beyond the spots in which they had passed out. Slowly, they all began to regain their senses.

Roger was one of the first to stand and survey the aftermath. "Henry, what are you doing here?" he called out when he spotted the leader of The Hastings Foundation.

On the device, Roger heard the machine whir into

functionality as the DNA-infused brew coated the spiral blades. The energy it was already generating was palpable. It was fully powered and ready to reshape the face of the continents.

"Seeing my grand project off. It wouldn't be right if I wasn't here," Henry said as Roger neared him.

"Right, I just didn't expect you to be here. I thought that you trusted me to see this through," Roger said.

"I had to be here. It's far too important to leave anything to chance," Henry said as he waved the mercenaries and techs to the side.

"But Henry, should anything go wrong, you could be implicated," Roger said as he reached out to him. Henry briefly placed his hand on the scientist's shoulder.

"You've got to trust me here. I know what I'm doing." Henry turned toward the device.

The scientist studied Henry. "I don't know who or what the hell you are, but you're certainly not Henry Hastings," Roger said. He brandished a handgun.

The heroes gathered, watching Roger intently. As the ground started to shift below them, they could barely manage to stay upright.

"The ground," Emilio said, looking toward his teammates.

"It's not me," Katrina said.

"The WaveMaker. It must be causing the ground to shake," CoCo said as the black beam of energy encompassed the device completely, making it impossible to see the WaveMaker or Rami.

"If Rami can't do this, that's it, right?" Emilio asked.

"Can't think like that," Pierce said.

CoCo neared Emilio. "What happened with the redheaded man?"

He grinned at her. "I gave him a dose of Pierce's blue calming juice."

She smiled in appreciation. "Nice."

"So who exactly are you?" Roger asked as he stepped toward the imposter, who sighed. The face contorted and looked like a melted peach candle as it reformed to reveal Josh.

"You are some sort of insidious Mod. It's lucky I saw through you," Roger said as he motioned for him to join the other Base 47 heroes. Josh reluctantly joined his teammates as Roger moved closer to the WaveMaker. "I won't let you destroy my chance to change the world."

Ericka grinned widely when she saw Josh was alive.

"This officially just got too weird for even us. Time to leave," Maru said. He used his power to alter the winds to float him up. "Margaux, grab the others and let's get out of here before it's too late," he said. She magnetically grabbed Dmitri, The Flame, and Timothy as they floated up.

"Come on, Ericka," The Flame said as she grabbed her hand. Ericka violently pulled away. "Whatever. It's your funeral."

"No, it's yours. I'm finished with going along with you just because you rescued me. I'm going to stand up for what's right," Ericka said.

"Figures! Villains always get away. Should we go after them?" CoCo asked.

"No. More important to help Rami here," Emilio said as the team gathered.

"Hollywood, what do we do? Say the word and we'll jump the old man," James said as he screeched to a stop next to the morphed Josh.

"And what about her?" CoCo asked as Ericka inched closer to them.

"I vouch for her. She was just caught up in all this," Josh said. She smiled at him.

"Keep going, Rami. You have to complete the WaveMaker. You will be responsible for changing the face of the globe forever," Roger said with a laugh as he walked toward Rami, whose skin was beginning to char and flake off. "You all may have powers, but I am in control," he warned the heroes.

"Oh my God. Look at Rami," Josh said.

"You think he knows what he's doing?" Emilio asked.

"Emma said it's up to Rami to save the world," CoCo said as she reached out mentally to Emma.

"There's nothing we can do at this point. Rami is the only one who can reverse the WaveMaker. We've got to let him do what the voice says," Emma thought to the team.

They looked around and felt the island shake again. James looked to Emilio, who told him to check on Etienne and Katrina.

"I hate feeling this helpless," CoCo said as she watched Rami and Roger war against each other. She turned to Emilio and said, "I wish we could combine our powers and help. Together we could make something special."

"Don't I know it," Emilio said, grinning. "But we haven't practiced combining our powers before and we can't risk screwing everything up."

"Can we risk doing nothing?"

"We're not just doing nothing. We're trusting Rami," he said.

The black beam grew in intensity. Through gritted teeth, Rami said to Roger, "I won't let you use me or threaten my friends. I know what's going on here."

"Rami, it is down to you. You have been chosen and you will lead the world into a new age. First, the Reckoning will change the face of the world, and then the New Dawn of Mankind will emerge. We are on the precipice of a new world, and you are the catalyst for the change. Now do what you were born for," Roger said.

The dark blackness enveloping Rami and the WaveMaker emitted a pulse, pushing everyone away.

Roger felt the ground shaking beneath him. Maybe no one was supposed to survive on the island. Even with Rami's power theoretically providing a safe space, the island could fall back into the sea. The complete test of the Ascendancy would be Roger's own survival.

"Rami, I know you must be scared, but this has all been foretold," Roger said as he neared him.

"Rami! Don't listen to him! We can still save the world without losing you!" James shouted over the deafening howl.

"James, it's okay," Rami said. The speedster relaxed.

"We can't just let him do this!" Katrina cried as she lifted her hands toward the machine.

"No," Emma thought to all. "It's up to Rami now."

"But we can take him now. That scientist is no match for all of us," Emilio thought back.

"As much as I hate to say it, I think Emma might be right."

"Etienne, shush. You're too weak right now," Katrina said as he lay in her arms, his body alternating between solid and phased.

"All we need is Rami to finish merging with the WaveMaker," Roger said. He pointed at Nicola and a tech. "You two, get out of there."

Roger looked at the device and smiled as he ran his fingers along the warm metal. The black beam grew larger and larger as the device began shaking.

"Waleed. Now!" Rami yelled over the rumble of the device, and his friend opened portals to the opposite side of the island for the team members. The Base 47 heroes began making their way to the portals.

"Don't forget the reporter," Josh said.

Waleed nodded.

"What's going on?" Roger asked as he pointed the gun at Rami.

"You won't shoot me. I'm too important," Rami said as his skin peeled off in layers, revealing new skin, which burned and renewed repeatedly.

Roger's eyes widened and he took a step back. As he did, Josh grabbed him and threw him to the ground. "Come on, Rami, we can all leave!"

Rami shook his head and pointed to the others.

"We have to take them too," James said as he cocked his head to the mercenaries, though he didn't sound happy about it. Josh looked long at James and then nodded.

"Take him too, death is too kind for him," Rami said, pointing at Roger.

Waleed's last remaining portal was for Josh. Waleed, himself, had already gone to the other side of the island.

"Come on, Rog. You're coming with us," Josh said through gritted teeth. He efficiently disarmed the scientist, and pushed the howling and screaming troublemaker through the portal, and it closed after them.

Rami looked around and a pained look spread across his face. Just him, Nicola and James left.

"I can run and save you," James pleaded. "Don't do this."

"It won't work," Rami said. "The moment this goes off, you won't have enough time, even at your fastest. You must save yourself. It's the only way."

Rami fought back a tear.

"Does it have to go off?" James asked the female scientist.

Nicola nodded. Tears rolled down her face. "It's too late."

"I have to do this. It's the only way," Rami said as he fought against the fear of certain death.

James remained, not ready to leave his friend's side.

"James, you have to go now. I've got this," Rami said as his eyes turned violet. Reluctantly, James picked up Nicola. He ran, but his heart just wasn't in it. He knew he was clocking in well below his top speed. Anything to give Rami a few more moments of precious life.

Rami watched his friend run, carrying the helpful scientist. When he judged they'd reached a safe distance from him and the WaveMaker, he closed his eyes.

"I am here. The Sentinel. I answer the call. I will save us all." Rami opened his eyes and the device began to slowly rotate, then to gyrate. Parts of the machine began to warp. The wind whipped around him and tore at his uniform. His body began to float inside the cavity created by the whirling spiral blades. His breath slowed as a rip in the air grew larger by the moment. Images flipped in Rami's mind. His parents. Books he'd never read. The face of his beloved the last time he saw her, on the day not so long ago when they last made love. As the flashes blurred together, he knew he was slipping away. He thought about all the things he had not done, and his regrets grew.

"I'm scared."

"I know you are," a voice replied.

"What happens next?" Rami asked as he touched the heated metal.

"Everything."

"Arian," Rami mouthed as his entire body lifted into the air and his heart stopped. The black beam zipped back down to the center of the WaveMaker and a white light enveloped the entire western portion of the island, obliterating everything near it.

CHAPTER
69

22 August

The dark sky lit up in the west, daylight bright. The explosion sounded like a thousand thunder booms all at once. Rami had sacrificed himself to save the world.

"Nooooo!" Katrina screamed. She threw her body on the ground, and she lay there convulsing. The air was thick with the energy of her grief.

"Josh! Get her!" Emilio shouted. Rocks began swirling around her, like planets in an unstable solar system spinning out of control around the sun. They prevented anyone from getting close. Josh approached her, but the rocks flying erratically around her drove him back.

"What is happening to her?" Emilio asked.

"She feeds off of emotions and Rami just died. No bigger emotion than that," CoCo said. She grabbed Emilio's arm to steady herself.

Suddenly, the rocks dropped to the ground and Katrina's body lifted off the ground. She hung limply suspended in the air. The entire area grew silent as if someone had clicked mute on the world.

"'Cause that's not scary," Josh said in the stillness.

The rocks again broke off from the ground and became a barrier between the team and the raven-haired girl.

"Ahhhh!" Emma grabbed her head in pain and screamed out as Waleed ran toward her.

"Look out!" CoCo shouted and dove toward Luli and her newborn to block an incoming rock from hitting them. But to CoCo's surprise, both she and the rock bounced off of the force field protecting mom and child.

"Lucky boy," Jiya said, easing herself into the protected area of the force field.

"Jiya. Stay close. My baby will protect us," Luli said.

Nicola rushed over to fawn over the newborn. "You had your baby!"

"Yes, he just couldn't wait," Luli said as she held him close.

"We've got to calm her down," Josh said and ducked, letting a grapefruit-sized chunk of lava harmlessly fly by.

"Any suggestions?" Pierce asked as he and his men dodged flying rocks.

"Emma! Can you get to her?" Josh asked.

The little Irish girl cowered behind the teleporter and shook her head.

"Too much psychic screaming. Can't focus," she said. Tears from the strain flowed down her cheeks. Waleed picked up the scared seven-year-old and held her close.

"We have to get out of here. Waleed, get us back to Base 47," Pierce ordered. His men took cover from Katrina.

"I can't. Not yet. Took all I had to get everyone here. I need a moment to recover," Waleed said. He sat next to Etienne, who was still injured from the earlier lightning strike that seemed to have short-circuited his ability to phase on command.

The rest of the team struggled to evade rocks sent

hurtling every which way by a girl who was now suspended in midair in a fetal position.

Maggie and Focus fled toward Nicola and Jiya, with their hands covering their heads.

"Stay here. Much safer," Jiya said over the roar of the wind.

"You okay?" Focus asked. He set his camera on the ground, filming Katrina.

"I have no idea. You do know we just witnessed that man saving the entire world, right?" Maggie said.

In the distance Roger and the remaining mercenaries were trying to escape.

Katrina began to spin counterclockwise in the air as the team desperately tried to bring her down. Anytime they got close, she instinctively emitted a psychokinetic bubble that pushed them away. Tears streamed down her face and her scream kept on. When she ran out of air, she took a deep breath and wailed again.

"There's no way to reach her," Josh said. He dodged the rocks and psychokinetic pulses from his teammate.

"Let me try," James said to the group. He focused on the situation at hand and ran toward her, using the flying rocks much like expert parkour enthusiasts would to leverage him closer to Katrina. As he reached out to grab her hand, she looked right through him, curled up in a ball and then splayed her body like a Jacob's cross. The movement sent a wave of psychokinetic energy all around her. James lost his footing and started to fall. Josh slipped between the rocks and barely caught him.

James gave a grateful look to Josh as he touched back down on the ground.

"This is hopeless. We can't get near her, and she is out of control," Josh said to CoCo and Emilio.

"The longer this goes on, the harder it will be to bring her back from the brink. Remember what Pierce did to her at The Hog Pit?" Emilio said in a hushed tone.

The wailing Canadian's voice faltered and they thought the worst might be over. But she cried out again.

"She's not going to be able to stop herself. She's going out of control. Emilio, use your luck to get her," CoCo suggested.

Emilio nodded, took a breath, and started out toward his teammate. He looked over and saw Pierce holding a familiar blue vial in a pump gun. "Etienne! Do something!" Emilio motioned at Pierce and the vial and then placed himself in front of Katrina so Pierce wouldn't have a clear shot.

"Merde!" Etienne said as he struggled to stand up. His body hadn't recovered from the lightning strike. His left hand phased right through his head as he took a breath. He shook his hands out and looked at Katrina wailing in the air. He stood and a huge rock ripped right through his chest.

"Thank God for that," he said as he instinctively remained phased to evade her psychokinetic pulses. He stepped on one of the rocks and slipped through. He took a deep breath and tried again. This time he could rise up. He stepped up again on another airborne rock, which he let spin him closer to her. He reached out and grabbed Katrina's leg. She tried to pull away but he had already made her body ghostlike. He pulled the terrified, grieving girl down into his arms and whispered into her ear. She stopped screaming and her tears slowed.

The rocks dropped back to the ground and the island took on an eerie silence.

"I've got you. It's okay," Etienne said softly.

She opened her eyes and saw the object of her crush was holding her in his arms. She looked over at CoCo, who smiled.

"See, sometimes all a girl needs is someone to hold her," Emilio said as he walked to CoCo and wrapped his arms around her.

"You ass," she said. She tilted her head and kissed him slowly.

Josh walked over to Emma and knelt.

"It's going to be okay. Somehow it's going to all be okay," he said to her.

The sky shifted red and the sun broke through the clouds.

Emma heard the voice in her head for what might be the last time. She beamed at her teammates.

"The voice told me that Rami did it. The earth has been given a second chance. All is in balance once again," she said.

Waleed stood. He opened a portal and the group passed through. In an instant they were back at Base 47 and the newborn island was empty and once again quiet.

EPILOGUE

I

23 August

"I can't believe they're keeping us here," Maggie grumbled to Focus. They had been confined to a suite at Base 47 since the showdown on the island. Worse, Pierce's men had kept their equipment, so they hadn't even been able to work on the story for TheModsBlog, and that feature would be the best one yet. Beyond viral. If they ever got out of here with their footage intact, that is.

Focus tried to calm Maggie, to no avail. She would vent and rant for a few minutes and then sit in silence, plotting her next move. He polished off the Granny Smith apple from his lunch and wiped his sticky hands on his blue one-piece outfit.

The door clicked twice and opened, revealing three people. They stepped inside and the door slammed shut.

"I'm so sorry about you both having to be here." The voice belonged to the three-and-a-half-foot girl who spoke in a soft Irish lilt.

"Maggie, sorry. This really is for your own good. We have to be careful with how we proceed," CoCo said, pushing her brunette hair off her shoulder.

"CoCo, I don't understand. We have to get this out to the public. They have a right to know. You saved the world!" Maggie said. She started to walk over, but CoCo held up her hand and Maggie stayed put, although she kept speaking. "You came to me. Asked me to cover this. To get your story out there. How can I do that if you won't let me out? How is the girl? And Washington? Is he okay?"

"Both are fine," CoCo said. "Washington was wearing body armor. He's a bit bruised but okay."

"This is bigger than any of us." The comment came from the third figure, Josh.

"Why? What is"—here Maggie's questions seemed to fail her, and she held out her hands, palms up, and gestured around the room before finishing—"this?"

"You have to trust me," CoCo said.

The door opened again and the room got very crowded.

Captain Pierce, in old dark-green army fatigues, entered, along with a squat but officious-looking man holding a manila folder. Maggie didn't recognize him. She addressed Pierce. "Where is our equipment and footage?"

"All of your footage and equipment will be returned to you in its entirety. With no damage or edits," Josh said.

Focus harrumphed as he looked at Captain Pierce directly.

"Maggie, I know you must be all sorts of mad about everything, but it will all be worth it," CoCo said.

Maggie looked from Pierce to Josh to CoCo and wondered what they weren't telling her. And who the still-unidentified newcomer was. "All right, so let's say I go along with you. What's the play?"

The squat man answered. "We are in a brave new world, Ms. Adams, and we want you to be a part of it."

Maggie rolled her eyes at the Aldous Huxley reference.

"And just who are you?"

"I'm with the UN and I have the ear of some of the most influential people in the world. People who care, uh, care greatly about how the Mods will affect the world. By tomorrow—"

"With the United Nations? That was awfully fast," Maggie shot back.

The squat man ignored her interruption. "By tomorrow your report on what happened on the island will go viral. You will be the herald of a fantastic future. We invite you to document the particulars of the powered people. We're at a very crucial point. The world needs you to help them understand the future of mankind. They trust you."

Maggie balked. "What else is going on here?" she demanded.

For a long moment, no one answered.

"And why is the girl here?" Maggie asked as she pointed to Emma.

"To keep everyone honest. You know she can read minds. She is our assurance to you that we will keep our promise," the squat man said.

Emma slightly nodded and her eyes began to glow violet.

The Mods looked at each other and seemed to reach an unspoken agreement. Josh answered.

"As you know, I bought Base 47 a few years ago and when the solstice happened and it was clear that there were more Mods, I listened to my better angel and offered the base to help them," Josh said, looking at Emma. "Without the training they received here, they would never have been able to prevent the catastrophe that almost happened. You know that firsthand."

"Ms. Adams, we have a golden opportunity for you," the squat man said, picking up the thread.

"Maggie, we need your help," CoCo said as she stepped back into the discussion. "There is a very real threat. As you saw on the island, not all of the people who got powers are good. We need to come together and police our own or the governments will step in."

"And that won't be pleasant," Josh added.

"I'm grateful that we got to tell you our side of the story, and now you have a greater understanding of the risks we take and the stakes we are fighting for." CoCo knelt beside Maggie.

"And what about the Mods who escaped?" Focus interjected.

"We're working on them," CoCo said.

"There is a proposal, which will certainly gain support, to force those with powers to register them. That is not what we want to see happen. That could lead to, uh, rounding up those people and shipping them God knows where. We've been down that dark path before," Josh said.

"There's a very strong possibility that registration will happen," the squat UN man said, speaking over the last of Josh's words. "As you can imagine, the story that emerges—your story—will be valuable as governments form their own task forces to decide what to do about these individuals with powers. Like, CoCo, for example. We may not be able to stop them, but maybe the UN can harmonize the process. Assuming that you want to help the people who saved your life."

"Are you trying to manipulate me into going along with this?" Maggie asked with wide-eyed disbelief."And just who are you, again?"

"As I said, I'm with the UN."

"Yes, but names. We're civilized. We introduce ourselves with names. And yours is?" Exasperation and sarcasm leaked out of her voice.

The squat man reddened. "John. Harris."

"And what is your title?"

"Vice chair for the committee on Mods."

"There's a committee?"

"This is getting us nowhere," Pierce grumbled. "Just listen to what the man has to say, Maggie."

She shrugged, then nodded, realizing this was not the time for that mystery.

"There is an opportunity to use the island situation as a grand opportunity. With your help, we can turn this into a great chance for the powered people to take care of their own." The man flashed the manila file folder at them. Maggie could see the label read SENTINEL.

"What—or who—is SENTINEL?" Maggie asked.

"It stands for Solstice Enhanced Network for Training, Intervention, Negotiation, Enforcement, and Leadership," John said dryly.

Before Maggie could form her next question, CoCo interrupted. "We are." She flashed a badge that gleamed in the fluorescent light.

"This organization will help us create a fully international colonization effort on New Atlantis and create a powered task force that will search out and contain powered problems," John said.

"And you think that you can counteract any dissent? Who will be in charge? Who will run oversight on this?" Maggie said. "CoCo, think about this. You don't know what you're signing up for."

"That's where you're wrong," CoCo said. "If we don't do this, it will be worse. You saw what happened on the island."

"CoCo—" Maggie said.

"It's done. I hope you understand what we are asking you to do," she said. She turned and walked out with Emma and Josh, leaving John and Pierce with the travel journalist-turned-blogger and her cameraman.

"Maggie, I know that you will do the right thing." John turned and walked toward the door.

The politician walked out. Only Captain Pierce, Maggie, and Focus remained.

"You'll be free to leave shortly, and we will return all your equipment and footage, as promised, so you can make your report, Maggie, Focus," Pierce said.

Focus looked at Maggie who looked back down at the SENTINEL file folder still on the steel table.

"Your move," Pierce said and walked out.

Focus watched Maggie intently as her eyes were on the door closing shut.

"So, Mags, what will it be?"

She turned her head to her partner, smiled, and pulled the file toward her, opening it.

EPILOGUE

2

24 August

"I know you entrusted me to ensure the WaveMaker success," Roger trembled before Henry in the great stateroom at the Hastings family home.

"We've already been through this and I no longer wish to talk about it," Henry said as he abruptly turned around.

Roger gulped and swallowed hard. He knew exactly what the penalty for failure, or, more precisely, for crossing The Hastings Foundation was. Kaczmarzyk and Giraud both paid the price with their lives.

"I could let you go on and on, but there are more important things to focus on. Sure, the Reckoning did not go as planned and we've lost Rami, but all is not lost," Henry said as he stood up and beckoned Roger to join him.

"I know you are confused about why you weren't immediately dealt with after the island disaster. Rest assured, it was a heavily debated topic. But in the end, I was convinced that you could still be useful to us," Henry said. Roger could barely look him in the eye.

"You are essential to the success of our next plan. Something that will truly revolutionize the world," Henry said, rubbing his hands together and grinning beatifically. He pressed a sequence in the keypad and a secure lab opened up behind the oak wall. Roger eyed this secretive state-of-the-art facility with awe and envy. If he'd thought the equipment at the labs at THF were top-notch, what he saw here left them in the dust. With the advantage of complete secrecy, Roger imagined what kind of advances he could accomplish.

"What is that?" Roger pointed at a statically charged blueish ball suspended in a two-foot cubic glass case. The case balanced atop a black pillar. The glass was triple reinforced and also protected by a bioprint index that would only allow one person—Henry—to open it.

"That, Roger, is a cryosphere. And it's the future."

EPILOGUE

3

27 October

Arian sat on her favorite stone bench in the shade by the waterfall in Jamshidieh Park in Central Tehran. She loved the change in seasons and the cooler weather suited her just fine. She flung a light pink wrap around her shoulder and fixed her head scarf. She sat across from an impeccably dressed young, married couple, and fidgeted as their eyes fixated on her.

"I am so glad that we could meet." Arian rested her hands on her growing belly, trying not to think about the life inside her. There was a sadness behind her eyes, reflecting a loss profound and deep.

"I know that this must be a difficult decision, but we are honored that you have chosen us to raise this child," the man said.

Arian, flooded with despair and grief and uncertainty, said nothing for a long time.

Sunlight gleamed off his silver watch. Arian noticed a strange pin on his lapel and wondered what the design denoted. Three stars were spaced at the points of an equilateral triangle around the perimeter of the circle with what appeared to be a mountaintop, or just the upper slants of the triangle connecting the star points on the inside of the circle. In a concave arc in the middle, three smaller stars were spaced across that mountaintop, reminding her of Orion's belt.

"That's an interesting pin," Arian said at last. The man smiled slightly and gently touched it with his hand.

"Been in the family for generations."

Deep inside, Arian felt the child move, and was saddened she couldn't share the happy moment with Rami. She thought back to the day she found about Rami's death. Several of his friends had shown up on her doorstep to share the tragic news. They threw around words like sacrifice and saving the world, but all she could focus on was that Rami was gone. She was still too numb, too raw, too full of grief to be capable of giving love to anything, possibly not even the baby her lost love had given her. Every thought she had of the baby was shadowed by the pain of knowing he or she would not grow up with a father, and of the weakness she felt, knowing there was no Rami in her future. And so she had sought out potential adoptive parents.

A slight gust brought Arian back to reality.

The sun slowly faded behind the mountains, and a haunting melody danced across her mind. It evoked memories of a song from her childhood about a lion and an eagle.

As the couple talked to her, speaking of their plans for raising Rami's child, she hummed the song, searching her mind for the lyrics. Something about the lion raising a baby eagle and the eagle never understanding it was anything else but a lion. Never soaring in the sky because it was never taught to fly. She didn't want be the lion. She wanted her baby eagle to rise to the heavens. In the end, it came down to a question of strength. Would she have the strength to give Rami's child love and roots with her, or the strength to grant him wings but never to know his mother, as well?

EPILOGUE

4

24 November

The tiny west African island of Santo Antao was in the midst of three straight days of rain. The redheaded man, drenched despite his raincoat and umbrella, made his way through a dilapidated hospital in the center of town. Bright blue and pink paint peeled from the walls, and stretchers in various states of decay rested haphazardly in the hallway. An acrid smell wafted through the entire building. Dressed in a loose-fitting polo and seersucker pants with a wide-brimmed hat, the redheaded man followed his contact as closely as possible.

Using the unlimited resources at the disposal of the Ascendancy, the redheaded man had scoured the Internet since the incident on New Atlantis, seeking unexplained activity or reports of unknown persons. All possible trails had been dead ends. Then two days ago he picked up some chatter about an undead guy who had washed ashore a small African island.

The locals had tried to revive him, but even though his vitals registered him as alive, he would not wake up. They sent him to the hospital, but kept him in a separate room because his condition frightened the other patients.

The redheaded man sent an Ascendancy operative to the island to check out the situation. When the operative confirmed his suspicions, the redheaded man made his approach.

"The body is in the last room, unattended," the operative said in a slow drawl. He shook his superior's hand and added. "Only the Sentinel Can Save Us."

"Through the Sentinel All is Possible," the redheaded man responded. Only the hardliners believed in the prophecies, and he knew better than to allow a hardliner to doubt him. He groaned as he pulled his sweat- and rain-soaked shirt away from the stinging rash on his chest. "Hot, wet, and sticky here, huh?"

"That time of the year, they say," the operative replied. "According to the chief of surgery, the locals collected money to take care of him. Charity case. Apparently he washed ashore shortly after the events on the island and they felt some sort of pull to help him," the operative explained as they walked through the waiting room. An almost antique television high in the corner behind protective bars related a story the redheaded man was familiar with. Onscreen, a news segment focused on the UN colonization scheme for New Atlantis. Details about the plan and of the newly formed SENTINEL group crawled across the bottom of the screen, as happened most often with news shows.

"Why didn't you want me to alert the Ascendancy about this development?" the operative stumbled as they turned the corner.

"Before giving anyone any false hope, it's better to erase all doubts," the redheaded man said as he pulled out a handkerchief and wiped his sweaty brow. It was pouring outside and muggy to boot.

As they walked in, the redheaded man saw dead flowers,

a few makeshift toys, and a crudely made cross of sticks and rope beside one of the doors. He asked about them.

"Some of the locals have taken to leaving little gifts at the door," the operative said as they reached the room. He opened the door and the scent of bleach blasted out of the room. At the far end of the room was one single bed. The occupant appeared to be attached to three or four monitors. The rain hit the roof like a symphony that timed along with the beeps of the heart monitors.

"And he has not said a word, or woken up?" The redheaded man scratched his chest.

"Not according to the doctor."

They made their way to the left side of the bed.

"We've been looking for him for a long time," the redheaded man said. He leaned over to confirm that the comatose man was actually Rami Kazemi. He held a finger below Rami's nose to check for breathing. The undead man twitched as though a fly had landed on him. For a moment, the redheaded man thought Rami was still conscious, just stuck somewhere deep inside himself.

"And the fee we agreed on?" the operative asked.

"You'll be well taken care of," the redheaded man said. He pulled out a syringe filled with batrachotoxin, a venom found in poison dart frogs in Central and South America that causes paralysis and death in minutes. He jabbed it into the short operative. "Stop struggling, you'll only make it worse."

"Why?" he croaked. The operative dropped to the floor, unable to move his body.

As his eyes began to glaze over, the redheaded man answered.

"Because the Ascendancy has failed for the last time. The Swarm shall succeed where you have all fallen short." He took out his encrypted satellite phone and placed a call.

"The package is secure."

The redheaded man unplugged the monitors and gently removed the IV line. He looked at Rami and marveled at his healthy glow. There seemed to be no atrophied muscles and he had seemed to respond to outside stimuli.

It had been three months since the conflict on New Atlantis. Three months since the Ascendancy failed to bring about the Reckoning and had lost the Sentinel in the explosion. And three months that the blasted rash had plagued him in the spot where Emilio had injected him with the blue fluid.

Today, the Ascendancy's opponent, the Swarm, was marking their return. As the redheaded man waited, he looked at the man—the Sentinel—lying in a hospital bed on an African island few had ever heard of.

"All this for you, Rami. You have no idea how important you truly are."

The redheaded man smiled, leaned down, and whispered softly into the ear of the comatose man. "You don't seem so special to me."

He looked out the window, noticing that the rain had subsided as the reds and yellows of the sky danced in a dazzling display of swirling acrobatics.

He rolled his eyes and added, "But it's not for me to decide. Your fate is already written in stone."

The Children of the Solstice
have only paused the wrath.
Soon, the Sentinel will rise and
finally the world will know
the truth so long denied.
The Sentinel will cleanse
the filth and cleave
the land from seas.

GRATITUDE

Writing a book is a mammoth undertaking. You'd think co-writing a book would halve the effort. It didn't. But collaborating allowed us to write the best debut fiction book we could make and still have fun with it. So, first and foremost, we're grateful that we're siblings who love and respect each other, and who can actually still be friends at the end of a project like this (which probably says more about our parents—thanks M&D—than it does us).

John Dylan DeLaTorre has given up so much time for this book. Baltimore says, "Your love and affection fills me up. Thank you for believing in me. Always."

We owe additional thanks to our friends and other family members who took "I have to write" in stride, who supported us, encouraged us, and asked not just how the book was coming along but when they would be able to buy a copy. Thank you.

Some of those friends went a step beyond by serving as our beta readers. Thank you for helping us spot problems in the draft when we were too close to the story to see them. You have helped us refine our manuscript and we are truly grateful for your help.

We also called in some professionals to help make this

book the best we could. Matthew Arkin of My Two Cents Editing provided an early critique that reshaped our approach to the entire book. Tiffany Munn provided an early critique that helped us flesh out the story line. Lourdes Venard helped us tighten our chapters and clean up our words through copyediting and proofreading. Thank you.

The book looks as great as it does because of Alex Sanchez, who drew and inked the cover art as well as provided the character sketches used for some of the chapter breaks as well as for promotional materials. John Kaiser designed the cover and logo and provided inks on supplemental artwork. Thank you.

It was a pleasure working with all of you.

With deepest gratitude,
Baltimore & Jennifer.

REVIEW

Many thanks for choosing our superhero book. Please consider writing an honest review *Awakening* and posting it on Amazon or Goodreads. There are few things more valuable for book sales than honest reviews from a variety of readers. Reviews are the best way readers discover great new books. We truly appreciate it.

ABOUT THE AUTHORS

Baltimore Russell is an actor, producer, and writer. He and his husband created the *People You Know* new media series, which aired on HereTV. Almost from the time he learned to work a pencil, he could often be found creating his own stories. He lives in New York City with his husband, John Dylan DeLaTorre.

Native Texan Jennifer Pallanich is a trade journalist who has bylined over half a million words about the oil and gas industry. She has published the nonfiction book *Flacks & Hacks: Trade Secrets Journalists Want PR Pros to Know* and loves to read good versus evil stories. An avid scuba diver, traveler, reader, and writer, she lives with a lab mix named Houdini and a cat named Possum.